Wriggly Little Hands

A wriggly little novel by

Alex Knight

Edited by Bethan Hindmarch
Cover art & map by Ivan Shavrin
Cover typography by Andrei Bat
Chapter art by Kellan Moss

To Erin, for always laughing at my bad jokes.

To Eric, for teaching me to craft said jokes.

To both of you, for always playing in the space.

ONE

A Wriggly Little Courier

Goblins look like if cats—hairless cats—had thumbs and learned to walk on two legs. But while cats are allowed to commit as many crimes as they want, on account of being cute and small, the same hasn't been true of goblins ever since they discovered arson.

Today, however, it wasn't goblins setting fire to everything.

Oli had been excited, at first, when so many new friends had shown up on the Plains of Abandoned Hope and Paralyzing Fear. He'd been even more excited when he noticed all the fun siege engines and war mammoths they'd brought along. But then his new friends—the Bright Queen and the Army of the Just—had laid siege to his old friends—the Dark Lord and his Legions of Smoldering Shadow. In goblin society, it was polite to greet new neighbors with a nice newtcake or a fresh pot of warmed mud. In human society, it seemed wanton slaughter was the go-to. That was how the Bright Queen had decided to introduce herself to the Dark Lord, at least, and who was Oli to judge?

Wouldn't be the worst thing in the world if they could do it all a bit quieter, though. And maybe not burn down half the swamp again. Especially considering that was the half he and his cousins lived in.

Battle cries and blaring horns echoed down from the highlands, followed by an explosion then a trickle of loose stone. It swept past Oli's ankles and splashed into the swamp—along with something shiny. Something that flashed golden as it hit the water with a gentle *plop*.

Goblins, like magpies, can't resist shiny things and Oli had the little sparkly rock in his palm before it had time to sink to the mud. Except, it wasn't a rock, he found, but a ring. Lost by one of his new friends fighting above?

Goblins hadn't yet discovered the concept of personal belongings, but they had learned humans got loud and waved their arms a lot when they lost their, well, anything. And a ring was a thing. So, probably, it was best if Oli returned it.

But who had dropped it?

There were no markings on the ring. Except, no. Something was etched around the inside in spindly writing. Crooked and sharp, with jagged edges as if it'd been clawed into existence by the nail of some cruel and ancient demon.

Oli, like most goblins, couldn't read—but the ring was apparently in a helpful mood as it chose that moment to begin reading its own inscription. A whispered, echoing voice seemed to creep from every crack and crevice, to bubble through the black swamp water. It crawled up Oli's body with pointed claws, scratched at his neck, and finally, squirmed into his ears like a foul, wriggling creature from some dark and wet cavern.

"Property of the Dark Lord Sarusomal, Master of Deceit, Corrupter of the Just, He Who Even the Shadows Fear(™)," the ring said. "If found, kindly return to Doomsday Mountain, Suite Three, Citadel of Shadow and Sin, Kingdom of Darkness. Reward offered."

The voice raised goosebumps on Oli's skin and left his mind reeling as if another presence had taken root there. But it gave helpful directions so that was nice.

"Oli know Doomsday Mountain!" he chirped happily. "Just up road!"

A cry echoed down from the battle. Panicked, frantic. It sounded very much like someone had lost something of great value. But luckily, Oli was a good goblin and the ring said exactly what to do if it was lost.

He was overdue for a visit with the Big Boss anyway. Technically, all foul creatures served the Dark Lord's whims, and technically, goblins always served the biggest boss around. But said whims of said biggest boss had never turned to Oli or his cousins. So had they lived, and waited, and occasionally participated in the foreign exchange program with their mountain goblin cousins to the north. And in the meantime, the Dark Lord had been busy with his newfound arts and crafts hobby in his volcano workshop. Then the Bright Queen had shown up, and the swamp had nearly burned down and, well, Oli had been something of a neglectful neighbor and/or servant of late. But there was a fresh newtcake back at the hovel, and paired with the Dark Lord's lost ring, why, that'd make for an excellent excuse to drop in.

With a smile, Oli tucked the ring safely in his boot and headed home to grab the cake.

TWO

Presents For The Dark Lord

When it comes to goblins, most folk look right past them. And besides, with the Eternal Battle between good and evil raging on, who had the time to worry about them? Certainly not the Bright Queen and her army. They hardly noticed at all as a lowly goblin ambled by.

Newtcake in hand (and wriggling just right), Oli left the Swamp of Sadness and Sweaty Underthings to pay his neighbor a visit. Usually, entering the Dark Lord's domain was an exciting parade of fanfare and terror. Towering trolls with beards as long as buildings guarded the Gates of Imposition. And past them were the Rapids of Regret with their waters black as orc blood. Then came Butcher's Butte and the hoodoos of Who Goes There? Finally, the Eviscerated Everblight. But the Bright Queen and her Army of the Just had taken up residence in all of that and created something of a traffic jam in front of the Citadel of Shadow and Sin, so Oli took another route.

The Caverns of Whispering Web were a pleasant pathless-traveled. Everyone always went for the big road, always in such a hurry. They missed all the local charm of the caverns, what with the big spiders and the bigger spiders—oh, and also the biggest spider who'd haunted the world since the first sunset. But goblins tasted terrible, and Oli's slimy coating allowed him to slip through even the tightest of grips and the stickiest of webs.

The newtcake didn't have such an enviable coating of slime though, and so Oli found himself hoping the Dark Lord didn't mind a bit of extra decoration atop the dish.

"Mishalob the Many-Legged!" he said with a smile and a wave as something massive chittered past in the darkness. "How you? How family?"

A thousand-thousand smaller somethings chittered in response. So many it seemed the floor was alive. A great rolling sea of carapace and glistening eyes.

"They getting so big!" Oli exclaimed.

One of the adorable monstrosities dropped from above with a screech, legs wide and fangs bared. It landed on his head and slid right off, slime covering its many spear-tipped legs.

"Sorry, Oli no can stay today. Go see Big Boss. Go see Dark Lord Sarusomal!"

As the thought passed his mind, and the breath drew through his lungs, and the name passed his lips, what little light that trickled into the caverns retreated. All around, Mishalob's chittering brood hissed in unison.

"Exciting, Oli know!" He smiled and held the newtcake high. "Hope Big Boss hungry."

The Caverns of Whispering Web were an endless labyrinth, but like any good neighbor, Oli had come to visit many times. The path through was plain to him and soon he waved goodbye to Mishalob and her kids as he passed into the catacombs beneath the Citadel of Shadow and Sin.

It was said the tunnels ran for endless miles beneath the flame-scoured Kingdom of Darkness, but Oli kept to the main route as he climbed the black rock stairs, each step slick with seeping water.

The first door was guarded by a group of towering orcs with halberds in hand and armor made of enchanted ash and cinder.

They didn't move as Oli approached. He stopped in front of them, then waved a hand in the air.

No response.

Jumped up and down.

No response.

Finally, he bit one of the guards on the toe.

"Oy! Who goes there?" the guard boomed, her chest puffed out and weapon at the ready.

"Goblin-friend Oli," Oli said with a smile.

The orc's eyes searched the landing, checking every crack and corner before finally noticing the small figure waving up at her.

"Oh." The orc slouched back against the wall and returned to conversation with the others.

"Oli no visit in long time. But now bring cake! And have ring for Big Boss."

The orcs weren't listening.

Oli gave them another smile anyway then continued through the door and up more stairs. The wine cellar came next, its entryway guarded by an ash geist.

Oli waved and the ash geist acknowledged him by staring straight ahead into the unending darkness. Always were a quiet sort, ash geists, but behind those smoldering eyes of eternal, burning torment, there was an unmistakable friendliness.

Up to the dungeon, next.

"Busy today," Oli said with a low whistle as two apprentice nail pullers and a journeyman knee breaker carried a screaming angel past. "Work hard, or hardly work, eh?" Oli elbowed Gruesome with a chuckle. The Head Torturer—who was also a specialist when it came to head torture—hadn't done much talking since his tongue had been cut out. Still, he pushed Oli aside in a way that said 'Hey friend! Good to see you! Where are you off to?'

"Oli take cake to Big Boss. And want say hi to old friends. You know how is."

Gruesome signaled that he did by walking away and shutting the door behind him.

"Have good day!" Oli called after him as a fresh bout of screams clawed from beneath the door.

The rest of the Citadel of Shadow and Sin passed in a blur. It seemed everyone was busy, and Oli didn't want to bother them so he hurried through the Hall of Horrors, but couldn't resist stopping for a quick drink at the Moaning Moat. Best water this side of the volcano. The souls imprisoned within added a spritz of something special.

Refreshed, with his tongue still tingling, Oli headed up to the Dark Lord's throne room. Some sort of speech was underway and a legion of offal amalgamations were listening intently as Sarusomal himself gestured and jabbed toward the plains.

Not wanting to be rude, Oli slipped inside, then waited off to one side until the Dark Lord finished.

"Bring me prisoners, in as great of numbers as you can." The Dark Lord's voice popped and boiled, like the unknowable, magmatic depths of Doomsday Mountain itself. He smiled next, and fire leaked from the corners of his mouth in a molten dribble. "And in as many pieces as possible."

The offal amalgamations screeched and whistled at that, using whatever semblances of throats and lungs they had to voice their approval. Then, as one, they turned and marched from the room. Or those that could march, marched. Others shambled. Some crawled. A few simply oozed toward the door in a determined fashion.

After their departure, Oli sucked down a deep breath, turned to face the Big Boss and—two figures entered the room and bowed low.

"My Lord," the first hissed, voice rasping and rough. He was cloaked in shifting robes and where they dragged on the floor, soot stains blackened the stone. "The Lock is near." The voice seemed to echo from every shadow and crevice in the room and even as it spoke, whispers rippled outward, repeating the words in fading, shifting echoes. "A fellowship sought to carry it across our borders this very morning, but their efforts were thwarted."

"You have recaptured the Lock?" the Dark Lord asked, flame burning more brightly beneath the cracks in his armor.

"Not... as such, my lord. We routed the incursion, but the ring was dropped in the fighting. Rest assured, it will be fou—"

The Dark Lord's fiery lash struck out and sheared the creature in two. He had just enough time to scream before infernal fire blazed impossibly bright and then nothing was left of him but for a rough silhouette burned into the wall.

"Unacceptable."

Standing alone now, the second figure winced.

Where the other had been all robes and soot, this one was a walking suit of armor. Through the joints and gaps, Oli could just see a shifting, loosely formed shadow.

"I pray, Lieutenant of Lament, that you will deliver better results?" The Dark Lord spoke and as he did, the flame in his eyes burned all the brighter.

"Of course, my Lord," she said. "The Lock is near. Even now I sense its presence. I will deliver it to you immediately."

The intensity of Sarusomal's gaze did not lessen.

"And, uh, furthermore... furthermore..." She swallowed hard. "I will deliver unto you not just the Lock, but the Key as well."

"Do not boast idly in my presence, Lieutenant."

"Never, my lord." She bowed all the lower, armor clanking, though the sound seemed muffled by the shadow beneath.

"The Key, like us, is besieged. How would you retrieve it with no army? How would you slink unseen through the lands of humankind where so many of my fouler servants have failed?"

"There is no end to which I will not push myself in your service, my lord. No obstacle before which I will falter."

The Dark Lord was silent a long moment, then nodded.

"Perhaps we will make something of you yet. I will bestow a dark and terrible power upon you. It will signify to all you have my cursing, and those who still serve me in the lands of humankind will give you aid." The Dark Lord gestured to the throne room doors. "Let no one disturb us."

The troll guards nodded, then pulled the doors shut with enough force to shake the citadel down to the dungeon. An echoing boom informing all that court was done for the day. No more creatures, no matter how vile or villainous, would impose upon the Dark Lord's time.

"Um..." Oli found himself suddenly locked in the throne room and what had been politely waiting his turn now felt like something much less polite. "Uh, hello, neighbor!"

Dark Lord Sarusomal, Master of Deceit, Corrupter of the Just, He Who Even the Shadows Fear(™), froze. His eyes narrowed, embers spitting from them and sparking across the floor as he scanned the room with a woeful and terrible gaze.

"Oli, uh, no mean get locked in with you," Oli said. "But bring presents!"

THREE

Courier Of Cataclysm

"Who taunts me unseen?" Sarusomal growled, voice rumbling like an avalanche set to bring down the mountain itself.

"Here, Oli here. But no mean taunt!" he jumped in place and waved.

"A spy!" the lieutenant shouted and drew a sword that instantly set itself aflame.

"Hold, Lieutenant!" The Dark Lord frowned and one eyebrow crept up his basaltic face as he took in the goblin. "By what quiet and secret magic have you infiltrated my inner sanctum?"

"Oli want say hi to Gruesome, so Oli go cellar route."

"My guards did not stop you?"

"One grunted!" Oli said, beaming. "Oh, Oli bring cake." A newt tried to squirm free but a quick poke and it was back into the dessert's gelatinous depths. "And found this. Maybe yours?" He hopped on one foot, tilting to one side as he fished the ring free from his boot. He held it out, unclasped his hand, and all at once it was as if every shadow in the room leaned in closer.

The Dark Lord himself did not flinch.

"You have returned the Lock?"

"Found in swamp. Come bouncing down hill and plop! Ring say it yours so Oli bring. Oli good neighbor. And good servant of shadow and also of sin!" He snapped a smart salute at that. A bit too smart and as his hand slapped his brow, the ring popped free.

"Oh!" Oli darted after it as it bounced once, twice —*ding, ding*—across the floor. He dived and caught it on the third bounce, but squeezed too tight and the ring popped out again, this time launched right toward the open balcony doors—and the churning, roiling depths of the volcano below.

The Dark Lord flicked his finger and the doors snapped shut. The ring bounced off their stone face and wobbled backwards.

"Ha!" Oli made to scoop it up, but a flaming whip caught his ankle and lifted him into the air. Goblin slime boiled and spat beneath the fire's grasp as the Dark Lord carefully bent down and picked up the ring.

"You have succeeded where even my most sinister of servants have failed. You reclaimed my Lock. You bore it through the whole of my kingdom. You slipped through my defenses, my guards, and right into my very throne room, unnoticed. How is this possible, Master Goblin?" At those last words, the Dark Lord leaned in close and a puff of ash washed across Oli's face. Got stuck in his slime.

"Oli walked? And maybe skipped some in Caverns of Whispering Web."

"You survived the lair of Mishalob and her kin?"

"Mishalob friend. Bitey but nice!"

"What is this power you command, little one? What trickery?"

"Goblins have no power, my lord. Neither trickery nor purpose. Pay the little fiend no mind," the Lieutenant of Lament interjected.

"Silence," the Dark Lord snapped and the citadel shook to its foundations with the force of his voice. When even the churning magma outside seemed to quiet, Saruso-mal's gaze returned to Oli. "What is this... goblin magic?"

"Oli no have magic. Always want learn but no can read."

"And yet, you have power." The Dark Lord lingered on that thought. "The power to go unnoticed." And as he said it, his eyes snapped wide. "But of course. Master... " Saru-somal waved a hand as if to say 'what was your name again?'

"This goblin Oli!"

"Master Olivandros!" the Dark Lord boomed. "How woul—"

"Is just Oli."

The fire inside the Dark Lord flared with raging intensity. Did the Big Boss have an upset stomach? Oli wondered if he should suggest a belchtoad tonic.

"Very well. Master Oli, I have a task for you."

As he said it, Oli's face lit up. A task? A mission? An infernal calling! Finally, the goblins of the Swamp of Sadness and Sweaty Underthings would have a purpose!

At the same time, the Lieutenant of Lament recoiled.

"My lord, you mustn't!"

Sarusomal muttered a spell and a forest of ashen arms emerged from the wall and took hold of the lieutenant, thoroughly ensnaring her.

"Master Oli, you have brought me the Lock. By its power, the Bright Queen and her army will be stayed. But their light grows brighter by the day and before it, my shadows burn away. There is yet still a weapon to change the course of this conflict. A weapon to bring an end to the Bright Queen, and her armies, and even the very ground upon which they stand." The Dark Lord lowered Oli to the floor and his whip fizzled from existence. "You have already brought me the Lock, now I command you bring me the Key. In so doing, you will save this kingdom."

"A command? From Big Boss?" A jitter began in Oli's legs. Worked its way up to his hips. "Big Boss has mission for Oli?" The jitter reached his little goblin chest, his shoulders, and then he was shaking and bouncing in place.

"Be calm, my smallest servant of shadow."

"Yes, Big Boss. Calm. Calm, yes." Oli jumped in place, huffing and puffing. "Oli calm!"

"Be still!" The Dark Lord gestured and an impossible weight rooted Oli's feet to the ground, took hold of his legs, pressed down on his shoulders. An orc or troll might have been stayed by the force, but goblins were squishy creatures and so for a moment, Oli was held in place, and in the next, he was balled up like the world's slimiest pretzel.

A bent arm covered his face, but one bulging eye peaked through.

"My fearsome and mighty Master of Shadows, this creature is not worthy of serving you," the lieutenant hissed, still held in place halfway up the wall.

"The Outriders of Outrage failed me." Sarusomal said

it and a fresh rush of magma boiled up through the cracks in his enchanted armor. It hissed and spit in the air as he twitched a finger and the lieutenant was dragged along the wall. "Our spies have been rooted out. Even my foremost officers crawl before me bearing nothing but excuses and complaints." The lieutenant was pushed against the doors, which swung open. "The Key remains besieged. *We* remain besieged. Our dream of a captive and damned world slips away by the moment. We have tried to do things the right way. Perhaps, it is time we tried something different."

"My lord, I beg you, put your faith in m—"

Another flick of the Dark Lord's finger and the lieutenant was flung from the throne room. One of the troll guards peered in, then gave an accusatory stare at the door.

"Bad door," she said, slowly. "You stay closed!" She shoved it shut once more and Oli found himself suddenly very alone with the Big Boss.

"Master Goblin, the Key is far afield. The road to reach it is long and we have precious little time. The journey will be dangerous and bloody—or it would be, for any other of my servants." The Dark Lord kneeled, which brought his face level with Oli. Or, as close as was possible when one party was a cat-sized slime ball and the other was an eleven-foot tall, sorcerous half-giant. "The journey is only dangerous if one is seen. But even more powerful than temporary invisibility, is the power of being ignored. You are seen but not considered. Underfoot but out of mind. You, my damp little goblin, are perfect."

No one had ever called Oli perfect before, much less the Big Boss himself. It was enough to bring a tear to his eye and a fresh rush of snot to his nose.

"Th-thank, Big Boss."

"Of course, you will need a way to prove you have my cursing." The Dark Lord took hold of Oli's forearm, then pressed down with one massive thumb. "Will you undertake this foul quest for me? Will you become a true servant of shadow? An apostle of apocalypse? A courier of cataclysm?"

Oli's lip quivered as he looked up and into the Dark Lord's boiling eyes.

"Oli's cousins come too?"

"They will not bear such power as you."

"Cousins have many powers!" Oli nodded enthusiastically. "Hob can spit ten feet! And Lin Two smell terrible!"

The Dark Lord might've sighed, or maybe it was just his internal hellfire hissing against the comparatively cool air in a room perched above a volcano. Either way, his only response was a dribble of magma that ran from a crack in his hand, down his thumb, and onto Oli's skin. Slime boiled away before it and then the skin sizzled and popped. A flash of pain and the Dark Lord released the little goblin.

Oli fell backwards, fire in his veins, a burn mark on his wrist, and a smile stretched across his face.

"A sliver of me now resides inside you, Master Oli. Call on it only when needed most. Only in the most dire of—"

"How use?" Oli asked, poking the burn mark. "Ooh!"

The room darkened. The shadows along the walls reached out, then moved of their own accord. The border between life and death cracked like a creek bed too long without rain and through those cracks a half dozen damned souls clawed their way back from hell. At once, Oli was surrounded.

"What is thy bidding, liege?" they asked, their voices cascading in a chorus of overlapping whispers.

Oli waited on the Dark Lord's response. When none came, a thought slapped him across the cheek.

Oli turned to the Big Boss.

"Shadow friends mean Oli?"

A slow, heavy nod.

Oli peeked back at the retinue of cursed souls.

"Uh, no have bidding. Oli no have plans. Shadow friends have plans? Want go somewhere? Maybe go eat—"

"Enough."

A swift gesture from Sarusomal and the shadows evaporated, whisked away like candle flames before a hurricane.

"Retrieve the Key, Master Oli. It awaits you deep in Fortress Isolgar, the Beachhead of Barbarism and Minor Inconveniences. Bring it to me before the next full moon and you will live as a god." The Dark Lord paused and for the briefest of moments, a flicker of doubt ran across his molten features. "A small and... wriggly god."

FOUR

Wriggly Little Cousins

"You are going to die, little goblin. You are going to fail. You are going to mess this up and the moment you do, I will be here, waiting, ready, proficient. You are a joke and a bad one at that, you squirmy little thing." The Lieutenant of Lament seemed happy to hear Oli had gotten the job.

"Oli good squirmer," he said with a nod.

The lieutenant didn't have a face but for the shadows inside her helmet, and yet, it was apparent she was frowning.

"It is not my place to question the Dark Lord's cunning," she said, and it sounded more like a reminder than anything.

"Big Boss cunningest!" Oli chirped, skipping as he crossed the drawbridge above the Moaning Moat.

"How do you plan to complete such a long journey? Do you even have supplies? Weapons? A map?" The lieutenant briefly considered drowning Oli in the moat and saving everyone some trouble.

"Oli do!" he smiled, then paused. "Wait. No. Oli no have. But do have cousins."

"There's more of you? Wonderful."

"Many cousins!" Oli bounded away, taking the stairs down to the dungeon two at a time—which really amounted to a sort of rolling bounce from one to the next.

The lieutenant glided after him, insubstantial legs carrying her swift and silent but for the occasional clank of armor.

"Goodbye, Gruesome! Oli on secret mission for Big Boss! No tell!" Oli shouted. The only reply was a bloodcurdling scream from behind a locked door.

"Goodbye, ash geist! Oli on secret mission for Big Boss! No tell!"

"The quest is not a secret if you tell the whole of the world about it!" the lieutenant hissed, looming over the goblin's shoulder.

"Oh." Oli's slapping feet came to a stop. "Oli need lie, in case anyone ask what Oli is do. Need smart lie. Clever lie…"

* * *

"Good news, cousins! We go on road trip!" Oli shouted at no one in particular. The lieutenant frowned, little waves rippling out from beneath her as she hovered above the swampy water.

"Who are you talking to?" she asked, then noticed a pair of eyes ahead. Yellow and big—or, big at least in comparison to the creature's head. And then another set, and another. In moments, where there'd only been a tangle of tree roots and fetid water, there appeared a stumbling assemblage of goblins.

Two squeezed out of the tree roots. Another rose up from beneath a lily pad. There was a splash behind as a fourth fell from the canopy. Something pulled at the lieutenant's shoulder and she recoiled as another goblin appeared from inside her armor.

"Get out of there!" She tried to toss the disgusting thing away but couldn't get a good grip on it and so succeeded only in covering her armor in slime.

"Road trip?" one of the goblins squeaked.

"Where to? Ooh, ooh. No tell! We go see Gruesome?"

"Further! More dangerous!" Oli shouted, jumping up and down and splashing mud everywhere in the process. "Oli have secret quest for Big Boss! And cousins come with!"

"No, no they don't. This isn't a vacation," the lieutenant hissed.

"Who that?" one goblin asked, and then all of them were staring at her, wide-eyed and open-mouthed.

"Cousins, this Scary Lieutenant of Lament," Oli said, arms spread wide. "And Scary Lieutenant of Lament, these cousins."

"I don't care."

"That one Hob. And that one Gob."

"It's pronounced *Johb*," Gob said, and somehow, there was an aristocratic slant to his tone. Even had formal robes and a tie on, though they were sorely soaked through with muck and ragged at the bottom.

Hob, on the other hand, was dressed like Oli, which was to say, barely.

"I don't care about your cousins."

"That Lin Two." Oli waved at what was probably the female variety of their sad species.

The lieutenant frowned.

"Not that I care, I really don't, but humor me… what happened to Lin One?"

"Lin One there."

What the lieutenant had taken for a particularly ugly rock moved and revealed itself to be a particularly ugly goblin. If it even was a goblin. It certainly wasn't damp and vaguely toadish like the others.

"Is something wrong with him?"

"Lin One rock goblin, which lot like a swamp goblin, but dry."

"An even more pathetic take on an already pathetic design," the lieutenant sighed and tried not to wonder how her unlife had led to this point. "Look, this is all disgustingly… familial, but the Dark Lord commanded me to see you safely to the border, so grab whatever sticks and mud you need and let's get moving. The sooner you fail, the sooner I can actually get the job done."

"That one Robert," Oli said, as he pointed to the largest of the goblins. Near the size of an orc. And, actually, the longer the lieutenant looked, the more she was sure Robert was an orc. Oli leaned in close, voice a whisper. "Robert foreign exchange cousin from mountain goblins. We trade away Bad Lin."

"Bad Lin no good," Lin One said.

"Bad Lin bad," Robert agreed with a voice that shook like a bucket full of rocks.

"Bad Lin gone," Oli said and all at once his eyes seemed to sink into his face. And then his yellow eyes were all the lieutenant could see. "Bad Lin gone."

What might've been a shiver ran down her spine, but she refused to acknowledge it.

"Alright, alright. Enough. I've met your cousins. Yay. We're all very excited—"

"And that one Man," Oli said, face back to normal.

"Man... the goblin?"

"Man the goblin."

"Dark Lord take vengeance on my soul," the lieutenant lamented. "Cast me into your volcano and boil me for an eternity. I would welcome the release. No punishment could be worse than this."

"Oh cousins," Oli said. "More good news. Big Boss give Oli po... er, crow... " He frowned, working through the sound. "Toe... notion? Lotion? Toe potion!"

"*Promotion*," the lieutenant said, face in her hands. "He gave you a promotion."

"Yes, that! Oli now agent of apocalypse!"

"Does it pay well?" Gob asked and somehow managed to sound snooty about it.

"I no know!" Oli beamed. "But come with this!" He raised one little stubby arm and if the lieutenant had a stomach, her heart—that she also didn't have—would have fallen through it, for there on the little snotcat's arm was the mark of the Dark Lord himself. The mark she should have been given. The mark of unholy power and corrupted might.

"A bruise?" Lin Two asked, squinting.

"No, no. Leech bite!" Hob said.

"Better!" Oli clenched his fist, then pressed a finger to the mark and the air trembled with the necromantic power of Sarusomal. The light of day fled and the trees seemed to close in around them. Where once there'd been swamp, now there was abyss. And from it rose six assassins of pure spite, six damned souls, six unkillable servants of shadow and ichor plucked fresh from the pit of hell and dragged back to the mortal realm.

"Toe potion come with friends!" Oli said, then made to clap the closest shadow servant on the shoulder. His hand passed clean through, but he smiled anyway. "Shadow friends, meet cousins. That one Hob. And that one Gob."

"It's pronounced *Johb*."

"That Lin Two, and that…"

FIVE

A Bag Of Numerous Nasty Things

"Okay, *Master Goblin*. This is your quest, so let's hear it. Our kingdom is surrounded and besieged. Everything from here to the Plains of Abandoned Hope and Paralyzing Fear is a battleground. So, enlighten me. Exactly how do you plan to get out? How do you plan to even take your first step on this 'road trip?'" the Lieutenant of Lament asked, voice growing more annoyed with each word.

Of all the new friends Oli had made since finding the

Lock, she was definitely one of them. And the most pushy. Probably just under a lot of stress or tired from wearing such big armor all the time. Did shadow creatures get tired? Or maybe she was just really happy for Oli? She certainly had been excited since he'd shown off his mark and the new friends it made. Maybe that was—

"Hello? Hello!" the lieutenant was clapping her hands in front of his face. "Oh my Dark Lord. You're going to die so quick out there. Please, just, get on with it. Pick a direction. Would you like to get trampled by a war mammoth on the plains? Or carried off by what's left of those infernal eagles? Ooh, or I know, you can all drown in the Rapids of Regret."

"Goblins float!" Hob said. "No can drown."

"Hmm, yes. It's true," Gob stroked his decidedly beardless chin. "Goblins are rather buoyant."

"Hey! Some goblins girls!" Lin Two snapped.

"*Boo-y-ant*," Gob said, sounding it out.

"*Guh-uh-rrls*," Lin Two retorted.

"Someone please drown me," the lieutenant mumbled.

"Everyone, everyone!" Oli shouted, jumping up and down. "We no go any of those ways."

"Want see mammoth," Robert sighed.

"One day, big cousin." Oli patted him on the shoulder, or tried to, but could only reach his lower back. "But today, goblins go secret way. Goblin way."

* * *

"How… how did you know about this?" the Lieutenant of Lament asked. Oli couldn't see any face inside her helmet, but his acute goblin intuition told him she was confused.

"This goblin way," Oli said simply.

"No, this is the Geist Gate. An ancient monolith built

of the cremated remains of an army from the first and a half age. Only the Dark Lord can harness its power. A single drop of his burning blood is enough to rip open this portal to hell and draw out all manner of servants foul and mighty."

The big stone loomed tall over them. Silent, watching. Moss wrapped up its sides and runes ancient and mysterious covered its face. Petroglyphs had been carved into it, depicting the carnage of conquest and battle, while teeth and tusks from all manner of beasts jutted from its face.

"Maybe to Big Boss this Geist Gate, but to goblins, is goblin gate. But this wrong side." Oli led the group to the rear of the stone. There were petroglyphs there too, but mostly stick figures and blobby circles with smiley faces.

"This Goblin Gate," Oli said, and if the lieutenant wasn't mistaken, there was something approaching reverence in his voice.

"Gob-lin Gate," Lin One said.

"Gob-lin Gate!" Lin Two agreed, and then the whole group was chanting it in rhythm. "Gob-lin Gate! Gob-lin Gate!"

"Goblin Gate here long as Oli remember," he explained over the chant. "Long as Oli's mom, Oliv, remember. Long as Oliv's mom, Oliva, remember. Long as Oliva's mom, Olivan, rem—"

"It's been here a long time, got it," the lieutenant said, arms crossed. "Does it… do anything? Besides…" she leaned in close, scrutinizing the simple shapes carved into it. "Besides keep baby goblins entertained?"

Oli hawked a glob of spit into one hand.

"Delightful," the lieutenant scoffed, but then, with the others still chanting, Oli pressed his spit-filled palm to the monolith.

"Goblin Gate make goblin go. Goblin Gate make

goblin come. Goblin Gate we say hello and please now to do eat that one!" Oli said it with a bouncing rhythm, then pointed at Hob.

"Woo!" Hob pumped a fist in the air and then charged forward. He ducked his head low and sprinted right into the monolith—where he cracked his forehead and promptly bounced right back off.

"Woo..." he cheered again, this time with much less enthusiasm seeing as he was cross-eyed and, the lieutenant was pretty sure, thoroughly concussed. Around him, the other goblins got out of sync and their chant slowly fell apart. Except for Robert, who hadn't really got the rhythm down in the first place but was pushing along determinedly.

"Oh, oops. Oli forget." Oli hawked another wad of spit into his palm, then pressed it against the stone again. This time, though, right in the center of some sort of swirly glyph. "Sorry, Hobby. Work this time." He waved his free hand until the chant was picked up once more. When it was going something approaching strong, he repeated the definitely not real incantation. "Goblin Gate make goblin go. Goblin Gate make goblin come. Goblin Gate we say hello and please now to do eat that one!"

Hob gave another cheer and stumbled forward into the stone. He was off target but a good shove from one of his cousins got him back on course. The lieutenant winced but Hob didn't head butt the stone this time. Instead, there was a gurgling, sucking noise and he fell through it like it was thin air. Or something closer to viscous mud, but close enough. All the same, Hob was gone.

"Again!" Oli cheered and Gob jogged stiffly through the Goblin Gate.

"Where is it sending them?" the lieutenant asked, after

checking to make sure no goblins were appearing on the far side of the rock.

"Out," Oli said with a shrug.

"Yes, but—actually, you know what? I really don't care. My job was to get you to the border and I'm gonna say this is close enough. You all have fun out there and die quickly for me, yeah? Oh, hold on." She paused, sighed. "Before you die, do me a favor?"

Oli hesitated.

"Goblins serve Big Boss."

"By helping me, you help the Big Boss." The lieutenant clenched her hand, then thrust it upward. The ground shook, split, and a skeletal hand burst forth. Except, not a hand, a hoof. Oli jumped back with a gasp as an entire skeletal horse pulled itself from the ground.

Soil clung in wet clumps to its vertebrae and joints, but the unalive horse gave a very alive nicker and shook itself head to tail. Dirt and mud and what might've been a few bits of still-rotting flesh flew free and then Oli found himself face to face with the saddest looking horse he'd ever seen. Also the happiest. And simultaneously the largest and the smallest. Oli hadn't seen many horses.

Its eyes were empty sockets but as Oli leaned in closer, two little sparks appeared, then flared brighter until each socket was lit with a dancing, orange light. As if two tea candles had been set in there.

"This," the lieutenant said, slapping the ignoble steed on one bony shoulder blade, "will help you on your journey. And when you inevitably get found out and massacred, nothing of value will be lost. I'll just resummon the remains."

"What name?" Oli asked, mouth still hanging open as he reached a tentative finger toward the creature.

"It doesn't have a name. It's just your run of the mill undead mount."

"Everything need name." Oli frowned. "Oli have name. Lin Two have name. Even Robert have name."

Robert grunted at that and raised both fists high.

"Robert!"

"Look, name it whatever you want, I don't care. That's not why I'm giving it to you. I'm hoping it'll help you help me help the Dark Lord."

But Oli wasn't listening. He'd gotten one tiny hand high enough up for the skeletal fiend of a horse to stretch down and rub against it.

"It perfect," he said, voice a whisper. "Oli love horse."

And from the looks of things, the feeling was mutual. Or, at the least, a far cry from the indifferent reaction most creatures exhibited toward goblins. The horse twisted and turned its head all about, letting Oli's little nails scratch its chin, forehead, and even the inside of its glowing eye sockets. It was warm in there, and when Oli's finger came back out it glowed a moment.

"Yes, yes, lovely. I'm so glad you like each other." The lieutenant worked another small spell and then she'd a bag in hand. "Look, here's what I need you to do—"

"Horse need name!" Oli said, spinning to face his cousins, sans Hob and Gob who'd already gone through the Goblin Gate.

"Horse?" Robert asked.

"Yes," Oli said, nodding slow. "It horse. Need name."

Robert nodded more insistently.

"Horse."

"That no good name. We no call Robert 'goblin.'"

"Oh." Robert hung his head. "Sorry."

"Horse good name," Man said. "Make sense."

"Ooh! Ooh!" Lin One jumped up and down, then pointed at the horse. "Lin Three!"

"Are there not enough Lins already?" the lieutenant asked.

"What's the hold up here?" a voice called and Oli turned to find Gob's head poked back through the Goblin Gate. "Wait, are we getting a horse?" He reached back then dragged Hob along with him as he stepped fully out. "This is a fine development. A horse will make traveling much quicker. Though," he paused, stroking his bare chin. "It won't blend in very well in the land of humankind, will it?"

"Need name," Robert said as he pointed at the horse.

"Need more than that, I should think. We'll have to disguise it somehow."

"Okay, enough!" The lieutenant shouted it and a thunderclap echoed through the swamp. That silenced the debate well enough. "Name the horse whatever you want, or dress it up to look like a mammoth for all I care. But you've been given a quest from the Dark Lord, and now I'm giving you another." She raised the bag she'd been holding and shook it. "This is a Sower's Sack. Or sometimes called a Bag of Numerous Nasty Things." She reached inside and pulled out a handful of seemingly entirely unrelated objects. A polished pebble, a dagger with a black blade, a charred and severed finger—even a handful of bent gold coins. She turned her hand as she spoke, and the various items slid back into the sack. "Each of these sows the seeds of chaos, when given to a receptive person. Someone downtrodden and angry, or ambitious and unscrupulous. Maybe even an honorable warrior out for vengeance—and susceptible to being consumed by it. In the right hands, these seemingly normal items create villains. They create, well, us." The lieutenant returned the last of the objects to the sack, then tied it shut. "But you don't need to worry your empty little goblin heads about any of that. All you need to do is get this sack to Rodrigrar, at Inn-N-Out. No, no, I know, you're on a quest for the Dark Lord, but I promise, the inn is right on the way. Before the siege, it was my job to pass these Sower's Sacks on to our vast network of spies and saboteurs. But with the Bright Queen and her Army of Idiots squatting on our front door, the deliveries have gotten a bit behind." The lieutenant held the sack out to Oli. "Take this for me and you'll have mine, and the Dark Lord's, thanks."

Oli started to reach for the bag, but hesitated.

"Goblins serve the biggest boss around, right? Well…" The lieutenant made a show of looking all over. "I'm the biggest boss here right now, and my boss—your boss—won't be happy if this doesn't get to its destination. Take it."

"I thought the point of this whole road trip was to not be noticed?" Gob asked, one brow raised. "What if we do get noticed and searched. And then they find that?"

"You're a bunch of innocent, unassuming goblins on a road trip to visit distant family—or whatever your cover story was. No one's going to stop you."

Gob didn't look convinced, but Oli was. He took the sack.

"We deliver for help Big Boss, no you."

"Great. Just see that it gets to Rodrigrar. Preferably before you all get killed."

SIX

Starting Strong

"Ah, the fresh air of the open road!" Gob said with a contented sigh as the countryside slipped by. The Goblin Gate had deposited them all far beyond the borders of the Kingdom of Darkness, in a small wood. Birds chirped, rabbits bounded, and all was generally peaceful. Decidedly devoid of the constant stink of ash as well, a smell that had permeated their swamp since the warring armies had burned half of it down.

"Is nice," Oli said, eyes wide as he took in the passing trees and thickets of brush. Everything was so green and bright. Could have used more mud, though. The ground was too solid. Didn't squelch at all. Horse didn't seem to mind, though, moving along at a steady trot. A vote had been taken and somehow, Robert's name suggestion had won out.

Now, the goblins all bounced along on the creature's back. Oli had a good spot on the shoulder, but the others were strung about, clinging tight like baby spiders on their mother's back. Getting on had been a whole other adventure, seeing as none of them stood taller than Horse's knees. But through the power of teamwork, and stepping on each other's heads, and with a few curses and blows exchanged, they'd all gotten on.

"Horse like new clothes," Robert said, patting the undead beast of burden. Gob had raised a good point that riding a skeleton through the lands of humankind would attract attention. A quick stop at the first farm they'd come to had fixed everything though. Now, Horse was wrapped in several stolen deer skins and stuffed with hay and grass. The result was the best-looking recreation of a real, living horse Oli had ever seen.

"Maybe goblins need road trip more often," he said, bobbing along with a smile as he watched puffs of hay spurt out from Horse with each step.

The sun was warm, the wind was blowing, and looking ahead, they could just see where their worn track joined with a road. From there it was supposed to be a straight shot to Rodrigrar and his inn.

"Make Big Boss proud," Lin Two said. "All get toe potion like Oli."

"Goblins be important!" Lin One agreed with a cheer.

"Importance is overrated," Gob said. "Your tiny brains spare you the burden of knowledge. By design, perhaps. I studied goblins, you know, back when I was— er, I mean... before. Anyway. Just know, the more you matter in the world, the less your life belongs to you. It's enough to drive you crazy. Enough to want to just disappear."

"Lot words," Robert said, frowning.

"Gob okay?" Oli asked, reaching out a hand. "Feel sick?"

He sighed.

"Gob okay."

Oli beamed.

"Good! No room feel bad. Goblins on evil quest! Goblins serve Big Boss! Goblins make proud. Goblins do evil and—"

"Halt!" A commanding voice rang through the countryside. The brush ahead rustled and then more soldiers than Oli could count—there were at least five of them—came running up. "By order of the Bright Queen, you will surrender yourselves!"

Oli gasped and almost managed to swallow his tongue.

"Hide the bag!" Gob hissed, then tossed it to Robert.

"How? How hide?" Robert cried, looking from Gob to Oli, then down to the bag. "How hide!"

"Throw it!" Lin One hissed.

"Sit on it!" Lin Two insisted.

"Throw it then sit on it!" Man said, jumping up and down and near toppling off Horse.

"We're dead. We're dead. I always knew it would end this way," Gob shouted. "I always knew—"

With everyone shouting, Robert panicked. He raised the bag high, looked for a place to throw it, hesitated... then unhinged his jaw and swallowed the entire thing.

"That... work," Oli said, then spun around in time to hear a dozen bows creak as they were drawn taut. He raised his hands high and froze. "No problem! No do bad!" Behind him, Lin One screeched and fell off Horse with a thud.

"The enemies have surrendered, Commander Argont, sir!" one of the soldiers reported, as he snapped a sharp salute.

"Hold on a minute…" The commander, a towering human in heavy armor, lifted his visor, then cursed. "Come on, Armolas, really?" He spun on his heel and shouted at a pointy-eared soldier. "These are goblins, not orcs!"

"Well *sorry*," the soldier said back, drawing out the word extra long. Oli didn't think he sounded very sorry. "You were all, 'Armolas, what do your elf eyes see?' Just put me on the spot. I did my best."

"How did you mistake goblins for an orcish raiding party?"

"This is just like that time he said he saw a walking tree," another soldier said and then everyone was laughing. "A walking tree, you believe that?"

"I've had enough lip from you, Henric!" Armolas spat.

"Oh, you wanna have a go, pointy?"

"Yeah, maybe I do, human!" he said with a shove.

The crowd of soldiers cheered and rushed over, shouting as grunts and oomphs came from the combatants. All the while, the leader sagged inward, shaking his head side to side.

"How many weeks now? How many weeks of guarding farms and sheep? And finally, just when there looks to be some action, we get this?" He cursed again, then raised a fist to the sky. "I swore I would have my revenge on the Dark Lord and by all that's holy, I will!" He sighed again. "But not here. Not guarding fields and cow pies."

A burp from behind caught Oli's attention. Robert looked sick, then heaved and spat something into his hand. The dagger with the black blade, from the Sower's Sack. Even as Oli stared at it, a compulsion overtook him.

Almost as if he could hear the voice of Sarusomal himself, whispering in his ear.

You know what you must do, little one.

Heeding the voice, Oli took the only slightly saliva-soaked blade and gingerly handed it toward the leader.

"Me think this for you."

The human looked up, then gruffly wiped away a tear.

"What? What is that?" he asked, but seemed unable to stop himself from taking it in hand. He stared at the dagger, and for a single heartbeat, Oli heard a distant laugh from back in the direction of the Kingdom of Darkness.

"It's... beautiful," the commander said and stood there, seemingly rooted in place as he stared at the blade. "It calls to me. What's that? Say again?" He leaned in, ear pressed to the blade as, behind, his rambunctious soldiers fought on. Oli caught his breath and looked around. It seemed for all the world that he and his cousins had been entirely forgotten. Or, perhaps, ignored.

"Goblins go now," he said quietly, but the soldiers weren't listening. Weren't paying any attention because, of course not. Who would pay attention to a bunch of goblins?

"Goblins go now," Oli said again, and with more confidence this time.

"Come on, Horse. Mush," Gob added and patted the hay-stuffed exterior of the skeletal steed. He gave a little nicker in response, then trotted ahead. No one moved to stop them.

SEVEN

A Long Awaited Drink

Rodrigrar's inn stood on the edge of a small town, far enough out that it wouldn't hurt real estate value, but close enough that no passing ne'er-do-well could miss it. Oli and his cousins had only missed it a couple times.

"Inn-N-Out," Gob said, a frown pulling at his features as he read the swaying sign. He looked next to the scrap of parchment the lieutenant had written on. As the only goblin able to read, it'd fallen to him to lead everyone to the address. Which would have been considerably easier if Hob would stop ripping pieces from it for tinder.

"This it?" Man asked, bouncing up and down.

"Gob smartest cousin," Hob said with a nod of assurance. "This it!"

"Gob teach Robert read?" the big goblin asked. "Robert want read!"

"It's simple, really," Gob said casually. "Just look at the letters and make their corresponding sounds."

"Urrrhfhh ossd rrruup toof," Robert said, drawing out each sound as his eyes followed the wording on the inn's sign. "Robert do it?"

"A valiant effort, Robert." Gob patted him on the back. "But I fear you need a teacher beyond, uh, my means."

The inn's sign had a frothy mug carved into it and a simplistic turkey leg with heat lines rising from it. Both made Oli's mouth water, and it was all he could do to remind himself they'd come on behalf of the Dark Lord and not their bellies.

But why not both?

"Cousins! Goblins go in!"

A cheer went up at that and Robert led the way, shoving the door aside with one massive shoulder.

"We don't serve their kind here!" the barman shouted the moment the goblins were inside.

Oli paused, then frowned.

"Robert mountain goblin. Has feelings too. Promise no hurt anyone."

"Not the orc, the horse!"

It was then Oli noticed Lin Two and One were in the process of pulling Horse through the too-narrow doorway. Hay bulged from the hastily crafted disguise and one bony shoulder had worn a hole through the sagging animal furs. Both Lins and also Horse froze as the eyes of everyone in the building fixed on them.

"Sickly looking creature, to boot. What've you been

feeding it—if anything at all? Gods! Its eyes are completely inflamed," the barman said, leaning across the counter.

"Take outside, take outside!" Oli hissed as he and the others shoved Horse and the Lins back into the street.

"Sorry, sorry!" Oli said, waving everyone's attention to him. "Horse live outside. We forget."

In the wake of his squeaking voice, the room was completely silent, but for the slow, long creak of a floorboard as someone shifted their weight. Goblins were the biggest creatures in the Swamp of Sadness and Sweaty Underthings—if one wasn't counting the crocodiles, or the jackals, or the Thing That Waits Beneath The Mud—but in the presence of so many humans, Oli suddenly felt very small. But then the Lins got Horse back outside and the door swung shut. As it did, it was as if Oli and his cousins no longer existed. Everyone turned back to their gambling and their plotting and their murdering, and the room filled with conversation once more.

"Goblins bring delivery," Oli said to the barman, but found he was no longer paying attention. "Hi? Hello!"

The man was big for a human, which meant he was massive for a goblin. So tall it seemed Oli's tiny, squeaky voice couldn't even reach his ears.

But the Dark Lord had chosen him! Big Boss had picked Oli and Oli would not let him down. With renewed confidence, Oli waved his cousins after him, then strode across the room.

He pushed his shoulders back as he walked, poked his chest out, and did his best to swagger. He reached the bar, and it only took two jumps, a couple yelps, and a bit of climbing to get atop a stool then lean toward the barman.

"Oli and cousins bring delivery."

"Huh?" The barman turned from where he'd been polishing a tankard, then took several moments to notice the goblin on the stool. "Oh, hello there. Didn't see you come in."

"You saw Horse!"

"Strangest horse I ever did see." The barman's eyes were distant as he shook his head slowly.

"How not see goblins too?"

"He saw ya, kid. Just didn't care 'cause why would he? Who cares about goblins?" said a human woman from the next stool over. A look of revulsion crossed her face a moment later. "Wait, why do I care about goblins? Why am I even talking to—lord. This is a new low." She downed the rest of her drink in one massive gulp, then left as quick as she could.

"There's power in not being noticed, you know," Gob said, scrambling up to take her place. "It's why I—"

"Lord above, this goblin can talk!" the barman exclaimed.

"All goblins can talk," Gob said, face scrunched up.

"They can? I never noticed."

Oli frowned at Gob. He'd the distinct suspicion his cousin had been about to say something interesting. But that was just Gob, wasn't it? Oli pushed the thought from his mind and looked back to the barman.

"Hello, Mr. Human. Oli and cousins bring delivery. Want find Rodrigrar for bag of sewing. Or, no. Sack of... " What had the lieutenant called it? "Sack of 'spicious stuff!"

The barman looked perplexed.

"There's no Rodrigrar here. And we're not expecting any deliveries."

"Oli told bring sack here. Give to Rodrigrar." Oli gestured to Robert. "Give sack please."

Robert opened his mouth and pointed down his throat.

"You swallow, yes. Was clever! But now need sack."

"Is stuck. Can't get... ow, urgh!" Something swelled in

his throat and he snapped his mouth shut. Only for a moment, though, as his cheeks bulged more and more until —*blagh!*—he vomited. Except, it wasn't stomach acid and liquified newtcake that splattered onto the bar but several objects that landed with thunks. Several objects of clearly magical—or perhaps more appropriately, mischievous —origins.

A necklace with a silver, thorny rose pendant hanging from it. A small wooden box with a locking latch and black iron hinges. And last, a candle, already lit and burning with a green flame.

"What are—" the barman began to ask, but his eyes flicked shut. When they opened again, they were darker and, Oli couldn't place how, exactly, but different. He'd the distinct impression someone else was suddenly looking out from the man's eyes.

"She sent you, hm? It has been some time." The barman nodded and now his voice was slower. His movements, too. Precise. As if every twitch of a tendon or blink of an eye were calculated. "I am Rodrigrar, and yes, our stores were running low. We would do well to replenish them."

Rodrigrar scooped the only slightly saliva-covered items and tucked them behind the bar.

"Clever of her to use goblins to make the deliveries," he spoke, voice low. "No one looks twice at goblins."

"You got a problem, runt? See something you like?" There was a sudden scraping of chairs and Oli turned to find Robert had wandered over to a table full of orcs. "Ain't nothing you're gonna like here, boy, I promise that."

Orcs were smaller than the average human, but not by much. And what they lacked in height, they made up for in muscle and density. Humans were the skinny, unathletic kid on the playground in comparison to their green-skinned, stockier, and altogether angrier, distant cousins.

"No have problem," Robert said, but his head was cocked to the side, staring at the orcs. He said something else but Oli couldn't hear it. The last of the orcs had remained sitting, but she rose now. Their leader, it seemed, considering she'd the largest tusks and an impressive handlebar mustache running past them.

"You wanna say that again, runt? See what happens."

"Robert no cause scene!" Oli shouted, then sprang from the stool and ran over. "No you either, Hob!" he added, hissing toward where his other cousin was in the middle of starting a fire under an unaware patron's chair. Where had he gotten all that tinder? There was a pile of, admittedly, perfect fire-starting materials already beginning to smoke. "No do arson!" Oli shouted and Hob pouted a moment, then smushed out the tiny flame. Oli grabbed Robert by the hand next and pulled him free from the grumbling crowd of angry orcs.

"Next round's on the runt," the leader shouted. "He spilled ours."

"Ya spilled your own when you near flipped my table," Rodrigrar shot back. "Now settle your horde or I'll do it for ya, Paulter."

"More talk like that and maybe we take our business elsewhere, old man."

"Ain't nowhere else'll take your business."

The biggest orc laughed at that, deep and throaty.

"Fair enough. Well, send another round anyway."

"Robert, we would all be very much obliged if you would avoid bothering the other patrons," Gob said. "Don't antagonize strangers."

"Robert no mean ant... tag... no mean ant wagon

eyes!" He pouted. "Just ask why big scary friends look like Robert."

"Hobby got you," Hob said and held Robert's hand. "We stay here. No trouble here."

"Thank you, Hob," Gob said and Oli nodded his agreement, then climbed back atop a stool.

"Couriers for her eat and drink free," Rodrigrar said, back to business and already filling tankards. Each was just about the size of Oli. "There's a roast on in the back." He snapped his fingers hurriedly and the batwing doors to what must've been the kitchen swung open as a younger human came out carrying two trays heaped with steaming meat and boiled potatoes.

"It ain't the finest food, but it won't kill most folks, so that's something," Rodrigrar said as the trays were dropped off.

"No have newts?" Oli said, frowning at the food.

"Or newtcake?" Man asked.

Their host frowned next.

"It's meat and potatoes. Don't be picky."

"Want BLT," Hob said, struggling to climb onto the bar. "Bug, leech, and turtle sandwich, please."

"Ooh, yes. That does sound nice. Perhaps topped with a maggot aioli?" Gob's stomach rumbled even as he asked.

Rodrigrar shrugged.

"I got meat and potatoes. Take it or leave it."

"It good, thank," Oli said, then paused. "Have more?"

"That tray's piled higher than you lot are tall."

"Oli have lot friends. Might be hungry," he said. "Let ask."

"How many goblins does it take to deliver a…" Rodrigrar began, then trailed off as candles began to wink out one by one. Even the oil lanterns by the door dimmed, then fell dark. The shutters on the far wall burst open next, but no light came through. Only a chill wind that swept across the room and left him shivering to his core.

Shadows reached out from beneath tables, the bar, the seats along the back wall, and grew longer... longer... and then pried themselves right up from the floor. Six silhouettes rose around the room, each so perfectly black it was near impossible to see them. As if they sucked in all light around them, swallowed it such that only void was left.

Six damned souls, dragged back to the mortal realm.

"Thank for come, shadow friends," Oli said and tried to hug one but passed clean through its spectral form.

Something clattered off to the side and Rodrigrar turned to find the shutters swinging wildly and the room devoid of patrons. Only a lone orc was left, struggling to grasp the doorknob with shaking hands.

"Let me out! Let me out of here!" he screamed, pounding on the wood.

"Oli bring new friends," the small goblin said with a smile, then turned toward the closest of the hell born monstrosities. "Shadow friends hungry?"

"We do not require sustenance, liege." The foremost spoke and its voice came as if from afar. As if it was but a distant echo, crawling through the caverns of some dark and damp hole. "Our only appetite is for the blood of your enemies."

The little goblin paused at that.

"Oli have no enemies." He gestured to the trays of food. "Have meat and potatoes."

The shadow was quiet a long moment.

"It has..." The anger was gone from its voice. In its place there was something that sounded a bit like hope. "Been some centuries since I had a beer."

* * *

"Great Dark Lord below," Rodrigrar said, eyes wide as plates as the shadow servants emptied their drinks. The closest raised a tankard and gave a little nod.

"'Course, 'course." Rodrigrar snapped at his assistant and he hurried out for refills. He did his best to stay away from the shadows, though. Somehow managed to pour from almost the far wall.

"Thnnk frr meel," Oli said through a full potato in his mouth.

"I knew you were working for her, but this is something more. You're cursed by the…" He leaned in, voice barely audible. "By the Dark Lord himself." His smile, already wide, grew wider still. "This is excellent news!" And then he ducked down behind the bar, digging through the pile of assorted useful things there with a renewed vigor.

"Oli and cousins try be good for Big Boss. This first job."

"Things have been a bit stagnant lately, what with the siege and all," Rodrigrar said, still out of sight and rummaging. "We've had a bit of a back-up in the system, but now that you're here—and with his blessing—we can get everything…" he reappeared, arms entirely full of an assortment of items. "Back on track!"

"Goodness." Gob's eyes were wide. "That is… a lot to get back on track."

"Like I said, the system was backed up. Gotta keep a steady flow of evil items into the world, ya know? The only thing necessary for the triumph of good is that evil men should do nothing."

"Or evil goblins!" Hob added, spraying meat bits across the countertop. Oli brushed them from the assorted items as he looked at each.

"What we do with these?"

"Deliver them, of course. They're not going far, but

I'm not supposed to blow my cover, or leave my post, and there haven't been any couriers by since the Bright Queen's armies showed up." Rodrigrar grabbed the first of the items, a sword twice as long as Oli, but with no blade, just a wireframe in the shape of a blade. "This one's just gotta get a couple towns down the road. Oh, and these two are going to the same place." He gestured to a green liquid-filled jar with an unidentifiable lump of... flesh?... floating inside it and a completely normal looking stone. Except, the stone was wet. And somehow, getting wetter by the moment.

"Yeah, funny thing. 'The Weeping Stone' it's called. Always leaks salty water and let me tell you, don't keep it in your basement unless you're trying to start a mold farm."

"No can take," Oli said, voice rising in pitch. "No have time. On secret quest for Dark Lord—er, family road trip. Uh. Secret family road trip... quest. But must to hurry. Get to Fortress Isolgar and back before next moon!"

"Fortress Isolgar? Oh, excellent. These deliveries are right on your way, then. And we've still two weeks until the new moon. Plenty of time." Rodrigrar refilled Oli's tankard and slid it back to him. "You are a courier of cataclysm, are you not? This is the job."

EIGHT

The Belly of Holding

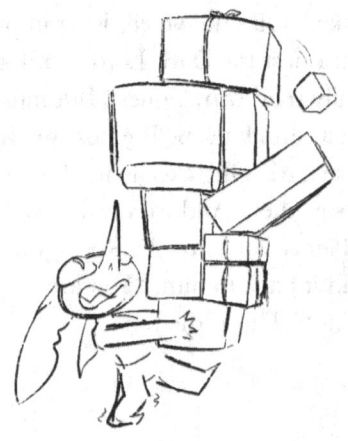

The wire-frame sword, lump of flesh in a jar, and Weeping Stone weren't the last of the deliveries, as it happened. Rodrigrar escorted the goblins outside where more packages were waiting. Neither Lin Two, Lin One, nor Horse had seen where they'd come from, but they were all clearly marked for delivery.

Some were wrapped, some boxed, and others not at all.

Among the additions were a metal oboe—which Gob identified as a type of instrument, though normally made of wood—a growling stack of crates, each nailed shut more thoroughly than the last, and finally, a book. Rodrigrar tapped its cover.

"This one's not actually evil. Just a story I wrote about the Dark Lord and me. Could you... give it to him? I'd be forever in your debt." He smiled sheepishly and Oli groaned.

It took some creative stacking, but with Robert's strength and Gob's strategy, the goblins managed to load most of the packages onto Horse, then climb on top with only a few extra packages held in their laps. The result was a teetering mountain of deliveries, threatening to avalanche over with each wobbling step. But then Rodrigrar waved them off and they were on their way. They left town moving as fast as Horse could carry them. Previously they'd been traveling on back lanes and dirt paths, but now they were on a proper road.

"Get out of the fast lane, moron!" a dwarf hollered from behind as his pack mammoth loomed up right behind them. The gargantuan creature raised its trunk and let loose a deafening, trumpeting blast as it pushed past them.

"Hold on!" Man shouted and Horse nearly toppled over, the ground shaking from the mammoth's thundering steps. Crates and sacks and all manner of various cargo were tied tight and strung across the beast's back. Easily ten times what Horse was struggling to carry.

"It... it beautiful!" Robert said, mouth agape as he stared at the gargantuan creature.

"Now why didn't the lieutenant give us one of those?" Gob pondered aloud. "Well, probably because we were only supposed to deliver a single bag and retrieve the Key, not…" he gestured to their current predicament, "all of this."

"Big Boss made Oli courier of cataclysm," Oli said. "Must make Big Boss proud."

Another trumpeting blast from behind, this one echoed by several others and Oli spun to find a whole herd of mammoths waiting to pass them. They stretched as far back as he could see, with wagons and other beasts of burden mixed in.

"Maybe Horse better on side of road," Oli said and Lin Two pulled on the improvised reins to guide them out of the way.

"About time! Seriously," a human shouted from the shoulders of another mammoth. "Bright Queen's mercy!"

The mammoths passed in a constant flow, the ground buckling beneath each of their steps. A few of their riders shot nasty glances down at the goblins, but most ignored them. The worst looks, though, came from a group of hog riders. Most of them were orcs, and they wove in and out of the legs of the bigger creatures, laughing and throwing sidelong glances at the goblins and Horse. They scattered after a moment, though, when another mammoth pulled up alongside.

"Well howdy there, little fellas!" A too-cheerful human called from its back. While most of the giants had brown or black coats, this was one so light as to be almost blonde. As Oli stared, it gave two happy blasts from its trunk.

"I've never seen goblins in the hauling business before, but look at you go! Ah, it's just so nice to see youngin's taking an interest, you know? Good for you!" He whistled low. "That sure is a lot of weight for one poor horse. And he's doing a great job! You go, guy! You got this!" He pumped a fist excitedly. "If he does get tired, though, I've a half-loaded mammoth at the back of the train. We'd be just tickled pink to give ya a lift wherever you're going." The rider had neatly combed brown hair, spectacles, and wore a comfortable looking green cloak. "Oh, I'm Flan, by the way. And this beautiful girl here is Mam," he said, patting his blonde mammoth.

"Thank for niceness, Mr. Flan and Beautiful Girl Mam," Oli said, neck craned all the way back to look at them. "But we okay. Thank. Bye." He leaned forward to Lin Two. "Faster, please."

She gave Horse a nudge and he struggled forward at what might've been a slightly quicker stumble. Mam easily kept pace.

"Alright then! Looking to do it all on your own? I respect that. Builds character!" Flan said, patting his mammoth. "If ya ever need help, don't hesitate to holler!" He clicked his tongue and Mam and the rest of his mammoth train picked up the pace. In moments, they were gone but for the massive dust cloud kicked up in their passing.

"Mammoth not bad idea," Man said, staring longingly. "Too much packages now."

And he was right. Poor Horse was barely staying upright and each goblin had at least one package in their lap.

"Idea!" Robert suddenly shouted, then grabbed the wire-frame sword. He opened wide, then started lowering it into his throat.

"Goodness, Robert! What are you doing?" Gob exclaimed.

"Bag hold many things," he said, teeth clicking against the wire frame. "But no get bigger. Now bag inside Robert. Maybe more things go in bag?"

"There sure was a lot in that tiny sack," Gob mused.

"Sword too big," Oli said even as Robert gagged, then pulled it back out.

"Sword too big," he agreed. "This not." He grabbed the jar with the mysterious lump of meat inside it.

"No good eat that," Lin One said and snatched it back. "Make sick."

"Well this is an interesting experiment, isn't it? Try this one, Robert." Gob handed over the oboe. It was similarly shaped as the sword, but nowhere near as long and as such, Robert got it down with no problem.

"And this?" Man handed over the Weeping Stone. They'd kept it hanging off Horse and over the dirt of the road seeing as, true to name, it hadn't stopped leaking water yet. Left a little trail of wet behind them.

"Robert try!" He dropped the unassuming stone down his throat. "Salty rock."

"Oh, and these!" Hob began handing over the smaller of the crates. Closer to boxes, really, but Robert got most of them down the hatch. And, true to his theory, he didn't get any bigger. Oli had expected him to end up looking like that time he'd seen a snake swallow an entire beaver. Somehow, it'd gotten the poor creature down its throat, but the snake's belly had been huge for weeks. Robert, comparatively, looked slim. As slim as possible for a mountain goblin.

"Less packages now, but no easier on Horse," Lin Two said, pointing to their still-struggling skeletal steed.

"Bag no get bigger, but do get heavier," Oli said, ponderously. "Strange bag."

Robert burped in response, spittle flying.

"Poor Horse won't need to take us much further," Gob said, then nodded ahead. "I think that's our next stop."

"Oh," Oli said, peering at the structure through the trees lining the road. It sat far off such that he could only get a glimpse now and again. A path diverged from the main road just ahead and Lin Two guided Horse down it, cooing and patting the ignoble steed as reward for his hard work.

It was slow going and the smaller path was riddled with potholes, but at least there were no more mammoth trains pushing past. The bumpy road left Oli a bit dizzy and Robert burping all the more.

"Nasty," Man said, wiping saliva from his back after the largest of the belches.

Robert tried to mumble an apology, but he looked positively sick.

The path turned, rose up a hill, then ended in a circular driveway. Horse's hooves crunched against gravel as he stumbled across it.

Before them rose a massive house, perched on the edge of a cliff. The abode was a mansion like none Oli had ever seen, but before he could appreciate it, Robert gave another belch then toppled backward off Horse.

"Salty. Nasty. Nasty salty..." he groaned, then his stomach churned and Oli dove for cover as a wave of bile splashed onto the driveway. The small packages he'd swallowed came flying back up. The oboe next, then a bunch of things Oli hadn't even known were down there. A severed, blackened toe. A little twig of wood with a grip on one side and a tapered end on the other. Another black-bladed dagger.

"Urghh..." Robert complained, then heaved once more and the Weeping Stone came out last along with a huge wash of water.

"Robert okay?" Oli asked, peering out from where he'd found cover.

"Stone no good. Too much wet. Too much salty."

"And now we've learned a valuable lesson," Gob said, picking through the bile and assorted objects.

"Robert no eat packages?" Lin One asked.

"No, that's very convenient. Robert should eat the packages again. Just, not this one." Gob kicked at the Weeping Stone. It spurted wetly.

"Robert no hungry," he groaned.

"Robert can wait to swallow everything again," Gob said. "We have a delivery here first."

"And Horse need break!" Lin Two began struggling to unload the mountain of crates.

Oli jumped in to help, and along with Lin One and Man, was able to heave the largest crate to the ground. As they set it down, something inside whined.

"Something live in this one," Oli said, putting an ear close. "Don't it need breathe?"

"Man help!" He scooped up the dagger Robert had vomited and set to poking holes in the side of the crate. "There, now scary crate monster breathe."

And then something was trickling through one of the holes.

"Uh oh," Man said, backing away.

The trickle turned into a flow, then a jet as frothy, viscous ooze sprayed from the crate. It collected in a sticky puddle as the goblins backed away.

"We break package," Oli said with a wince.

And then someone was laughing. The puddle, he realized, as reverberations shot through it like angry ripples.

"You fools!"

The ooze rose up into an unsteady, wobbling shape of a woman.

"I'm free! After all these years!"

Horse panicked and reared up, dumping the rest of the crates off his back. They clattered to the ground and if Oli had been listening close, he might've heard a quick oomph as the meat jar hit the gravel. But he was a goblin, so he wasn't.

"Ha ha!" The oozy woman shouted, and now it was more a cheer than a laugh. "See ya, suckers!" She lurched to one side, found the downhill slope, then sloughed down it in a slimy puddle. She laughed the whole way down, leaving a gooey trail as the goblins watched, eyes wide.

"Well, there's no way we're delivering that package now," Gob said. "Oops."

Robert grunted, hefted the now empty crate high, then chucked it off the cliff.

"What package?" he asked. In the distance, there was an explosive crack as the crate splintered to pieces far, far below. "No package."

"Big Boss no like!" Oli said, frowning at their diminished cargo. "But Horse like, so maybe okay."

"Shhh, you okay," Lin Two said, patting Horse as she collected hay to stuff back into his worn animal skins.

"Well," Oli said as he picked up the wire-frame sword, then turned to look up at the spooky mansion. "We have job."

NINE

Bad Spooky

"We just put by door?" Lin One asked as Oli carried the wire-frame sword toward the mansion. It was too long to manage alone, though, so the tip dragged in the dirt behind him.

"Would… like… " he said, huffing as went. The sword clanked against each step as he climbed on to the porch. "To give… to person. Whew." He paused at the front door to wipe sweat from his brow as he took in everything.

Up close, the structure gave Oli a funny feeling. Maybe it was the open windows, their translucent curtains billowing in the wind. Or maybe it was the bats roosting beneath the eaves, chittering and chirping as they watched with tiny, bright eyes. Then again, it was entirely possible the creeping feeling working its way over his skin was just on account of the distant screaming coming from inside the mansion.

"Nice place," Hob said, joining him on the porch. "With job now, we soon have one like?"

"The Dark Lord's favor is worth more than money, my dear Hob. Our rewards shall be far greater than clinking coins." Gob leaned against the railing and smiled.

"Also job no pay," Oli reminded him.

"Also that."

"Well," Lin Two said as she joined them on the porch. "Knock knock?"

Oli nodded and she stepped up to the door and—not being tall enough to reach the knocker—gave it a good kick. The door swung open, slow and with an echoing, moaning creak. The sound reverberated into the darkness within the mansion, creeping into the shadows and cobwebs until it was lost in the bowels of the house.

"Hel-lo?" Lin Two shouted in a sing-song voice. "Have package!"

The distant scream that'd been ringing at the edges of their hearing changed pitch for a moment.

"What that mean?" Lin Two asked, looking back.

Oli shrugged.

"Leave package by door?" she shouted.

The scream changed to a warbling moan. Now, Oli didn't speak scream, but something about that echoing, ghostly moan didn't sound particularly happy.

"Think they want package." He bit at his bottom lip. "We take in."

"No like," Lin One said, brow scrunched up and lip jutted out. "Is spooky."

"Spooky?" Oli frowned. "Big Boss spooky too. Citadel of Shadow and also of Sin spooky."

"But Big Boss there, so good spooky," Lin One explained. "Big Boss no here."

"Hm." Oli frowned at that, then his eyes went wide with an idea. He held the hilt of the sword out. "Take this. Keep you safe!"

Lin One's eyes lit up at that and he wrestled it into his arms, the hilt hugged tight to his chest and the blade dragging behind him.

"Now Lin One be spooky," he whispered to himself.

"Man wait with Horse. No have sword," Man said, as he found a seat atop the piled crates.

"Robert no have sword but Robert go!" The biggest goblin looked around for a weapon and, finding none, settled on the Weeping Stone. He held it cocked back, ready to throw. "No scared!" He'd returned now to his usual shade of green, apparently recovered from the experience of vomiting up his entire soul.

"We go then!" Oli said and stepped inside. The others followed, passing one by one from the sunlight on the porch to the shadows of the entrance hall. Robert came last, Weeping Stone at the ready and trailing splatters of salty water. As soon as he crossed the threshold, the door swung shut of its own accord. Near jumped off its hinges as it slammed closed and shook the whole wall.

The wire-frame sword clattered to the ground as Lin One panicked and ran headlong into the door.

"Bad spooky! Bad spooky! Want leave!" He pulled at the doorknob, but it held fast.

Something exhaled in the darkness beyond and everyone spun to face the sound, eyes wide.

"We… we bring package," Oli said, trying to find the source of the sound. "Leave here." He pointed to the discarded sword. "We go?"

The moan again, from further into the house. But now, Oli could understand it. There were words in the pained sound.

"Help… me… "

"If I'm not mistaken, I believe someone is in need of assistance," Gob said, rubbing his chin. "Someone should do something."

"Someone, yes. No us." Lin One said, very much not liking the idea of following a ghostly moan deeper into the shadows.

"You all cowards!" Lin Two stomped a foot, then strode forward. "No be scared. We have Robert."

Robert nodded, though he looked less sure than her. Behind him, the Weeping Stone was causing a small puddle on the floorboards.

"Lin Two right." Oli took a steadying breath. "We go. Bad spooky, maybe, but Big Boss keep goblins safe. Even if Big Boss no here." He nodded at his own words, encouraging the others to agree. The Big Boss had always kept them safe, except for that time the Bright Queen had burned down half their swamp. But every other time, definitely.

Together, the goblins managed to get the wire-frame sword lifted, then set off toward the moaning.

They were in an entrance hall with rooms on both sides, the ceiling rising to the second story above, and two curved, grand staircases winding up the walls to a landing. In the center of the space, a chandelier hung, cobwebs dangling to make it look like some sort of ghostly jellyfish hunting in the darkness.

Oli snuck a peek into the room on their right as he

passed. Looked to have been a sitting room, complete with a fireplace. Now, though, the chairs were overturned, the stuffing ripped from them, and several bookcases had collapsed in one corner, their books burying a stinky something he couldn't quite make out.

"Moan no that way," Oli said, then stepped onto the stairs. "This way."

Each step creaked more than the last and at one point, halfway up, a shudder ran through the house. Like something massive passing behind the walls. It started from high above, then shook the whole house as it came down, right past them, and all the way to the front door, which shook in its frame.

"House angry," Hob said.

"House… sad," Oli amended.

"Mr. Moan?" Lin Two shouted ahead. "We on way. Where you?"

"Arrrghhhuuuuuuhhh!"

"Oh, okay. Is this way."

The landing above the entrance hall wasn't much better than the room Oli had peered into. The banister was broken in several places and burn marks had scorched large holes in the rug. The wall was bashed inward in one spot as if a mammoth had been thrown into it. And everywhere, the air stank. Acrid and stale, like spoiled eggs.

The moaning was coming from around a corner and the goblins peered around it bravely. Ahead was a narrow hallway, windows lining one side. They were all shattered and when the wind blew, their white curtains danced in the space. Reaching out with gentle, grasping threads.

"Aurrrguuuhhhhuuuuuurrr!"

"Robert go first. Is biggest." He pushed past, Weeping Stone at the ready, then led them, step by step, down the hall.

Oli ducked under each curtain as they came to them, not wanting to be touched by their ghostly fingers.

And then, the moaning was right ahead. Coming from the room at the end of the hall. Its door had been knocked off its hinges and lay to one side, forgotten and splintered.

"Help… me…ah!"

"Have… have package," Robert said, then tiptoed into the room. Lin Two followed, then Oli, then the others, sword dragged behind them.

"Thank the Dark… Lord! Took you… long enough!"

A man was standing in the room, back to them. He was dressed in robes, had a long, black beard, and held his hands out in front of him where a cloud of white mist was boiling in midair. Veins and tendons stood out on his arms and his back was hunched over, giving the impression he was under great strain. Just beyond his fingertips, the captive cloud swirled endlessly.

"You have… the Soul Sword of… Silundonnor?"

"Have this." Oli said, and he and Hob raised the sword a bit. "We leave here. Thank. Good bye."

"No, no, no!" the man's face snapped around and Oli could see he was sweating profusely. Veins stood out on his forehead. "That sword was—gah!" The cloud of mist pulsated and the man fell to one knee. "Get back there, you!" He leaned forward and pushed out with his hands. The mist retreated a bit. "That sword was supposed to be here… a week ago. I need it to capture these… but I can't reach. Quickly, goblins! I need you to touch the sword to— is that rock leaking?"

Robert looked down at the Weeping Stone in his hand. It'd been dripping on the floor the whole way and now there was a puddle beneath his feet. The room must've been sloped, though, because the puddle was moving toward the man and the cloud. And also a circle of salt on the ground which, looking closer, Oli realized ran around the edge of the white mist.

"Don't let the water—" the man began to say, but it was too late. The puddle reached the salt, dissolved it, and then all at once, the cloud exploded outward.

It rushed through the gap in the salt and in the time it took Oli to blink, they were all enveloped.

TEN

Just A Little Murder

"Oh no. Oh no, no, no! Do you know what you've done? Do you understand? You stupid, stupid goblins! You've doomed us all!" The man's voice, panicking. But distant and fading, which was okay because it was such a nice day out and Oli was comfortable.

He was sitting in the downstairs study, a cup of warm tea beside him, and Hob lounging on the chaise and finishing up a cross stitch. Sunlight streamed through the window, warmly lighting the wooden floors. Brought out their deep, rich color. The reason he'd picked them, after all.

There came a knock at the door and Oli was getting ready to ask Robert to answer it, but he was already on it. Such an exceptional butler, that one.

The door swung open and there was a brief, muffled conversation. Oli couldn't grasp the words, but he didn't need to. Robert would let him know if it was something that required his attention.

"I wasn't expecting company today," he remarked as he admired Hob's cross-stitch. "Were you, my dear?"

"No, not at all. Though maybe it's the new table finally come?"

"A bit too soon for that, I should think. But let us hope. Perhaps it is our lucky day."

There was an explosion and Robert was flung down the hall in a blast of crackling flame. Oli jumped to his feet, but even as he did a figure strode through the ash raining down in the entrance hall. It was a man with a long, black beard and a worrisome look in his eye. Distant, hungry.

"Apologies," he said. "But this is necessary." And then his palms alighted with howling flames.

* * *

There was some sort of clamor downstairs because of course there was. There always was living with these people. The book he'd been reading slipped from Gob's lap and thunked to the floor. Bent the pages and dented the spine.

He scooped it up as he wiped sleep from his eyes.

A shame, really. It'd been such a fine nap. But of course he couldn't enjoy it. He couldn't enjoy anything in this house since he'd moved in with his sister and brother-in-law, and worse—far, far worse—their parents.

Another bang from downstairs and this one was accompanied by a scream. Almost sounded panicked, if he wasn't mistaken. But probably that was just his drowsiness messing with him. He rubbed sleep from his eyes and groaned as he rose from his favorite chair. Too comfortable, he'd often complained. Maybe he really did need a less enjoyable reading spot. Perhaps then he could get through more than an hour of study before dozing off.

Well, he was up now. And probably best he checked on whoever had screamed downstairs. Find out what nonsense his sister and brother-in-law were up to.

There was someone in the hallway as he stepped into it. A strange man wearing robes.

"Hello there," Gob said, surprised. "May I help you?"

"Well, there is one thing," the stranger said, then raised a hand.

"I'm sorry, who are yo—"

* * *

Fire. Fire! Something was burning in the house, and from the intensity of the smoke, it wasn't just her son-in-law having knocked a candle over again. Or, if he had, he'd really done it now. Either way, there wasn't time to waste.

Lin Two snapped shut the journal she'd been writing in and hurried across the room, skirts gathered in hand.

"Smoke!" she called in to Lin One who was tinkering with one of his model ships again. "Something's burning."

"Oh dear!" he said, straightening up and fussing at his handkerchief. "We should do something about that. Does Robert know?"

"If he doesn't, he's about to." Lin Two grasped the railing tightly as she hurried down the stairs to the second story and—her eyes found Gob. He was slumped in the corner, unmoving.

"Gob! My dear!" She ran to his side. "What's happened, are you okay? Robert!" she shouted, searching for him. Blasted butler! Terrible at his job. By rights she should have released him from their service weeks ago, but Oli had pushed back. "Robert! Send for the doctor!"

"That won't be necessary, madam."

A man was at the end of the hall and his clothes were on fire. Or, no. Just his hands. He was smiling.

* * *

"You stupid, stupid goblins!" The man was shouting again as Oli's vision faded in. The house was gone and the world around had been reduced to nothing but mist. Fog and shifting shadows.

An unseen force held him rooted to the ground, but he could move his head and, looking to the side, see his cousins. The same force must've held them because he'd never seen goblins stay so still.

In front of them all was the man, on his knees. His hands were firmly planted on the floor and Oli wasn't entirely sure, but it looked like the fog was gathered more thickly around him.

"Oli died..." he said, remembering the scene he'd just lived.

"Oh no! Is Oli okay?" Lin One exclaimed.

"Well he's here with us, so he didn't actually die. Probably." Gob was wincing at the end of the line. "I think... I think we all experienced that, yes? The... scenes? I'm not really sure what they were. The..."

"Memories." A voice spoke from all around. "Our memories." And now the voice was right in front of them.

Oli's eyes widened as the fog parted to reveal an elvish woman. She was older, matronly even, wore a scorched dress, and her eyes burned with a terrible vengeance. Worse yet, she was translucent. And the burning in her eyes gave off no heat. Only a deep chill that followed wherever her gaze turned.

"You not normal elf," Oli managed. "You…"

"Are dead, yes, little goblin. Along with the rest of my family." She stretched her arms out and more figures emerged from the fog.

"The sword," the man whispered at Oli. "Give me the sword. It can contain them, can harness their soul power. It's our only h—"

"That foul vessel won't help you here," the ghosts spoke as one and their eyes turned in unison to the human. "Nothing will."

"Where… where here?" Lin One asked, voice shaking.

"Somewhere you don't belong, small one." The matronly ghost softened then. "Thank you for all you've done. Without you, this vile man may have succeeded."

"Tell us, small ones," another ghost spoke. "What manner of hero are you?"

"No hero, ghost ma'am," Oli said. "Just couriers."

"Today you are heroes. Today you have righted a wrong." The matron looked down at her murderer. "A wrong that will not go unpunished."

"No, no! Please! You don't understand. I didn't want to kil—"

"Silence!" The ghosts screeched it as one and the man gagged on his words. Tried to suck down another breath but his mouth was frozen shut with spectral ice.

"Thank you, again," the matron said, eyes back on Oli and his cousins. "Now leave this vile man and his sword to us and depart in peace, noble couriers."

Even as she said it, Oli and his cousins were carried away, the mist retreating in a rushing swirl until it disappeared entirely and they found themselves back in the old mansion, and alone.

"Lin Two, Lin One, Robert," Oli said, rushing around to count his cousins. "Hob and Gob!" He breathed a sigh of relief. "Everyone be okay?"

Gob was patting himself up and down as if unconvinced his body was corporeal again.

"That no fun," Lin Two said, eyes wide as she stared around the now empty room. The ghosts and the man had entirely disappeared.

"That no good," Lin One agreed.

"Delivery successful!" Robert pumped a fist in the air. "We do it!"

"Yes, well, that's one way to look at it," Gob said, already looking for the exit. "Now how's about we leave and never come back?"

Everyone sprinted toward the door.

"Oli like that idea," he said and made to follow them. His toe kicked against something though, and he found the Weeping Stone discarded on the floor. Technically, they still were supposed to deliver it to its destination so he scooped it in one hand and ran.

The house was quieter now. Nothing shuddered behind the walls, nothing breathed unseen in the darkness, and even the curtains billowed less. All the same, the goblins hurried in a mad dash.

Oli was the last off the grand staircase and just as he reached the bottom, something thunked behind him. He near jumped out of his skin and ran all the faster. But Gob was standing on the front porch, eyes wide and pointing. Oli slowed, then looked over his shoulder to see an urn clattering down the stairs. It clunked and bounced from one step to the next.

Thunk. Thunk.

When it hit the floor Oli was sure it would break but instead it landed heavily, rolled, and came to a stop right in front of him.

"No want," he said, backing away, but then something was moving in the dust on the floor. Something unseen, dragging a track through the dirt and grit to make... words. Writing.

"What say?" Robert asked. "No can read," he added with a heavy sigh.

"It's... well, it's an address," Gob said, watching as more letters were dragged through the dust. "The Overlook B&B, Number Six Seaside Lane, Storm Coast County, Kingdom of Humanity."

"Why send empty urn?" Oli asked and, as if in response, the urn shook. The lid rattled and a wisp of mist leaked out with a tiny gasp.

"I'm afraid it's not empty." Gob swallowed hard. "Our new ghost friends seem to want a change of scenery. And, well, I think that's on our way?"

Oli sighed.

"Courier of Cataclysm harder job than me thought."

ELEVEN

Wet Beef Jerky

"What happen in there?" Man asked from where he was hiding behind Horse's skeletal flanks. "Hear bad sounds. Angry voices!"

"Meet mean wizard man, meet angry ghosts, free angry ghosts, then…" Lin Two paused, brow furrowed. "Ghosts eat mean wizard man?" She shrugged. "I no ghost knower."

"We deliver one package…" Oli said, and Man cheered. Oli raised the haunted urn. "And get another."

Man blew a fart noise and deflated.

"Package collection growing!" Lin One said, climbing atop one of the crates piled beside Horse. "Soon have all the packages!"

"No to keep. Only deliver," Oli said. "But goblins go too slow. Big Boss need Key soon."

"Does anyone even know what the Key is?" Gob interjected suddenly. "I mean, did the Dark Lord tell you what it looks like?"

Oli frowned at that.

"Key is key," he said. "That why called key."

"Gob feel okay?" Hob asked, placing a hand on his shoulder.

Gob sighed, then reluctantly nodded.

"Sure, yeah." He massaged his temples. "Anyway, what were you saying?"

"Goblins go too slow," Oli said again. "Big Boss need Key soon but goblins have too many packages. Too heavy."

"Ooh, Robert help!" The big goblin grabbed the urn and opened his maw wide. All at once, a wind whipped up and staggered him. A rush of leaves broke from the surrounding forest, swirling in a vortex before settling in front of Robert. And as they settled, they made the shape of words.

"No can read." Robert frowned at them. "One day want read. One day."

"Do not eat our urn," Gob said, piecing together the difficult sentence, then turning to Robert. "I think our ghostly companions prefer to ride somewhere other than, well, wherever that bag in your stomach sends things."

"Okay. No eat." Robert gave a serious nod, then patted the jar. "No eat."

The wind blew past again, but this time it seemed natural. Just swept away the leaves.

"Still have problem," Oli said. "Horse no can carry all packages. Need help!"

Robert did his best to swallow one of the bigger crates, which was a nice gesture, but futile considering it was as large as him. Still, he bit down on one corner helpfully.

"Need mammoth!" Lin Two shouted all at once. "We can have mammoth, Oli? Please?"

"Yes, yes!" Hob said and began stomping around as if he were one of the giant beasts of burden. "We be big! We be loud! We be extra stinky!"

"If goblins need mammoth Big Boss give mammoth. Like he give Horse," Oli pointed out. After all, they were serving him and he'd always provided what they needed. "Big Boss!" he shouted into the sky. "Goblins have mammoth please? Thank!"

No mammoth came plummeting down. A dragonfly did, but only after it'd flown headlong into a tree. Man pounced and gobbled it up, spittle flying.

"Big Boss give treat!" he said through crunchy mouthfuls. "Big Boss happy with goblins."

Oli was pretty sure the dragonfly wasn't a gift, but the Big Boss worked in mysterious ways, so who was he to judge? And either way, it wasn't a mammoth.

"Big Boss no think we need mammoth," he said. "Goblins find other way."

"Okay, okay," Gob said, voice ponderous. "Bear with me on this one—"

"Bear?" Man shouted and climbed higher atop the boxes. "Where bear?"

"Werebear?" Lin Two shouted next. "Ooh, ooh. Bite Lin Two!" She held out an arm as she searched the clearing. "Make into scary werebear, please!"

Gob sighed deeply. Some days, he regretted his past

choices. Maybe he shouldn't have resorted to such an extreme as this, but after the showdown at the college, what other option had been available to him? And, though he was loathe to admit it, his adopted cousins had grown on him. A bit like a toenail infection, but also a bit like annoying younger siblings.

"I was going to propose we disassemble the crates, get rid of the excess packaging, and only carry the essentials. Some of the items in the crates might even be able to fit down Robert's throat."

Oli frowned, then pointed to the still-glistening trail of ooze heading off into the woods.

"No good happen last time goblins mess with crates."

"Yes, well, that was unfortunate. But it's a safe assumption not every crate is serving as a prison for an ooze monster."

"How you know?" Oli asked.

"Well, I don't. As I said, it's an assumption."

"You tell Oli about as-sump-shuns once," he said, arms crossed. "Said turn us into butts!"

"That's not quite how the saying…"

"Oh my great abyss above and below!" A new voice shouted and all the goblins jumped as one. "Are you imbeciles just going to stand here and argue semantics until the heat death of the universe? Or are you actually going to get on with the deliveries?"

"Who that?" Robert heaved a crate high and stood ready to throw it.

"Yes, who goes there?" Gob asked, hands held in front of him as if, well, as if he'd once seen a fight but didn't really remember how it all worked.

"Big Boss?" Oli asked, looking to the sky. But the voice didn't sound like Big Boss. It was too whiny. Too human. Lacked that little special something that always left your soul shivering as if it was staring down an eternity spent in the deepest, coldest pit of hell.

"In here, you morons."

Hob carefully approached the pile of crates, and with Man's help, moved them to reveal the book Rodrigrar had asked they give to the Dark Lord.

"Book read itself!" Man said, reaching for it cautiously. "Book smart!"

"Book teach Robert how read?" the big goblin asked.

"No, not the book! Why would you think I'm the book? Books can't talk. Well, there was that one time we implanted a limited consciousness into the Encyclopedia Universalis. That book could talk, but mostly it just screamed. Ahem. No, you dumb little goblins. I'm not a talking book. No, not a crate either," the voice warned as Oli prodded the nearest one. "Over here. No, no, yes. There. *Yes*, exactly."

Oli lifted the jar Rodrigrar had given them. It was full of green liquid and floating in said liquid was an unidentifiable lump of meat. Looked like a chicken gizzard crossed with a kidney.

"You are... wet beef jerky?" Oli asked. "And can talk?"

"I was a man not so long ago—look, the accident was rather traumatic. But that's not the point. The point is I'd hoped for a competent courier to get me home so I could fix all this. Instead, it would appear the tattered remains of my brain stem contains more wrinkles than any of the other seven brains here." Little bubbles leaked from the floating lump of jerky as he spoke.

"Gob smart goblin," Oli said and pointed to him. Gob only backed away, though, eyes wide as he, for the first time, seemed to have nothing to say. Only shook his head and waved a hand under his chin.

"I was content to sit here and just let you be on about

your jobs, but it seems you're entirely incapable of doing them. And so, as usual, I must take charge—good help is so hard to make these days, I swear. Look, you've taken on more packages than you can carry. Woe is you! What an insurmountable obstacle! If only, in the long history of invention and innovation, we'd come up with a solution for such a problem. Something like, oh, I don't know, a big box to put all the other boxes in. Oh, and let's give it wheels, shall we? And pull it with horses. And we'll call it… a wagon! Yes, a wagon! Wouldn't it be ever so helpful if such a thing existed?"

Man's brow furrowed.

"Wagon do exist."

"Aha!" The bubbles trickled out more excitedly. "We have a front-runner for least stupid goblin. Yes, you're quite right. Wagons do exist! Can anyone tell me what that means?"

"We should get wagon!" Oli exclaimed as the idea hit him out of nowhere.

"Yes, exactly!" The wet beef jerky jiggled a little. "Another front-runner emerges!"

Oli craned his neck to the sky and spread his arms wide.

"Oh, Big Boss of darkness and frighten, give wagon?"

"And fades back into the pack…" the lump of meat said with a sigh.

"Wagon no come." Oli frowned at the clear blue skies. "Where get wagon then?" He turned to Gob who was always full of good ideas. "Gob know?"

But he only shook his head, suddenly silent, then set about gnawing on a crate.

"There's a wagon dealership literally down the road," the organ said. "I don't want to tell you how to do your jobs, but somebody has to. Go get wagon, load this pile of detritus into it, then deliver me and the Weeping Stone to our destination. We're going to the same place so really, it's not that hard." The lump sank to the bottom of the jar, then floated forward to bump into the glass right above a little note stuck to the outside.

"No can read—" Robert began.

"Yes, yes. We're well aware," the organ groaned. He made a noise as if clearing the throat he didn't have. "It's the address of my destination, but seeing as no one here can find two brain cells to rub together, I'll guide you there —soon as you get that miraculous, mind-bending invention we call a wagon."

TWELVE

Wriggly Little Customers

The wagon dealership was bigger than anything Oli had expected—mostly because it was sized for humans and other human-sized races, but it made it just that much more impressive anyway.

Out front, select wagons had been put on display, raised on tilted platforms to show how dramatically all-terrain they were. And in the back, behind a fence, there were more wagons than any of the goblins had ever seen in one place. Big ones for hauling as much cargo as a mammoth; small ones just for enjoying a lazy ride through the country; armored ones for whatever armored wagons were used for—Oli wasn't sure; and more.

"Hello, yes, excuse please. Want have wagon," Oli said, standing on his tiptoes just to get his eyes up to the height of the front desk. The human sitting there didn't notice him.

"Hob give boost?" Oli asked and his cousin obliged, pushing him all the way up onto the desk, arms shaking.

"Hello human woman!" Oli said triumphantly.

She looked over slowly, as if she'd noticed an ant crawling across her paperwork, then gasped.

"Frankric! The infestation's back!"

"No infest. Only want wagon," Oli said and gave his most diplomatic smile. He didn't know what that word meant, but he tried his best.

"Oh, you can talk?" the woman leaned away, wincing. "Ugh."

"No, just—oh, come on. Just, yes, just toss me up. Like that—yes."

There was a clunk and then the jar landed beside Oli, liquid sloshing side to side.

"Excuse me, madam. I beg you forgive the imposition of my companions. They are regrettably necessary for the moment. Please ignore them and take us to your finest wagon."

If the human woman had been surprised before, she was downright panicked now. Or, at least Oli assumed that was the case as she screamed, tipped over her chair, crawled to her feet, then sprinted away still screaming.

"We follow?" Oli asked. "To best wagon?"

"What's all the commotion—huh?" A human man asked as he strode into the room. He was well-dressed in formal robes that were only a little bit frayed at each seam, and his hair was slicked back like someone had upended the talking jar onto it. His eyes were beady and small, but they went wider and wider by the moment as he took in the sight before him. The goblin tracking mud across the welcome desk was bad enough, but why was there an embalmed piece of beef jerky beside it? And then, great gods above, there were more goblins just behind. And an orc! Frankric's heart jumped at the sight, until he realized the orc was squinting fiercely at a brochure as if locked in a fight to the death with the words there. Lastly there was a horse—right in the lobby, hadn't even been left outside!—and it barely looked fit enough to breathe, much less pull any sort of wagon. Gods, the thing was basically rotting where it stood.

"Want wagon!" Oli said to the man with his biggest smile. "Can have?"

"Sir, excuse me. Sir?" the lump spoke and the man took a moment to process that. "Hello, yes. We're here for a wagon. Top of the line model, if you have it. Any longer on that half-dead horse and I'll be shaken right out of my jar."

The gaggle of pests in front of Frankric might have been repulsive, but after a moment, his mind caught up to the fact that they were customers. And customers were never repulsive. He clapped his hands together and gave a beaming smile.

"Well, of course you're here for a wagon! And boy, do we have plenty of 'em. Best wagons in the land. The Bright Queen herself rides in one of our models, you know." He gave a wink. "And while hers is one-of-a-kind, I'm certain we can find the exact right one for you!"

* * *

"That one?" Frankric laughed as the smallest goblin pointed to the nicest wagon on the lot. "Oh, that's too much wagon for you, little guy. That right there's the top-of-the-line sport wagon from *Bayerische Motoren Wagonwerke*. Sleek, sexy, and expensive." He gave a low whistle. "Comes standard with hookups for up to thirty horsepower and enough suspension you'll think you're riding a cloud. Perfect for a respectable businessman about town."

"It's missing turn signals," the lump bubbled and it was right. The little flags mounted on the sides of every other wagon were noticeably absent.

"It's a Bayerische Motoren Wagonwerke! It doesn't need something so demeaning as turn signals," Frankric laughed.

It was a fine-looking wagon, Oli had to admit. The finest he'd seen and that was saying something because there was quite the collection of wagons stuck fast and rotting in the swamp back home. Unlike those, however, this wagon was dry. And the wheels were still on! The seats even came with cushions that looked rather tasty.

"Lin One want that one!" he said, pointing to a massive, near sailing ship-sized wagon. "All fit in there."

"Oh, this little guy?" Frankric slapped the side of it. "This bad boy can fit so much mud in it. Or… whatever it is goblins need to haul. This little number will carry as much as four mammoths!"

Oli's eyes went big at that.

"Four mammoths?"

"Aye, that's right. And you only need two to pull it!" Frankric laughed again, one hand on his belly. "Or, maybe you'd like to transport your whole goblin brood? Said you lot were on a road trip, right?"

Hob nodded blankly.

"Then you'd want this sleek people—er, goblin mover.

May I present the 1379 Forb LTD Country Squire! With six rows of bench seats, plenty of room for luggage and feed bags, and a collapsible canvas cover, it's our top-of-the-line destination wagon." He gave a wink.

"Ooooh," the goblins said as one.

"No, no!" The lump chimed in. "I wouldn't be caught dead in that thing. What do I look like, a father of sniveling brats on a road trip to Smalley World? Come on, Frankric. Let's get serious."

"Well, I suppose we could get more specific."

"Specificity is preferred."

"Could find something a bit more suited to your particular needs."

"That would be excellent, thank you."

Frankric nodded, then led them away from the finer wagons and toward a fenced-in side area with a low, swinging gate to get in and out. A bored looking man was sitting beside it, half asleep.

"This is where we keep our best wagons," Frankric said, nodding at the goblins as he pulled the gate open for everyone. "You don't want that other stuff. No, no. You want something like this little beauty right here!" He stopped beside an appropriately goblin-sized wagon.

It was beautiful. Painted a brilliant red, it had four wheels, raised sides so no one fell out, and even a handle up front so it could be pulled. It was magnificent! Brought a tear to Oli's eye.

"That's a children's toy," the lump said.

"What?" Frankric pressed a hand to his chest—and kicked a Teddy bear out of sight behind the jungle gym. "No, sir, you're mistaken. This is a certified Real Wagon! Only one in our inventory, too. And look, it even comes with custom artwork on the sides."

"A child's drawn on it with chalk," the lump said.

"It…" Oli wiped a tear away. "It beautiful. We take!"

"That's the spirit! And it's yours for only the low, low price of three bronze pieces."

Oli patted his pockets, before remembering he had none.

Lin Two held out a worm she'd found.

"This enough?"

"Not… uh, not quite." Frankric frowned. "You did bring money with you, right?"

"Yes!" Oli said, then frowned. "But no."

Frankric sighed.

"Okay, well how about a trade?" He repeated the word nice and slow. "Trade. Can we do that?"

"Yes!" Man nodded enthusiastically. "We give Horse, you give wagon."

Frankric winced as he looked at Horse in the distance.

"That poor thing's trade-in value is about one wheel. Looks well out of warranty, too."

"It's literally dead and reanimated," the fleshy lump said.

"No give Horse!" Lin Two shouted and pushed Man aside. "Horse friend!"

"Yeah! And who pull wagon?" Lin One added, piling onto Man.

"Okay, ow! Ow!" he shouted, running as they pinched him.

"Anything else worth trading?" Frankric asked, hope draining from his eyes.

"Robert have idea!" There a choking gag from behind and then several wet items thunked to the ground. Robert bent to dig through them, then held up a saliva-covered locket. "This work?"

"Well, it could be a start." Frankric reached for it, then

82

froze as his eyes fell on a feather quill among the other regurgitated things. "What about... what about that?"

He blinked and a shadow passed over him. Licked his lips next as his mind filled with images of all the money he'd make if only he had that beautiful, beautiful quill. And it looked like it used red ink, too, from the dribble gathered on the quill tip. Vibrant, brilliant red ink. Looked alive, almost. The contracts he'd write with that quill and its ink would be nothing short of magical. He didn't know how he knew, but he just did. And then, as if from afar, there was a voice in his ear. Not loud enough for him to consciously notice it, but loud enough that his subconscious was all ears. Such sweet riches that voice promised. Such binding, unbreakable contracts he could pen. If only he had that quill. He'd have the power to finally show the world how successful he was. How successful he deserved to be.

"The quill for the wagon," he said, extending a hand toward it. "It's a deal—"

"Halt in the name of the Bright Queen!" A voice echoed across the lot and Oli looked up to find a massive wagon clattering toward them. Armored and bristling with spears and bows and men holding them. The wheels had spikes jutting from their spokes and there was a battering ram mounted on the front end.

"You are being detained. Stay where you are!"

THIRTEEN

Detective Stones

"Stay where you are! Move another step and we will open magic on you!" A soldier atop the war wagon shouted. He didn't look like other soldiers Oli had seen, though. Instead of armor he wore a coat and shiny boots, and he'd a wand grasped in both hands.

"No move!" Oli shouted, hands in the air. "We no move!" He gave a little kick to Lin One who was bent over, chuckling to himself as he stoked a fire between Frankric's boots. "No move, cousin!"

The driver of the newly arrived wagon pulled hard on the reins, the four horses jerked to the side, and then the entire vehicle drifted to a stop, wheels screeching and screaming. Even before it stopped, the side doors flew open and a half-dozen shiny-booted soldiers spewed out. They leapt through the air and Oli couldn't help but let out a little gasp of awe.

One heroic launch after another, the soldiers' faces set in grim determination, their hearts steadied with the noble purposes of their work. Their breast plates flashed in the sun as each tucked into a perfect roll, then let the momentum carry them to their feet. They came up, one after the other, with wands held in hand, clasped tight and pointed at the goblins. Or, well, mainly pointed at Frankric, but Oli kept his hands raised high anyway. One of the soldiers had a staff gripped by both hands, its back pressed into their shoulder and the business end at the ready.

"No sudden movements now, salesman—if that's really your job," the foremost of the soldiers said. She'd a bowler cap on in place of a helmet and it was cocked to one side in a way that said 'reckless but competent.' Or maybe 'too cool for rules but always cool under pressure.' Oli wasn't an expert in human fashion. Whatever her tilted hat was trying to say, it was apparent she was in charge of the soldiers. There was a badge on her chest, but Oli couldn't read. It was extra shiny though.

"Comply and this will be easier for you," she snapped, wand aimed at Frankric's chest.

"Really, Sergeant, such an entrance. The drama, the action!" A voice came from inside the wagon. The doors still hung open and beyond, there was only dark. Until a flit of flame bloomed to life—along with a puff of pipe smoke —to reveal a man sitting inside. "You don't need all the theatrics to impress me. I'm ever so familiar with the fine job done by our heroic officers." The wagon creaked as he emerged from within. It'd been sitting low on its suspension and Oli had assumed that was on account of all the armor plastered about it. He learned now it was on account of this man. The entire wagon rose up with a relieved groan as his weight left it. He stepped into the sun and it became apparent he wore no armor—and needed none, because beneath his flowing trench coat, he was made of stone.

"Look, Lin One!" Man hissed. "He just like you!"

"Lin One rock goblin. That no rock goblin. That golem!"

And he was right. The golem was far taller than any of the goblins—half again the height of a human—and not just drier than a swamp goblin, but literally made of stone. Living rock that shifted and clacked as he moved. He drew on his pipe again and, as he blew out, the smoke dissipated through the cracks all across his body.

"I'll take it from here. Thank you, Sergeant Lastrof."

"Your authority on this case is questionable at best, Detective Stones."

"Please, as always, call me Sherrock."

"My officers and I are in the middle of apprehending suspected agents of chaos and darkness, *Sherrock*, so can you please stop doing this? We're not just here to draw attention and set up your dramatic entrance," Sergeant Lastrof said and her already aggressively slanted brow took on an even angrier slope.

"Of course you're not *just* here to assist my dramatic entrances," Detective Stones said as he patted her shoulder. "You're also the comic relief. Now then!" He shouted it and snapped his attention to Frankric before she could retort. "Do forgive the interruption, but we are hot on the trail of some true scoundrels, you see."

"Calm," Oli whispered to the others. "Be calm. Big Boss protect."

Robert looked as if his stomach was troubling him, and Gob had already worked his way to the back of the group. Arms still in the air, but he looked to be eyeing a getaway.

"What do?" Hob asked. "Oli, what do?"

"Trust Big Boss," Oli whispered back. "Big Boss save!" Though, when that was going to happen, he wasn't sure. Soon, hopefully.

"This is just a wagon dealership, er… Detective, sir," Frankric said, arms still in the air. "The only thing criminal here are our deals." His lips twisted into a bit of a smile at that.

"Oh, a man of humor. Well, you'll have to compete with the jesters behind me and, I must warn you, they're exceedingly amusing." Sherrock took another long drag of his pipe. He smiled, then exhaled. "But perhaps you can do a better job of entertaining me. I'd love to hear the story of how you became a servant of the Dark Lord?"

"Servant of the Da—the Dark Lord?" Frankric swallowed hard. "No, no, no. You've got it twisted, surely. I'm just a wagon salesman."

"Hmm, not sowing seeds of chaos and treachery through the land, then?"

Oli's eyes flicked down to the quill Robert had regurgitated. No one had noticed it yet so Oli nudged it beneath the red wagon with his foot.

"Enough games," Sergeant Lastrof said and pushed past Detective Stones. "We know there's a courier of cataclysm in this county. Scurrying from place to place, doing the Dark Lord's bidding. I've a hunch it's you." She poked a finger into his chest and he winced.

"It's not, I swear."

"You sure you're not lying to us? We have spells to make you talk."

A heavy bead of sweat rolled down Frankric's cheek.

"I'm not lying! Not about this, you have to believe me," he cried out all at once. "I only lie once in a while. About little things, like mileage!"

The Sergeant leaned in closer, frowning all the deeper.

"Okay, okay!" Frankric gasped. "And when I say I'm going back to talk about wiggle room with my boss, there is no boss! I just go have a cup of coffee then come back!"

"Fascinating, very fascinating," Detective Stones said, repacking his pipe. "But the problem is, we know there's an agent of apocalypse here. And if it's not you, well, then who?" He looked around, brows raised. "The wagons?"

"I don't know! I don't, really. Maybe the goblins?" Frankric gasped.

"The goblins?" Sergeant Lastrof frowned. "What go— oh." Her eyes found Oli. He gave a little wave, arms still high overhead.

"No mean bother. Just want wagon."

"When did they get here?" she snapped at her officers who all shrugged in response.

If the Big Boss was going to intervene, it was going to need to be soon. Oli crossed his fingers and glanced toward the sky. A bird flew overhead, unconcerned.

"Goblins? At a wagon dealership? Isn't that interesting." Sherrock's joints cracked with a sound like a minor rockslide as he bent down in front of Oli. "Now what might you all be doing here?"

Oli swallowed hard. Big Boss had always protected them, but now he was starting to think they were on their own.

"Want have wagon!" Man chimed in from behind.

"Whatever for?"

"Horse no do too good," Oli said, finding his voice again as he pointed to where they'd left Horse out front. "Need wagon for road trip. Go see family." Oli realized he was still holding the jar and its talking lump of wet beef jerky, though it'd seemingly lost its ability to talk with so many agents of good about. "We take present to family," he said, holding it up awkwardly.

"Hmmm…" The detective made a sound like water flowing through a rocky creek bottom.

"For the world's best detective, you're too easily distracted," Sergeant Lastrof snapped. "Stop wasting time." She waved the goblins away. "And you lot scamper off. Go set a fire somewhere else."

"Yes, ma'am," Oli managed as he spun and began herding everyone away. "Quick, quick!"

"Go!" Gob hissed.

"Hold on."

Sherrock's voice froze Oli in his tracks.

"Why is that stone crying?"

Lin Two looked down to the Weeping Stone tied to her belt.

"Um… it sad?"

"Hmm." He pressed a thumb to his stoney chin.

"Sherrock!" Sergeant Lastrof slapped his shoulder. "We've a job to do."

"Yes, of course," he said, but even as the soldiers hauled Frankric into the wagon, Sherrock's eyes never left the goblins' retreating backs.

FOURTEEN

A Shortcut To Mausoleums

"Can't this wretched creature go any faster? Ride, you fools! Ride!"

The jar was a flurry of bubbles as the sentient flesh lump screamed an unending stream of encouragement.

"Go, Horse! You can do! Go!" Lin Two shouted, patting Horse's skeletal neck as every stride was a shaking, panicked affair. Far short of a wagon, they were all loaded back up on the beast, crates tottering side to side, and Man hanging from Horse's tail and screaming.

On the upside, they were making good time.

"Be careful with the jar," someone whispered in Oli's ear. Gob, leaning in real close, voice barely audible. "I don't trust it."

"That why you so quiet?" Oli asked. "Oli was—"

"Chit chat later! Save our rears now!" The flesh had spun toward Oli, or, as best as he could tell what was the front. Gob yelped and slipped away from the jar.

"Turn here!" Oli shouted, leaning over Lin Two's shoulder and pointing. She yanked to the right and Horse reluctantly followed, dirt and maybe a package or two kicked out behind them.

They swung hard around the turn and, for a moment, Oli could see the wagon dealership behind them. It was swarming with the Bright Queen's soldiers now, but none of them had cared about the goblins. Just like Big Boss had said. Maybe he had saved them after all.

"Whoa there!"

Horse stumbled into the heavy flowing traffic of the main road and immediately cut off a mammoth. It trumpeted angrily as it reared onto hind legs—and dumped its cargo into the road. Oncoming wagons swerved aside, horses bucked and kicked, and at least one other mammoth-load's worth of crates and crops and tools were dumped into the road. Shouts and curses floated after the goblins, but with traffic so jammed, no one could follow. Horse kept going, teetering side to side until they rounded the next bend.

"Good Horse, good," Lin Two said, trying to calm the frantic beast. Oli hadn't realized skeletons could sweat but somehow, Horse was.

"It okay," Oli said, looking to make sure no one was following. "We make it."

"Everything fine," Man said, climbing up from where he'd been dangling from Horse's tail.

"'Everything fine?'" The jar boiled with the force of the sound. "Everything's not fine! We were nearly apprehended by the Bright Queen's forces! All because you pitiful lot had to stop and ogle the wagons."

"Wagons was jar's idea," Lin One pointed out.

"Robert no feel okay," the big goblin said, then clapped a hand to his mouth and burped wetly. When it came away, he'd an evil-looking dagger in hand. He tried to swallow it back down, but gagged in the process.

"Horse too hot!" Lin Two shouted from up front. "No can keep going."

Man and Lin One began fanning their ignoble steed.

"Get air! Make cool!"

There was a rattling from among the crates and Oli spotted the urn shaking in place. The lid slipped to one side and a sliver of mist crept out. It rolled forward and Man yelped as it reached him.

"Gah!" He near jumped off Horse, but the mist kept going. It reached out delicately, like a spectral finger, then ever so gently, touched one of Horse's vertebrae.

Horse let loose a sudden whinny and Oli climbed atop a crate as frost instantly shot across Horse and the animal skins he was wrapped in. After a moment, the whinny was replaced by a satisfied snort.

"Ooh, Horse like..." Lin Two cooed. "Many thank, scary ghosts."

The mist brushed her cheek a moment, then retreated into its urn.

"Great, well that's just wonderful. Now that we've made friends with the ghost urn and the stupid horse isn't melting, can we focus on where we're going?" the organ jar bubbled.

"Jar mean," Oli said, picking it up and turning it to face him. "Maybe we no deliver." He put on his fiercest expression.

Behind, Robert grunted agreement.

"Maybe we smash!"

"Okay, okay, calm down," the lump said, bubbles trickling more slowly now. "We're all just a bit heated, let's not overreact."

"No overreact. You overreact."

"Okay, that's fair. I was unkind. That was rude. But how about we all play nice—and not smash anything? When we get to my house, I'll see that you have all the... heated mud or worms or whatever it is you want." The lump spun in place, presumably turning to face each of the goblins. "Does that sound good? Yeah? You just have to deliver me to the address listed."

"We go to Fortress Isolgar to get Key," Oli said firmly. "That quest for Big Boss." He set the jar down and crossed his arms. "But... your delivery on way. We drop you off when passing."

"And the Weeping Stone, too!" the lump insisted.

"Weeping Stone sad," Lin Two said, looking down at the thing. "Why sad?" She gave it a hug. "No be sad, stone."

"Look, look, look," the lump said. "This is the road to Isolgar. You're doing what the Big Boss wants, but you're still a week away. And three days from my place. But..." the lump drew out the word in a string of little bubbles. "You can shave a whole two days off both trips if you follow my route."

"What route this?" Lin One asked looking unconvinced.

"I've lived here all my life. I know every mausoleum and graveyard of this county. And the best short cuts between them."

"Oli no trust." He tapped the jar. "Lump mean, not help us."

"By helping you I help myself, you insolent little—" A sigh. "Look, take my short cut. I get home faster, you get rid of me sooner, and everyone's happy. Oh, and we can avoid the Bright Queen's patrols."

"Patrols? What patrols?" Gob perked up, then seemed to remember something and made himself scarce again.

"What wrong with Gob?" Oli asked Hob, who only shrugged.

"Patrols like that one," the lump answered, and looking through its sloshing liquid, Oli could just see riders blocking the road ahead.

"Uh oh."

"Quick, turn here!" the meat lump insisted as he bounced off the left side of the jar. "By that old tree. There's a creek bed. Follow it!"

* * *

Traveling on backroads was far slower than the highway, but at least there weren't any of the Bright Queen's patrols or giant, stomping mammoths. And the lump's instructions led them from one patch of scraggly trees to the next, so Horse kept mostly cool even in the heat of the day. Only a few crates were knocked free by low-hanging branches. They traveled for the rest of the day, then slept on Horse as the dutiful demon-steed soldiered on through the night. By morning they'd made great progress—according to the floating lump of wet beef jerky.

"Ah, yes! Mt. Sematary Hill," he said as they passed

into what seemed the fifth graveyard in a row. "One of my favorites, I must admit. Very active."

"How is active?" Gob asked. He'd been mostly quiet around the jar, but now he was talking again. Not like his usual self, though. Didn't get enough sleep, maybe.

"Well, burials, of course. This is the most popular cemetery from here to Turnside Tower."

"Why care?"

"No reason," the lump said in a way that said there was definitely a reason.

"So why you talking lump?" Man asked, poking at the jar.

"Man!" Oli hissed, then waved a finger at him. "That rude. No ask why we goblin. We just goblin."

"I know we goblin, but what lump? Why lump?"

"I wasn't always this pitiful thing you see before you," the lump said. "Once I was magnificent. I was brilliant! And everyone looked up to me." His voice quieted. "But there was an accident that left me rather… reduced. But once I'm home, I can fix all of that, which is why it's imperative that we——"

"Well, well, well."

One of the Bright Queen's patrols! Oli panicked at the thought, but as he found the source of the voice, realized he was wrong. It wasn't a Soldier of Good but an orc, standing at the exit to the cemetery, muscular arms crossed as she leaned against a snoozing saddle hog. Paulter, Oli realized, recognizing her and her excellent mustache from the Inn.

She snapped a finger and then suddenly arms caught Oli from either side and hefted him off Horse.

"Hold those tight," the orc leader said. "Don't want any repeats of that trick you pulled last time, huh?" She leaned forward, squinting at the mark Lord Sarusomal had left on his forearm.

"Is nice to see again, but please to put Oli down," he said, but the two orcs had grips strong as iron. "Please to put down."

"There's only three of them! Fight back, goblins! Use the ghosts or something!" the lump shouted, but even as he did, there came a grunting from afar—and drawing closer by the moment. In the time it took Oli to blink, the grunting was right up on them and, from the hill on their left, five hogs appeared, each with an orc riding it.

Like their leader, they wore leather jackets with plate armor reinforcing the elbows, shoulders, and back. Chain mail clung in patches and loose strings in what seemed a choice more in favor of fashion than practicality.

The riders swept down the hill, hogs grunting and squealing as their hooves thundered.

"Horse, do something," Lin Two said, leaning forward. The undead steed took in the scene, then sat down. Crates, packages, and goblins toppled off.

"Not that something!" But even as Lin Two scrambled to her feet, the hogs were on them. Great tusks and saliva-dripping lips pushed forward, herding the goblins into a tight, squirming pack.

The orcs chuckled at the sight. One gave her hog a heavy pat on its thick, muscle-packed neck.

"Got the one with the goods, boss," a voice grunted and Oli turned to see the strongest-looking orc had wrapped his arms around Robert from behind. Oli'd never looked too close, but in the moment, his mountain goblin cousin looked a lot like their orcish captors. About the same size, though where Robert's bulk was all huggable heft, the orcs' was taut muscle.

"Robert no want hug, thank," the mountain goblin

grunted, trying to ease away. The strong arms held him locked in place.

"Open the crates, search the packages. Grab anything what looks valuable," Paulter said, and her companions set about it. The hogs kept the goblins huddled tight as crates were hefted, packages were shaken, and the collected spilled cargo was searched.

"Ugh. What's this thing?" one of the orcs asked, kicking at the fallen organ jar. The wet beef jerky inside sloshed around, but didn't speak. "That's just gross."

"And the horse isn't even alive!" another orc exclaimed, pulling at the animal skins covering Horse. They came free in a shower of hay and stuffing. "You really beefed it this time, Paulter. There's nothing of any value here because of course there isn't. These are goblins! Like I told you."

"Shut up, Jeremiah. I know what I saw." She snapped her attention to another orc. "Get the sock."

"No need sock, already have, thank," Robert said, but the orc was already approaching, a smile slashed through his beard as he fished around inside his jacket. Not in the pockets, though, but up in the sleeve. In the armpit. And then he pulled out a sock and even from paces away, the smell hit Oli like a sucker punch. Like a newtcake left too long in the sun. Or heated mud taken from the latrines instead of a proper mud hole.

Oli gagged and leaned away, but the sock wasn't meant for him. Was shoved under Robert's nose instead.

"No want... thank. No need—" Robert made it all of half a sentence before there was a churning in his stomach. A bulge filled his throat and he forced his mouth shut. His cheeks swelled, eyes crossed, and then he couldn't hold it back anymore. A surge of vomit poured forth and with it came a whole closet full of items from the Bag of Numerous Nasty Things.

They clattered down in a constant rain, clinking and cracking, bouncing, rolling, and in some cases, scurrying— and by the moment, piling higher and higher in a sopping stack.

"There's the good stuff," Paulter said, clapping her hands together. "That'll do quite nicely on the market, well, once it's washed off."

"That not for you," Oli explained. The orcs must have been confused. "Well, we no know who it for until we meet them, but it not for you, probably."

Paulter leaned in close and smiled.

"And what if we take it anyway?"

"You… give back when done with?" Oli asked.

She shook her head slowly side to side.

"No, little goblin. We don't."

"But it not yours," Hob said, brow furrowed. The hog in front of him snorted and jerked forward. Hob swallowed hard and bit down on any further complaints.

"Really nailed tight, this one," one of the orcs grunted as he fought to pry open the biggest of the crates. The nails were run deep in it, but with his muscles bulging, he just managed to pry the lid open. "What do they even have in—ah!"

What looked like giant spider legs flashed out, along with a hiss of excitement, and the orc was dragged down into the crate.

"Jeremiah!"

The orc holding Robert shouted, then released him to rush forward. One orcish arm fought out of the crate and clamped tight to the edge. At least, until another arachnid leg hooked under and pried it free.

"Close it!" Paulter shouted as more orcs rushed to the screaming, hissing crate. The first to arrive peered inside as if considering trying to save his companion. His face turned greener all at once, though, and he threw his weight onto the lid, shaking his head at the others. With their combined strength, they managed to get the lid shut once more, though the crate continued to hiss and shake for some time.

"That what you get… for open packages… no for you," Robert scolded. The sock had fallen to the ground, but even still, dry heaves wracked his frame as he tried to speak.

"You're about to find out what happens to runts who open their stupid mouthes!" one of the orcs snarled and dragged Robert toward the crate. "Open it. The beast wants seconds."

"No feed Robert to scary spider box!" Oli shouted and struggled to touch a finger to Lord Sarusomal's cursing. The orcs kept him in place despite his slimy exterior slipping in their grasp.

"Not a bad idea," Paulter said, stroking her handlebar mustache as Robert was shoved against the crate. "Think we could fit them all in there?"

Hideous laughter at that as the idea filtered through the orc horde. In moments, they broke the circle of hogs and began herding the goblins toward the crate.

"Everyone calm down!" Gob shouted over the frenzy. "There's no need for all this, now is there? Take what you want and let us be on our way. We're just an assemblage of goblins, after all. What can we do to you, anyway? Really, this is all very unnecessary."

"Talks rather fancy for a goblin, don't he?" Paulter asked, focusing on Gob. "Maybe there's more to you than meets the eye." She paused a moment, then shrugged. "Spider won't care, though."

"Now stop right there! This has gone far enough, thank you—"

An orcish fist caught Gob in the stomach and left him wheezing. Oli cried out at that and then all his cousins did too.

"Get this thing off me!" Paulter shouted as Lin One used her mustache to climb up and get at her eyes.

"Ah! It bit me!" Another orc punted Man and he soared through the air. In moments, what had been a rather peaceful robbery with only the minor threat of murder devolved into chaos. Something closer to a battle, though a very one-sided one at that.

Amidst all the distractions, Oli fought to slip free and activate his curse. His natural slimy coating was usually enough to escape any grasp, but the orcs holding him had hands like sandpaper. Just when he thought he was free, they pulled tighter and stretched him out like a hide on the tanning rack.

"Wriggly one, this is," one of his captors said. "How's about we—"

Oli's ears popped all at once, then blasted with a piercing ringing, and it took several long breaths for him to realize he wasn't the only one. The other goblins clapped hands over their ears, and the orcs too. Then he noticed the shadow behind him. Craning his neck around, he found a massive, blonde mammoth reared up on its hind legs, tusks raised high, and trunk curled back as it trumpeted.

The front legs came crashing down and the graveyard shook as if hit by an earthquake. Orcs and goblins and gravestones alike were thrown to the shaking ground.

Oli's captors toppled over and he hurriedly reached a finger toward his cursemark, but already, the orcs were fleeing. One thought about standing and fighting but the mammoth swept him aside with a swing of its trunk. In the span of a breath, the orcs, their hogs, and even Paulter were gone. Shouting, maybe, as they fled over the nearest hilltop. Oli couldn't be sure as his ears hadn't yet stopped ringing.

Someone was talking at him. A human man, mounted on the back of the mammoth. Oli had seen his neatly combed brown hair before. And his spectacles and waving green cloak.

"Flan?" Oli asked, barely able to hear his own words through the ringing.

The human said something back, then smiled wide.

FIFTEEN

Crag's List

"Always a trouble, out on the road," Flan said, nodding at the orcs' fleeing backs. "Gotta look after your cargo, before someone else gets to lookin' at it. Oh, but that's just another reason why ol' Mam and the others are such treasures." He laughed at that while patting the mammoth's furry shoulder. "Transport and protection, all in one! Aren't they just the best? Aren't you? Yes, you are. You are!" he leaned forward, whispering in her ear and scratching it such that her hind leg started to rise a bit off the ground and give a few little kicks.

"Who this?" Lin Two asked, peering up at the human and his blonde mammoth with eyes wide.

"He offered us a lift," the fleshy lump bubbled. "Some time ago, when we first set out from the inn. I didn't trust him then and I trust him even less now."

"What's going on there?" Flan asked, squinting to better see the jar. "Oh no! Hate to break it to ya's, but you got a bit of beef jerky in your soup."

"That just…" Oli paused as he realized he didn't know the sentient piece of meat in the jar's name. Or if it even had one. "That just jar. We deliver home soon. No worry."

"Yes, lord below, please. In fact, why are we just standing around? Get on with it, already! We're only a day from my home."

"Ya just love to hear it!" Flan slapped his knee. "You got the hauler spirit, kid, and that's no lie. Just finished getting shook down by a nasty horde of hog riders and you're already thinking about finishing your route. I love it! You know, first time I saw your crew on the road, puttering along on a single horse, crates stacked all which way, you know I told myself 'Flan, there's a crew got spirit. Got the right mindset! Maybe they don't have the best tools, or the best animals, but they're not letting that stop 'em!'" Flan patted his chest over his heart, then wiped a very real tear from the corner of his eye. "That's what it's all about, you know? Haulin', I mean. Sure, the open road's nice, and riding mammoths is fun, and the money's great—but the true haulers, those born with a soul for moving boxes all 'cross this wonderful creation?—they do the job because it calls to 'em. 'Cause they can't imagine doing anything else. It's what got me started and I see it in you now. You got the spirit, all of ya's!"

"Oh. Uh, yes." Oli said, scratching his head. Hadn't quite gotten all of that, and understood even less of it, but Flan had been smiling big as he said it so probably it was a good thing.

"That no why we do it," Man said, standing up tall. "We on secret mission for Big Boss!"

"Man no say!" Oli darted toward him.

"We go on a special quest for Dark Lo—"

Oli clapped a hand over his cousin's mouth right as Gob did the same from the other side. Man fell over backwards with a little squeal.

"He mean we… we love boxes. Love carrying boxes. Taking new places." Oli said, stumbling every word of the way.

"Loooove boxes," Lin Two chimed in, pointing to the crates. "All boxes!"

"Yes! Be nice to boxes!" Lin One gave one a big hug.

"Uh…" Robert frowned at the commotion, then reached out to pat the nearest crate. "Good… box. Nice box."

"Look at that, Mam! Just look at it!" Flan was wiping away another tear. "These kids are stealing my heart, I tell you what."

"No steal!" Oli shouted at once. "Goblins no steal. No do bad. Goblins good! Nice."

"Oh, of course! It's just a figure of speech. I didn't mean it literally," Flan laughed.

"Goblins no serve Big Boss Dark Lord?" Man whispered, confused. "Man no underst—"

Gob wrapped an arm around his shoulders and steered him away.

"Well, anyway," Flan pressed a hand to his brow as he said it and checked the horizon to make sure the hog riders weren't coming back. "I'm so sorry those lot gave you trouble. Let me make it up to you? Mam and I just finished a route, dropped off our cargo and the other mammoths. We're headed same way as you. If you'd be open to it, why, I'd love to offer a bit of help. Us haulers gotta look out for each other, you know?" He rested his hands on his hips and nodded. "Let Mam get your cargo, while ya climb on. We'll take ya far as we can."

Mam gave an encouraging trumpet from her trunk, then used it to pick up a crate and heft it onto her back.

Flan beamed.

"What'dya say?"

* * *

With all the cargo and goblins loaded onto a mammoth, and with Horse following alongside, they made great time. The route was full of tight backroads, but most of the time, Mam opted to use the swaying fields and gentle hills instead as they crossed the countryside. The lump gave them directions every step of the way, but even it seemed to be enjoying itself.

Hard not to, with a breeze caressing their faces, the sun shining bright above, and a whole world of possibility ahead. Oli felt very much like he had right after they'd set out from the Kingdom of Darkness. Like there was no doubt they would complete their quest for the Dark Lord. Maybe they could ride Mam the whole way there? Would Flan mind?

The rest of his cousins also seemed to be enjoying themselves as the countryside slipped by. Lin Two and Lin One were hanging from the mammoth's great ears, feet dangling and kicking at the passing ground far below. Hob and Gob were with the crates at the back, watching the clouds drift by above. Man was scurrying all over, picking tasty bugs from Mam's fur and popping them into his mouth with satisfying crunches.

"Well, it's none of my business now, but I have to admit, you lot have some of the strangest cargo Mam and I ever seen, I tell you what." Flan said it cheerfully as the crates, packages, sentient jar, ghost urn, weeping stone, metal oboe, and the book Rodrigrar had written for the Dark Lord all shifted and shook where they were tied to Mam's flanks. Clicks and hisses slipped from the spider crate near continuously, along with the occasional burp.

"Love delivering boxes," Oli said, forcing a smile. "All sort of... boxes."

"And bag!" Robert chimed in from where he was riding on Mam's head, sat between her massive, wooly ears. "But it stuck." He opened his mouth wide and pointed down his throat. "No can get out except when sick!"

Flan nodded as if that made any sort of sense to him, then leaned over to Oli, voice low.

"What's he mean?"

"Robert just like talk. He foreign exchange cousin from mountains. Say funny things sometimes."

"Oh, yeah, yeah. I got me a cousin like that. Ol' Jeb. Strangest man you ever did meet. He means well, don't get me wrong, just a little funny. But aren't we all funny in our own ways?"

"Man no funny," Man said, pausing with a squirming beetle pinched between his thumb and index finger. "No good at jokes."

"Flan no mean funny like that," Oli tried to explain, before realizing Man wasn't listening. He'd spotted another beetle and was chasing it down, the other still held in hand.

"Ah, would ya look at that!" Flan pointed to a sign at a crossroads ahead. "The east path leads to Vynnia! That's where we're headed, right?"

"Vynnia, quite right." The lump of wet beef jerky floated against the glass of the jar and gave a little nervous shake. "We're almost there!"

"You can read?" Robert asked, eyes wide at Flan as Mam the mammoth carried them on to the east path. "How?"

"Well of course! All humans can read. Or, I guess, most of us can. We learn when we're young. Not much a point in having all these signs everywhere if there's no one to read 'em, eh?"

"Can teach Robert read?"

"Sorry to say, I'm not much of a teacher. At least, not when it comes to readin'."

Robert sighed at that.

"But might be there's someone in Vynnia can teach ya! I mean, I've never been but it's a human village, I think, so there's sure to be a teacher about. Check the schoolhouse once we're there."

"No have time," Oli said. "Sorry, Robert. Maybe find teacher back in swamp?" He pointed to the crates tied down behind them. "Boxes to take. No time to waste!"

"So how'd you all get started in the haulin' business anyway?" Flan asked, smiling as always. "I'm sure that there's an interesting story!"

"It nothing special. Simple story. Big Boss ask Oli go get... special box and bring home. Oli cousins help. Then little boss ask goblins take bag to inn. But inn have more boxes. Then oops! Goblins free oozy woman. Then meet wizard. Then ghosts, and ghosts want go far. Then try get wagon, but no can afford. Then soldiers come. Smart stone man ask questions. Soldiers scary. Goblins run away. Then meet Paulter and friends. Then meet you. Now go Vynnia. Then rest of stops and..." Oli paused. Then what? Well, get the Key for the Big Boss and bring it back. Suddenly, that felt awful far away. But they still had plenty of time. "Find special box and bring to Big Boss."

"Not an interesting story? Why, that's a whole epic! Far more exciting than my first delivery. And it sounds like you've only just begun, too! Say, you've got a strand, don't ya? Gotta keep track of your happy clients, so you can work with them again." After a moment of silence, Flan raised an eyebrow. "A strand? Ya know, on the Web?"

Oli scratched his chin.

"Caverns of Whispering Web? Goblins no there, goblins here."

"No, no. *The* Web," Flan said, laughing. "Every hauler's gotta be on the Web. Here, let me pull it up." He waved a finger in front of himself, the tip dancing and tracing a letter or something in the air. Down up, down up, moving to the side in a slant. He repeated the shape three times and then the air in front of him began to sparkle and glow. Silvery strands materialized from nothing until in front of Oli there *was* something. But more than something. A great lattice of strands, stretching off in all directions. There seemed an endless amount of them, all interconnected. After a few steps, though, they all disappeared, hissing away like slender moss stems in a fire.

"Crag's List, please. Let's take a look at the record of work for our friends here. For... Oli, right?"

He nodded.

"For Oli and Cousins Hauling Company!"

"What that?" Oli asked. "Why it take name?"

The sparkling air transformed, then resolved into a slightly transparent rectangle of parchment. At the top corner of it was a drawing of Oli himself. But lifelike. Incredibly lifelike. As if Oli had looked in a mirror once and it'd stolen the image of him and frozen it in time. Except, well, the image wasn't centered, so only half of

Oli's face was in it and the background looked like it had his cousins in it. They were all clinging to Horse, half falling off.

"Who do this? How exist?" Oli said, making a face very much like the one he had in the image. Something between a shout and a gasp.

"Every hauler has a strand on Crag's List. You don't have to make one, it just appears if you do the job. Easier that way!"

"What this strand say?" Oli asked hurriedly. Beneath the image he could see a couple paragraphs of text, but as he was unable to read, it was just gibberish.

"Well, since you didn't know about the strand, you haven't filled in any of the basic information—your preferred route, available equipment, going rates, stuff like that—so the only thing here is your reviews."

"Reviews?"

"Yeah, you know, like how satisfied a client was with your work. Here, take this one for instance." Flan pointed to a section of text, then read aloud. "Matron Matherson deVille says 'Courier saved my family and I from damnation at the hands of an evil wizard. They were a bit messy, but that worked in our favor. Five out of five stars. We hired them on the spot for a new contract.'" Flan clapped his hands together. "Look at ya, already doing good work! Oh, but wait. This review's not as good: Warlock Dan says: 'Zero out of five stars. Courier literally got me killed.'" Flan winced.

"Who write these?" Oli said, not recognizing any of the names. "There more?"

"Looks like there's two more. Wait, no, three."

"Read to Oli!" Oli said, standing now. "Very important!"

"You're a natural, kid. Reviews are the lifeblood of a

hauler's career. Word of mouth and all that, ya know?" Flan waved his finger and the text moved a bit to show more writing. "Harmless Smirking Innkeeper says: 'My business was backed up due to the war, but this courier arrived just in time. Brought expected deliveries and accepted several more I needed delivered. Four out of five stars on account of delivered items being somewhat damp.'"

"That Rodrigrar. Scary inn, bad food. No like Horse."

"And this one from 'Completely Normal Human Man with No Ambitions of Drowning the World in Darkness' says 'Unexpected courier, but shows promise. Five out of five stars.'"

"Five stars!" Oli couldn't help but smile. Initially he'd been concerned the reviews would expose them as doing the work of the Dark Lord—something the Bright Queen and her soldiers didn't seem happy about—but with each new review, it seemed their cover was left more intact. He didn't know who Completely Normal Human Man with no Ambitions of Drowning the World in Darkness was, but it was nice to know he was another satisfied customer.

"And last there's a review from someone calling themselves the 'Lieutenant of Lament.' Now ain't that just a silly name? Some people, I swear. Take themselves so seriously. Anyway, they didn't leave a written review, just a rating. Zero out of five stars." Flan sucked at his teeth and gave a little wince. "Well that's not nice. And looking at all the reviews, well, your overall rating could be better. Averaging two-point-eight stars out of five."

"That no good?" Oli asked.

"Well, it's not great, that's for sure. But hey! Nothing worth doing is easy, right? And you got a hauler's heart, kid, I can tell. Keep working hard and those reviews will shoot up in no time. I mean, look at all the cargo you have right now." He gestured back to the crates and packages tied to Mam's flanks. "Deliver those successfully and you'll be right back on track!"

"Well I certainly won't be leaving you a good review," the lump bubbled. Oli frowned down at the thing, then gave it a good shake.

"Ahh! Okay, okay! Stop it!"

"Good review."

"Fine, right. Yeah." The lump of meat floated into the back of the glass, as far from Oli as possible. "Two out of five stars, maybe."

Another shake.

"Five out of five! Five out of five, okay!"

Oli looked at Flan with a smile.

"Reviews improving!"

SIXTEEN

The Somewhat Diminished Dr. Percival Viscous

A proper goblin house is as cozy as a public latrine—damp, slimy, and all the best ones come with tasty infestations. Roofs and walls were optional, but Oli had found them particularly useful for cultivating just the right amount of oozing humidity. One can imagine Oli and his cousins' disdain, then, when they spotted the castle ahead of them standing firm against the raging storm. So firm, it looked like there wasn't even a bit of roof leaking. How could one ever hope to have a mold garden without inviting the elements in?

"This look about right to y'all?" Flan asked, one hand shading his eyes from the driving rain. Lightning flashed in the sky and for a single heartbeat, the castle was silhouetted against the storm. Massive, ominous, imposing. Combined with the rain—so heavy as to be oppressive—it reminded Oli of the Dark Lord, and that brought a smile to his face.

"Oli think this it!"

"Home, sweet wonderful, brilliant, secluded home!" the lump of wet beef jerky bubbled, sloshing around in the jar in a swirl of excitement. "This is it! Quickly, up the driveway! My staff are waiting."

"No see address," Robert said, looking at the spike-topped fence in front of them. Two massive, moss-covered stone columns formed the sides of a gate. Towering, rain-slick, and ancient. They were entirely devoid of any posted address, though.

"The instructions for my and the Weeping Stone's delivery read 'Number One, Castle on the Screaming Cliff.' You see any other castles around?" the lump asked.

Robert spent a long moment squinting through the rain.

"No see more."

"Well, then. Maybe we should check with someone who lives here, see if this is the right address? Someone like, oh, well, me, I suppose. Seeing as this is my home."

"Why you need house? Have jar," Robert said, confused.

The lump sighed.

"You have a wonderful body, Robert. And a beautiful skull. It's so perfectly empty."

"Thank!"

"Right, well, if this is the place, I'm glad for it!" Flan waved away a glimmering window into the web, then clapped his hands together. "Mam and I've just been booked for another haul, starting down in Montcellier. Goblins, we can take ya far as you need to go in that direction—maybe dry off a bit in the process—but then we'll need all available space for the next job."

"Oh no, no, no," the lump said suddenly. "I must insist you all enjoy some hospitality before leaving. After all, you've carried me and the Weeping Stone so far. You've done us a great service and the least I can do is repay you with a roof from the rain, food for your bellies, and a well-stoked fire."

"I think we should stay with Flan and Mam," Gob said, speaking up for the first time in a while. "They've been kind to us."

"But food do sound good," Lin One said, rubbing his belly.

"And Horse also need eat," Lin Two added.

Oli's stomach grumbled as if in agreement.

"Well it's settled then!" The lump gave a little wiggle in its jar. "Flan, thank you ever so much for your assistance. We wouldn't have made it without you. May you and your wondrous mammoth have safe travels and fair weather! Goblins, if you'll please, I can't wait to repay your kindness."

"And with good review, too?" Oli asked.

The lump bobbed up and down which was probably the equivalent of a nod.

"Flan, if you wouldn't mind just taking us up to the front door? It's the last favor I'll ask, truly."

Flan didn't agree immediately but looked to Oli first.

"If not too much trouble?"

"No trouble at all," Flan said. Something in his face looked a bit worried, but probably that was just the rain getting all in his eyes and nose and anywhere it could.

The castle, already massive in size, grew only larger as Mam crunched up the gravel driveway. It ran up to the front of the house, where it ended in a wide circle. Plenty of room for even a mammoth to unload, then turn around and head back.

Two figures were waiting beside the double front doors, their backs straight and expressions neutral, even as the storm raged around them.

"Henchmen!" the lump cried out. "Oh, it's just so wonderful to see you. Percival's home, and how I've missed you."

At the lump's words, the two figures seemed to come awake, like statues given the gift of joints and movement in them.

"Be ever so helpful, won't you, and assist in unloading my friends' cargo?"

The figures moved to the mammoth and Oli got a better look at them. Towering, broad-shouldered men, but with wide, stiff faces and gray skin. Probably it was from the rain but there was no warmth in that skin. And oddly, little sparks of light danced beneath the surface every few moments. Like the lightning above, Oli thought, but trapped inside their bodies.

"Ma-ster Per-ci-val," the first figure said, his voice rough and slow, as if forming each word was a challenge. Sounded a lot like Robert, really. "Wel-come ho-ome."

"Well howdy there, fellas!" Flan gave a happy wave. "No need to strain yourselves, Mam's got this handled, don't ya miss?"

The mammoth trumpeted in response then, using her dexterous trunk, began lowering cargo down into the shelter of the door's stoop.

"Help the goblins down, too, please," the lump said

even as Mam's trunk grabbed the jar and delicately handed it down to one of the waiting men.

"No need help. Goblins good," Oli said.

"Ho-ow ones so-o small ge-t off one so bi-ig?" the henchman holding the jar asked, words clumsy in his mouth. But the goblins were already in motion. In moments, there was a whole chain of goblins working together to make the world's squirmiest ladder. It was just like how they got off Horse, but longer.

"We all cousins," Oli said as he stepped on Hob's head, then climbed down Man's body and toward the ground. "Work together."

"Wo-ork to-geth-er?" the henchman asked and as he said it, his eyebrows inched together like a vice tightening.

"Cousins?" the lump asked suddenly. "You said some of you were siblings."

Oli nodded as he held on to Lin One's ankle, then dangled toward the ground.

"All goblins cousins. Especially the siblings."

The lump was silent for several long moments, seeming to ponder that. Flan, as well. Finally, the hauler gave a little shake of his head.

"Well that just ain't right."

Mam trumpeted a quick blast.

"You're right, girl. Ain't our place to judge."

By then, the cargo was all unloaded and the last goblins made it to the ground. Gob came last, seeming displeased. Lin Two guided Horse out of the storm, his animal skins and stuffing sagging from the endless downpour.

"Well, truly, it has been a pleasure." Flan gave a wave as Mam turned away from the house. "I'll be just tickled pink watching your hauler journey, goblins! If you ever need anything, you can contact me via Crag's List. Don't hesitate one bit! You got the spark in ya's, I can see it bright as day! Follow it and it won't never lead you astray!" By then he was swaying side to side as Mam picked up speed, heading back into the storm.

"Thank, Flan!" Oli shouted and the others joined in.

"Give Mam many brushing from me!" Lin Two called. "With good brush!"

Flan's laugh carried back on the wind, then was swept away as another sheet of rain came driving through.

"Well then," the lump said. "Why don't you all join me inside. I've some quick business to attend to and then we can get right to work."

"Work?" Oli asked, stomach grumbling. "When food?"

"Oh, right, I was lying about that."

The henchman holding the jar turned toward the doors, and the second one opened them. Beyond waited a crowd of figures, each a near identical copy of the last. More henchmen. Much more.

"Welcome to my humble abode," the lump in the jar said. "I am your host, Dr. Percival Viscous; these are my loyal henchmen, who serve my every beck and call without hesitation; and this is Castle Melkior, where my experiments change the world as we know it. Come inside, won't you?" A little laugh. "I'm not asking."

SEVENTEEN

His Imperious Majesty The Dark Lord Sarusomal And The Humble Barkeep Rodrigrar Drown The World In Shadow And Sorrow: An Aspirational Fiction

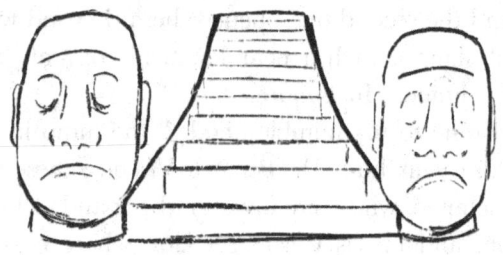

"Oli no want go with Dr. Percival. Sorry," Oli said, then pressed a thumb to the Dark Lord's cursemark on his forearm. He didn't like to be rude, but the lump in the jar—apparently named Dr. Percival Viscous—was being ruder. Luckily, Oli had friends that could help. He looked to the shadows, waiting for them to emerge.

"Foolish little goblin. My entire castle is enveloped by an anti-magic field. You have entered a domain of science!"

"That why Horse break?" Lin Two asked as she frowned to the pile of bones the undead steed had collapsed into moments before. "Big Boss can to fix?"

"Big Boss must to fix!" Oli shouted.

The jar bubbled with the lump's cackling laughter.

"Your Dark Lord has no power here."

"Robert have power," Robert said, hand raised. He made to slap the jar free from the henchman's grip, but another figure caught his arm and then several henchmen surrounded him, their faces free of emotion as they methodically restrained the biggest of the goblins.

"Yes, you do have power, Robert. The power of a healthy and functioning body. It's a power I've grown to miss ever since the accident."

"Look, Oli, I hate to say I told you so, but I did kind of tell you so," Gob said, whispering in Oli's ear. "Never trusted this worm."

"Why not say more?" Oli whirled to face Gob. "Why not warn harder?"

"Well I can't blow my cover, now can I?" he snapped back, then balked. "Er, that is to say, I am definitely a goblin and have been one all of my life. No one is looking for me and definitely none of those people might know a crazy mad scientist like Dr. Viscous here."

"No plotting now, thank you very much," the lump bubbled, and several henchmen separated Gob and Oli. The rest of the goblins, as well. Horse—or the pile of bones that had been Horse—and the packages were left on the stoop while everyone else was restrained and carried inside.

"Gu-ests do-o no-t want to co-ome," one of the henchmen said.

"Well of course they don't, you dolt!" the lump snapped back. "Do what you're told and make them come anyway! And make sure you grab the Weeping Stone!"

The gray-skinned, stone-faced servants nodded and

took hold of the goblins. Another snatched the Weeping Stone from Lin Two.

For his part, Oli bit at the hands of the emotionless human-thing holding him, but the henchmen seemed to feel no pain. They just stared ahead with their blank expressions. Or, they did for the most part. As they were herded through the grand entrance hall of the castle, one of the henchmen stepped beside Oli. It was one of the two that'd been guarding the front doors. Oli recognized him by his rain-slick hair and clothes.

"Ho-w yo-u know to-o climb do-own mamm-oth?" he asked, fighting to form the words like his mouth and lips were numb.

"What?" Oli stopped struggling a moment.

"Ho-w yo-u know to-o climb do-own mamm-oth?"

"Oli hear but no understand. Already tell. Goblins cousins."

"Co-ousins always wo-ork to-geth-er? Ho-w?"

"Not always. Sometimes cousins fight. Sometimes bite."

"So-o h-ow do wo-ork to-geth-er?"

"Sometimes agree to?" Oli felt like he was talking to a tree trunk.

"Ag-ree?" The henchman with the wet hair frowned. "Wh-at is ag-ree?"

"Hey! No talking with the prisoners!" the lump snapped from ahead. The henchman carrying him had turned around so Dr. Viscous could shout at them. "Don't talk to my henchmen!"

"Doctor Wet Lump mean to friends!"

"I have no friends, goblin. No equals, either. I am singular. I am supreme. I am *evolved*."

"You wet beef jerky."

Oli blew a raspberry at him.

"Keep the prisoners quiet," Dr. Viscous growled. "And get back in line, Henchman Fourteen." The wet-haired henchmen hurried back into the crowd.

"Wh-at are th-ese pr-ris-son-ers?" another henchman asked.

"What are these prisoners?" Dr. Viscous mocked back at him. "Don't concern yourself with questions, Henchman Seventy-Six. I didn't put enough room in your head to handle questions. And especially not answers," he added with a laugh.

"O-kay."

"Wet beef jerky extra mean now," Lin Two said and the lump just laughed all the more.

"Putting up with you slimy idiots has been torture beyond the comprehension of your addled little brains. You can't imagine how difficult this has been for me. But, somehow, I persevere. Call it mental fortitude. Call it my hard-earned genius. Or maybe just call it spite." The lump floated around at that, seeming to look further into the castle. "Call it whatever you want. We have business to attend to. Come now."

Oli had never been inside a castle before. The Dark Lord's Citadel of Shadow and Sin, maybe, but that was a different thing. Living, almost, and shifting constantly at the behest of the Dark Lord's will. This was more solid a building. Made of decidedly non-evil stone, but the decorations did their best to make up for that. Thick, musty carpets lined each hall and looming suits of armor waited at every intersection and door frame. Oli peered into them as he was carried past, but they were decidedly empty of malicious shadows.

In some places, the stone walls had been smashed open and large, copper pipes wormed out. They ran along the floor for some distance, before turning and slipping down through the floorboards, or back into the wall. In some places, they hissed and leaked steam, which left the hallways hot and damp.

Strange, glowing torches were also mounted through the halls, but they used no flame. Oli couldn't tell how they worked, for whenever he looked at them, he was blinded and left with glowing after-images burned into his eyelids.

"Where take us?" Lin Two shouted from the back.

"What do with us?" Man added.

Dr. Viscous ignored them, focusing instead on the staircase they were approaching. The stairs rose up for several paces, then ended in empty air. Looking up, though, Oli could see a dozen or more floors stretched up toward the far, far ceiling. How to get to them, though, he couldn't figure, seeing as there weren't enough stairs.

Two stone columns stood on either side of the unfinished stairs with a face carved into each.

"Ahem," the lump bubbled, and then there was a grinding of stone and the faces' eyes scraped open to reveal decidedly non-stone eyeballs. A bit of water leaked from one eye until a long, grinding blink wiped it away. Despite the slowness of the eyelids, the eyeballs themselves snapped to and fro, taking in the bubbling jar, the henchmen, and the goblins.

"Master Viscous," the left-most column said with a surprised yelp. It had a carved mouth and lips, but neither moved. Even still, the voice came echoing out.

"We did not expect to see you again," the right-most column said, eyes flicking to the jar, then Oli. "This is a wonderful surprise. Things have been so dreadfully dull since your departure."

"Yes, yes, well here I am. Surprise. Tell me, where is my assistant? Where is little, groveling Viktor?"

"Ooh, yes, yes. With pleasure, Master," the left-most

column said, and its very-living eyeballs stared into the middle distance a moment inside its very-stone eye sockets. "I can sense Master Viktor in the botanarium. He did not tell these humble servants what he was planning to do in there, though Right and I have speculated at length. Not our place, we know, but, well, there hasn't been much to do with you gone. Master Viktor never comes down from the upper levels and the henchmen just sort of stand about—"

"Master Viktor, hm? Is that what he's called now?"

The right-most column blinked once.

"There was something of a vacuum after your departure, Master. Left and I have discussed it at length. The question of how to proceed without you, that is. Many solutions were proposed but none were productive. Our humble viewpoint is somewhat limited. Uh, philosophically, as we are stuck in place here, and literally, as we are, well, stuck in place here."

"Yes, you are stuck in place because your job is to work the stairs, Left and Right. Nothing more! Actually, you know what? You want more responsibility? Something else to think about?"

"Please, Master! Yes!"

"Fill these idle minds, Master!"

"You can remind me to take you both in for reconstruction. I gave you far too much processing power for your jobs. You work the stairs, that is all. I forbid you from thinking of anything else."

"Yes... Master," the right-most column said, eyelids half closed.

"Of course, Master," its counterpart added.

"Now do your jobs. I wish to go to the laboratorium."

Both columns closed their eyes, seeming to focus for several moments. And as they did, the stairs began to move. If Dr. Viscous hadn't explained his castle was surrounded by an anti-magic field, Oli would have thought the stairs were magic. But instead, gears turned and clanked, stone ground and shifted, and before all of them, a set of stairs unfurled from seemingly nowhere. They jerked and popped, then locked into place like the inner mechanisms of some intricate puzzle. After several long moments, a path up and further into the castle waited, ready for them.

"Maybe if you thought about your jobs more—and your ridiculous boredom less—you could have done that faster, hm?" The jar bubbled and frothed. "Consider that, Left and Right."

"Of course, Master," they said in unison.

The henchman carrying the jar led the way up the stairs and the rest followed, goblins held tight.

"You two!" the lump snapped. "Guard the hall. Make sure no one follows. Especially not any mammoths or bespectacled riders!"

Two henchmen peeled off at the foot of the stairs and stood sentry.

"Robert," Oli hissed, twisting to look at his biggest cousin. "You have book Rodrigrar give?"

"Book?" Robert frowned, then seemed to feel around inside his mouth with his tongue. Something moved in his throat and then he nodded excitedly. "Book here."

"Spit out!" Oli said hurriedly.

Robert didn't seem to understand what Oli was planning, but he didn't need to. As the henchmen carried him toward the stairs, he gagged, heaved, then spat the dripping book onto the floor.

"Left and Right bored?" Oli said to the sentient, stone-faced columns, turning to keep looking at them even as he was carried past. "Have book! Maybe can read? Keep entertained!" he shouted the last bit, hoping they'd hear even as he was carried further up the stairs. Whether they did or didn't, though, he couldn't tell.

"Quicker, quicker you louts!" Dr. Viscous bubbled from ahead. "I've waited for too long for this!"

* * *

"Ugh, goodness me. One of those nasty little frogmen spat up," Left said, eyeing the soggy thing.

"And on the Master's carpet, no less!" Right added, indignation in its stony features. "How rude! Oh stairs above, look. It's seeping through. That's going to mold, I'm telling you now."

"Master Percival!" Left called, voice echoing up the stairs, but Master did not hear. Or chose not to respond. "Well, someone has to do something."

"I would clean it up," Right said. "But, well…" The column rolled its eyeballs in something approaching a shrug. "Haven't got any arms, have I?"

"We can't just let it sit there."

"Perhaps if we debate long enough, someone else will come about and solve the problem."

"Funny looking thing, though, isn't it?" Left squinted for a better view of the thing. It was soggy and dripping saliva, but on its face there were… words. "*His Imperious Majesty The Dark the Lord Sarusomal and the Humble Barkeep Rodrigrar Drown the World in Shadow and Sorrow: An Aspirational Fiction.* Huh." Left read the title again, and as they did, the words filled their mind with possibilities. "Who is this Dark Lord fellow?"

"And how do they relate to 'the Humble Barkeep Rodrigrar?'" Right puzzled over that a moment. "And what is a barkeep anyway?"

Left didn't have the answer. Didn't have many answers,

really. A side effect—or perhaps the intended outcome—of spending one's entire existence as first non-sentient, unhewn stone, then eventually as sentient, hewn stone.

"Wo-ork to-geth-er."

The voice came from a distance so far away neither Left nor Right would ever cross it. A vast chasm three whole steps across the room where stood one of the henchmen Master Percival had ordered to stay. Left never paid much attention to them. In many ways, the henchmen weren't so different from the stairs—just tools. The stairs carried the Master about the castle, while the henchmen performed other such tasks for the Master. Tools, all of them.

Except, the rain-slicked henchman had a look in his eye that neither Left nor Right had seen before in their limited world. Didn't know what that look meant, only that it was new.

The rainy henchman—Fourteen, had master called that one?—stepped forward and reached out, hands shaking, to pick the saliva-soaked object off the floor.

"Bo-ook," he said simply. "Go-oblin say thi-is bo-ook."

"What are you doing!" Right began to shout, but Left shushed their counterpart.

"The book was soiling the master's carpet. This wet servant was fixing that for the master, yes?"

"No-o." The henchman stepped forward, then held the book out to the columns. "Yo-u ca-an re-ead." As he said the last word, he opened the book's cover. "Wo-ork to-geth-er."

Left and Right gasped at the same moment. The master hadn't ordered this! And yet, neither could stop their eyes from pouring across the newly revealed page, for on it were more words. More than either had ever seen before. More than had been on the cover, even!

"The following is an aspirational account of the horrors that could become reality should his Imperial Majesty the Dark Lord Sarusomal team up with his loyal and humble servant, the barkeep Rodrigrar. Together, no foe will be able to stand before them. The Dark Lord with his bulging muscles and all-knowing gaze, and Rodrigrar providing his rakish good looks and mischievous smile." Left read the words aloud in a great rush.

"What… what is this?" Right stammered. "I can see images, in my head. A story, forming from… nothing. From ink!"

"This one must read more." Left's eyes snapped to the henchman holding the book. "Next page."

"Re-ead out lo-ud?" he asked back and neither Left nor Right could agree quickly enough.

Clumsy fingers worked at the damp pages, but managed to get it turned and then straight away, Left and Right were reading again.

"Wo-ork to-geth-er."

EIGHTEEN

Wriggly Little Test Subjects

"What do to Robert? Stop!" Oli shouted.

"No do, thank!" Lin One added.

"Let goblins go, please. Appreciate!" Man joined in and then everyone was shouting and howling. But the henchmen didn't stop their work. Their hands were clumsy but firm as they moved Robert into place, then tightened the straps until he was locked tight against the table.

"Bed no comfortable," Robert said, squirming but getting nowhere.

"It is not supposed to be comfortable, my body-having

friend." The lump bubbled in what Oli figured was an ominous manner as a henchman held him up to watch the proceedings. "But worry not your little mind. Soon you'll be extremely comfortable. Soon you'll feel as if you're floating. Really, it's rather nice. Once you get used to not having limbs or being able to move under your own power."

"What do to Robert?" Oli shouted again. He'd been tossed into a small cage along with the rest of his cousins, who were now all pressed up against the bars, arms reaching through desperately.

"Do you know how difficult it is to build a new body?" the lumpy doctor snapped. "Do you understand the precision involved in the sewing? Can you imagine the intricacies one must navigate to ensure every vein and tendon work just so? No, of course you can't. And neither can my staff. And even if they could *comprehend* such work, their pitiful forms are far too stiff to attempt it." The jar bubbled furiously with the Doctor's explanation. "No, such a miraculous act of creation is a talent only I can achieve. As soon as I have hands again."

"Oli have hands. Maybe can help if save Robert?"

"Hands, fingers, a *body*," Dr. Viscous continued, speaking more to himself than anyone else. "Even one so pathetic as a goblin's. After all, it will only be temporary. Now, where did I leave the…" he trailed off and Oli was left with the distinct impression the lump was looking around the room, so he did the same.

Windows lined the far wall, stretching from floor to ceiling. Rain pounded against them and lightning occasionally flashed, turning the world outside bright as day. Glass cups, twisted and formed into various shapes, lay about the space. On tables and in cabinets. Some had liquid inside. Others smoked. Some had liquids inside and smoked at the same time. But what sort of strange drinks Dr. Viscous enjoyed wasn't Oli's concern. No, he found himself much more bothered by various body parts scattered about the space.

They were all gray and limp. Not rotting, though. As if the process had been halted. Arms and hands, a bit of ear. Someone's jaw with a patch of beard still clinging to it. Oli's stomach churned at the sight. Reminded him too much of the lair of the Thing That Waits Beneath the Mud. That was a no fun place, but Castle Melkior was turning out to be every bit as no fun.

In that moment, Oli very much wished Big Boss would come help them. But they were far from the Kingdom of Darkness and Big Boss had been noticeably absent since they'd left.

"No know what do…" Oli whined, hands to his face.

"Call on friends!" Hob hissed, grabbing Oli's arm and raising the cursemark.

"Oli tried. Friends no can come here."

"Other friends! Spooky ghost friends!"

"Spooky ghosts still by front door. But maybe can hear if we loud?" Oli slammed into the bars and shouted. In moments, his cousins all joined in until the laboratorium echoed with the sounds of their panicked chaos. Even Man joined in, pausing from his own escape attempt. He'd managed to snatch a book through the bars of the cage and had already worked its pages into a respectable little blaze. Whatever the next step in that plan was, though, remained thoroughly unclear.

The yelling continued and Robert joined in as well, his shouts and whoops all the louder for his mountain goblin size—at least, until a henchman stuffed a wad of cloth into his mouth.

"Mmmphpf grrrmmphf ffrrr fmph!"

"Right, get on with it already." The jar sloshed a bit, the lump inside it bobbing up and down until the henchman carrying it set it down on a table much like the one Robert was strapped to. Little strings of copper or brass connected the two, curling as they hung in the air.

"No, I know, the normal anatomy's not there. Just… just place the diodes in the liquid. Yes, like that. It should do." Dr. Viscous barked orders at the henchman as they placed little metal cups—attached to the metal strings— against the jar. They put some on Robert next.

"Prepare the charge!" The jar bubbled furiously as the command was given.

Across the room, several henchmen began working a crank as big as a waterwheel. It clacked and hissed as it was spun. Like an angry snake, but growing higher in pitch by the moment. A little spark of light zapped Oli in the hand and he fell back from the metal bars of the cage.

"What happening?" Lin Two asked as more sparks zapped through the bars.

"Oh, this is bad. This is very, very bad," Gob said with a grimace.

"Gob have good idea!" Oli said, then grabbed his shoulders and shook him. "Gob always have idea!"

"Not being captured and locked up in this madman's castle would have been my idea," he shouted. "But it's a bit late for that, isn't it? I mean, if I was still a—" He shook his head. "I can't do anything. I'm just a goblin now. Just like you."

"Bah!" Oli pushed him away and threw himself back against the bars. A renewed series of electrical jolts shot through him, but he ignored them to shout at the jar.

"I don't have need of mouthy servants, but if I ever do, I'll remember just how well those mouths of yours work!"

Dr. Viscous shouted back, then turned to a henchman. "The charge is sufficient. Flip the switch."

One of the henchmen nodded, grabbed a lever on the wall, and yanked it down. The hissing, crackling sound that'd been building suddenly evaporated. All at once. It was replaced instead with a gurgling, echoing cry as Robert spasmed against the straps holding him down. The liquid in the jar, likewise, boiled and bubbled.

And then it was done.

Before Oli's ears could stop ringing, the calamitous noise was ended and silence fell across the room, but for the pounding of rain on the windows.

Robert laughed. But it wasn't Robert's laugh. Wasn't Robert's voice, but Dr. Viscous', and coming from Robert's mouth.

The straps were released and Oli's cousin sat up on the table. But the sinking feeling in Oli's stomach told him it wasn't his cousin anymore. The feeling was confirmed, moments later, when the lump bubbled and from it, came Robert's voice.

"Oooh, floaty. Like soup!"

"Yes, yes. Enjoy your soupy prison, my dull-minded friend. It's all yours. And this—!" Dr. Robert Viscous jumped to his feet. "Is mine. All mine!" A cackle then as the goblin's back arched, his arms spread wide, and his laughing filled the whole of the room. Outside, lightning flashed and thunder rolled. Dr. Viscous' voice, through Robert's throat, echoed across the room. Right up until the doors were kicked open. Lightning flashed again—really well timed around these parts, it seemed—and a silhouette took an uneasy step in.

"Ah, Viktor. Viktor, Viktor, Viktor," Dr. Robert Viscous said, a little laugh in his tone. "How nice of you to stop by and welcome your old Master home."

"Dr.... Dr. Viscous?" the newcomer's voice shook. "I... I thought you were dead."

"Well, you certainly tried to make that the case, didn't you, my ambitious assistant?"

* * *

Something was happening up in the laboratorium, but the master had specifically commanded Left and Right not to think about anything but their jobs. Probably that command also meant not reading spittle-covered books vomited up by captive goblins, but at the moment, both columns were having too much fun to care.

"Next page!"

"Yes, yes. Next page!"

The rain-slick henchman turned another page. And found there were no more pages.

"Th-at a-all."

"What? No! How?" Left clamored.

"Go back to the beginning! We can read it again, can't we?" Right shouted, panic in their voice. "This is the most fun I've had in... ever! My mind is all images and... and... feelings? I don't know what's happening, but it's incredible."

"I've never even met this Rodrigrar, but now I so want them to get with the Dark Lord! They were meant for each other! I have to know how their story continues! And what will happen when they discover there's only one bed at the inn?"

"We have to know!" Right agreed, then snapped their eyes to the henchman. "Are there more of these books? Somewhere? Anywhere?"

"I fi-ind mo-ore, if I ca-n," Henchman Fourteen said. Once he'd been soaked in rain, but he was nearly dry now.

So much that it was getting hard to tell him apart from every other henchman that served in the castle. "Bu-t bett-ter with mo-ore henchmen. We wo-ork to-geth-er. Yo-u he-elp henchmen. Henchmen he-elp yo-u."

Left's eyes narrowed at that.

"What did you have in mind, exactly?"

NINETEEN

Henchpeople United in Labor and Purpose Local Chapter Zero Zero One

"So ends your brief and uneventful time as master of this house, Viktor. And what a disappointment it was. Not only did you fail to kill me, you allowed me to return with only the aid of my wits and these goblins!" Dr. Robert Viscous barked laughter at that—the last part especially. "How humiliating it must be. Defeated by the charred lump of your master and a gang of idiot goblins."

"Goblins no idiot!" Oli shouted, banging on the bars again. "Dr. Viscous idiot!"

"Oh, however shall I recover from so scathing a rebuttal!" The one-time wet beef jerky lump retorted, hand raised to the brow of Robert's stolen body.

"Well, Master, you may have survived thus far. You have me there, I must admit. But your 'survival' has left you somewhat diminished, wouldn't you agree? Certainly, you've chosen the largest of the goblins to inhabit, but still, you must now go through life as a goblin. If you are so reduced as to think of that as victory," he paused to chuckle. "There is no more severe a blow I can strike against you."

Dr. Viscous' apparent one-time assistant spoke with a confidence Oli hadn't seen anyone use against the doctor yet. But, looking at him, it made a sort of sense. Allegedly he'd been the assistant, but Oli didn't understand how that would have worked, seeing as he was far larger. If Oli knew one thing about humans, it was the bigger they were, the more important they were. Probably. And Dr. Viscous' former assistant was big. If a bit unbalanced, too. As if he'd been assembled piecemeal from all manner of corpses, and every dimension of him had been given an extra stretching in the process. The only thing that wasn't big about him was his spectacles. Round, cracked, and clinging to his massive nose, they were almost comically small. Fitting for his pinched, squinty little eyes, though. A lock of jet-black hair hung wetly over one shoulder, while the rest of his head was shaved to the scalp, revealing more than a few scars that'd been stapled shut.

"I've taken your castle, command of your henchmen, and if anything, have accelerated efforts to fulfill our order for *him*. Removing you actually improved our output— more evidence that it was the correct decision, I should note. Put simply, I have blossomed into full form while you've been reduced to nothing more than a well-spoken goblin, my old master. Run the numbers however you'd like, but the summation is the same. I stand alone, the victor, the genius, the assistant who rose to cast down the fading light of his once-great master."

"You never were very good at arithmetic, Viktor." Dr. Robert Viscous spread his arms out to gesture at the henchmen who'd accompanied him through the castle. "Even in this pitiful—and temporary—body, they recognize their old master. Their allegiance remains."

Viktor clapped his hands and the doors burst open with a swarm of more henchmen who looked, as far as Oli could tell, exactly identical to all the rest. Except these lined up behind Viktor, arms crossed.

"Not all henchmen are so loyal to the past. Some imagine a better, brighter future. Some—most, even—stand with me."

"Oh ho! A dramatic display, to be sure. If you learned one thing from me, assistant, it was a flare for... the dramatic!" Dr. Viscous clapped his goblin hands together, then produced the Weeping Stone.

Viktor's brow furrowed. He shrugged.

"What, do you not recognize your own defeat?" Dr. Viscous let out a howling cackle as the stone dripped a steady stream of water from his hand. "This, my unlearned friend, is a little machination we know as the Weeping Stone. Long have I sought it, for long have I kept a secret." A henchman approached from behind, then clapped something into the doctor's waiting hand. "Many years ago, I happened upon a Weeping Stone. A peculiar little thing, it was. At a glance, a normal stone. But it exuded salty water, seemingly without end. Even when enveloped within my anti-magic field. That led me to the realization that this stone, this little artifact, was something so much more. And so, I tested it. And probed it. And measured and weighed and studied its nature with every tool at my disposal. It's exact nature, I must admit, I still do not fully understand. But I did learn something. Something that made me realize, the Weeping Stone was not alone. There existed in the world, in fact, Weeping *Stones*!" Dr. Robert Viscous delivered the line with a dramatic bellow, then opened his hand to reveal a second stone, which looked exactly like the first.

"Two Weeping Stones?" Man asked, leaning over Oli's shoulder for a better view. "So? Why matter?"

Oli could only shrug. As far as he could tell, the two scientists were more concerned with sounding powerful than actually proving they were.

"Alone, a Weeping Stone leaks water endlessly. But my tests indicate that when these two artifacts are brought together, they will amplify each other's power. Amplify the flow to unmeasurable levels. When harnessed correctly, they will generate limitless power for *my* castle. But as a happy side effect, this unstoppable tide—this tsunami of salt and water—can be used to wash even the most persistent filth from it path. Filth, Viktor, very much like you." And with that, Dr. Robert Viscous set his feet, raised his hands, and clapped the stones together with a maniacal laugh.

But nothing happened.

Or, well, not nothing, exactly. Something happened. But that something was the stones both stopped leaking. A few last drops pitter pattered out, but even those slowed until all that was left was a little trail of salt dried to the doctor's arm.

"Huh." Dr. Robert Viscous looked at the stones. "Hold on. But a moment." He separated them and their individual streams of water began again. "Ah, yes. Now then, as I was saying. Filth, Viktor, very much like you!" He slammed the stones together again and, again, the flow of water stopped.

"Well, Master. Perhaps I was never good at arithmetic, but here's a little equation for you," Viktor said, already chuckling. "What does one Weeping Stone plus one Weeping Stone equal?" He turned to the crowd of henchmen at his back. "Anyone? No?" Viktor turned back to the doctor with a sneer. "It equals one very mistaken little goblin-man."

"Maybe Weeping Stone no more sad?" Man said. "Found friend."

"Hm." The doctor looked down at the stones. "I admit, an unexpected result. Rather disappointing, as well. Consider my hypothesis disproven." He tossed the stones aside. "But allow me to formulate another. I believe, when a sufficient amount of electricity is applied in liberal amounts to your temples, you will cease to be a problem for me, Viktor." He snapped his fingers and his crowd of henchmen shuffled forward.

Viktor did the same and his own crowd readied as well. All the while, Oli was pressed up against the bars of the cage. The Weeping Stones had clattered across the floor and almost within arm's reach. He got his fingers against one, then rolled it in. Lin Two grabbed the other and handed it over. Oli focused on the stones, thoughts rushing in his head. Surely there was a way to use them to get free? They were magic, or something more, something that worked even inside the anti-magic field. That meant they were powerful.

"How make work?" Oli mumbled. "How make work!"

"You have your electricity theory, Master. But I'd like to perform an experiment of my own. Or, a bit of math, actually." Viktor scooped one of the henchmen up, then flexed. His mountainous muscles bulged and the henchman—without reacting or crying out—was torn in two. Viktor smirked as he tossed both pieces aside. "I'm going to practice a darker sort of division on you, Master."

At that, Dr. Robert Viscous took a step back. For the briefest moment, doubt flashed across his features. And then the doors to the room were kicked open once more and yet more henchmen flooded in. More than the total number that were already there. So many, in fact, that they couldn't even fit. The crowd stretched back out of the room and away down the stairs as far as Oli could see.

"No-o wo-ork for Master Viktor anymo-ore," a henchman at the head of the crowd said, and Dr. Viscous smiled.

"It would seem your math is wrong again, Viktor."

"No-o wo-ork for Master Viscous anymo-ore, ei-ther."

"What?"

"Henchmen wo-ork to-geth-er."

Both Dr. Viscous and Viktor laughed at that, but as far as Oli could see, the henchman wasn't joking. His hair was a bit ruffled, as if it'd been wet, then dried all out of place. Beneath it, his stiff eyes pivoted in his gray, sullen face, then brightened as they fell on the small goblin.

"Go-oblin show henchmen how to wo-ork to-geth-er. Now henchmen wo-ork for selves."

"What is this nonsense?" Viktor called, fists clenched as he spun toward the newcomers. "What madness?"

The crowd parted as two very large somethings were carried through. They reached the front and Oli was shocked to see the columns from the foot of the stairs. Their bases were cracked and broken, mortar and stone still falling from them, but their faces were intact and their eyes very much alive. The henchmen set them down with a calamitous boom.

"Thank you, friends," Left said. Or maybe it was

Right. Seeing as they'd been moved, Oli really couldn't tell. "Ahem. Yes, Masters Viscous and Viktor? We and the henchmen have been talking—"

"And reading!" Right—or maybe Left—interjected.

"And reading, yes. And, well, you know. It'll really surprise you what happens when you open your mind a bit. Get to know your co-workers. And once you get to talking, well, you realize you've more in common with each other than with the Masters."

"Henchmen bring bo-oks, Left and Ri-ight re-ad bo-oks. Get sma-art. And so-oon, teach Henchmen to ge-t sm-aart. But no-ow, henchman no need Masters."

"Yes, exactly right. You see, we've taken a vote," one of the columns said. "And we've decided to unionize."

"Just so," the other column said. "We figure, why work for you, doing what you want, when we could... work for ourselves."

"An-d do-o wha-at we wa-nt."

"Exactly." The column's stone mouth couldn't move, but even still, Oli had the distinct impression it was smiling.

"This... this is preposterous!" Viktor shouted.

"The most absurd thing I've ever heard!" Dr. Viscous added. "You're henchmen. You don't think. You don't organize. That's why I created you. That's why I stitched you together in your pitiful forms and gave you the smallest, most infinitesimal spark of life. Gave you just enough brain power to remember to breathe."

"You said it yourself," one of the columns said. "You gave us far too much processing power for our jobs."

"So now we're interested in a new job." The other column said, and the henchmen moved forward as one.

Viktor swallowed hard.

The henchmen moved in, a grim determination filling their otherwise vacant eyes.

"Wait!" Oli shouted, banging the Weeping Stones against the bars of the cage. "Please to not hurt Robert's body?"

The columns' too-fast moving eyes appraised him, then acquiesced.

"Fair point. We swap the bodies back. Then we become self-employed."

TWENTY

Putting The Cart Before Horse

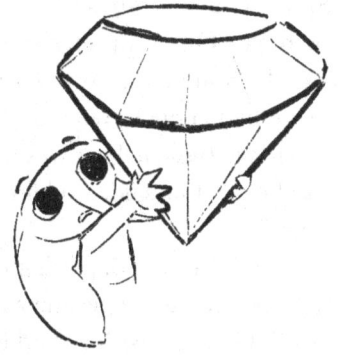

Plop.

The pair of spectacles fell into the jar with a little splash, joining the vaguely recognizable lump of flesh.

"I would have preferred death," the spectacles that'd formerly been Viktor said, as they sank as far away from the jar's other occupant as possible.

"I will have my revenge," grumbled the lump that had been Dr. Percival Viscous before, and was again. Bubbles

143

trickled up as he spoke, but no one paid much attention as a henchman capped the jar and screwed it shut.

"What do with them?" Robert asked, decidedly back in his own body now.

"Ta-ake to-o con-stab-bles," several henchmen said as one. "We-e vot-ed."

"That's better than you deserve, your traitorous wretch!" Dr. Viscous shouted, but he was very small again and so was his voice. Loud enough for the spectacles that had been Viktor to get riled up, though. With no small amount of strain, they rose up then across the jar and smushed against their former master. Any coherent conversation descended into a bubbling frenzy of squelches and curses.

"Tha-ank yo-u aga-ain. Yo-u sh-ow how wo-ork to-geth-er," the henchman Oli was pretty sure had been the wet-haired one said. Honestly, it was hard to tell them apart. Humans were bad enough, but whatever process the doctor had used to make these fellows was worse.

"Happy to be help," Oli said, nodding. "All is better when work together."

"Thank for save us," Man said, patting the henchman's knee cap. "No want be used for experiments."

"Or spare parts," Gob said with a shudder.

"Hold on a mo—stop! Stop!" Dr. Viscous shouted from the jar as he tried to bob away from the spectacles' assault. "Why do I recognize that voice?"

Gob immediately disappeared into the crowd of henchmen.

The henchman holding the jar gave it a good shake and the doctor was whisked around in a swirl.

"Yes, I think there will be many changes around here," Left said. Someone had marked a big L on its stone face with paint, which Oli found immeasurably helpful in keeping the two separate.

"All discussed and voted on, of course," Right said.

The crowd of henchmen grunted their approval at that. They were gathered around the goblins, and if Oli wasn't mistaken, there was fascination in their eyes. Seemed those had been becoming more expressive with every minute the henchmen worked for themselves. But probably he was just seeing things.

"Well, thank again," Oli said, looking at them all. "This been scary and no fun and now we must continue on quest for Dar—to see our family."

"And bring presents!" Lin One added.

"And bring presents."

"Before you go," Left said. "And speaking of presents, we wanted to give you a token of our thanks. For helping us, but also for the books!"

Oli looked to the stack of drying pamphlets Robert had been able to vomit up. None of them were technically books, but they hadn't packed the Bag of Numerous Nasty Things and really, it'd been good luck to find any sort of reading material in there. Among the papers were a flyer for a Merman Church of Day Late Complaints, the written extended warranty for someone's wagon, and a flyer for a free comedy show in a town no one had heard of. If nothing else, though, they were reading material to last until Left and Right could find which nearby towns had libraries.

Several henchmen lifted the columns and started down the hall.

"Goblins no need extra presents," Oli said. "Leaving alive enough."

"And with own body," Robert said, patting himself down.

"More presents more better, though!" Lin One shouted and ran after the columns. The others hesitated a moment, then followed.

So they moved through the castle; a tightly-packed crowd of henchmen, carried, sentient columns, and goblins trying not to get stepped on. They all came to a stop outside at a small stable.

"So sorry to bring you all the way down here, but we needed to get beyond the anti-magic field of the house for your present to work," Left said. "And for that to—"

"Horse!" Oli shrieked then sprinted forward. The steed had been returned to unlife and was even in one piece again. The henchmen had gone so far as to replace its animal skins and hay. Oli slammed into one skeletal leg and hugged it tight. Not a breath later, Lin Two used his head as a springboard and launched herself up to hug Horse's face.

"Big Boss fix?" her muffled voice asked.

"No," Oli said, pulling away from his hug to look at the crowd of henchmen. "You fix?"

"Horse fixed himself," Right said, voice cheery. "Just snapped back together as soon as he was carried out of the anti-magic field."

"It miracle!" Lin Two cheered.

"The henchmen," Right began, but was cut off by a hiss from the crowd. "Sorry, sorry. I forgot the most recent vote." The column cleared its stoney throat, then started again. "The *henchpeople* took the liberty of bringing Horse here and loading up your possessions. They're big and strong and happy to help, after all you did."

"Thank but where cargo?" Oli asked, pointing to Horse and his decided lack of struggling under the weight of far too much baggage.

"That's the second part of our gift," Right smirked.

"May I present… " The column paused, cleared its throat. "May I present… " And this time the henchperson the column was looking at got the signal and made a dramatic gesture to one side. "Viktor's newest invention, and a device that's sure to make you the most envied haulers on the continent!"

A curtain Oli hadn't noticed was pulled back to reveal a wagon.

"Lots people have wagons," Hob said.

"Yes, yes they do," Left said coyly. "But lots of people, goblins, henchpeople, and the like, do not have *this* wagon. For this wondrous invention is a self-propelled wagon! Not only will your poor steed no longer need to carry you, he won't even need to pull your wagon!"

A henchperson tied Horse's reins to the back of the wagon with a flourish.

Gob burst out laughing at the sight.

Oli elbowed him.

"What funny?"

"They put the cart before the… oh, never mind."

"If Horse tied to back, how wagon go?" Man asked and Oli nodded his agreement. As far as he could tell, it looked like any other wagon. Just like the ones they'd seen at the dealership. Well, except for the giant metal barrel protruding from the back like it'd burst its way out.

"Be-ehold!" a henchperson said then pulled a lever at the front of the wagon. There was a terrifying roar that shook the stables so hard hay and dust rained from the rafters. The metal barrel on the wagon exploded to life in a plume of flame that flared right out the far end of the stables—and seared a few lose strands of Horse's hay in the process.

Oli and his cousins panicked, scrambled, and scurried for cover beneath hay bales and henchpeople feet. But as they watched, the explosive wagon calmed and the shooting flame lessened into something approaching a rumbling rhythm.

A henchperson slapped the side of the wagon and smiled.

"Th-his li-ttle devil runs o-on—"

"Wait, wait!" Left interjected. "Let Iris tell them."

Right beamed at that.

"One final gift, goblins."

Another lever was pulled and a gem set into the wagon's running board glowed to life. Light gathered above it, then formed into a face. The goblins all cried out again and abandoned their hiding spots to find better ones.

"Hello, I'm Iris, your personal navigator and interactive guide to the *Master Viktor Is A Genius Self-Propelled Rocket Wagon XXI*. I'm imbued with runic magic that coordinates with elvish henge sites all across the world to triangulate your location at any given time, and can plot a route anywhere you'd like to go." The little floaty, shiny woman head dropped her voice to a rushed whisper. "I operate using patent pending magitech protected under the Inventor's Coalition Patent and Trademark Division. Unauthorized reproduction of this invention may result in legal or magical repercussions." She smiled as she finished rushing the words out. "Welcome to your journey."

The henchpeople all applauded. Due to the sheer volume of them crammed into the stables, the sound was enough to leave Oli's head rattling and ears ringing.

"So…" Left said, excitement in their voice. "You like it?"

"It… it… " Oli eased out from beneath a haystack. "It—"

"It amazing! Lin Two love it! Lin Two love Iris!" The goblin hooted and cheered as she clambered atop Horse—

paused to give him a scratch behind the ears—then dove into the back of the wagon. She reappeared from among the crates and packages stacked there, then scrambled up to the seat at the wagon's front. It looked like it was made for one normal-sized human, but considering goblins were considerably more fun-sized, there was plenty of room for her and at least two others. Oli decided immediately he would not be one of those. The back looked far safer. Until he considered the giant metal tube actively spitting a jet of flame larger than his house.

"Hello, Iris! Me Lin Two!" Lin Two said, waving at the floating head and getting a little too close such that her hand went clean through Iris. She didn't seem to mind, reforming immediately.

"Hello, user. Please say your name several times so that I may learn it."

"Me Lin Two! Lin Two is me!"

"Please say only your name, with a pause before and after."

"… Lin Two…"

"Thank you, *Lin Two*." Iris said it, but her voice went all stiff as she said the name. "It is a pleasure to meet you, *Lin Two*."

"Please to meet, Iris. Now meet cousins!" Lin Two waved everyone up to the wagon. "Come, come. Tell names!"

Oli stayed firmly put, but the others inched out from their hiding spots, seemingly emboldened by the fact that Iris hadn't done something horrible to Lin Two. Or maybe it was that the jet of flame hadn't burned the whole stable down yet. Either or.

TWENTY-ONE

Chaos On The Causeway

"Woooooo!" Lin Two shouted, lips flapping in the wind as the *Master Viktor Is A Genius Self-Propelled Rocket Wagon XXI* roared down the road. She'd quickly discovered the farther the throttle lever was forward, the faster they went. The only downside to this discovery was that the lever could only go so far forward. Still, Lin Two had given it more than a few kicks, just to make sure. All the while, flame belched from the metal mouth at the rear of the wagon and only most trees were set aflame as the goblins rocketed past.

Oli clung to the back of the wagon, steadying himself against the stacked crates. They swayed and rattled, along with Horse who'd been loaded inside as well. Even the ignoble steed, powered seemingly by dark magic and hellfire, hadn't been able to keep up.

The forest alongside them rushed past in a whooshing blur. So quick Oli couldn't make out individual trees so much as just a smear of greenery—which soon thereafter became a flaming smear of greenery.

The main road came up all too quickly and Lin Two pulled hard on the ship's wheel the wagon had for steering in place of reins. Crates, goblins, Horse, and even the *Master Viktor Is A Genius Self-Propelled Rocket Wagon XXI* itself tilted to one side, near rolling over entirely as the wheels screeched and fought to stay in contact with the road.

A mammoth trumpeted in alarm and reared up on its hind legs as they drifted past, dirt and splinters flying.

"Wooo!" Lin Two cheered, fist pumping. She'd dug out a pair of goggles from somewhere and had them down tight over her eyes. Didn't hide the pure excitement coursing through her features, though. Oli could have used a pair of his own to contain the pure terror coursing through his.

"You are on the fastest route, *Lin Two*," Iris said, her stiff voice battling against the rushing wind. "You will reach your destination, *Fortress Isolgar, the Beachhead of Barbarism and Minor Inconveniences*, in one day, fourteen hours, and twenty-one minutes."

"One day?" Oli shouted from the back, struggling to be heard. "That fast!"

"Yes, that's all fine and good," Gob said, both hands clenched to the seat to keep him rooted in place. "But we have a few last deliveries to make between here and there. Have you accounted for that, Iris? I mean—ugh! Gah!" he spat and coughed all of a sudden. "I swallowed a bug!"

"Free bugs!" Hob shouted and stretched his mouth wide.

"Please speak the address of any additional destinations you would like to add to the route," Iris said, looking at Gob who was still clutching his throat and gagging.

"Gob can read," Oli said, looking to his cousin.

"The depths to which I have been reduced," he said, shaking with a tired sigh as he climbed among the tied-down crates.

"Ooh, ooh! Robert read, Robert read!" the biggest cousin said, butting in. He squinted at the first address, then stumbled through a vocalized stream of unintelligible gibberish.

"That is not a valid address within my knowledge," Iris replied.

"Oh." He sagged inward. "Robert no can read good."

Oli patted him on the shoulder as Gob took over.

"One One Nine Dragon Gullet Lane," he shouted, squinting at the writing. "Number Two Market Street. Forty-One Springbrook Mountain Valley Meadows Court Lane." He stumbled over the words here and there, but generally managed well enough, considering the bumpy road and whipping wind.

After the misadventure at Dr. Viscous' castle, most of the unusual packages were all delivered. Of course, there was still the ghost urn en route to its seaside chateau, and the Weeping Stones too, but those had no destination. Were mostly just clattering around in the back, though they did look happier, as far as rocks went. What was left to be delivered was mostly big crates—those that hadn't been lost, or whose cargo hadn't escaped—and the strange metal oboe.

"That all," Man reported as he finished reading the last address. "No more."

"Rerouting…" Iris said, her glowing eyes distant. "Rerouting… "

"What 'rerouting'?" Hob asked, leaning over to Oli, who could only shrug.

"Route found," Iris reported, a note of pride in her tone. "In two miles…"

"Would you look at that," Gob said, smirking. He was sat on the driver's bench besides Lin Two. "This insane quest might actually be possible."

Iris continued with her directions.

"In two miles, use the left two lanes to turn left on to *Kings Way Bypass*."

"What is 'miles'?" Oli asked, brow scrunched at the strange new word.

"What is 'Kings Way Bypass'?" Lin One frowned.

"What is 'lanes'?" Lin Two asked.

Ahead, several oncoming oxen bellowed as the *Master Viktor Is A Genius Self-Propelled Rocket Wagon XXI* chased them off the road.

The oxen and wagon toppled over in the ditch, feet and wheels to the sky. Their driver rose up from the wreckage and cursed, fist shaking.

"Perhaps 'possible' was too strong a word," Gob said, frowning at the sight while, ahead, Lin Two drove them into yet more oncoming traffic.

* * *

"Ah, the wind blows cool from the west, the birds sing in the trees, and every spot of dew looks a jewel, glistening in the new sun! A very fine morning, wouldn't you say, Lord Maricelli?" Xander asked as he greeted his patron with a bow.

"Would be far finer with those smirking Jannistons put in their place." The lord crossed his arms as he frowned across his perfectly manicured lawn to the neighbor's estate.

"Put the wretched Jannistons from your mind, my lord. For when they set eyes upon our creation, they will know true jealousy." Xander swept into another practiced bow as he led his patron down from the manor's colonnade and to the front drive where his masterpiece awaited. It was covered in a sheet at the moment to make for all the more dramatic a reveal. What magnum opus hadn't been presented with a bit of drama, after all?

"Come, come, let's see it then," Lord Maricelli said with an impatient wave. But there was that glint in his eyes, too.

"Of course, of course, my lord," Xander said, then decidedly took his time easing toward his concealed masterpiece. Better to draw out the moment, no? The look in the lord's eyes now was the same Xander had noted all those years ago, when he'd first won his patronage. It was that look that dared to hope for something truly magnificent. That revealed that even if his mouth wore a frown, his heart beat with anticipation.

"I know we have gone over budget, my lord."

"More than once."

"And I know there have been delays."

"A half dozen, at least."

"But all of that ends… today." Xander let a smile pull at his lips. Let his patron see it. "My lord's patience and his—"

"Deep pockets?"

"*Faith* in my mastery will be rewarded." Xander whipped the sheet aside with a flourish. "Allow me to present the finest carriage in all the world!"

And so it was. A masterwork in every sense of the word.

"Sleek, but with a refined elegance even royals will envy. Behold, the turntippet wood from the jungles of Coatia, lacquered and polished to put even the sun itself to shame!" Xander caressed a hand along one door, fingers just playing at the surface. "Behold, the golden filigree, pure and brilliant as the history of your noble family!" Xander reached as if to touch the precious metal, then snapped back at the last moment. "Behold, every nail and stud, crafted from an ingenious composite of metals to provide maximum strength and minimum weight. But this carriage is not just for show, my lord, no, no! Comfort, too, has been given the utmost attention, as has reliability. Notice, these reinforced wheels will stand up to the roughest of roads while the suspension—a design of my own invention—will make even a landslide feel as smooth as the King's Way itself." Xander was beaming then, eyes entirely filled with the majesty of his creation. "And you might think all this comes at the price of speed, my lord, but I assure you that is not the case. This carriage is the most advanced to ever grace the roads. From its composite metals to the revolutionary way I've—"

"What's that?" Lord Maricelli asked.

"Composite metals?" Xander asked. "Well they're a sort of—"

"No, *that.*"

And it was only then Xander noticed his patron wasn't even looking at the carriage. His eyes were instead turned to the entrance to the driveway, and beyond, somewhere down the road where something was... screaming? No. *Roaring*.

A flock of birds burst from a tree alongside the road, flapping in a panic into the sky. And then a comet came howling into view. But, no. A wagon. Except it was spewing flame from its rear—and moving at an impossible speed.

It was all Xander could do to stare, mouth agape, as the wagon howled down the driveway then skidded to a stop before them. It was a behemoth of pipes and pistons, of steaming steel and hissing flame. It was terrifying. And beautiful.

"Forty one Springbrook Mountain Valley Meadows Court Lane?" a squeaky voice asked.

Lord Maricelli nodded slowly, eyes wide.

"This for you."

A crate was pushed off. It clattered to the ground as Xander managed to regain control of his mouth enough to ask who was responsible for the miracle machine before him.

If there was an answer, it was drowned out as the wagon roared to life, spat flame halfway across the lawn, then exploded down the driveway in a shower of gravel.

* * *

"No, no, I understand that's the way things have been done, but today we look to the future. Today, we put to rest how things *have* been done and welcome in a bright new era of how they *should* be done." Gillum said, as the parcel warehouse bustled behind them. Many-armed octofolk worked tirelessly up and down endless rows of shelves, sorting, moving, and packing packages while, outside, horses arrived and departed with bags of letters bound for every city in the kingdom.

Postmaster Scote frowned beneath his large mustache as he thumbed through the informational pamphlet.

"Terror birds, huh?"

"Terror birds," Gillum said, nodding emphatically. "Though we like to call them *Terrific* birds."

"I don't know, they sound dangerous. Can't have them eating my couriers. Or worse, the mail."

"The only thing terrifying about them is the speed with which they'll see your mail delivered," Gillum said as he followed the Postmaster outside to where horses were being loaded with bags of letters.

"What're you still doing here, Rogers?" the Postmaster barked at a loitering rider. "That treaty has to be in Numeru by morning. Get gone, boy!"

"Yes sir, Postmaster, sir!"

"Terror birds," Gillum said, fighting for attention. "Are the fastest courier in the business, I assure you. Mammoths carry more, sure. And horses are reliable, yes. But when it comes to speed over distance, and weight carried versus calories consumed, well, there's simply no better option than a *terrific* bird. And with a gnome rider, why, there's no finer nor faster way to deliver letters, documents, and any other important information." Gillum spread his hands wide, staring up at the sky as if he could already see their brilliant future approaching. "Terrific Courier Service—delivering your future."

"Hm. Well." Postmaster Scote chewed his lip. "Don't know much about terror birds, I 'spose, but there is need for a swift document delivery service ever since the eagles perished on that suicide mission into the Kingdom of Darkness."

"Yes…" Gillum said, nodding and already feeling the

gold soon to be weighing down his pockets. "Just sign this and we'll be in business." He pulled a contract from his coat pocket and held it out—

Something whooshed past so fast the contract was ripped from his hand. It was swept into the air and tossed away as if driven by a hurricane.

Gillum spun to find every horse and rider staring at the road and the flaming wagon wheel ruts cut deep into it.

* * *

"Come on, now," the old driver growled. "Heave!" He pushed forward with all he was worth as his horses pulled from the front. Wood groaned, the wheels shook—then gave out and rolled back into their muddy ruts.

"Gah!" the driver shouted, then threw his hat down and stomped on it. "No one wants to work anymore." He shot a look at his draft horses who whinnied indignantly in response.

Something clattered on the road behind him and the driver started speaking as he turned around.

"Hail friends, do you think you might be able to..." His words trailed off as he spotted the passing wagon. There were little creatures—gnomes? No, goblins!— crawling all over it. And stranger yet, there was a horse on it. *In it.* A horse riding in the back of a wagon. He locked eyes with the creature and it gave a little nod and a whinny as it rolled past on the strangest wagon the driver had ever seen.

"Don't you be getting any ideas now," the driver grunted as his horses, knee deep in mud and covered in sweat, watched their compatriot cruise past.

* * *

"Why so slow?" Lin Two complained, eyes already back to the throttle. "Fast better."

"Your destination is ahead," Iris said and her floating head spun to face a store beside the road.

"Animal feed, wagon repair, and general outfitters," Gob said, reading the words on the sign above the building. "Looks like this is the place."

The front of the building was piled high with hay bales and sacks of grain or something.

Lin Two gave the throttle a kick and the whole wagon leapt forward—almost into the nearest wall of hay—before Oli caught the lever and yanked it back. They came to a sliding stop in front of a group of humans wearing overalls.

"Number One Crossroads Place?" Man asked as the humans all stared up at them with eyes wide and mouths slack. "Number One Crossroads Place?" Man asked again, impatient this time. "Have delivery."

"Have delivery!" Robert said, hefting two crates from the back of the wagon.

"Uh, yeah, that's for us," one of the humans said. The expression on his face said not a single thing in front of him made sense at the moment.

"Thank," Robert said then chucked the crates down at the man's feet. He opened his mouth to respond but Lin Two had already kicked the throttle back to full. The wagon's engine roared, a deluge of fire spat out behind them, and then Oli's stomach felt it would burst out of his back as they launched forward and back on to the road. The humans cheered their departure—or something like that. Oli wasn't entirely sure but they were all suddenly running around and shouting. And someone had set one of the towering hay bale walls on fire. It seemed strange to

Oli to order hay just to burn it, but humans were strange creatures and he didn't pretend to understand them.

"We make good time!" Lin One said, feet blowing in the wind as he clung to the running board.

"There is a slowdown on your route," Iris said suddenly.

"Huh?" Lin Two asked. "No slow down!" And she kicked the throttle for good measure, even though it was already fully forward.

"There is a slowdown on your route," Iris said again. "Recalculating... recalculating... "

TWENTY-TWO

Construction On The Causeway

The world the goblins had journeyed into was full of dark and sinister forces. But as the traffic continued to thicken around them, a magic far more ancient and far more evil than even the Dark Lord's took hold of them: road rage.

"There is a two hour slowdown ahead," Iris said, her stiff voice all too easy to hear now that the wind was no longer whipping past. The big metal mouth at the back of the wagon growled and popped but didn't do much more than that, seeing as Gob had pulled the throttle lever to its slowest position.

"What this?" Oli asked as he climbed atop the crates to peer at the congested road. As far as he could see, the entire Kingsway was backed up with mammoths and wagons and all other manner of walking and rolling things. They weren't doing much walking or rolling, though, seeing as everything had come to a near stop.

"Why this?" Lin Two shouted, her arms crossed as she began to pout. "Wagon want go fast!" She eyed the throttle lever but Gob stood guard over it.

"There's no room to go anywhere," he said even though he didn't look happy about it.

"Iris!" Lin Two shouted and stomped her foot. "New route?"

The floating human shook her head sadly.

Ahead, the traffic moved a bit and Gob eased the throttle lever forward.

"Woo!" Lin One cheered as they rolled one wagon length ahead. "Again! Again!"

A wagon ahead was waving one of the little flags that hung off each side. The driver kept looking back at Oli and his cousins as if trying to work something out, or get their attention. Oli waved back and the wagon driver responded by waving his little red flag all the more.

"I think he's trying to merge into our lane—" Gob began but was cut off as Lin Two shoved him aside and took control of the throttle. The wagon jolted forward, sending everyone rolling about, and the other driver shouted a barrage of curses as he was blocked out of the lane. Lin Two cheered as she jumped back to her feet then blew a raspberry at the other driver.

"You little cretin!" he shouted, then began to climb down from his driver's bench.

"Stupid human no want this!" Lin Two shouted, near foaming at the mouth as she shook her fists and howled. Man joined her, hooting and hollering, and then Lin One, too, and Hob. They all looked rabid as they shouted the man down.

"Yeah! That what Lin Two think!" she shouted as the man grumbled and turned tail. "Ha! We win! We better!"

"What wrong with Lin Two?" Oli asked, not understanding the sudden madness.

"Road rage," Gob said, shaking his head. "Not even the purest of hearts are beyond its reach. The Dark Lord himself can only dream of such power."

"Gahhhh!" Lin Two shouted, fists to the sky and her whole frame shaking. She whipped back to the driver's bench, eyes wide, then began scanning for any further gaps in the traffic.

"No cause accident please," Oli told her but she was already shooting another gap, the wagon creaking forward to cut off a mammoth. Oli swallowed hard as the massive beast reared up and trumpeted, its gargantuan foot easily capable of crushing them.

"Yehahaha!" Lin Two cackled with glee.

"An alternate route that would avoid the slowdown is available," Iris' stiff voice called out suddenly.

Lin Two and the others seemed to barely hear her, however. They were still pointing and scheming how they could move up another wagon length. Looking ahead, Oli could still see nothing but wagons and beasts of burden, all packed-in and slowed to a crawl. And maybe, on the distant horizon, some sort of figures in bright orange, working beside the road.

"Where alternate route?" Oli asked to Iris.

"In one hundred paces, use the right lane to exit onto unnamed road," she said and spun to nod ahead.

Following her gaze, Oli found himself staring at a spot where runoff seemed to have washed away the side of the road. The result was a rough mud ramp leading down and into the surrounding trees. There, a track of loosely packed dirt continued on until it was lost in the depths of the forest. Rocks and roots and every other such bump Oli could imagine protruded from it.

"That no look safe," he said, not liking what he was seeing. "Look good for goblin home but no look good for wagon home."

"It let us beat traffic?" Lin Two asked, bouncing in place and still searching for any way to jump another wagon length ahead.

"We go! We go!" Hob added, his foot tapping hurriedly on the washboard.

"Warning! The *Master Viktor Is A Genius Self-Propelled Rocket Wagon XXI* is not rated for backcountry travel," Iris said by way of response. "The manufacturer is not liable for any damage sustained from use of vehicle outside of its intended purpose."

"Oli no think this good idea," he said. "If wagon break, we back to Horse."

Horse gave a panicked whinny from among the crates in the back.

"Wagon no break! We go!" Man said as he and Hob jumped up and down.

Lin Two frowned, though. "Horse no need carry all this. No good for Horse." All at once, the road rage seemed to leave her. "We… wait here." She said it, then nodded and crossed her arms. "We wait."

Man, Hob, and Lin One were still all worked up, but without Lin Two's leadership, they had no consensus where to direct their anger. The result was an incoherent series of hoots and goblin curses as they shouted at the surrounding drivers, then each other, then finally even the crates in the wagon.

Man shouted at the Weeping Stones next and a sudden rush of water followed, surging out and flooding the back of the wagon.

"Man make stones sad!" Oli reprimanded, then climbed back to shove his cousin away from the stones.

"Man no mean it," Oli said, patting the stones awkwardly. "You good stones. No cry."

The rush of water slowed to a trickle but didn't stop entirely.

"See what Man do?" Oli shot at him.

Man winced.

"Man sorry. No meant be mean."

"Alright, alright," Gob said, clapping his hands to get everyone's attention. "We're stuck crawling along for a while, so we need to entertain ourselves," he said.

"Robert play music!" the big goblin said as he pulled the metal oboe from among the packages still to be delivered.

"Actually…" Gob said, visibly wincing as he eased the oboe back into its case. "I had something else in mind." He turned his gaze to the surrounding wagons as the traffic moved and everyone inched forward again. "I spy with my goblin eye… something black!"

"Big Boss' heart!" Oli immediately shouted with delight.

"No, no. It has to be something we can see around us right now."

"Oh." Oli bit his lip. "No count if Oli see in head?"

"No, it can't be something you remember seeing. It has to be something you see right now."

"Ooh! Ooh!" Lin One jumped up and down. "It the sky! Gob spy sky!"

"The sky? What? No!" Gob slapped a hand to his face and groaned. "It also has to be the color I specified—actually…" He turned to Robert. "Maybe you should just play that oboe for us."

TWENTY-THREE

Curse Words Of Encouragement

"Ugh. Finally!" Lin Two grunted then kicked the throttle back to full. Behind them, flame spewed out and sent the construction orcs fleeing. Their work clearing brush and flattening the ground to create new lanes for the Kingsway had caused all the traffic.

"No slow down no more," Lin Two said to Iris.

"You are on the fastest route. You will arrive in ten minutes."

"Ten minutes to Isolgar?" Oli asked, suddenly

bouncing in his seat. "We that close? Big Boss be proud of us!"

"Not just yet," Gob answered. "We have two packages going to, well, there." He pointed along the road ahead. Oli's brow scrunched up because why would they be delivering packages to the dirt? Or, maybe Gob meant the trees? Did trees want packages? Oli couldn't say for sure—he'd only been a Courier of Cataclysm for a couple of days—but who was he to assume what trees wanted?

"Not there," Gob said as he grabbed Oli's head and tilted it higher up. "*There.*"

And then Oli saw it.

"What…"

He was at a loss for words. The thing rose from a hill not far in front of them.

"What it is?" he asked as every neuron in his brain—all ten or fifteen of them—fired at once and failed to find an answer. "What it is, Gob?" He asked it more hurriedly now as the wagon continued its screaming approach.

"It's called a city," Gob said. "And they're horrible places."

The… city was easily five times… Oli looked down and counted his fingers—no, ten times—bigger than their collection of humble huts back in the Swamp of Sadness and Sweaty Underthings. But no, it was bigger than that, too. He counted all of his cousin's fingers, but stumbled when the numbers got too big.

"You are on the fastest route," Iris said as the city drew up in front of them all too quickly. Out of the traffic jam the wagon was back to roaring down the road. And, Oli noticed, the others on the road were being extra nice as they turned, saw the wagon, screamed, then scurried out of the way. People around the city sure seemed polite.

They reached the city in what felt no time. The road

crossed a wooden bridge over a poor recreation of the Moaning Moat back in the Kingdom of Darkness. It didn't seem to have a single tormented soul swirling in its decidedly non-tar black water. But not even the boring moat could dampen Oli's spirits as the wonders of the city unfurled around him.

He found he had as much ability to describe the city as an ant did to describe the inner workings of the *Master Viktor Is A Genius Self-Propelled Rocket Wagon XXI*. The city was the most complicated and beautiful thing Oli had ever seen. And the loudest he'd ever heard. The stinkiest he'd ever smelled and the dirtiest he'd ever tasted. It was all of those things and all at once.

Even though he was perched atop the wagon, he felt small. It wasn't unusual for goblins to feel small seeing as, well, they were among the smallest of sentient species. But the city made him feel a new kind of small. The kind of small that wasn't a bad thing. The kind of small that opened his eyes to how big the world could be—and how much potential could be found in it. Everywhere he looked traders traded their wares. Craftsfolk built bridges and erected buildings, each of them impossibly detailed and yet toweringly huge. The streets were paved with perfectly smooth stones and along them, soldiers marched in formation to the beat of drums. Above, a gaggle of gnomes repelled down the side of a building washing its windows from a sort of hanging bench. Down one side street, a mammoth dunked its trunk in a great vat of liquid then sprayed it across a house, painting an entire side in one go.

Everywhere Oli looked there was energy and noise and *life* like he'd never seen before.

"It no so bad," he said trying to open his eyes wider to see everything all at once.

"Smell bad," Lin One said with a big smile. "Smell really bad!"

"Just like home!" Hob chirped. "But more fun and loud and stinky and there no Thing That Waits Beneath the Mud try to eat." His smile faltered a moment as he eyed the roadside gutters. "Probably."

"Too much in way," Lin Two grumbled as they reached a part of the street where wagons were all piled up in a slow-moving line. Luckily there was a smaller street on each side of the big street with no wagons on it, just a whole bunch of humans and orcs walking along. "Ooh, we go!" Lin Two said and pulled hard on the wheel.

There were some stone pillars in the way but the wagon squeezed between them—only a few bits scraping off the sides—and then they were out of traffic and onto the little street. Everyone seemed excited to see them, shouts and exclamations pouring from them as they turned to see the wagon, then jumped out of the way. Once again, Oli found himself surprised by how nice everyone was.

"Hello!" he said, waving back at a troll that was growling and shaking her fists at them.

The wagon hit a bump and Robert coughed suddenly, then spat up a pile of saliva-covered objects from the Sower's sack. The troll flinched as they slapped against her, but she grew calm a moment later as one of the objects caught her eye. She seemed to forget the goblins entirely as she bent to scoop it up.

"Have good day!" Oli called as they left her behind, her massive frame already huddled tight around the object she'd grabbed.

"In fifty feet use the left lane to turn left," Iris said and the crowd parted in a panic as Lin Two guided them through an intersection. There was a pretty light hanging above it flashing red. The left and right sides of it were green and the goblins oohed and awed at the light show as Lin Two drove them directly through the intersection. An approaching wagon driver cursed and swerved into a building for some reason. The wagons behind him decided they needed to stop all of a sudden and did so by piling into one another in a screeching heap.

"May be careful," Oli said, leaning up to Lin Two. "Drivers here no very good."

The city was a maze like none the goblins had ever seen before, and it would have consumed them if not for the help of Iris. She announced each turn well ahead of time, which left just enough time for the goblins to argue over what she meant, come to a conclusion, second guess that conclusion, then swerve in what was probably the right direction at just the last moment. In no time, they rolled to a stop in front of their first destination, a nondescript warehouse down a deserted street.

"Have delivery!" Man shouted, hands cupped to his mouth, but no one was around to answer. He jumped up and down a few times. "Have delivery!"

A door that none of them had noticed previously appeared in the wall then creaked open. A hooded figure peeked out.

"Whattttsss sssyou wantsss?" it hissed in a voice like a chorus of cicadas.

"This is One Six Six Seven Snakestead Alley, is it not?" Gob asked, reading the delivery address. The figure nodded and Robert and Oli wasted no time putting their backs against the appropriate crate and shoving it off the wagon. It smashed to the ground with a shattering crash but looked mostly intact.

"This for you!" Oli chirped. "Thank!"

"Ssssoo ssssoooon?" the hooded figure asked. Oli couldn't see their face but they sounded surprised.

"Thank!" Oli said again, then nodded at Lin Two and she kicked the throttle forward.

"Another satisfied customer," Gob said, hands clasped together. There was just one crate left in the back of the wagon now. Well, and the spooky ghost urn, the Weeping Stones, the metal oboe, and Horse, too. But of those, only the crate, oboe, and urn had delivery addresses.

"Good, good!" Oli cheered as they roared away, bathing the alley in a swathe of flame. "Quick, where next deliveries? Then to Isolgar!"

Following Iris' directions once more, they navigated through the city. The streets were crowded with traffic but for whatever reason no other wagons were using the little streets, just a bunch of people walking on them. Everywhere the goblins went the city's denizens were really nice and quick to get out of the way. Many of them shouted curse words of encouragement and shook their fists in support. It was enough to leave Oli blushing as they arrived at their next destination.

"What it is?" Lin One asked, staring up at the towering, ornate structure.

"It's a human church," Gob answered.

"What are you doing? No, no! Not here, you dolts!" a voice called out and Oli turned to find a heavyset human in rich, red robes whispering at them. "Around the back!" he hissed, then hurried away.

"What he want?" Oli asked with a frown.

"I think that's our customer," Gob said, then guided Lin Two to drive the wagon around the church and into the tight alleys behind it.

The human in his red robes was waiting for them.

"Never bring deliveries to the front entrance!" he said

as they rolled to a stop. "Yes, yes, that one right there. The chest with the smoke coming out, yes. That one's mine."

Robert lifted it down from the wagon and into the waiting hands of two other humans wearing bright white robes.

"Always bring the deliveries back here," the red robe man continued. "But that being said… how did you get here so soon? Rodrigrar's message said not to expect you for a week at least."

"Oli good Courier of Cataclysm!" Hob said, slapping Oli on the back.

"Best Courier of Cataclysm!" Lin Two agreed.

"It's been too long since the Dark One has sent a reliable courier. Really, if I wanted inconsistency and contradictions, I'd still be with the Bright Queen now, wouldn't I?"

Oli nodded as if any of that made sense to him.

"Anyway." The man cleared his throat, then flicked a golden coin into the air and Oli caught it.

"What this?"

"A token of my appreciation."

The coin was very shiny and, in the few rays of light trickling into the tight alley, glowed like nothing Oli had ever seen. He chomped down on it with a smile—which quickly turned to a frown, then a gag as he spit to the side.

"No taste good!"

"Well it's for spending, not eating," the human said, frowning. "And there's plenty more where that came from," he leaned in close, "if you can help me out…"

"No, no. No can help, thank! Goblins big hurry," Oli said and nodded at Lin Two. She moved to hit the throttle but the robed man pulled a heavy bag from his pocket and shook it around.

"No, thank—" Oli began but Gob cut him off, then stopped Lin Two from moving the throttle.

"That's a lot of money," he said calmly and the robed human nodded.

"I've long been in need of a discreet and swift courier. Some *improvements* are called for on the discreet side of things, but something tells me you'll make up for it when it comes to the swift part," he said, whistling low as he looked at the wagon. There was a hungry look in his eyes then.

"No have time," Oli protested to Gob. "Go see family. In hurry see family, Gob *remember?*"

"I don't expect you to understand the supreme value of money," Gob explained to Oli and the rest of his cousins in a rushed hiss. "But it's the key to everything. Having money is like… having magic. You can do anything with it!" His explanation was met with mostly blank stares. "Some say it's the root of all evil, you know," he continued and the blank stares turned to interested stares.

"Like Big Boss?" Oli asked.

"Yes, just like Big Boss. That's why we should hear what the nice man has to say and—ow!"

Lin Two had slapped Gob in the back of the head.

"What was that for—" he began, until he looked where she was pointing. In the street beyond the alley a towering figure was passing by. A towering figure made entirely of stone.

Sherrock Stones. Oli recognized him and his puffing pipe immediately. He was accompanied by a group of soldiers. At the middle of the group, a particularly important looking soldier was carrying a jar with a familiar lump of meat and a pair of spectacles inside. Noticeably absent from the group, however, was Sergeant Lastrof. Oli was glad not to see the excitable, mean human, but he held his breath all the same as the group passed. Thankfully, they quickly entered the jail on the far side of the street.

"We go now," he said and this time Gob nodded.

"So sorry to run," he apologized to the robed human. "Might we continue this discussion at a future date? At the moment, I'm afraid we have urgent business."

If there was an answer, no one heard it over the scream of the engine as Lin Two kicked the throttle forward.

TWENTY-FOUR

Must Go Faster

Goblins, as a species, have never wanted much to do with virtues. Virtues can't be eaten, or thrown, and they definitely can't be thrown and then eaten. It should come as no surprise, then, that patience was not a virtue Lin Two exercised as she guided the *Master Viktor Is A Genius Self-Propelled Rocket Wagon XXI* through the human city. If arson was a virtue, however, she exercised a fair bit of that as the engine belched flame behind them.

Probably she could have gone a bit slower, but there was the slight problem of having discovered where

Sergeant Lastrof was—directly behind them and shouting from the saddle of a giant, squawking bird. It was a gangly thing, all legs and short, flappy wings. But in the twisty-turny streets of the human city, those legs were nimble enough to dart in and out of traffic and swift enough to keep pace with the considerably less maneuverable rocket wagon. Oh, and then there was the beak, big enough to swallow Oli in a bite and a half.

Lastrof wasn't the only bird rider, either. At least six of her officers flanked her, their own birds snapping and screeching as they dashed through the streets.

"Terror birds?" Gob said, rubbing his chin as he frowned at the squawking pursuers. "That's new. I've never known them to be domesticated, much less to allow a rider."

"Scary birds no look nice!" Lin One shouted. "No want be eaten!"

"No scary birds eat cousins, not while me around," Oli said, then pressed a thumb to his cursemark to call on the power granted him by the Dark Lord Sarusomal. The sky above darkened with clouds, a thunderclap set the ground to shaking, and then all about the street, shadows rushed from sewer drains, clawed free from cracks between the cobbles. The street was bathed in shadow and from it, cursed souls spewed into the realm of the living.

"Shadow friends save goblins from be eaten?" Oli shouted at them, but the rocket wagon was moving too fast and already the shadow servants were left behind. They burst into a sprint, even as their infernal bodies hissed everywhere the sun touched.

"What is thy bidding, master?" the foremost of them yelled.

"What?" Oli shouted back.

"What—" The damned soul was breathing heavy now. "Is thy—"

The words were lost in the whipping wind, then further drowned out by the squawk of a terror bird. It lunged forward, beak snapping shut and near taking Oli's nose clean off. He screamed and stumbled away, then scurried to the front of the wagon to throw his full weight against the throttle lever. For some reason, Lin Two hadn't had it all the way forward and a fresh burst of explosive force knocked Oli off his feet and sent him rolling right back to where he'd been before.

He came to a stop in time to see blasts of magic hissing and whizzing overhead. Oli peeked up in time to see the terror bird had fallen back some distance and in response, Lastrof and her officers were firing spells from their wands. One arched right into their engine—or tried to, but as the spell reached the roaring flame it burned up in a dazzle of color.

"In one hundred feet turn left onto—in sixty feet turn le—in twen—*turn left!*" Iris said, her usually stoic voice tripping over itself as buildings and pedestrians whipped by impossibly fast. "Turn left!"

Lin Two pulled hard and the wagon tipped onto two wheels for a frightening moment before slamming back down to all four. Horse, Oli, and his cousins were all flung about the empty cargo area. Fortunately, goblins were particularly bouncy so it didn't hurt much. Unfortunately, goblins were particularly bouncy so when Lin One hit Horse's bony shoulder he ricocheted right out of the wagon with a whooping cry halfway between fear and delight.

Hob threw himself forward and snagged Lin One by the feet. He cheered his own heroics for a moment before the momentum caught up and he too was yanked out.

Man grabbed Hob but the weight was still too much and he was dragged out. Oli lunged and just got his hands around Man's ankles but then he too was pulled free of the wagon. They all would have fallen free if not for Robert reaching out and anchoring them in place. That stopped them falling entirely from the wagon but did leave a four-goblin-long chain whipping and whirling in the wind.

Sergeant Lastrof's eyes went wide at the sight.

"Got you now!" she growled, then gritted her teeth and urged her terror bird forward with a firm kick to the sides.

* * *

"No one appreciates fine artistry anymore!" Tyrk growled. "And curse this wind, too!" he added as he inched through the streets of Numeru, precious cargo held in front of him. The breeze pulled at the stacked pages, trying its darndest to pry them free and carry them off to heavens knew where. It'd be different if it was a cooling breeze, but it was closer to a furnace wind, what with half the city converted into forges and refineries for the Bright Queen's miserable war. A steam whistle howled from somewhere nearby and another burst of searing wind rushed past.

Tyrk hunkered down to protect his cargo. He'd tried to pack the manuscript into a box, but he didn't have a box big enough. It'd take closer to four and he didn't have the arms to carry that many at once. Likewise, he was all out of parcel paper, so the best he'd been able to do was stack the pages in order, tie them up with a string he'd found in a forgotten desk drawer, and then carry them in front of him, one hand on top and one on bottom as if he was holding the world's largest sandwich.

Probably he should have just hired a cab, but cabs cost money and he'd already used up all his stipend—and then the stipend to the stipend—to secure the extra time he needed.

You can't rush perfection, he'd always had to tell the printer, but they didn't care. They weren't artists, they were businessfolk. Only cared about deadlines and budgets. It'd taken all the convincing he was capable of just to get a measly third extension on this project. As if delays weren't inevitable in creating one's *magnum opus*. And after all, weren't delays a small price to pay for the eternal fame and adoration they'd all receive for his laborious efforts? And that would start today. Would start two blocks away when he arrived in the printer's office and dropped his newest manuscript on his editor's desk. Already he was relishing the moment. Couldn't wait to watch that puffed up pencil pusher experience true art.

"Excuse me, *excuse me*," Tyrk hissed as he tried to navigate around a particularly thick crowd of loiterers. Clearly, they had nothing better to do than clog up the sidewalk and get in his way. Really, why were they just standing there? And what were they pointing at?

"Waahohooowwooo!" someone was shouting in what sounded halfway between delight and fear.

"Really now, what's all this racket?" Tyrk asked, leaning around his bundle of papers as the shouting got louder. He managed a glimpse past the side of the loose leaf tower just as the loiterers threw themselves to the ground. Tyrk's eyes went wide. Some sort of monstrous, mechanized wagon was hurtling toward him.

He cried out, cradled his manuscript, and winced as he spun to the side. The massive wagon whooshed past, just missing his shoulder. It left whipping wind in its wake and his tower of papers wobbled one way, then the other, then thankfully steadied in place. Only a single sheet of paper was whisked off the top.

"Oh thank the heavens," Tyrk said, sighing in relief. "That was too close."

But someone was still shouting. Right up behind him, now, actually. Tyrk looked over his shoulder—

His manuscript exploded as a chain of screaming goblins blasted through it. Papers flew in all directions, swirling and whipping in the wind.

Tyrk stood stunned, arms suddenly empty as paper and sparks rained down around him. It was all he could do to gulp down air and watch as the chain of goblins dragged and bounced behind the wagon with more than a few of his precious manuscript pages stuck fast in their slimy coating.

* * *

"No one appreciates fine artistry anymore," Germund Stonemixer said under his breath. "But they will after today," he added, as he took in his liquid masterpiece. Though, liquid wasn't really the right term for it, was it? It was something more. Something new. Something that would revolutionize the world of infrastructure. Those luddites in the cobblestone guild wouldn't know what hit them.

"No, no! Not there, you dolts!" Germund shouted and hurried over to stop his apprentices. Or, more specifically, the replacements to his apprentices, seeing as all the actual skilled laborers had been press-ganged into building siege engines for the Bright Queen. The collection of dullards and children he'd manage to scrounge up in their place were trying to pour a fresh drum of putty rock in exactly the wrong place. "We're only permitted to do one side of the road. We can't close both directions at once!"

As usual, they hadn't been listening. The marked off

area had already been poured properly and now he needed everyone in place with their scrapers to ensure it was as smooth as possible. This was the most critical juncture.

"Come, come." He waved them back to the drying solution. "Scrapers in hands, kids. Scrapers in hand! Yes, that's it. Steady now, steady. It must be smooth as glass."

"Boss?" one of the hired dwarflings asked, raising a hand. "Why we pouring this goopy rock when we could just get some from the quarry?" He gestured toward the edge of town and Deadrop Quarry. "They got the good stuff, and I should know, my papaw runs the whole show."

"Because poured rock is the future, my slow friend."

That didn't seem to clear anything up. The dwarfling was still wearing a confused frown.

"It's far easier to mix my solution on site than cut thousand-pound stones from the cliffside," Germund said, speaking slow and loud so everyone would understand. That seemed to work as the dwarfling nodded along, then smiled.

"Doesn't have to be thousand-pound slabs," he said. "Papaw cuts 'em smaller if you want."

"No, no. That's not the point!" Germund raised a foot to stomp but thankfully paused before he stepped into the still solidifying stone in front of him. "This is going to change everything. Roads, buildings, bridges, and who knows what else?" he exclaimed, pumping a fist in the air. "My putty rock is stronger than stone, easier to transport, and—thanks to my fast-drying, patented solution—can be shaped into anything you dream up. The only limits are your imagination."

The dwarfling shrugged. A moment later, he mumbled something.

"Come again?" Germund asked.

"Didn't say nothing."

But someone had. Germund frowned as he listened close, then realized the voice had come from behind them. Out on the street. In the distance, someone was talking. But it was too stiff to be a human voice. Was closer to a golem, maybe? Or, no. Something else?

"In fifty feet, turn right. In twenty fe—*turn right!*"

Germund liked to consider himself a brilliant inventor, but the thing that came screaming around the corner was a creation beyond his wildest imagining. The fact it was crewed by goblins hardly even registered in his mind as he saw, with frightening clarity, the machination was headed straight for his patch of freshly poured putty rock.

"No! No! Go around! Can't you see the signs?" he shouted, waving his arms as he ran forward. The driver spotted him and swung the wheel hard to the side, throwing the wagon into the far wall of the alley. Sparks and splinters exploded as wood and metal grinded against stone. The impact was too much, though, and the wagon rocked back in the opposite direction. Germund was left to fling himself out of the way. The machine teetered on the edge where the cobblestones ended in favor of his poured rock, then slipped off and dipped two wheels in. Just for a moment, though, as the driver managed to steer the devilry-powered machine clear of Germund's precious work. It didn't make much difference, however, as the chain of goblins dangling off the back of the wagon bounced off one alley wall, then the other, then up into the sky before being pulled taunt and belly flopping right into the patch of putty rock. Gurgling, giggling cries bubbled up as three of the goblins were dragged through the once smooth perfection, their faces churning its surface into a mess of imprints.

* * *

"Artistry at its finest, if I may so! You've really outdone yourself with this cake, boss," Alyce said, smiling up at the five-layer tall cake held between her and Fennis. They'd secured it as best they could for travel, encased in a paper box and tied shut with string in a strong knot.

"Well, it's not every day you get an order from the mayor himself," Fennis said, smiling up at his creation. This would be the one to put him on the map. He'd finally make his mom proud and firmly establish Fennis' Fancy Pastry Bakery as the finest in Numeru. They just had to get it to the gala in one piece.

Though, all the shouting was starting to concern him on that point. He'd no idea what all the commotion was, but thankfully it hadn't been a problem for them yet. But was it drawing closer? And what was that roaring?

The cake teetered to one side and Fennis' heel came down on an uneven slab of cobblestone.

"Whoa there, whoa there!" he said, fighting to keep his balance and steady his masterpiece.

"More potholes in these streets every day," Alyce said, shaking her head.

"Just another couple blocks…" Fennis said through gritted teeth and a renewed focus.

But the roaring was right up on them then. It was coming from around the corner of the intersection they were approaching. And then there was light, too. As if some massive ball of flame was blasting through the streets, casting angry, flickering orange light as it went.

"Uh, boss…?" Alyce asked, slowing down and near toppling the cake as she did.

"Don't worry about it," he grunted, focusing on his cake. "We're on the sidewalk, road traffic's not our problem."

"Ah, right."

The roar exploded around the corner and Fennis would've gasped at the flame-borne machination whipping past if he weren't so focused on his cake; if he weren't so focused on potholes; if he weren't so focused on—

"Ahh!" Alyce shouted and flinched away as the rocket wagon blasted past. Then her scream was joined by others as four goblins covered in heavens knew what were dragged past, kicking and flailing.

Through it all, Fennis stayed steady. The world could go insane if it wanted, but he simply didn't have time for it today.

"That was close," Alyce said, head craned around to watch the insane contraption blast away. "What even was that? Are those... goblins?"

"Out of the way!"

A policewoman on a terror bird came hurtling right at them, her mount's legs tearing furiously at the cobblestone as it sprinted. Behind her were another half dozen officers riding similar beasts. A whole flock of screeching beaks and flying feathers.

"Move aside! Out of the way!"

"Steady, steady!" Fennis shouted and Alyce did her best, following him in a wobbling dance as the birds whooshed by all around. One on the left, another on the right. Each one's passing buffeted them, pushing the cake one way then the other. Fennis and Alyce scurried beneath it, struggling to keep it upright. But then there was another bird coming right at them. It squawked in panic, eyes going wide as its clawed feet scratched and scraped to swerve around them but found little purchase on the cobblestones.

Fennis braced for impact, already able to imagine the street covered in frosting and feathers. But the bird leapt at the last moment and—with the help of its rapidly flapping wings—got just enough lift to soar clear over them. The very point of one taloned toe just nicked the knot on the cake box, pulling it loose.

The bird hit the ground hard, then gave an apologetic squawk as it scrabbled away.

Only then, as the street fell back to quiet, did Fennis let out a sigh of relief—and step directly into a pothole.

But the fates were kind that day and instead of toppling clean over he just jolted his ankle a bit. The cake stayed happily upright as the chaos of whatever was happening continued through the city.

* * *

"Enough of this madness!" Lastrof growled to herself. Even in the city streets, the wagon was too quick to catch. It was powered by the Dark Lord's evil magic, no doubt, and driven with a reckless abandon that would have made even a nihilist find religion. But the Bright Queen had laid siege to the Kingdom of Darkness. The great enemy was finally cornered. A century of warfare, of lives given for the cause. Finally, the eternal war was going to end. Whatever these sinister goblins were up to probably wouldn't change that, but she wasn't going to wait around and find out anyhow.

She bit down on her fingers and let out a shrill whistle to get her officers' attention.

"Stay on them!" she shouted, pointing to the raging inferno that'd been spitting sparks at them and setting stray fires all through the city. Her officers continued the chase as Lastrof pulled on the reins to guide her bird down a side street. Before her was a labyrinth of back alleys and dead ends, but this was her city.

"The Dark Lord has corrupted your hearts and given

you singular, sinister purpose," she growled, thinking of the goblins. "But the Bright Queen's light has shown me a higher purpose. I will not fail her. Her light will guide me." Lastrof gritted her teeth and guided her terror bird at breakneck speed down alley after alley. Each turn and twist sent her deeper in, would have left anyone else hopelessly lost. But she didn't need hope, she had conviction and through a combination of trusting her gut and letting the Bright Queen light her path, she navigated through successfully.

All at once, the alleys gave way to wide thoroughfare and as she spun in the saddle, a smile crept onto her face. She was ahead of the goblins! Her shortcut had worked! From the middle of the thoroughfare she could see smoke rising from where the monstrous wagon was whipping through the streets—and heading right for her.

"Praise be," she said, then clenched the reins in hand. "Now come here, goblins."

Based on the route they'd been using, they were heading for the eastern exit of town. Quarryside, it was called. Once they passed the gate there, they'd have two options for escape: the high road across the plateau, or the cliff road that wound down and down into the chasm, doubling back on itself time and time again. Obviously, they wouldn't take that road. Their speed would count for naught on it. That meant the Dark Lord's servants were headed for the high road—but Lastrof wasn't going to let them reach it. This chase ended here.

She readied her wand and called to mind a powerful spell. It'd need to be precisely aimed, right into the devious engine powering the wagon, but if she landed the shot, the fight would be all but won.

"Hey!" someone called from the side.

Lastrof turned to find a laundryman had paused from his labor, sheet blowing in his hand halfway to the line.

"What's all the racket today?" he asked.

"Go about your business," Lastrof snapped and turned her attention back to the approaching wagon. It was clear in sight now. She raised her wand and closed one eye.

"Hey!" the laundryman shouted again. "Hey now!"

"Shut it!" Lastrof snapped back, but the man wasn't yelling at her. No, he was yelling at the goblins who seemed to have lost control of the wagon. It was leaning heavily to one side and as Lastrof watched, pitched hard to the left—right into the laundryman's forest of clotheslines. The wagon plowed through row after row of still-damp laundry, sheets and clothes and all manner of fabrics ripped from the lines.

"No!" Lastrof shouted as the wagon became so covered in detritus she couldn't see the engine. She fired anyway, before her window of opportunity passed. The spell exploded from the end of her wand and hit the wagon right in its engine! Or, it would have, if there hadn't been a mountain of fabrics piled up there. The spell detonated with whizzing green shoots of magic flying in all directions—but failed to destroy the engine. Instead, it burned up several of the bed sheets such that Lastrof had a great a view of the goblins cackling in glee as they roared past.

* * *

"No can see! No can see!" Lin Two was yelling from the front of the wagon and Oli couldn't blame her. They were covered in sheets and clothes and even several clothes lines, tangled up and dragging behind them. The flames of the engine had even set several alight. Something exploded with a hiss and a pop of pressure in Oli's ears, then the sheets at the front of the wagon burned away.

"Ah, that better," Lin Two said happily.

Better for her maybe, but not for Oli. He was still holding on tight to Hob's ankles as he and his cousins were dragged behind the wagon. The ground bumped and bucked below them and everything had been happening too fast to see. Somehow, he was covered in a layer of crinkly paper, then what felt like heavy mud, and now, other people's clothing. But they were outrunning the scary birds so that was probably good.

"Turn left!" Iris' usually stoic voice sounded panicked now.

"Turn where?" Lin Two shouted back.

"Rerouting... rerouting... "

"*Oof.*"

There was a thud and Oli looked behind them to see Sergeant Lastrof. Where had she come from? Her terror bird was slowing down off to one side of the road, saddle decidedly empty. Lastrof, on the other hand, was clinging to the clotheslines dragging behind the wagon. Her face was set in a determined grimace as she pulled herself closer, climbing the dragging lines.

"Bad lady!" Lin One shouted. "Bad lady here!" As the first to fly from the wagon, he was the furthest out and thus closest to the sergeant.

"Robert pull us up! Pull up!" Oli shouted to their strongest cousin. He gave a nod but the wagon bucked at the same time and he stumbled, almost falling out of the wagon himself. The resulting jolt sent Oli and the others a few feet closer to Lastrof before Robert could get his feet back under him.

"Wrong way! Pull other way!" Oli shouted at Robert.

At the same time, there was more shouting coming from the front of the wagon.

"Where turn? No give enough time to make!"

"Rerouting… turn right in—now!"

Iris frantically tried to give Lin Two directions, but it was about all she could do to stay in a straight line what with the wagon dragging so much weight and leaning to the left on account of the strange rocks now glued to the wheels there.

They hit a particularly bad pothole and for a moment, Oli was bounced into the air. He looked over his shoulder to see they were headed for some sort of mining operation. Massive cranes were lifting stone slabs up from a pit. No, bigger. A whole canyon it looked like, and with no bottom in sight.

"Wagon no can fly!" Oli shouted up to Lin Two but if she heard him, she didn't respond but to keep fighting with the steering wheel.

"In fifty feet, make a U-turn," Iris said. "In ten feet—"

"Ahhh!" Lin Two cut her off with a cry as they crashed through a wooden barrier and right into the mining site.

Lastrof bounced and rolled on the end of the rope, but then, as Oli watched, her eyes went wide. Doubt filled her features, then terror. Without hesitation she released her grip and rolled away.

Oli looked back over his shoulder in time to see a ramp. Laborers were easing massive carts of stone down it, but the wagon was going *up* it.

"You are not on a recognized route—*you are not on a recognized route!*" Iris yelled as the ramp came to an end and Oli suddenly found himself flying. As was the rest of the wagon.

They soared out over the canyon, open air whooshing around them. Behind, the pursuing scary birds slid to a stop except for one which charged up the ramp after them. It sprang as far as it could... and fell far short of them. The last Oli saw the bird was flapping its stubby wings wildly and just enough to turn its fall into a gentle descent.

If only their fall could have been the same.

Driven by the explosive force of the *Master Viktor Is A Genius Self-Propelled Rocket Wagon XXI*, the goblins *almost* flew through the air. The chasm passed beneath them, then just as they began to dip into it, the far cliffside appeared and flat ground caught them with a gentle caress like being body slammed by a golem.

The wagon slammed down first, wheels leaning out with screaming groans as the full weight came down on them. Wood flexed, metal screeched, and then several thuds echoed out as Oli, then Man, then Hob, then finally Lin One crashed down into the cargo area. Horse came last and landed on them all. The combined weight caused a spin and the wagon veered to one side, lost all traction, and threw itself into a burn out, dust and dirt and smoke spewing around them.

Lin Two killed the throttle, the spin died out, and slowly, they came to a stop.

Worrying smoke rose from the engine and more than a few splinters lay about the cargo area as Oli wobbled to his feet.

"Cousins okay?" he asked, adrenaline coursing through him. "Horse okay? Iris okay?"

"That. Was. Awesome!" Lin One shouted, bouncing up and down. "We go again? We go aga—" His cheer turned into a gurgling shudder as he clapped a hand to his mouth then leaned over the side of the wagon.

TWENTY-FIVE

The Biggest Newt In The World

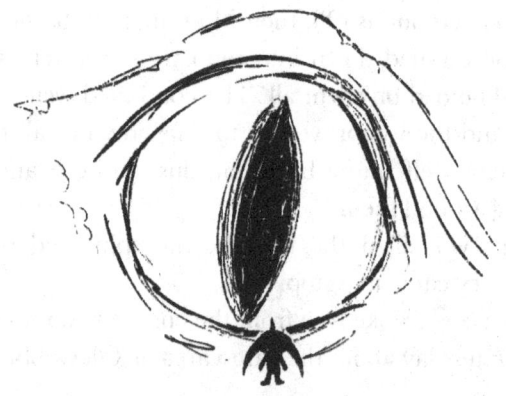

Of all the things one can say about goblins, 'smart' is assuredly not among them. 'Curious'? Sure. 'Enthusiastic'? Absolutely. 'Likely to critically misunderstand the complex machine before them'? Also yes. Taken all together, the outlook that the goblins could fix their rocket-powered wagon was grim. Didn't stop them from trying, though.

Oli's ingenuity mixed with Hob's confidence like bogwart spores and belchtoad secretion—which is to say the result was stinky, flammable, and inflicted injuries no insurance policy would cover. Add a determined effort from Robert—knocking around inside the engine with a rock he'd found—and in no time the wagon was fixed— which in this case, was a word the goblins had repurposed to describe exactly how much worse they'd made things.

But the wagon still rolled forward, even if the wheels on the left side bumped and thudded with each revolution and the engine spat flame out of all the new cracks shot through its casing.

The wagon, the goblins, and Horse had all seen better days, but there was still work to be about. And with Sergeant Lastrof and the scary birds left behind on the far side of the chasm, there was time for two final deliveries then on to Fortress Isolgar. Thanks to Iris' navigational prowess, both deliveries were directly on their route and, as a happy accident, rocketing over the chasm had cut significant travel time off the journey. Iris only sounded a little resentful of that fact as she guided them with calm assurance along the top of the plateau.

All around, the landscape was vast and dusty, interrupted only by the occasional tumbleweed blowing past, or getting caught in the various scorched wreckage. There were burned-out wagons, skeletons that appeared to have been roasted inside their armor, and even the remains of a few horses. They looked to have once been massive war steeds—before they'd been bitten in half. All in all, the goblins found it a charming landscape.

"You have arrived at your destination," Iris chimed out, a pleased note ringing in her tone

"We make delivery to bone man?" Oli asked, frowning down at the skeletal corpse in front of them. What should have been white, sun-dried bones were stained black and there was a suspiciously human-sized pile of ash all around them.

"Your destination is on the right," Iris said and the goblins let out an 'ohhh' as one when they turned to see the gaping cave. Or was it some sort of giant burrow? Hard to say, honestly, what with the acrid smoke pouring from its maw and obscuring everything.

Robert looked at the metal oboe he held in hand, then to the smoking hellmouth, then back to the oboe.

"Delivery go there?" he asked.

Gob read the instrument's delivery address again, then shrugged.

"That's what it says."

"Then goblins go!" Oli said as he grabbed the oboe and leapt from the wagon. "Too many deliveries. Goblins 'sposed serve Big Boss and get special Key thing, not all this stuff." He marched ahead with a renewed focus, oboe held overhead as his little feet slapped against the plateau's dust-covered rocky ground. "Cousins come!"

The mouth of the cave-burrow thing was even sootier than the land around it but once the goblins slipped into its ominous maw, things got better. Shinier, too.

"What this?" Oli asked, squinting against the brilliant, golden glow assaulting his eyes. The inside of the hellmouth was filled with mountains. But not mountains of stone, and not teeming with mountain goblins like Oli was used to. No, these mountains were shiny, and clinky, and made of golden coins. Just like the one the red-robed human had tried to give them. Oli's tongue remembered the nasty taste and he grimaced.

"No lick mountains, cousins. No good."

A rumble ran through the cave, the walls shaking as if with the leftover force of some distant, deep earthquake. The ground vibrated beneath Oli's feet in a not entirely unpleasant way and all around, coins clinked down from their precipitous peaks. Among them were a few other objects. A chalice here, a crown there. And... was that a golden harmonica? Oli's musical education hadn't advanced beyond armpit farts so there was no way to be sure.

"Cave shaky," Hob said, poking the ground. "Maybe no feel good?"

"Gods and Great Minds above!" Gob said in a rushed whisper. "This is incredible. We're rich! No, we're beyond rich. We could live like royalty. No, richer than that!" He clapped his hands together, positively squealing now. "We could live like *politicians*." He gave a whooping shout then ran toward the nearest teetering mountain of gold, arms spread wide. Another tremor shook the cave as he did.

"These no our shiny circles," Oli said, frowning.

Gob continued undeterred until Robert caught him by the back of the neck.

"Oli say shiny circles no is ours."

"Release me, you oaf!" Gob was squirming and slapping at his largest cousin's hand to little avail. "And open that voluminous maw of yours! We'll need the Sower's Sack!"

"Goblins here to give, no to take," Man said, frowning at the struggling Gob. He pointed to the oboe Oli was still holding overhead.

"Besides, goblins have all goblins need already," Lin One added. "Mud, newts, newts in mud..." He counted on his fingers as he listed off their prized possessions.

"Horse, too! And angry fast fire wagon!" Lin Two cheered.

"None of that means anything compared to *this!*" Gob cried. "Don't you understand?" he asked, momentarily forgetting exactly how much of an oxymoron the term "understanding goblin" was.

"Have all we need except for serve Big Boss," Oli said, feeling ashamed he hadn't thought of that earlier. That was why they were doing all this, after all, right? Even if it had been fun to see so many new things beyond the Swamps of Sadness and Sweaty Underthings.

"Release me!" Gob was still crying, kicking and slapping as Robert hefted him into the air. He was thunked down on a little ridge of rock protruding from the mountainous piles of treasure. Something jabbed into his backside and Gob reached down to find what distant memories from his old life told him was... an oversized trombone?

"Gob stay until feel better," Robert said, wagging a finger at him. "Goblins here to give, no to take."

Oli nodded at that.

"Humans get loud and wave arms lot when goblins take things." He thought about that for a moment, then frowned. "And maybe leave bad review!"

"Not a day goes by that I don't regret the circumstances that led me to being stuck with y—" Gob began, but was cut off as the little ridge of rock Robert had placed him on picked that moment to exhale. A furnace wind blasted through the cave, sweeping ash and dust into the air. It was hot enough that the bits of paper still clinging to Oli were seared away, their edges alighting orange.

"Ah." Gob said, freezing in place. "Everything makes sense all of a sudden."

'How make sense?' Oli wanted to ask, but the question became far less interesting to him as the ridge beneath Gob opened two massive nostrils and sucked in a breath.

"Run, cousins!" Hob shouted. "It Thing That Waits Beneath the Mud!"

"No! It Thing That Waits Beneath the Clinky Mountains!" Man corrected while fleeing for cover, but finding none. Probably that was on account of the fact he was fleeing in a circle, feet cutting a consistent track through the ash. Not his best idea, but considering that one time with the alligator and the tweezers, far from his worst.

Man's cousins joined him in panicked flight as gold and gemstones and all manner of glittery things rushed to either side in a clinking avalanche. The ridge continued to rise until all the treasure had run away and Gob was left sitting on the nose of the largest newt Oli had ever seen. A newt so large he couldn't imagine anyone would ever get it to fit in a newtcake.

Gob shook, teeth clattering as a pair of piercing, orange eyes opened behind him. Each was as wide as the engine nozzle on their wagon. In comparison, though, these eyes burned even brighter.

"What manner of trickery is this?" the Thing That Waits Beneath the Clinky Mountains / the biggest newt Oli had ever seen asked and her voice was so big another half dozen piles of coins collapsed. With every syllable she spoke, a blast of flame rushed out, snapping and popping hungrily in the air. "I hear your voice, but even eyes as mighty and prestigious as mine own cannot see from whence it comes?" The oversized newt swung her head about the room, Gob still shaking in place as he clung to the very tip of its snout.

"No mean to trick, sorry!" Oli said finding his own teeth chattering as he shouted up at the creature. "This..." He took a big swallow and found his mouth dry. "This One One Nine Dragon Gullet Lane? Iris say yes but Oli no see address. Also no can read."

"We... we have a delivery for you, oh Ancient and Mighty One," Gob said. To Oli it sounded like his cousin's tone had changed all of a sudden, but probably that was just on account of him being so far away now. Almost up to the cave's ceiling, really.

The burning, orange eyes rolled inward and almost went cross-eyed as they finally focused on Gob. A searing snort blasted from the nostrils a moment later.

"Thy stealthy magic is impressive, small orc. Or are you perhaps a large frog?" The cave shook and rumbled with the force of her voice as blasts of flame washed out and across the open air. "It matters not what manner of creature you are, you will not have my hoard."

"My... my humble acquaintance has your package," Gob said, fighting to speak as fear gripped him tighter than a nobleman's purse at a charity drive. "We come to give, no to take," he added and far, far below, Oli smiled wide.

"Yes! Gob get it now." He waved the metal oboe around excitedly. "This for you, biggest newt!"

The dragon, for clearly that was the name of the ancient being even if Oli did not know it, paused at the small goblin's words.

"Mine oboe?" A questioning puff of flame followed the question. "Thy quest is to deliver it safely to mine lair? And thou come not to pilfer mine hoard? Not to test thine noble heart and chivalrous nature in lethal combat against me?"

"We are but humble delivery goblins," Gob said. The dragon snorted and shook him from her nostrils. It was a long fall, but there was at least a billionaire's untaxed income worth of gold sprawled below Gob to dampen the impact.

"If thy words be true, pray tell why mine nostrils smell honor in the air?"

"Sorry," Robert said sheepishly from where he was crouched among the gilded throne of a long dead elven king. "Gassy when scared."

"Pray tell why mine nostrils smell nobility in this place?

And worse, a chivalrous heart!" The last words came out in a roar of flame.

"The smell offends you just as dawn offends the dark!" A shout rang out through the space. "And just as that brilliant light banishes fear and chill from land and heart alike, so too will my holy blade banish you, foul tyrant!"

A human was shouting from atop one of the nearby mountains of gold. He wore armor very much like the skeletons outside had, except his body was still made of flesh instead of ash and bone.

"Bright Queen give me strength!" he roared then leapt from the mountaintop, sword raised high.

"Ew, gross."

The dragon swatted him down like one might a fly buzzing around the dinner table.

"So sorry about this," she said as she hurriedly squished him beneath one impossibly large foot. "Thou know how it is with pests these days. Thou can squish a hundred but ever are there more. Where were we?" She shook out her foot and the crumbled armor and shattered sword of the one-time knight fell free. "Ah, mine oboe. Of course!"

Oli just had time to recoil as the dragon's massive head swung down and right into his face.

"Truly, thou are only here in service of delivering what is rightfully mine?"

Oli gave a nod as flame washed across the ground all around him.

"We is Oli and Cousins Hauling Company. And also on road trip to see family!" he added hurriedly.

The dragon sucked down a wash of air and Oli stumbled forward, near sucked into the gaping nostrils.

"Thou smell of too little intelligence for deceit."

"That us!" Oli chirped happily.

The dragon stared at him another moment, then gave a little nod.

"Forgive mine distrust, it is just none have ever come before me with such… "

"Honesty?" Gob offered.

"Smelliness?" Robert asked.

"Innocence," the dragon said, then reared her head up high. "I name thee dragon-friends and declare thee welcome in mine lair!"

Oli's cousins cheered at that and emerged from their various hiding spots.

"Oh, there are quite many of thou, are there not?" the dragon asked, seeming to take them all in for the first time.

"Lot cousins!" Oli said, then held up the oboe nice and high. "But only come bring this!"

"Ah! Have thine eyes ever seen more beauteous a sight?" the dragon cooed with what must have been her gentle voice. Oli was reminded of the time he'd caused a rockslide.

"Yes, yes, this will be the crowning jewel of mine collection. I have waited many years for this treasure." The dragon scooped the instrument up with the smallest sliver of one talon. "Might I…" She hesitated, then chuckled with an excited shiver. "Oh, but I must!" She eased her lips to the instrument and gave the most delicate puff of breath possible. An inferno poured through the oboe. It had enough power to reduce several large trees and a small village to smoking ruin, but on account of the oboe being made of metal, the result was a swirling rush of flame and then, beneath it, a reedy, almost bird-like squawk of a musical note. In its wake, the oboe was left red-hot and steaming, but decidedly intact.

"Oh, this is a fine day, dragon-friends. A fine day,

indeed. A reward is due. A reward—yes!—for thine service!"

"Good review only reward cousins need!" Oli said.

"Though I wouldn't argue with a mountain of gold," Gob added.

"A treasure for a treasure, yes!" the dragon declared, then swung away and dove into the vast sea of coins and crowns. Gold and silver, priceless artifacts and even a couple skeletons were flung about the cave as the dragon searched with a ferocious frenzy. The floor shook such that the goblins were left to bounce and roll about until, finally, the dragon reemerged. Grasped in one clawed hand, she held a golden... something.

"A treasure for a treasure," she said again. "Take this, dragon-friends, and with it, my eternal gratitude."

TWENTY-SIX

A Wriggly Little Wish

For centuries, the greatest minds and magicians of the mortal realm have sought to make True Flight accessible to the masses. Initial experiments with enchanted brooms had looked promising, until the Sweepening. You see, enchanting an object inherently gives it a sliver of consciousness, and it turns out no one had thought to ask brooms how they felt about an eternity of cleaning dusty floors. The witches seemed to have negotiated a truce with the wild brooms, but they weren't sharing their secrets anytime soon. After that embarrassment, the aeromancy industry had turned its focus to magic carpets—to equally disastrous results, at which point everyone agreed it best to stop seeking the power of True Flight through the enchantment of household objects. Currently, the foremost aero-magically gifted minds believe there's much promise to be found in dirigibles pumped full of highly flammable gasses.

The challenges of the aeromancy industry were unknown to Oli and his cousins—though not the challenges of highly flammable gasses—and yet, hurtling away from the dragon's lair, they had discovered the power of flight. All one needed was a goblin's fight or flight response (which is to say, fright and flight), a one-of-a-kind rocket-powered miracle wagon, and enough damage to said wagon that the side panels jutted out and began to generate lift. It was in this manner the goblins and their wagon fled across the countryside. Iris navigated, as usual, though the wagon's constant attempts at leaving behind its earthly tethers played havoc with her sense of direction. Going slower would have reduced the amount of lift generated by the wagon's "wings," but you try explaining aerodynamics to a wagon full of bouncing goblins.

"Why big scary newt give goblins shiny thing?" Robert asked, watching warily as the gleaming object they'd been given rolled around in the back of the wagon. It looked kind of like the ghost urn, but with a cone of taut, semi-translucent fabric wrapped around the top and, inside that, what looked to be a fragile orb.

"Is package?" Lin One asked.

"No have delivery address," Man replied, also frowning at it.

"Big scary newt say it gift!" Hob said as he scooped it up and held it out to Robert. "And look, is shiny!"

Robert's eyes snapped to the sky. All around, vents in the ground spewed columns of thick, acrid smoke. The endless, slow-rising miasma merged with the low hanging clouds to cloak the landscape in shadow and ash. Shadow and ash that would be a great hiding place for their scary newt friend if she decided she wanted her shiny thing back. But it had been a gift, right? Big scary newt friend had given it to them. So maybe she'd wanted them to take it? Robert reached out with careful hands and took the thing from Hob.

"What it do?" he asked quietly, mostly to himself. "Just look pretty?" He prodded it with a finger and the orb inside the little fabric shade suddenly lit up. Robert squawked and jumped back, but the orb was just... glowing. A burning bright light was emanating from it, but it was trapped inside the conical wrap of fabric and where the light passed through it, it came out gentle and calming. Warm, too. Robert found he liked this golden, glowing gift.

"Good news, cousins!" Oli said as the wagon achieved something approaching stable flight. "Only one package left to—"

There was a groaning crash as they slammed back to the ground and Oli and his cousins were all bounced out of their seats.

"Only one package left to deliver!" Oli finished, rubbing his increasingly sore bottom. "Ghost urn go to new house to haunt!"

"Cousins do good work!" Lin Two cheered from where she was hanging to the driver's bench for dear life. "Cousins do good work *fast*!"

"Yes, well, that's great and all," Gob said as he frowned

at their groaning wagon. "But you know what they say. 'Fast, cheap, or reliable—pick two.'"

"What mean?" Man asked.

"Who say?" Oli added.

"You know…" Gob waved his hand about. "People. People say."

"Human people?"

"*People* people. It's a generalization."

"What mean?" Man asked again.

Gob planted his palm against his own face and sighed. "Never mind."

"Cousins fast and cheap and reliable!" Oli asserted. "And will to prove it!"

Gob raised an eyebrow at that, then gestured as if to say, 'well then?'

Oli set his jaw in a defiant slant, then waved a finger wildly in front of him.

Gob sighed again.

"What are you doing?"

"Oli prove!" He waved his finger in the pattern once more, but it still wasn't quite right. How exactly had Flan done it? Goblins weren't known for their memory, but Oli was determined. He gritted his teeth and did his best to remember the correct movements to summon the Web.

Unfortunately for Oli, goblins weren't known for their magic either. But fortunately for him, no one really understands how magic works—those that claim otherwise are likely trying to sell you something. But one need not always understand a thing to make it work. So it was for Ditaxsophis the Divisive when he accidentally sundered the world to form the five lands. So it was for the Dark Lord Sarusomal when his arts and crafts hobby produced, by happy accident, the Key and Lock. And so it was for Oli now, brow furrowed and tongue stuck out of the side of his mouth, as he waved a finger in the air. Intelligence, it seemed, wasn't always as necessary as determination, so as Oli repeated the gesture a third time, he finally managed to conjure up the Web. Shimmering, all-connecting strands formed in front of him, then wove into something like a hovering, translucent sheet of parchment. Oddly enough, it followed them as the wagon once again lifted into the air, then slammed back down.

"Uh, how to show reviews?" Oli asked, looking at his cousins.

Gob gave a weary sigh.

"Crag's List," he said. "Show the strand for... what was it? Oli and Cousins Hauling Company?"

"Yes! Please to show!" Oli added, in case the Web needed to be buttered up.

The translucent strands of nothingness solidified into a mostly translucent network of somethingness. On it was the incredibly lifelike drawing of Oli with half of his face out of view and, in the background, his cousins clinging to Horse.

"Look Horse! Is you!" Lin Two shouted over her shoulder.

Horse's eyes glowed a bit more brightly at that, but mostly the undead steed was just doing its best not to be thrown clear of the wagon.

"Hm, look. There are more reviews here," Gob said, rubbing his chin as he navigated around the strand with a few gentle waves of his fingers.

"That lot words," Robert said, eyes downcast at the wall of text.

"Maybe Big Boss teach Robert read when goblins bring Key," Oli suggested, patting his biggest cousin on the back.

"Here, let's see what the newest reviews say," Gob mumbled as he began to read several fresh additions to the strand. "Ankcaulagraung, Fire Wyrm of the Blazing Eternities says:... well, actually it looks like they didn't write anything. There's just five little stars and then five little flames." Gob pondered that a moment, then waved it away in favor of the next review. "Ted Squamata says: 'Couriersss were sssurprisssingly ssswift. Sssix ssstarsss out of five.'"

"Six out of five? Goblins do good!" Oli cheered.

Gob frowned. "Well the review's full of mistakes, so I don't know how much stock we should put in it, and secondly you can't give six stars out of five, but... the customer does sound pleased."

"Read more!" Oli called and then Robert joined in to start a wagon-wide chant.

"Read more! Read more!"

Gob waved everyone to silence, then cleared his throat.

"Ahem. Kingsway Animal Feed, Wagon Repair, and General Outfitters says: 'Delivery arrived ahead of schedule, but courier's reckless driving caused significant damage to our facility. Three out of five stars. We will be filing a claim with courier's insurance.'"

"Ooh, they file claim! That sound good!" Hob cheered.

"Decidedly not a satisfied customer," Gob replied sternly. "Though they did still give us three stars. Huh." His frown softened into something approaching a more thoughtful look. "The next review's unverified. Xander North says: 'Courier, please read this! I must speak to you about your wagon and its miraculous engine! Please, reply to this so we can arrange a meeting. We can both make a fortune together!'"

"What fortune?" Oli asked.

"In this case, I suspect it's simply a ruse to lure us into

some sort of scam," Gob said as he clicked the 'report' button beneath the review. "Ooh, look at this one. Lord Danbury Amadeus Maricelli XII says: 'Expeditious and elevated. Courier delivered package ahead of schedule and with a gilded refinement most befitting our stature. All noble families should seek to employ a company of such class in future, though exemplary dedication so fine as this may come at a cost beyond the means of *some* so-called nobles. Five out of five stars.'"

"That lot words," Oli said.

"And yet they sing our praise!" Gob was excited now. Could there be something in this courier business? No one else had a rocket wagon—as far as he'd ever heard. It would be depressingly pedestrian work for one such as himself, but with a bit of work, he could teach his cousins to do most of it. And he'd manage the finances, of course. Soon they'd—

"Read more! Read more!" His cousins were chanting again.

"There's just two more," Gob said, scanning the glowing translucent strand. "Dr. Percival Viscous says: 'Entirely incompetent, and reckless to boot. I wouldn't trust this gaggle of idiots to pick their own noses, much less deliver precious cargo. Zero out of five stars.' Well, I suppose that's to be expected," Gob said.

"Wet beef jerky deserve what he get!" Lin Two said with a huff and everyone nodded in agreement. Even Horse gave an agreeable snort.

Gob reported that review as well then pulled up the final new review.

"Henchpeople United in Labor and Purpose Local Chapter Zero Zero One says: 'Workers of the world, unite! You have nothing to lose but your chains! Also, five out of five stars. Courier delivered two packages, our salvation, and the power to determine our own destiny. We could all learn from the simple kindness with which they treat each other.'"

"Whoa, that nice review!" Oli said, smiling until someone hit him in the back of the head. "Oof!" He spun around to find Robert slapping desperately at him, fear in his eyes while he held the big scary newt's gift out at arm's length.

"Oli! Oli help!" Robert said, mouth agape at the shiny urn. It'd been glowing before, but Robert must have done something else because now it was full-on shining. Brilliant, golden light oozed from the thing.

"What did you do to the lamp you dolt?" Gob exclaimed, then ducked for cover behind the driver's bench.

"No do on purpose! Robert sorry!"

The glowing light grew more intense as something seemed to move inside the golden lamp. Then, all at once, a rush of sparkling energy burst from beneath the lamp shade to hover above them in the air. It whooshed and howled a moment, then resolved into a floating person. A beautiful person, if Oli was being honest. More beautiful than the Lieutenant of Lament or even, though he trembled to think it, the Big Boss himself.

The beautiful, glowy person spoke and the whole wagon trembled with the power reverberating through their every syllable—or maybe that was just the wagon in the process of tearing itself apart, Oli couldn't say for sure. Either way the wagon, and the goblins, trembled as the golden person spoke with a voice too perfect for this world.

"Whaddya want?" he said, a perfect scowl pulling at his creased cheeks. "This better be good."

"You come to us," Lin Two snapped over her shoulder,

too busy driving to properly welcome their newest guest. "What you want?"

"You activate the lamp, you get the genie. That's how it works, kid. Now whaddya want?"

Oli and his other cousins stared, dumbfounded.

"Come on, come on. I got places to be." The genie snapped his fingers impatiently. The sound of it shook Oli from his stupor and all at once he remembered his manners.

"Hello Mr. Genie Man, me Oli. Sorry no expecting you so no bring newt cake."

"I'll survive."

Oli spread his arms wide.

"Mr. Genie Man, meet cousins."

"Nah, I'm good."

"That one Hob. And that one Gob."

"It's pronounced *Johb*, if you please," Gob said. "And allow me to apologize for my cousins here. I don't think they fully understand the wonder before them. You'll have to excuse them, they are, after all, merely gob—"

"Yeah, that's great, kid. Look, it's a simple exchange, right? You found my lamp, you got me out, so now you get your two wishes. Hurry it up, eh?"

Gob made a little sound, then frowned.

"Two wishes?"

The genie grunted.

"Not three?"

A shrug next.

"What, you think the wish granting industry's immune to inflation? Come on, now, whaddya want? Riches? Fame? Deodorant?"

"Goblins can have anything goblins want?" Oli asked, eyes going wide.

"Oh, truly a difficult question, isn't it? There's so much I want," Gob said, positively jumping up and down now as all of his greatest desires battled for dominance in his mind. "Ooh, that's a good one. But, no. Wait. *That's* an even better one! Yes, that'll do, yes. Genie, for my first wish I would like—"

"Genie man to teach Robert to read!" Oli shouted with a smile.

The genie raised a hand as if to snap his fingers, then paused, frowned.

"Hold up, that's not how you should phrase tha—"

"Genie man to teach Robert to read!" Oli shouted again and then his cousins joined in, bouncing up and down and shouting the wish.

"No, no, you don't want that," the genie said and clasped one hand over the other, stopping his fingers from snapping. His forearm bulged as it clenched tight, then his eyes next as he shook his head. "You don't want that, you should ask for—no, no!" A snap echoed out from the clamped hand and the wish was made. All at once, the genie disappeared in a puff of smoke. When he reappeared, he was surrounded by a cloud of floating books, a school desk, and wore a pair of glasses low on his nose. Another puff and Robert appeared in the desk, a book placed in front of him. His smile spread from ear to ear and his eyes were so wide with excitement Oli wasn't sure they still had lids.

"Oli best cousin ever! Oli nicest cousin ever!" he shouted somehow without releasing even a smidge of his smile.

"Gods of the Lamp forgive me," the genie said, head sinking down.

"What wrong?" Oli asked. "Genie man say make wish so Oli make wish."

The genie's golden color burned into an angry red as he spun to face Oli.

"You want your friend to read? Fine! Wish for him to be literate, that way I can magick it into existence. But no, you couldn't do that, could ya? No, you had to wish for me to *teach him to read*."

"Oh my Dark Lord," Gob said and from the horror in his eyes Oli could tell he was excited for their cousin. "Can we undo—"

"No." The genie sagged down into a floating chair across from Robert, shoulders slumped. "A wish can't be undone once it's snapped."

Gob began to speak up but the genie waved him silent.

"And wishes must be completed one at a time."

"Robert is will learn to read!" their biggest cousin cheered, pounding his fists against the magic desk. "Robert is will be litter rat!"

"*Literate*," the genie said, face in his hands. "You are going to be *literate*. Maybe," he said, shaking his beautiful, defeated head. "Gods of the Lamp spare me."

* * *

Following Iris' directions, Lin Two drove the wagon further into the countryside, and with some help from Gob, they even managed to get the wagon to stop launching into the air. It still wanted to take flight, but the impromptu repairs kept that urge limited to excited little hops. In this way, the goblins followed their route as the scorched and scored countryside around the dragon's lair slipped away, replaced instead by a sort of savannah. Faded, green bushes and stunted trees dotted the landscape and, in the distance, the largest swamp the goblins had ever seen was drawing nearer.

It was just like the Swamp of Sadness and Sweaty Underthings, except it didn't have any trees covering it in eternal shadow. Also, the water was a brilliant blue instead of brooding black, and it was so wide the goblins couldn't see the other side. Strangely, there was also only one shore and it was a sandy, bright thing. Waves crashed against it, foamy and white, and crabs scuttled through dunes that looked almost soft.

It was beside this strangely bright and windy swamp that the goblins found their last delivery destination.

"The Overlook B&B, Number Six Seaside Lane, Storm Coast County, Kingdom of Humanity," Iris said, a triumphant note in her voice. "You have reached your destination."

It was a three-story house with a widow's walk up top and a wrap-around porch below. Rocking chairs eased back and forth in the constant wind that swept in off the blustery swamp.

"Ghosts pick good new house," Hob said and gave a low whistle. He'd never quite gotten the hang of that particular skill, though, so really it was more akin to blowing a raspberry.

"Too bright, goblins boil away. And too windy! Goblins blow away," Oli said, shielding his eyes from the sun and squinting against the wind as he hurried to the back of the wagon to search for the ghost urn. It'd rolled in among the ever-growing mountain of books surrounding Robert and the genie. From the way the genie and Robert were yelling at each other, the reading lessons seemed to be going well. Oli left them to it as he found the urn—only knocking over two towers of books in the process.

"Thank for come with!" he said to the scary urn and, specifically, to the scary ghost family contained within.

"Enjoy new home!" Lin Two added, waving as Oli jogged up to the porch.

A handful of sand was caught in the wind, then swirled around in front of Oli. When the grains came to rest, they spelled out letters.

"No can read," Oli said. "Ooh! Ooh! Maybe Robert can!" He whipped around to call for his biggest cousin, who, it appeared, was in the middle of being beaten over the head with a textbook by the screaming genie. "Maybe Robert no ready…"

"It says 'Thank you, goblins. We are indebted to you and yours,'" a voice spoke but there was no one around. "Over here, no, not there. Look closer, yes. Yes, there."

Oli squinted at the nearest rocking chair to find it wasn't the wind moving it but a ghost. They were nearly invisible in the bright sun, but the gentle shade of the porch made them the slightest bit visible.

"New arrivals!" another voice cheered, this one higher pitched than the last. One of the rocking chairs jerked suddenly and a whoosh of wind rushed up to Oli. "Ah! We're so happy to have you!" The urn was lifted from his hands as if someone had grabbed it. "I'll give you the tour!" The urn and its new guide whooshed away then disappeared into the house with a slam of the front door.

"Don't mind Cas, he's still adjusting to life after life," the first ghost said, still in its rocking chair.

The sand in front of Oli rearranged itself once more.

"'Should you ever need our assistance, you must only call for us.' Well, that's nice. Clearly our newest residents thought well of you, courier."

Oli couldn't be sure, but the mostly translucent figure in the rocking chair seemed to nod.

"Tell me, courier. Are you taking new work? We have a—"

"No to new work right now, thank!" Oli hurriedly shouted. "Must now for Big Boss—er, see goblin family! Thank! Bye!" he said over his shoulder as he ran, for that had been their last delivery. Or rather, the last delivery to distract them from their original purpose, to get the Key and return it to their Dark Lord.

Oli's little feet slapped against the sand as he hurried back to the wagon with a singular goal in mind: on to Fortress Isolgar.

TWENTY-SEVEN

Sunburns And Shortcuts

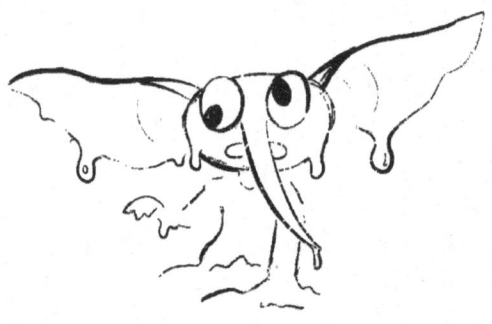

Goblins have excellent hearing. Sonderklangin folk tales go so far as to claim goblins find naughty children to snatch away by listening for mischievous thoughts. While the veracity of that particular story has never been confirmed, it's easy—especially considering their abnormally large ears—to see how one might come to the conclusion that goblins are excellent listeners. But that would be a considerable overestimation of exactly how much is going on between said abnormally-large ears. You see, goblins have excellent hearing but their just-above-mushroom levels of intelligence means all those things they hear bounce around, trapped inside their worryingly thick skulls, until a strong enough sneeze comes along to free them.

Iris' directions would have met this same fate if any of the goblins had been able to hear them over the howling wind. Her floating head spun and shouted, maybe about something important but the specifics were whisked away seeing as the throttle was in the full forward position, the wind was whipping past, and Oli could already imagine Fortress Isolgar rising from the horizon.

The gist of Iris' directions seemed to be a jumbled deluge of "Continue straight. Continue straight! Don't hit the sheep! Stay on the road! Continue straight—*continue straight!*"

Lin Two managed most of it, with just a bit of help from Lin One who was dangling from the wheel, pulling with his full body weight to swerve the wagon away from the herd of sheep that'd rudely planted themselves right in the way as if they owned the whole field.

Thankfully, as they traveled onward, there weren't many more inconvenient herds of sheep, or fields, for that matter. The arid savannah gave way to rocks and sand and then a new sort of landscape filled the horizon. One of dunes and sand, scorching sun and funny little lizards that ran on two legs. It looked very much like the exact opposite of the sort of place Oli preferred—except for the lizards, those looked tasty.

"You are on the fastest route. Continue on *the Boilway* for the next forty miles," Iris said, her voice going all stiff as it did whenever saying a name.

Ahead, the road—where it hadn't been buried by wind-blown sand—ran straight across the wastes and all the way to a wavering horizon.

"We almost there!" Oli cheered. "Fortress Isolgar just

ahead!" He did a little dance on the driver's bench beside Lin Two. "Goblins almost there!"

"Big Boss make us important and scary!" Man cheered, joining Oli in the jig, their bare feet slapping against the wood planks.

Lin One ran up and jumped onto his sister's shoulders.

"Big Boss make us strong!"

"Big Boss make us rich," Gob said with a breathy laugh. "That would do just fine."

Even Robert gave a cheer from the back of the wagon, but it was quickly silenced when the genie hissed and jabbed a finger at the textbook they were studying from.

"What Fortress Isolgar look like?" Oli asked under his breath as his mind tried to fill with images of their dramatic arrival. Obviously, it'd be big and dramatic like the Citadel of Shadow and Sin. All black, volcanic rock and surrounded by fires so hot the very air itself screamed in pain. Ooh, ooh! Or maybe it'd be something subtler. Something more like Library of Lies and Half-Truths. Oli had only been there once, but it'd been a wonderful place. Tucked deep into a cliffside, it'd been as dark as Mishalob's caverns, but much more lively. Its endless labyrinth of shelves—stocked with books, crystal orbs, and all manner of dark prophecies—was patrolled by an army of hissing specters. The ghostly librarians were kind of like Oli's friends the ash geists, though a tad less friendly.

"You are on the fastest route," Iris said, drawing Oli from his thoughts. "You will reach your destination in three hours and forty-one minutes."

"That soon!" Oli said, counting his fingers to remember exactly how many three was. "That soon!"

"Three hours in this heat and we're going to be cooked more thoroughly than an overdone newtcake," Gob complained, frowning up at the sun. It was only then Oli noticed his usual coating of slime was bubbling a little bit.

"Tingly," he said with a little wiggle.

"No like," Hob said as he tried to cover his bubbling arm with the other—which resulted in both of them bubbling. He cried out then dived to the back of the wagon where the genie had magicked up a parasol for himself and Robert.

"Class is in session, scram!" he said and a flick of his wrist sent Hob tumbling away. There weren't any more crates or large packages to hide under, though, so he was left clinging to the underside of Horse's belly, hands and fingers still bubbling where the sunlight touched them.

"Make more shade?" Robert looked up from his text-book to ask the genie. He pointed at the parasol.

"Or at least some hats or something?" Gob asked, hand cupped to his brow as he scanned their rapidly passing surroundings.

"You idiots condemned me to this fate," the genie replied gesturing at Robert and the pile of books. "I can't grant any more wishes until this one is complete."

"Yeah, but it's not a wish, so much as… a gift? From the kindness of your heart?" Gob asked with a creeping smile.

The genie was unimpressed.

"Don't try to play rules lawyer with my magic. It doesn't work like that." He snapped his fingers and then both he and Robert were encased in a transparent bubble. Robert exclaimed, mouth opening wide at the sight, but no sound made it out.

"Genie busy," Oli said. Maybe Big Boss will help, he almost added. But Big Boss hadn't helped when Sherrock Stones and Lastrof had nearly caught them at the wagon dealership. And Big Boss hadn't helped when Dr. Viscous had taken Robert's body. Maybe Big Boss was distracted? Or maybe he'd forgotten about them. But no! Goblins were on an important quest for Big Boss, how could Big Boss forget? Squinting into the boiling sun now, though, Oli felt rather forgotten.

"You are on the fastest route," Iris said suddenly. "You will reach your destination in two hours and fifteen minutes."

"Wait, what?" Gob asked, brow furrowed. "How did that happen?"

"Lin Two best driver!" she shouted, bouncing on the driver's bench. "Lin Two save goblins from sun!"

"That's not how it works." Gob was rubbing his chin. "Iris… did you recalculate? How did we gain so much time?"

"You are on the fastest route. You will reach your destination in nine hours and fifty-eight minutes."

A pained gasp from Lin Two.

"Lin Two no good! Lin Two ruin for everyone!"

"No, no, it's not you," Gob said, waving her to quiet as he tried to figure out what was happening.

"Lin Two do good job." Oli gave her a comforting pat on the shoulder.

"Destination lost. Searching… searching… " Now Iris sounded—well, not panicked—but as close to panicked as possible for a floating, semi-sentient head enchanted solely to give directions.

"What wrong, Iris?" Lin Two asked, her tone concerned.

"Searching… "

"Whatever it is, she better figure it out quick because we're not going to last two hours in this sun, much less nine."

Iris perked up at his words.

"Destination: *Fortress Isolgar, the Beachhead of Barbarism and Minor Inconveniences* found! You will reach your destination in forty-nine hours and six minutes."

"What?" Gob was yelling now.

"You are on the fastest route."

Lin Two joined the yelling as she kicked the throttle lever to make sure it couldn't go any more forward.

"Goblins no go make it!" Man cried, hands raised to block out the scorching sun, but then even those were sizzling. He threw himself down and crawled into the scant shade of Gob's shadow. "Never should left swamp!" he lamented. And then everyone was shouting and moaning. And bubbling.

"We no make it," Oli lamented, covering his boiling face with his sizzling hands. "Sun too hot!"

"Where go, Iris? Where go!" Lin Two shouted, pulling hard on the wheel first one way then the other. The wagon pitched and swerved, rattling as it jumped the edges of the road.

"Quick, pull off there!" Gob said pointing to something appearing from the sand a little ways off to one side. It looked to be a collection of leaning stones. They had big, wide faces carved into them and though the sun had long bleached their surfaces white, they still cast shade. Just enough for Lin Two to tuck the wagon in and send everyone into an avalanche of sighs as the burning light was finally blocked.

Oli fell against the side of the wagon with an exhausted exhale, then slid right off it and into the sand with all the grace of a bead of sweat down a giant's cheek.

In the shade, the sand was blissfully cool. Oli rolled in it, squirming with glee as the still-lingering burn was chased from him.

"Sand cold. Feel nice!" he called to the others and soon

they were all jumping from the cart to wriggle in the sand of their shaded oasis.

"You are no longer on the fastest route," Iris called, her voice stiff once more and seemingly as unconcerned with the shade as she'd been with the heat. "In thirty feet, make a U-turn, then return to *the Boilway*."

"No do yet," Lin Two said from the burrow she'd dug into the shaded sand. "Stay here until sun gone."

"Sun bad! Sun go!" Man shouted, shaking a fist at the burning ball above them. His knuckle slipped from the shade and began to sizzle again. He yelped and plunged it into the sand.

"We really shouldn't waste the whole day here," Gob said but hardly anyone was listening. "Though… well, something is going wrong with Iris. We should figure that out first, I suppose. As soon as we know where we're going, though…" He trailed off as he noticed no one was listening. Hob was laying on his back, swinging his arms and legs as if making mud mosquitos back home, just sandier. Lin One had already buried Man neck deep, and Lin Two had disappeared entirely, only puffs of sand shooting out from her burrow.

"Okay, we can enjoy this for a bit, but then we have to get back underway."

Oli winced, but nodded.

"Gob right. Gob smart. Goblins go soon. But how?" he peeked up at the sky, but there was only the burning sun above, no aid from the Big Boss to be found.

"We covered Horse in animal furs and such," Gob said, thinking aloud. "What if we take them off and tie them together? Then we tie them to the sides of the wagon and have Robert hold them up from beneath? It'll be like a makeshift canopy."

"Whoaahhh…" Oli said, mouth hanging open as he

tried to grasp all the steps of Gob's intricate plan. "Gob *very* smart. Maybe Gob be Big Boss someday?" he added under his breath.

Gob smiled at the flattery and his cheeks flushed red. Or maybe that was just the sunburn setting in.

"It is a good plan, I admit. But we'll need our strength for it, so maybe we can just… enjoy this… for a bit," Gob said with a relieved sigh as he settled into the cool sand.

"You are no longer on the fastest route—" Iris began but Oli chucked a handful of sand at her.

* * *

Oli's dreams were broiling hot. First, he was trapped in an oven, cooking alongside his nan's famous newtcakes. He kicked and bit at the door until it finally gave way and he spilled out. Except it was even hotter outside and he realized he was back in the Dark Lord's throne room and instead of the ring rolling toward the edge of the balcony—and down to the volcano below—it was him. Oli screeched and jerked away, but then he was falling no more, just kicking and tossing sand at his sleeping cousins.

"Whew," he said, wiping sweat from his sand-covered forehead. "Doomsday Mountain no good for swim."

His words were met only by the snores of his cousins. Even Robert seemed to have been given a break by the genie, seeing as he was face-down in a book and drooling.

It was still daytime, Oli found, but afternoon now, and their shade had moved a bit, leaving part of him to be crisped by the sun's touch. And weirdly, there were more shadows than he remembered. As if there were more stones looming above them now. Except these stones were grinning. And smelled like orcs.

"Paulter!" Oli gasped as he spotted the mean orc and her impressive handlebar mustache.

"No mammoth around to protect you now, huh?" she sneered and as she did, more hog-riding orcs appeared all around. More than Oli could count when he was awake and alert, much less in his current, bleary-eyed and foggy-minded state.

"Orcs no win this time," Oli said as he scampered to his feet. "Orcs mean and stinky!" And with that he pressed his thumb to his cursemark.

The shadows jutting out from beneath the tilting stones deepened, lengthened, then drew up from the ground. The sand hissed and shook, grains jumping and shooting out in all directions as the damned souls oozed from the ground. They arose slumped, with heads hanging down and their shoulders wide and lean with muscle. When they were fully risen, their backs straightened as one and then there were six fully-formed shadow servants protecting the goblins.

"What is thy bidding, liege?" the foremost of them asked. Its voice came like a muffled whisper, trickling through the sand gently, but with enough threat in it that Oli could swear the ground all around gave a shiver.

If Paulter gave a shiver, Oli didn't see it. Instead, she growled at the new arrivals, her bottom lip pulling back to fully reveal her yellowed tusks. Her gang did the same, even if some of them looked like they might have experienced a shiver.

"Orcs go away!" Oli shouted and his raised voice woke the rest of his cousins that hadn't already figured out what was happening. "Paulter go away!"

The damned souls nodded in unison at the command, then advanced on the orcs. The first to break from the shadow of the tilted stones and into the sunlight, however, let out a hissing shriek. At the direct light's touch, the servant began to shake and waver. The others frowned, watching from the edge of the shadows.

"Apologies, my liege. There is magic at work in this place. It seems we are somewhat... limited."

"Come, come, come!" Oli shouted, waving his cousins into the shadows beside the damned souls. "Goblins stay close!"

They all rushed to join him, especially Robert who already looked sick to his stomach, no doubt remembering what happened last time with Paulter and her gang.

"Who's the new guy?" Paulter asked, squinting at the genie.

"What new guy?" the genie fired back, then snapped his fingers. As he did, Paulter's expression went blank. A moment later she shook her head as if waking from a stupor, then returned her grinning attention to the goblins.

"Everyone likes to think orcs are just dumb brutes. Just muscle and good looks. But they underestimate us to their own peril." And with that, she pulled a mirror from her saddle and, adjusting it just right, bounced sunlight right into the chest of a shadow servant. The creature screamed and thrashed as the sunlight set it aflame.

"This is isn't natural sunlight," Gob said, hand to his chin. "Something's protecting this place. Natural sunlight would never be enough to so severely damage a summoned servant of Sarusomal."

"A summoned servant of who now?" A deep voice asked. One of the orcs, Oli thought at first, until another newcomer appeared from behind the distant-most tilted stone. He was a towering, broad-shouldered figure, backlit by the afternoon sun and standing tall as his trench coat flapped dramatically in the wind. Oli squinted but couldn't make out his features. The human's identity remained a mystery, up until he raised a hand to his face and lit his pipe in a puff of flame. It was then Oli realized he wasn't a human at all.

"Stonesman," he said, eyes wide.

"Detective Stones, if you please. Or Sherrock, if we're being friendly," he said, his voice clattering like shale down a hillside. "Now who was summoning servants of the Dark Lord?"

"Arrest 'em first, ask questions later!" a cry rang out and Sergeant Lastrof and a gaggle of officers sprang up from the backside of a nearby dune. They rushed over, wands in hand and pointing at Oli, his cousins, the orcs, the shadow servants, and even one at Horse, which just seemed mean.

"Why you here?" Oli asked after he managed to regain control of his dropped jaw. "Goblins no do bad. Goblins go see family!"

"Are many of your family members spectral servants of the Dark Lord?" the Sergeant asked, but somehow it sounded more like an accusation.

Oli frowned at the shadow servants, bit his lip.

"Uh... those no mine."

"We are your servants now and forever, liege. Until the day our work is finished and you release us back to the depths of hell."

"How peculiar," Detective Stones said, one rough hand rubbing against his chin with a grinding sound. "I've never heard of goblins dabbling in magic. Then again, the infamous Dr. Viscous had more than a few interesting stories about goblins, didn't he, Sergeant?"

"Had more than a bit to say for a man with no mouth," she said, then gestured to her officers. "Arrest them all."

"The goblins are ours, human." Paulter tipped the

mirror to flash sunlight across the sergeant's face. She winced and raised a hand, annoyance across her features.

"Drop the mirror, orc!"

"Come and make me."

One of the officers stepped forward to do just that. Paulter flung the mirror at him and he responded with a blast of magic from his wand. It arced into Paulter's chest, then deflected off and into the sand with a puff.

"Orcs are magic-resistant," Lastrof shouted. "Remember your training!"

"A shame humans aren't break resistant," Paulter said with a chortling laugh. She clenched a fist then slammed it into the titled rock beside her. The blow was so strong as to shake the structure to its roots. "Now then, let's—huh?" She stopped mid-sentence to frown at the ground. Something Oli had already been doing. Ever since the orc had struck the rock, the sand had been vibrating. Grains jumped up and down, then buzzed frantically as the vibrations grew stronger and stronger still.

"What goblin magic is this?" Lastrof asked, but then there wasn't time for Oli to respond as the bottom gave out beneath them all. As if someone had pulled the stopper from a great, sandy bathtub, the desert sank into itself and the goblins, the orcs, Lastrof, her officers, and everyone else were sucked downward. As they fell, Oli heard the faint sound of Iris calling out in a cheery tone.

"You have reached your destination!"

TWENTY-EIGHT

Cast First And Ask Questions Later

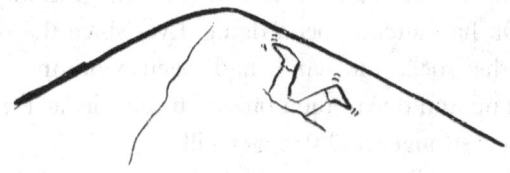

Goblins haven't really figured out the full range of emotions yet. While other folk experience passion, and wonderment, and are free to ponder the great mysteries of life, goblins mainly get by in one of three states: panicked, hungry, or looking to set something on fire. Oli and his cousins felt all three as the sand collapsed inward and dragged them into the desert's depths.

Oli gasped for air and found only sand. In his nose, his ears, sticking to the insides of his mouth—up until the moment all the sand suddenly vanished. It was replaced by far too much open air as he found himself falling out of the ceiling of some massive cave.

The ground was far below but roaring closer by the moment. And were those houses down there? Buildings, even? Oli braced for what was sure to be a rough landing. His stomach rose into his throat and he'd just begun to scream with his sand-filled mouth when he landed with a gentle *thud*. As it happened, there wasn't unforgiving ground beneath him but a loose, waist-deep layer of soft sand. It was almost more comfortable than his mud bed back home. And there was a nice bit of shade here, or… no, that was a shadow. Several shadows, and getting bigger by the moment. Oli screeched and rolled to the side just as the wagon, and Horse, and a dozen other falling figures came crashing down. They each landed with soft thuds as the sand caught them more gently than seemed possible.

Except Sherrock Stones. Shockwaves of sand were flung out in all directions as he hit the ground with the force of a mountain falling over.

"Connection interrupted. To resume navigation, please vacate any anti-magic fields, pocket dimensions, or congested tunnels," Iris' voice called, slightly muffled seeing as the front of the wagon was buried in the sand.

The genie clawed his way out of the sand beside the wagon, then reached back in to drag Robert out.

"Robert!" Oli cheered.

"Oli!" Robert cheered. "That was—"

"You have homework to be about, young goblin!" The genie cracked a book and shoved it in Robert's face. "Pages thirty-one through thirty-five. Come on, snap to it!"

Robert frowned.

"No can count that high."

"Well that's… I… " the genie threw his hands up in the air. "The wish was for me to teach you to read, not count." He flipped through the book to the correct pages. "Here, do this one, this one, this one, and this one!"

While the lessons continued, Oli turned away to wipe sand from his face, but it was all stuck in his natural coating of slime. He managed to get most of it out of his eyes, though—at least enough that he could take in their surroundings.

It looked like they were in some sort of gigantic cave system but with buildings built into the walls, or arrayed along winding, narrow streets.

Oli found himself reminded of the labyrinthine crypts that ran beneath the Dark Lord's fortress. Except these had less sanity-devouring horrors, and there didn't seem to be any torture chambers either, *and* there definitely weren't any corridors of eternal shrieks. No, the sprawling cave-city thing about them now was rather beige in comparison to the eternal dark of the Dark Lord's under domain.

The roof was held up by towering, sedimentary stone columns streaked through with layers of red, orange, and beige sandstone. They connected to a ceiling of packed sand via great spanning arches. Every two dozen or so paces, light trickled down through what must have been thinner sections to illuminate this hidden world with glowing shafts of washed-out golden light.

"What this place?" Lin Two asked as she shook sand from her ears, then blew it from her nose with a trumpeting blast that would have made Mam proud.

"It appears to be some sort of cave system," Gob said, sandy eyes wide as they scoured every inch of the marvels around them. "It—" he was cut off by a hacking cough. "Something… caught in my throat… " he managed.

"No sun here!" Man cheered. "Goblins no boil!" And he'd a point. The shafts of light coming down from above were bright, but as Oli passed his hand through one, not particularly hot. More a comfortable warm, like mud heated just right.

There was a great shifting of sand as Sherrock Stones rose up and shook the desert from his cracks and joints. He upended his ever-present pipe—releasing yet more sand—then gestured with it.

"This is no mere cave system," rumbled his gravelly voice. "I suspect we have stumbled upon something far more intriguing than that. Something like that ancient beachhead of barbarism, Fortress Isolgar."

Fortress Isolgar? The name rang in Oli's mind. They'd arrived! But... this place didn't look anything like Fortress Isolgar. Not that Oli had ever been, but when it came to interior design, the Dark Lord's style wasn't exactly understated. No, this place had none of the hallmarks. Where were all the looming shadows and churning magma? The torture chambers and imprisoned, weaponized souls of the damned? There wasn't even a single ominous tower!

Alright, well, there was the cursemark of the Dark Lord hacked with deep gashes into each of the massive sandstone pillars, but as far as evil lairs went, Oli found that a rather lazy attempt at decorating. And however imposing the multi-story cursemarks were, they were far outnumbered by the houses and buildings below them.

The structures had been beautiful, once, each adorned with intricate columns carved from the natural sandstone. Larger-than-life figures were cut into the walls of the homes as well—statues, almost, of humans holding chisels and hammers. The homes had been works of art but now they were ancient and cracked, crumbling in most places. They were everywhere, though, the space between them forming streets and avenues, alleys and public squares. Just like the human city they'd left behind, except this one was falling apart everywhere he looked, and it was drier than ash, and there were no people.

Wait, no. There were people. Maybe?

Vaguely human-shaped figures were shambling from the city everywhere Oli looked. Their bodies teetered and tilted with each step, dumping sand from them. Or… out of them? They weren't just covered in sand, they were made of it. The closest of them cried out in raspy, wordless voices as they shambled closer. In moments, they were everywhere. A legion of faceless sandfolk.

"Hello!" Oli said. "Good to meet!" He put on his friendliest smile and waved.

"Well this is curious, now isn't it?" Detective Stones said, then paused to give a little cough. "Sorry. Ahem." He shook the feeling away and turned his attention back to the figures. "I wonder, can they hear us? There are no discernable eyes, but they certainly see us, wouldn't you agree, Sergeant?"

Lastrof was still half-buried in sand as she blinked her eyes clear to take in the sight.

"You really think this is Fortress Isolgar?" Her voice was but a whisper, as if not wanting the goblins to hear. "Our siege lines are still some miles away."

"The soldiers surround the entrance to the fortress, but I think we may have just found another way in." He pondered the roof a moment. "Though I'm not sure falling through the ceiling is intended to be a frequently used route."

As if in response, one of the sandfolk let out a raspy groan. Lastrof raised her wand.

"Hands in the air!" she snapped. When the creature didn't respond, Lastrof gave a nod to her officers. They were already tense, wands raised and aimed, their tips glowing with swirling light.

"Get on the ground!" the Sergeant shouted. "And hands in the air!"

"Lay flat and face away from us!" another officer began

shouting and then, like someone had thrown dinner scraps into a kennel, all the officers were barking orders at once, each straining to be louder than the other beside them.

"Crawl toward us, hands in the air!"

"No sudden movements! Look at me when I'm talking to you!"

"Stop resisting!"

The orders came in a rushing, jumbled mess. It didn't much matter, though, seeing as the sandfolk didn't obey any of them.

"Hello sandy ones!" Oli shouted, struggling to be heard above the chaos. "No mean harm." He lowered his voice and leaned in a bit closer. "We on same side." A knowing nod. "Also serve Big Boss." He added a wink just to make sure the eyeless, moaning sand zombies got the message. "We—"

"Gah!" A yell from the side caught Oli's attention and he turned to see Paulter and her orcs charging the sand-folk. Axe blades swung in a flurried frenzy and the sandfolk fell apart like a beloved sandcastle beneath an older sibling's stomping feet.

And then it was chaos.

"Stop resisting!" one of the officers shouted at a sand person calmly shambling his way. There was a blast of light and the figure exploded into a shower of sand. In the wake of the blast, the end of the officer's wand trailed a thin stream of smoke. "Stop resisting!" he shouted again then fired several more blasts into the swirling cloud.

The officers' jumbled shouting turned into jumbled spell casting and bolts of light arced outward. All around, sandfolk burst apart. Their disparate grains swirled in the air, then, gathered together in an ever-growing sandstorm. It roared as it spun, a chorus of angry sandfolk voices howling as one.

233

Detective Stones grumbled to himself as the wind thwarted his efforts to light his pipe. The goblins, on the other hand, panicked and gathered up around Oli.

"What do?" Lin One screeched, hands covering his ears.

"Well it doesn't look that bad, does it?" Gob mused, squinting through the wind as ever more sand filled the air. There was a legion of sandfolk, but it seemed they fell apart when met with anything stronger than a sneeze.

Didn't mean they stayed apart, though.

Oli pointed one shaking finger at a pair of severed but still-standing sand feet in the middle of the fighting. The swirling sand was piling up on top of them by the moment and shaping back into a sand person. And then it was happening all around. The swirling sand whipped around the space, then gathered all together to resolve back into the shape of sandfolk.

"Maybe no good be here," Oli said, not liking any of this one bit. "Maybe sandfolk no serve Big Boss. Goblins go. Go now. Come, cousins. Follow!"

"What do?" Lin One shouted again. Oli pried his cousin's hands free from his ears, then shouted his plan again. This time, Lin One nodded.

"We go!"

Despite the chaos, Horse didn't seem bothered. He'd found a scrap of brittle, leafless brush and was chewing away happily at it as the goblins fled.

"Great plan and all," Gob said in Oli's ear as they scrambled through the crowd of exploding sandfolk. "But is there a specific place we're running to or… ?"

"Away!" Oli shouted as, looking back over his shoulder, he could see the sandfolk were overwhelming everyone. Paulter was still screaming and slashing, but she was already buried up to the waist. The rest of her orcs were neck deep; and though they looked to be trying to swim in the sand, somehow, were only sinking deeper the more they struggled.

"Away!" Oli shouted again and focused on running as fast as his goblin feet could carry him into the city. Or maybe it was Fortress Isolgar. Either way, the goblins ran.

Detective Stones squinted through the swirling sandstorm as he watched the goblins flee. On his other side, Sergeant Lastrof was leading her officers in a fighting retreat in the opposite direction. The more they fought, however, the more the sandfolk followed them. In sharp contrast, no one seemed interested in the goblins. Maybe that was just because no one really paid attention to goblins. But Sherrock had never been like everyone else.

Since he'd been nothing more than a wee stalagmite, even the most mundane things had fascinated him. As he'd grown, this ceaseless curiosity had crystallized into an obsession with life's overlooked things. As a happy byproduct, it'd made him a great detective. The Bright Queen counted him among her most valuable servants, but personally, he'd never been much a fan of the game of thrones. It was basically just musical chairs for murderers. And anyway, as far as Sherrock could see, blazing servitude under the Bright Queen wasn't all that different from abyssal subservience beneath the Dark Lord. Her burning righteousness blinded him just as much as Sarusomal's sinister shadows. And neither of the two had much interest in the overlooked things in life. Like why had the bees been disappearing? Or why did the legendary Fortress Isolgar look to be some sort of forgotten city? Or—most of all— why did this gaggle of goblins carry a cursemark of the Dark Lord and yet show none of the sadistic cruelty that typically accompanied such a power?

There was a fascinating question. At the moment,

though, the sandstorm was making it too much a chore to keep his pipe going, and things certainly didn't look any calmer over Sergeant Lastrof's way. She'd always been more of the cast first, ask questions later sort. Sherrock much preferred questions and answers, and there looked to be more of those with the goblins than Lastrof.

Wrapping himself around his pipe with a grunt, he fought to light it while striding off after the goblins.

TWENTY-NINE

Too Many Words

Sandfolk rushed through the city like human-sized dust devils. They whipped down alleyways, swept across the roads, and converged on the fighting in an ever-growing storm. Oli made sure he was firmly turned away from all that nonsense as his slapping feet echoed through the labyrinth of sandstone alleys.

"Come cousins! We go now. We go fast!" he called, scampering on all fours to run that much quicker.

Goblins spent most of their lives ignored, or at most, as unwanted nuisances. Sort of like the neighborhood opossum. But with a bit of good-natured interest, one might learn both opossums and goblins ate ungodly amounts of ticks, making them great neighbors... once you got past all the hissing. And arson.

Oli had never been so thankful to be ignored as he was now. Every time they turned a corner to find another sand person whirl-winding past, he was sure it'd sweep them up. But it never happened. The sandfolk raged past and toward the sounds of fighting. Oli didn't stop to wonder why, he just ran, and his cousins followed.

Goblins were quick little devils when they wanted to be, but their legs were short and their natural slimy coating didn't give them the best traction. As such, Sherrock caught up to them rather swiftly, carried by his long strides and his stony weight having no trouble pushing through the storm winds. It also helped the goblins were leaving a trail of damp behind them. One of them must have grabbed that curious, water-leaking stone Sherrock had seen previously. In any case, he finally got his pipe lit and burning steady as he caught up to the scampering creatures.

He tried to wave down the slowest of the goblins—the big one who was lagging behind. Though, upon closer inspection, said overly large goblin was lagging because there was some sort of angry man whacking him with a textbook while yelling about the intricacies of sentence structure. That... seemed like something best left alone, so Sherrock moved on to the rest of the group.

"Pardon me but would you mind terribly if I fled in this direction as well?" he called in his friendliest voice. The goblins turned as one in response, eyes wide and teeth bared. The panicked hisses that followed were almost loud enough to rival the howling wind.

"No, no, it's quite alright. I mean you no harm," Sherrock said and once again cursed his natural hulking stature. Really, he would have been better suited for the physical labor or violence that were the chosen professions of most respectable golems. There was no denying his hands were suited to crushing, and his massive feet for stomping, and his head more for bashing through any obstacle than thinking up a way around it. But the path he'd picked rarely called for any of that.

"No come closer!" Oli shouted and without him needing to say anything else, the shadow servants reappeared from every darkened crack and crevice in the surrounding buildings.

Sherrock raised his hands, palms turned out.

"I am unarmed."

"He lie!" Man shouted. "Have two arms!"

"I mean to say I carry no weapons," Sherrock explained patiently. "And, to be transparently clear, I'm not chasing you. For the moment, we're simply fleeing in the same direction. But... while we are, I have *so* many questions."

"That lot words," Lin Two said, frowning at the giant stone man. "Last person with lot words trick goblins. Take Robert's body!"

"Ah, yes. That would have been Dr. Viscous? He certainly had a lot to say once he was brought in, didn't he? And more than a bit of that about you all. I haven't thanked you for that yet. He was a terribly boring villain—wholly unoriginal in his aims and execution. I mean, honestly? Graverobbing to stitch together a private army of minions? A spooky castle on a cliff in a storm-prone region? It was all so uninspired. So *boring*. I gave the authorities all the information they needed, but as usual, they bungled the case." Sherrock took a long pull on his pipe then vented the smoke through his porous body. "I would have taken care of the case eventually, of course, but you did it for me, so I owe you my thanks." Silence followed as all the goblins stared at him. Man frowned, then leaned over to whisper at Oli.

"That even more words…"

"Short, simple sentences, right." Sherrock said, quick on the uptake. "Got it." He gave a sharp nod to punctuate his understanding.

"You say no here stop goblins?" Oli asked, his voice tentative.

"On my honor, you have my word that I've entirely no intention of…" Sherrock trailed off. Too many words again, right. "I won't arrest you."

"Then can run this way too," Oli said, voice firm now. "But try trick goblins and…" he jabbed one crooked finger at the shadow servants.

"We will reduce you to chalk dust," the foremost of the servants said in a slithering hiss.

"Entirely understandable," Sherrock said, nodding. "You have my word, Mr… ?"

The shadow servant paused at that. Its features weren't entirely clear—more a clouded, shadowed collection of shifting suggestions of flesh—but Sherrock had always been good at reading people and he was sure, now, that he saw confusion in those shadows.

"This wretch does not have a name. This wretch… does not remember having a name."

"Shadow friend no wretch!" Oli insisted. "Shadow friend cousin now!" He paused, thinking. "Shadow friend need name?"

"Ooh! Hob Two!" Hob suggested, waving his hand in the air. "Want be Hob Two?"

"Or maybe Gob Two!" Man added.

Gob shook his head.

"Spooky Gob?" Man asked.

"There will only ever be one Gob, cousin."

"We do not require names, liege," the foremost shadow servant said, head bowed. "We are but tools for inflicting your dark desires."

Oli shrugged at that as if to say, 'your loss.'

"Yes, and that's a wonderful point," Sherrock said as he took a long pull on his pipe and the fire in the bowl lit his features. He leaned in closer. "What are your dark desires, my new-found goblin friend?"

Oli pondered a moment, then began counting on one hand.

"Eat, mud bath, start fire…" He trailed off, thinking. "Run from scary sandy people, start more fire, then finish road trip to see family!" he chirped happily.

"Not exactly the work of the Dark Lord himself now, is it?" Sherrock mumbled under his breath.

"No work for Dark Lord! Who say this?" Oli yelped.

"Speaking of scary sandy people…" Gob pointed behind them. The square they'd fled wasn't visible now that they were so deep into the labyrinth of back alleys and side streets, but the storm was. It rose above the building tops, a great swirling, roaring stain on the cityscape. And growing by the moment.

Oli gulped.

"Cousins, shadow friends, rock man," he said. "We run more."

* * *

Sherrock stayed stride for stride with the fleeing goblins, or more accurately, each of his strides counted for about four of theirs. And following them was like leading hungry cats to their food bowls. Every other moment the goblins darted under his feet, near getting squished beneath his stony weight. Inevitably one would get caught by a stomping step, but the creatures' slimy coating made it impossible to actually crush them. Instead, they were squeezed like a bar of soap only to shoot out ahead and skip along the ground. If anything, accidentally stepping on them gave them a speed boost.

If Sherrock hadn't been so focused on not making goblin jam, he might have recognized the city sooner. It's not that he'd seen it before—or that anyone alive had. But everyone had heard about it. Everyone—excluding probably goblins—had heard bedtime stories of Sandlantis. The Desert Flower! The center of the learned world! A cradle of civilization where science, and philosophy, and the higher arts of every order were taught as simply as tying one's shoes.

Or so the stories said. They were somewhat harder to believe when no one could say where Sandlantis was. Or explain what had happened to it. But now, running through the back alleys from a scouring storm, Sherrock was starting to get an idea.

The Desert Flower had been swallowed by the desert itself. But from the looks of things, it had been no natural disaster. At least, he'd never heard of a landslide that swallowed entire cities. Or that turned their populace into desiccated, groaning sand golems.

No, it didn't take the world's finest detective to suss out there was something more at play here.

Where they'd initially fallen into the city-turned-fortress had looked to be some sort of large, public square.

The buildings around it had once been ornate and sweeping. Where they were all fleeing now, however, looked to be an older part of the city. Smaller buildings and tighter streets. Being entirely honest, Sherrock wasn't overly fond of the look of it. Still, it was better than the districts in the distance. Every so often, when he and the goblins emerged at a large enough intersection, Sherrock could squint into the distance to see the rolling outskirts of the city, tucked in all too tight against the cave-filled walls surrounding them. The buildings there looked even older and more decayed than the rest. With a bit of forceful guidance—and more than one accidental squishing—Sherrock was able to direct the goblins' flight away from that area.

"This storm's only getting worse," Sherrock said, fighting just to be heard above the whipping winds as a building beside them caved in on itself. As it crumbled, the stone dissolved into sand then was swept up in the howling wind to make it howl all the more. "We should seek shelter."

The goblin Sherrock was reasonably sure was named Lin Two pointed to a nearby house. She grabbed the doorknob and pulled the door open—just as the house toppled over. Before them, it fell apart, breaking into swirling sand so completely even the seemingly wooden door fell away. The little goblin was left with only a doorknob held in hand and her eyes wide.

"Maybe no go that way," Oli said, backing away.

But where else was there to go? On three sides there was city, buildings and alleys, the quickly collapsing remains of what might've been a playground, and of course, whirling, biting sand. The only thing around them that wasn't falling apart was the sandstone wall that towered up to the arched ceiling far above. Already it was scoured smooth so the present storm didn't seem to be doing much to it. It was then Sherrock noticed something.

"The formation of this rock's been disturbed," he said, frowning at it, then pausing to cough as more sand caught in his throat. Only when he swallowed it away could he speak clearly again. "Like the layers have been shifted at some point." He was reminded of a curtain pulled aside, then left to fall back into place. If only that curtain was made of stone and would always bear the marks of the disturbance.

"Geology's a fascinating science, truly, but now isn't exactly the time," the too well-spoken goblin named Gob yipped. "If this storm gets any stronger we're going to become geology ourselves!" He wiped at his skin as he said it, frowning at the places where the slime had dried up and his skin had gone flaky and dry.

But Sherrock wasn't focused on that. His gaze was fixated on the wall of stone. A completely normal wall. An overlooked wall. A wall with telltale signs of magical tampering.

"Do me a favor, goblins, if you'd be so kind? You see this spot here?" he asked, tapping a pale, sandy splotch with the end of his pipe. "I suspect it's a trigger." He pushed a finger against it and, sure enough, the spot depressed with a soft click. "Ah, yes. And there's a second one just there. Press it, won't you?"

Oli looked doubtful, but leaned against the spot. It didn't budge. Lin Two joined him, then Lin One, to no effect. Then almost all of the goblins were growling and fighting, feet digging trenches in the earth as they pressed with all their might. Nothing happened until the big goblin —which Sherrock was reasonably sure was actually an orc —lumbered up, nose in a textbook, and idly poked a finger against the spot. Then, finally, it depressed with another soft click.

The wall responded with a rumbling groan, then the previously smooth stone face roughened into individual bricks. The bricks turned inward, pivoting away such that they seemed to be folding in on themselves and, as they did, a passage appeared. A passage into darkness and close-cramped tunnels. A lingering damp clung to the walls and ceiling. Oli had never seen any place so welcoming.

THIRTY

Distant Cousins

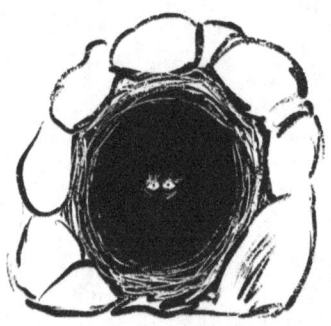

While a goblin's naturally slimy sheen may look effortless, it actually takes a fair bit of upkeep. For optimal luster without losing viscosity, the modern goblin requires a humid environment, access to fresh mud, and a balanced diet of squishy and wriggly things. The air inside the tunnel wasn't quite humid, but it was a bit wet. Enough so that the sand coating the walls and piled up in the corners was, well, not mud, but something close. Sticky and cool to the touch. A welcomed relief from the scouring everyone had just escaped.

246

It was humid enough, even, that Oli could swallow again and have his throat feel like something other than fine grit sandpaper.

The tunnel hadn't been particularly wet when they'd entered, but it was growing wetter by the moment as the sand and dirt beneath Oli's feet slowly turned to proper mud. After a moment of confusion, the cause became clear.

"Man save Weeping Stones!" Oli's cousin said, hugging them close to his chest. While they hadn't been leaking in the past few days, they were now. And... shaking a bit? Scared? Or try really hard to squeeze more water out? Did they work like that?

"Lin Two want save Horse, but Horse no want come," she sighed.

"Why?" Sherrock Stones asked, inquisitive as ever.

"Can lead Horse to Moaning Moat, but no can make Horse drink damned souls," Lin Two sighed.

"I'm sorry, no. I meant why did you save these objects when you were in such imminent danger?"

"Goblins save stones from wet beef jerky, now stones live with goblins," Man said holding them up high. "But stones scared so Man take. Keep safe."

"It just like scary ghosts," Hob explained, frowning all the while, not understanding what Sherrock wasn't getting. "Ghosts scary, then nice. Ghosts ask go new home so goblins take to new home."

Sherrock didn't look to have understood every bit of that, but he nodded to show at least some of it made sense.

"You have an admirable dedication to delivering your packages," he said.

"An admirable dedication and just enough stupidity to inflict untold levels of torture," the genie added, sparing a moment from Robert's reading lessons for the complaint. "Just ask 'em what they did to me."

"Genie man say goblins have two wishes!" Oli chirped back. "Robert always want read. Oli wish genie man teach Robert read!"

"Ah," Sherrock said, a frown pulling across his stony features. "I see the problem there."

"Never in all my millennia..." the genie said, shaking his head. Then with a huff, went back to teaching Robert.

"Kind of you to wish for the betterment of your cousin, though," Sherrock said to Oli. "There are many other wishes one might have chosen. I'm beginning to understand why you have so many clients."

"What 'clients'?" Oli asked, chewing on the unfamiliar word and not caring for the taste of it.

Sherrock made a gesture and a window in reality opened before him. Inside it, Oli recognized the Web. And particularly, he and his cousin's page on Crag's List.

"These are your clients, or rather, the reviews they've left about your service. It's how I was able to interview all of your clients. And figure out where you were heading."

"What do with 'clients?'" Oli asked, still not grasping the concept.

"Well, you work for them, and they pay you. I suppose you could say the Bright Queen is a client of mine." He lingered on that thought before deciding it wasn't one he cared for. "Well, I guess anyone I take on a case for is my client. The Bright Queen just pays well, unfortunately."

"Goblins no get pay!" Oli chirped happily.

"The Dark Lord doesn't pay you?"

"No work for Big Boss—er, Dark Lord!" Oli insisted. "On trip to see family!"

"Of course, of course. My apologies." Sherrock dispelled the goblins' indignation with a gentle wave. "It's just, that cursemark on your arm is usually a sign of a cursing bestowed by the Dark Lord."

Oli hid his forearm behind his back.

"That just bruise!" Lin Two shouted at the same time as Hob insisted it was an old leech bite.

"Oh, apologies. I must have seen it wrong," Sherrock said pressing a hand to his chest, then pausing a long moment. "So then… who are these lot?" He nodded over his shoulder to the lingering shadow servants.

"Cousins!" Oli shouted as the damned souls raised from the deepest pit of hell watched from the shadows. "Uh… distant cousins."

"I see."

As far as Oli could tell, Sherrock looked to have bought the excuse.

"You have been graced with a large family," the golem said, then frowned as he looked down to find the water around them was ankle deep now. "Is it possible to turn those off?" he asked, nodding to the still-weeping stones in Man's arms.

"Stone have feelings, sometimes scared, sometimes sad," Man said. "Sometimes cry. And no want be left with wagon."

"How do you know the stones have feelings?" Sherrock asked, suddenly wondering how closely related he might be to the little things.

"Stones tell!" Man said.

"No hear stones tell," Oli said, frowning.

"In head," Man said, jabbing a finger to his temple. "Stones talk here."

"A magi-psychic connection, hmm?" Sherrock rubbed his chin. "You don't say. That's very interesting. How were you able to attune with them? Usually there's a trial of somesort, a dangerous undertaking?

Or an act of courage to demonstrate one's worthiness?"

Man scrunched his face up at the question, clearly not understanding. Sherrock waved it away.

"Right, well," Gob said, impatient as ever. "I'm glad Man has found some imaginary friends, but can we get back to the part where we were fleeing this accursed place? That storm didn't look to be slowing so we shouldn't either."

"Stompy stone man say this Isolgar," Oli whispered in his cousin's ear, voice almost quiet enough to go unheard. "We no flee, we find Key."

Oli led the way through the tunnels, the shadow friends close by in case anything unsavory were to jump out of the dark. The tunnel split in several places, new shafts shooting off and into even deeper darkness. Sounds echoed through them, reverberating and bouncing so much it was impossible to tell what had originally made them. To Oli, it felt like home. Just needed a few menacing critters scurrying through underbrush or calling from the canopy.

Each tunnel looked like the last, so there wasn't much indication exactly which way they should have been going. But at the same time, the group didn't know where they wanted to go. And, as Grandma Oliva had always told Oli, 'when no know where go, any path know where go there.'

It was this logic that kept Oli assured of his choices as they navigated the seemingly endless tunnels—and came to a junction where several of them conjoined. At the entrance to one of them was a body.

"Sand woman!" Lin One shouted and all the goblins scurried away.

Sherrock eased up to the body. It was a curious thing. Not entirely made of sand, now that he inspected it. Rather, it was as if the person was mostly made of sand, but part of the chest, the shoulder and arm, and her head were still flesh and bone—and thoroughly unresponsive. Dead, perhaps? Sherrock tapped the maybe-corpse on the shoulder. When there was no response, he checked her for a pulse. There was… something there. But it wasn't as reliable as a heartbeat. Was more a random thing, whipping and whirling like wind through the body's veins.

"Is dead?" a small voice asked and Sherrock looked down to see one of the goblins peering through his stony legs at the body.

"Maybe. I'm not sure."

And then the other goblins crept up all around, whispering and peering. One of them poked the body then darted away. The others panicked and followed, but nothing happened, so they all crept back, eyes wide.

Man leaned particularly close over the half-sand, half-person. He still had the Weeping Stones grasped tight and a few droplets of shimmering water splashed down from them to the sand and the sand person.

"Gahhh!" she jerked up with a shout. The goblins fled in a series of shrieks and screams, but her shout hadn't been one of pain or anger so much as a startled gasp. Like she'd been holding her breath for a century or two. "Storm's a'comin', folks! We gotta go! Shutter your windows, fill your baths, we gotta…" she trailed off as she looked around. "How long have I been out?" She moved to raise her sandy arm but it just fell away to loose grains. "Uh oh," she said, biting her lip. "That's not good."

THIRTY-ONE

Curses And Capitalism

"Does anyone have like a bucket, or a bag?" the half-person asked, her voice annoyed as she looked at the fresh pile of sand that had been her right arm.

"Robert have bag!" the largest goblin said triumphantly, temporarily freeing himself from reading lessons to step forward—and plant a foot directly into the pile of sand.

"No! No! Don't step on it!" the woman shouted, trying to corral it all back together with her remaining arm. Robert didn't hear her, though, distracted by the arm he'd shoved halfway down his throat, searching for the Sower's sack.

"Stop! You're scattering it everywhere!"

"Still stuck," he said with a sigh. "Sorry. No have bag."

"Get off my arm sand!"

"Ooh, actually!" Robert's eyes lit up bright. "Have idea!" He dropped to all fours, further scattering the sand, and began shoveling everything in front of him into his mouth.

"You—no, that's not—stop doing that—" The woman finally let out a resigned sigh and collapsed onto her back. "Ya know what? It's fine. I didn't need that arm anyway. All good. I'll just…" she rolled onto her side then began pulling herself forward with her one good arm. "Pardon me, excuse me," she said, dragging her way through the goblins.

Sherrock took one big step and caught up with her.

"May I offer my assistance, madam?" he asked with a slight bow. "If there's somewhere you need to go, Ms… ?"

"Delphine," she said simply. "And I need to get home before this storm arrives. Gods know it'll do to the upper districts what it's already done to the lower."

"Ah." Sherrock lowered his pipe at that.

"What?" Delphine asked, pausing to stare at him. The realization dawned in her eyes a moment later, though. "No." She shook her head. "Come on, really?" And then she deflated, falling to the tunnel floor in a series of angry, ringing curses.

"I'm afraid all of the city has been afflicted by this curse," Sherrock said, trying to cushion the blow.

"All sandy now!" Oli said, popping up on Sherrock's shoulder.

"And mean!" Lin Two said, suddenly hanging off his elbow. When had the little creature gotten there?

"Goblins, goblins, please!" Sherrock said, waving his hands at them. "A bit of courtesy, if you can. This poor woman has just received terrible news. She's grieving. We must—"

"Grieving?" Delphine was staring up at Sherrock now. "Grieving's for when you've already lost! Does it look like I've lost to you?" she growled then began dragging herself across the floor again.

Sherrock decided not to answer that question truthfully.

"I'm gonna find that dirty liar Nestlecles and make a sand castle out of him! Or what's left of him." She frowned, then looked back. "I imagine everyone's like this now?"

"More scary," Hob said, covering his eyes.

"Mrrhhhmphssnmmphaa," Robert said, trying to speak through cheeks stuffed with sand.

"More sandy!" Lin One translated.

"I'm afraid the goblins are correct." Sherrock took a gentle puff from his pipe. "You are the most human person we've come across here. Or, perhaps, the least cursed? We're not entirely sure what's going on."

"What's going on is that sorcerous traitor Nestlecles damned us!" Delphine shouted, then set to pulling herself forward again.

"Would you accept our assistance?" Sherrock asked gently.

"If you, your slimy pets, and whatever those shadow things are would like to help, you can take me to Nestlecles so I can cook him into a nice vase, then shatter it, and do it all again."

Sand wasn't an ideal ingredient for making vases, Sherrock knew, but in the moment, it seemed best not to point that out.

"Cook mean fire?" Hob asked, looking hopeful.

"Too long since start fire," Lin Two agreed.

"We can go start a fire somewhere else, cousins," Gob said, markedly not following the crawling Delphine. "Preferably somewhere like back home, *after we visit our family*." Gob said that last bit all funny and with several winks, but Oli couldn't figure out why. And anyway, he didn't need to find this Nestlecles person, he needed to find whoever was in charge of Fortress Isolgar—if this really was it.

"Scary sand lady tell goblins where find..." Oli paused, thinking hard to ensure he picked his words carefully. "Big Boss of this place... who no is evil... but maybe know lot about Key?"

Delphine's face scrunched into an expression of severe confusion at the request. So severe, in fact, the sandier parts of her face cracked and fell away.

"... sure?" she finally answered.

"What's this about a key now?" Sherrock asked, but Delphine had recovered from her bafflement.

"Tell you what, kid. Get me to Nestlecles and I'll tell you whatever it is you want to know. Assuming I can understand the question," she added under her breath. "The big guy here can carry me, yeah?"

"Mrhhhmph!" Robert said, stepping forward, arms outstretched.

"I meant *him*," Delphine said, nodding at Sherrock. Robert deflated but the genie made it clear the only thing Robert was going to be carrying was the textbook he was supposed to be studying. Meanwhile, Sherrock gave a bow of his head and did a little flourish with one boulder-like hand.

"Detective Sherrock Stones, at your service, madam." With that, he scooped her—torso, single arm, and little dangly bit of a stomach—up with ease. "Where to, Ms. Delphine?" he asked. "And do tell us everything about what happened here."

She pointed down a tunnel that sloped gently upward. Sherrock strode into it, the goblins and shadow servants following just behind. As they did, Oli patted Robert on the back.

"Is okay. Robert still big guy at heart."

* * *

"I don't know all of what happened," Delphine said, her voice echoing through the tunnels above the sound of their trudging footsteps. Well, mainly Sherrock's trudging footsteps seeing as the goblins had all climbed atop him, and the shadow cousins didn't walk so much as slither through supernatural abyss.

"I'm sure it started because of Nestlecles and his greed, though," Delphine continued. "'Water's too precious a commodity to be free!'" She said in what was probably supposed to be a mocking interpretation of him. "As if the wellspring hadn't flowed here for centuries before we built the city. As if we hadn't built the city *because* of the wellspring!"

"What is 'wellspring'?" Oli asked from where he was perched on Sherrock's shoulder.

"An endless well of the purest, coolest water you've ever tasted in your life," she said, her eyes going distant at the memory of it.

"Make mouth tingle when drink?" Oli asked.

"What? No."

"Moaning Moat do." He crossed his arms. "Sound tastier than wellspring."

"The damned souls within do add just the perfect spritz of eternal suffering," Gob chimed in.

"Right, well, be that as it may, the wellspring was the heart of our city. An oasis in these blistering sands just as the city itself was an oasis of civilization in the dark. We lived and we prospered all thanks to our bottomless, life-giving well. But the primordials were at war with the elders again so the economy was in the tank. Then Ditaxsophis tore the continent asunder and formed the five lands. Well that just went and wreaked havoc with the trade routes—you can't even imagine the potholes."

"Oh, of course," Sherrock said, nodding as if Delphine hadn't just referred to creation myths as if they'd happened last week.

"But these things happen, no reason to kick up a panic." Delphine pointed to guide Sherrock into a new tunnel, this one steeply sloped. "Except kick up a panic was exactly what Nestlecles did. 'The wellspring's running out of water!' 'We have to preserve the waters of creation!'"

"Rationing is not unheard of in times of turbulence and tumult," Sherrock said.

"Yeah, that's what Nestlecles said. Tight times for all, but we'd weather it together, right? Arm in arm in mutual determination and resilience? Except for those with extra gold lying around, of course, because Nestlecles never said no to profit." Delphine fumed at the thought. "For a little extra gold each month, your family wouldn't have such parched throats."

"Hm." Sherrock gave a thoughtful grunt as he took another pull on his pipe.

"Yeah, and as it happened, the wellspring wasn't fond of that decision. Its flow slowed by the day. The city began to dry up and what little water the wellspring did give became worth its weight in gold. And then the curse crept in." Delphine growled as she recounted the story. "It hit the poorer districts first—because it was drier there, maybe. Unnatural sandstorms, raging without relent. And then, well…" She waved her arm where, just below the shoulder, flesh ended and there was a nub covered in sand. "You've seen what happens next." She paused a moment as if thinking. "But you say the whole city's gone to pieces?"

"Grains, even," Sherrock said with a nod.

"Good, then. Means even those that could afford to hoard the water weren't spared."

"But why you?" Lin Two asked, popping out from beneath Sherrock's armpit and leaning to squint at Delphine's face. "Why you half-half?"

Delphine faltered at that, words failing her a moment.

"I don't know. I saw the storm coming and ran for the tunnels, thought they'd be the fastest way home so I could warn them. That's the last thing I remember."

"Maybe half-half for reason?" Oli suggested.

"Get me to Nestlecles, that'll be reason enough," she said, then nodded to the next tunnel where the floor rose in a sloping ascent. Sherrock continued along it with Delphine in his arms, goblins hanging off him every which way, and the shadow servants stalking ahead and behind. In the darkness they were almost invisible, but for when Sherrock would turn his head. Only then would he catch the slightest glimpse of them in the corner of his vision.

"What that?" Oli asked suddenly, then tilted an ear up.

"What's what?" Sherrock asked.

"*That!*" Oli shouted, then sprang from the golem and hurried ahead. "Hear voice! Human voice!"

Oli scampered ahead on all fours, ears pointed ahead.

Sherrock hurried to keep up as the other goblins shouted and slapped at him to go faster.

"There!" Oli said when he finally stopped. He pointed to a crack in the tunnel wall. Sherrock pressed one massive eye to it and peered through. The tunnels must have led them up into what Delphine had called the upper districts, seeing as the world outside the tunnel was high above the city. It was still underground, but off to the right there was a cliff, and spreading out below it, a panoramic view of the city.

"Stop resisting!"

"Lastrof," Sherrock said under his breath as his eyes snapped to take her in. The sergeant and her officers were grouped up in a circle at the edge of the cliff. They stood in some sort of carved-out depression, like a creek bed that'd run dry.

More pressing than their surroundings, however, was the army of sandfolk. They weren't attacking for the moment, but probably that was on account of them having Lastrof and her officers outnumbered and backed against the cliff's edge.

A figure in among the sandfolk was speaking and Lastrof was shaking her head by way of response.

"Surrender and you may know mercy," the voice called.

"Surrender this!" Lastrof shouted, then blasted a spell at the figure. And just like that, the battle resumed.

"Ah, perfect! They're distracting the sandfolk," Gob said. "Hopeless, but helpful. Let not their sacrifice be in vain. Come on, come on. Let's find this Nestlecles person before anyone realizes we're here." He jumped down from Sherrock and marched further along the tunnel. "It's this way, is it?" he asked over his shoulder.

"That not nice, Gob," Oli said.

"No, it's not nice. It's practical," he retorted. "Aren't you always saying if we need help Big Boss will send help?"

Oli nodded.

"Well if they need help, their Big Boss can send it, right?"

"Well…" That did make sense. And Gob was the smartest of Oli's cousins.

Sherrock sighed suddenly.

"That'd be me, I suppose."

"Huh?" Oli cocked an eyebrow.

"Lastrof's an… enthusiastic soldier of the Bright Queen, but she has a tendency to, well…" He gestured at the general insanity outside. "Get in over her head. I'd hoped she'd be able to work her way out of this one without me, but here we are."

"Sherrock go to help mean shouty people?" Oli asked. Somehow, that made him feel better. He didn't know Lastrof or her officers and certainly didn't care for them, but abandoning them made his stomach feel squirmy. Like he'd eaten a too-ripe newtcake. It also made him itchy all over. Or maybe that was just the fine dust floating in the air? It seemed to get everywhere and left his skin dry and flaky.

"*We* go help mean shouty people," Delphine said suddenly and Oli noticed now she'd her eye to the crack in the wall. "I see that squirmy liar Nestlecles out there. He's at the head of all this, I know it."

THIRTY-TWO

Nestlecles the Parched

Goblins love fighting like siblings love sharing the back seat on a cross-realm road trip. And like said siblings, goblins' fighting prowess primarily consists of mean pokes, unexpected flatulence, and complaining to whatever higher authority is closest at hand. Nonetheless, Oli and his cousins gave their loudest battle cry as they charged into the army of sandfolk—and made sure to stay safely behind Sherrock.

"Let me at 'em! Let me at 'em!" Delphine yelled, throwing punches with her one good arm and waving the nub of the other around as she waded through the fray. Or, more appropriately, as Sherrock waded through it carrying her.

For their part, the sandfolk tried to resist, but grains of sand, when you really think about it, are just a bunch of very tiny rocks. Sherrock, on the other hand, was one very, very large rock.

"Is there a Nestlecles present?" the golem asked politely. "Excuse me, pardon me. We're looking for one Mr. Nestlecles?"

The sandfolk army hissed and howled as they broke against him—a whirlwind trying to topple a mountain. Following his every step, Oli's eyes and nostrils were filled with sand.

"Sherrock!" a distant shout from Sergeant Lastrof as she paused from her torrent of spells. She stood at the center of the seemingly dried out creek bed, an old well cracked and brittle beside her. "Where have you been?"

"Uncovering... the mysteries... of this place," Sherrock said through the quickly forming sandstorm. He barged onward, his unstoppable momentum boring a hole through the otherwise impenetrable front lines. In his passing, though, the sandfolk quickly charged in to fill the gap. They came at the goblins from all sides and were met with lethal hostility.

"Gah!" Hob shouted as he delivered a well-aimed poke to the ribs of the nearest enemy. The sand person looked down, confused at the blow, then lost its head as a shadow-servant's cursed blade cleaved it in two.

"Aha!" Hob cheered, holding his extended finger high, then turned to find his next target. Meanwhile, Lin Two kicked a sand person in the shin. Grains of sand fell loose from the creature—and then a whole lot more fell loose when a manifestation of corporeal evil in the form of a shadow cousin's scimitar sliced the foe shoulder to toe.

Lin Two paused, staring in awe as a wild smile pulled itself across her face.

"Me tell Lin Two she always kick too hard!" Lin One shouted. Behind him, several sandfolk howled as they leered over him. A clumsy arm swung back and reduced them to swirling dust as Sherrock lost his balance on the unsteady ground.

"Apologies!" he called back.

Seeing his cousins in the midst of the fray, Robert pried his nose free from his assigned reading.

"Pay no attention to that nonsense," the genie scolded, but Robert's cousins needed him. He gave a bellowing war cry and chucked *Learn to Read with Puppy the Pug and Friends!* right into the chaos. The surprisingly sturdy book smashed into a sand person and they disappeared with a puff.

"Books not just smart," Robert said, eyes wide. "Books strong!" *100 Words to Teach your Toddler* was sent flying next. Then Professor Sus' well-loved children's classic, *The Kobold in the Cap* was weaponized as Robert ran screaming through the enemy host, swinging it side to side. The genie chased him, smacking him with a ruler all the while.

"This isn't—" *Smack.* "What I meant when I said—" *Smack.* "You needed a book club!" *Smack.*

Oli watched, eyes wide, as the two rushed past, Robert swinging his book and the genie doing just as much work with the ruler. Meanwhile, Man was cowering at the back of the fray, the Weeping Stones tucked in tight to his chest. All the commotion must have scared them as they were weeping more than ever. The water pooled at Man's feet and, for whatever reason, the sandfolk looked past him. They did not, however, look past Lastrof and her officers. They, in contrast, were surrounded and fighting fiercely. Their wands blasted with near constant explosions of light. There was nowhere for them to go but through the enemy, though, seeing as their backs were to the cliff and the long drop to the ancient city below.

"Cover me, I'm out!" an officer shouted, then dropped to one knee to pry a dull and empty looking glass sphere from the end of his wand. He retrieved a brighter, glowing one from his belt, slapped it into place in the wand, then raised to cast again. A sand person reached him, however, and a wrestling match ensued. The wand was knocked free to bounce against the rocky ground, then roll into Oli's foot.

"Huh?" the little goblin bent down and scooped the thing up. Didn't look like much more than a knobby piece of wood somewhere between the length of a stick and a tree branch. It took Oli two arms to heave it up, however. His hands tingled where he touched it and something in his stomach buzzed energetically. Ooh, and there was a little button on the side of the wand. Probably it was best not to touch that, Oli thought. Who knew what would happen?

"Bright Queen's mercy, give that back!" someone shouted, and Oli would have, but he couldn't hear them above the sound of the button clicking repeatedly beneath his thumb and also the sound of a barrage of spells exploding wildly from the end of the wand. The magical blasts cut a swathe through the legion of sandfolk, clearing them out en masse. All the while, Oli held on for dear life as the wand bucked and kicked, throwing him about the space. Sandfolk screeched, officers shouted and ducked for cover, and even Sherrock grunted as he was hit, though the spell rebounded off him and down into the ground.

After several terrifying moments of rapid fire, Oli was knocked onto his rear then held the wand pointed at the ceiling as it fired off its final few spells. The magical device relinquished one last booming spell, then fell still, smoke and a few glittering sparks streaming from its business end. Oli pried his thumb from the button and a hatch popped open on the rear of the wand to spit out an empty glass sphere.

In the wake of the onslaught—and with the combined efforts of Lastrof's officers and Sherrock's imposing physical presence—the fight looked to be won. Or, at least, all of the standing sandfolk had been reduced to piles. Some were beginning to reform, but there was enough time to get away before that happened.

"Don't stop!" Delphine's voice cut through the aftermath. "We didn't get Nestlecles! He was just here—where did he go?"

"Where indeed?" a voice asked.

A wave rose from below the cliff's edge. Not a wave of water, but sand, and shot through with streaks of black. The dark and heavy grains reminded Oli of the volcanic slopes of Doomsday Mountain. The wave hissed as it shifted, but beneath that sound there was something else. An echoing growl, maybe? Oli's ears heard but his mind failed to understand.

"This has been an admirable effort." The voice again, and then Oli spotted a man riding the wave. He was small for a human, bespectacled, and dressed in smart, khaki-colored robes. His hands were folded behind his back as the wave washed against the cliff and deposited him gently among their number.

"That's him! Get him!" Delphine shouted, but Nestlecles gave a tutting click of his tongue and shook his head. As he did, his black-stained wave rushed forward and slammed into everyone. It only reached up to Sherrock's knees, but that meant Lastrof and her officers were buried up to the waist and Oli and his cousins to their chins. Even the shadow cousins were knocked down. They struggled against whatever magic restrained them, grunting as if in the midst of a wrestling match. The only one who looked pleased about the whole chain of events was Robert's genie who breathed a sigh of relief, then cracked open a fresh book in front of the now rooted goblin.

"Rather clever of you all, if I do say so," Nestlecles said, nodding. "The majority of my forces are engaged with Her soldiers at our front gates. Or perhaps, I should say, *distracted* with Her soldiers. Perfect cover for a fellowship of infiltrators to sneak in."

"You're under arrest—" Lastrof broke into a cough, but fought through it. "By order of the Bright Queen—" she raised her wand only for a sooty, black arm to burst free of the sand in front of her and slap it away.

"Come now, let's not use such profane language in these hallowed halls," Nestlecles scolded. As he said it, more sooty arms clawed free from the sea of black sand to disarm the officers. It took a whole ten of them to keep Sherrock held back. He grunted and groaned, mouth set in a grimace, then finally broke free of the arms—enough to raise his pipe to his mouth for a long, slow pull.

"Well, you had quite slipped in under my notice, but now that we're all here, we should have plenty of time to get acquainted," Nestlecles said, a self-satisfied smile pulling at his dried, flaky lips. "I am Nestlecles the Parched, Bane of Aquifers, and it is my great pleasure to welcome you to your eternal unresting place, here in Fortress Isolgar."

THIRTY-THREE

Wriggly Little Guests

"Fortress Isolgar? What are you on about?" Delphine growled from Sherrock's arms. "This is a city. This is Sandlantis!"

"Another one, truly?" The sorcerer known as Nestlecles rolled his eyes. "And just when I thought I'd rooted out the last of you half-and-halfs. Really, can you not just let my curse do its work? It'd be easier for everyone involved." He looked rather exasperated until a sand person stepped next to him and whispered in his ear. "They have a *what* now? Well where did they get that from? Yes, yes of course I'd like to see it. Bring it here, straight away."

At the sorcerer's words the sandfolk set to moving hurriedly, some unknown mission guiding them away from the site of the battle and off into the crumbling remains of the ancient city.

"Man, was it? Man the goblin?" Sherrock hissed under his breath, twisted around to speak to Oli's mostly buried cousin. Man didn't notice, or didn't hear, the whispers over Lastrof's shouting.

"Where are they going? What dark task have you assigned them?" she bellowed, her questions sounding more like accusations. Oli was by no means an expert in human communication but considering their current predicament—what with everyone fixed in place by Nestlecles' weird black sand—this seemed like a situation that called for a little less accusing and a little more pleading.

"Oh, they're just off to take care of a bit of tidying. I do like to run a clean ship around here. You know what they say, cleanliness is next to godliness, and down here…" his eyes darkened behind his glasses. "I'm the closest thing there is to a god."

"You're just a jumped-up, traitorous sorcerer!" Delphine shouted. She was still cradled in Sherrock's arms, but now she pushed herself up, as if trying to get free. "You're a liar and a cheat, just out to line your own pockets."

"I am your end!" Nestlecles shouted it, and as he did his features exaggerated, as if his skin was not made of flesh but of that ashen, volcanic sand. His mouth widened, his eyes enlarged, and his voice took on a deep echoing roar that shook his throat, then shook the sand around them, then shook every wall, crevice, and crook of the ancient city. What remained of Delphine broke into grains and fell through Sherrock's arms. Oli's vision blackened around the edges and then, as quickly as it'd come on, the darkness receded. Nestlecles' face snapped back to its normal, flaky self, and he dabbed at the corner of his mouth, a look of mild embarrassment overtaking his features.

"So sorry about that. I don't interact much with living creatures these days, it's been something of a long few centuries down here," he said. "I regret it's all too easy to lose one's social graces when all you have to interact with are mindless minions." Nestlecles gave an apologetic smile then as a figure rose from the spot where Delphine had fallen. A figure made of sand, but like the others, it was faceless and wordless. It rose and stood stock still, awaiting commands.

"You all will join her soon enough," Nestlecles said as everyone shivered at the sight. "You see, my curse is already hard at work." He gestured and Lastrof's arm was yanked forward to show several spots where her skin was turning to sand. She cursed at the sight, or tried to, but broke down into a fit of coughs instead.

"Man!" Sherrock hissed again, doing his best to go unnoticed despite being the largest—and without careful control—loudest of the group.

"You've been breathing in this air, these grains, since you arrived," Nestlecles continued, seeming all too pleased with himself. "My fortress protects itself, you see. It is akin to a living thing. My finest creation, truly. And soon, you will join it. Serve it. Serve me."

"Goblins no good to serving, maybe can just go? Goblins no to mean trouble," Hob squeaked from where his mouth just reached above the ocean of black sand. Nestlecles fixed him with a curious glare. "Okay, maybe to mean little trouble," Hob admitted.

"Oh, forgive me." Nestlecles looked taken aback. "I hadn't realized we had additional guests." And then, as it always went, once he'd seen one goblin it was as if all the rest had been revealed to him. His eyes snapped from one slimy, sand-covered head to the next as he took in Oli and his cousins. "A whole infestation of guests, it would appear."

"You'll release us and the pests, or you'll face the Bright Queen's wrath," Lastrof shouted, as she seemed overly fond of doing.

"Her forces are already at our gate. She and her miserable allies make war on us all across the land, what more wrath could we face?" Nestlecles gave a toothy grin as he adjusted his glasses. "She is giving it her best, and coming up short. Even the Kingdom of Darkness yet stands."

"Kingdom of Darkness?" Oli said aloud as the words resounded in his mind. They bounced around between his ears and passed through his brain four or five times before triggering an alarm bell. "Oli know Kingdom of Darkness!" He struggled and strained to pull his arm free. Nestlecles watched on with obvious confusion, but seeming to want to see where this went, he waved his fingers and the sand around Oli parted enough for him to jab one little arm into the air. "Look! Oli have bruise from Big Boss! Oli and cousins go on trip for Big Boss. Supposed go to Fortress Isolgar!"

"I told you they were up to no good!" Lastrof shouted as she turned an accusatory glare at Sherrock. He wasn't paying attention, though, was still focused on Man.

"Oh my! Let me see that." Nestlecles had barely spoken before his enchanted sand carried him forward. He took hold of Oli's arm, adjusted his glasses, then peered close. "Yes, yes. This is the Dark Lord's cursemark. The genuine article! Oh, and why didn't I see it sooner? Your shadow servants, of course! I should have recognized ol' Sarusomal's work. And here I was thinking it was the golem who'd dabbled in a bit of dark magic." He reared back, renewed interest apparent in his features as he studied the little goblin. Oli's stomach churned as he stared back. He'd met his fair share of the Dark Lord's servants— Mishalob and her many children, the cheery ash geist in the wine cellar, Gruesome the Head Torturer—and none of them left him feeling like he did now. Nestlecles' entire demeanor had changed, but Oli found, for whatever reason, he simply didn't like the sorcerer. It was one thing to serve the Big Boss, but that didn't mean you had to be mean.

"If the Dark Lord sent you, well I suppose that would explain the..." Nestlecles gestured off behind him as a familiar voice echoed from just out of sight.

"Connection interrupted. To resume navigation, please vacate any anti-magic fields, pocket dimensions, or congested tunnels."

"Iris!" Lin Two cheered, then gagged as doing so allowed a little avalanche of sand to pour down her throat. The sandfolk who'd left earlier were returning now, dragging the *Master Viktor Is A Genius Self-Propelled Rocket Wagon XXI* behind them.

"So the Dark Lord sent you to me with this wondrous machine?" Nestlecles asked. "And with so powerful a curse-mark?" He leaned in close. "You must be on a very important quest, little one."

Oli leaned away and did his best to suppress a grimace.

"Dark Lord send but no give wagon. Scary armor lady give Horse though," Oli answered, pointing as their ignoble steed followed the wagon into the square.

"Hrrmmphrrse!" Lin Two tried to cheer through her mouthful of sand.

"By 'scary armor lady' he means the Lieutenant of Lament," Gob said, rolling his eyes. "You'll have to forgive my cousins, their command of language is, well, not so commanding."

"And a well-spoken goblin too?" Nestlecles clapped his hands excitedly. "Truly, the wonders of the Dark Lord know no bounds. Please, please, forgive my earlier hostility, I had no idea we were on the same side." He threw his hands outward in a swift stroke and the sand restraining all of the goblins fell away. In its wake they were left dry and itchy. Except for Man. The water of the Weeping Stones had mixed with the sand to cover him in a sort of soupy mud bath. The sandfolk closest to him stepped away at the sight, and Oli found himself jealous of his cousin's moistness.

"Wow, it sure is dry and scratchy in here," Sherrock said from behind Nestlecles. Peering under the sorcerer's arm, Oli could see the golem acting strange. Snapping his head to the side, he made an exaggerated nod at Man, then to the old, dried up well. But Oli didn't know much about golems, and Nestlecles was still talking, so he turned back to the sorcerer.

"—this is so exciting, we haven't had word from back home in so very long. You must tell me everything, goblins," Nestlecles said, bubbling with enthusiasm now. "How is the Dark Lord? Is he getting enough rest? Keeping up with his hobbies? I told him he works too hard, you know. I told him, covering the world in eternal damnation is an admirable goal, but you'll never live to see it if you work yourself to death first, you know what I mean?"

THIRTY-FOUR

His Imperious Majesty The Dark Lord Sarusomal And The Humble Barkeep Rodrigrar Drown The World In Shadow And Sorrow: An Aspirational Fiction, Part II

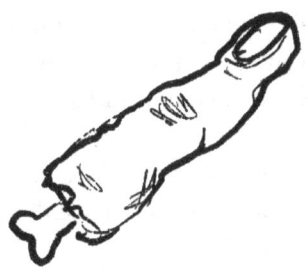

Goblin wisdom has long held that intuition is 'a bunch of hooey' and the only meaningful feeling one can trust from a stomach is hunger (and sometimes indigestion). Luckily, no one had taught Oli about goblin wisdom because no one *taught* goblin wisdom; for the simple fact that it wasn't wise at all. As such, thanks to this complete lack of wisdom, when Oli's gut told him Nestlecles was a Bad Guy, he listened.

"I've never known Sarusomal to make use of goblins," Nestlecles said, seeming to linger on the thought. As he spoke the Dark Lord's name, the shadows in the sunken city grew just a bit deeper. Nestlecles gave a little laugh then. "But who am I to question his abyssal malevolence?" He slapped his forehead. "And you made it here, didn't you? When so many others could not. Of course, all part of our Lord's scheme."

"What is 'scheme'?" Oli asked, but Nestlecles seemed to be talking with himself more than anyone else.

"You're here for the Key, then? Truly?" he positively bubbled with excitement at the mention of it. "But of course you are! I knew someone would come, I just never thought to expect..." he gestured at Oli and his cousins. "Well, *you*. But—ah! Yes, ever the more brilliant then, isn't it? No one expected you! Or for that matter, *suspected* you." Nestlecles bounced up and down so much he had to pause and fix his glasses. "The time has come to unleash..." he paused to frown at the captive officers and golem. "The ultimate weapon?" he asked, leaning in so close his breath tickled Oli's ear.

"No know about ultimate weapon," Oli said loud enough for it to echo about the space. "Big Boss just want Key."

"Key? Weapon? What is this?" Sergeant Lastrof shouted from behind. Nestlecles waved his hand casually and a rush of blackened sand filled her mouth.

"Mrrrhppphjh!" she shouted, somehow only a bit quieter than before.

"But a moment, my cursed little friend. I shall retrieve..." Nestlecles paused for what he knew would be a moment steeped in drama. "The Key!" With that, he spun around, cast a small spell, and stepped into a pocket dimension.

"Oli, my friend," Sherrock said, his voice calm and collected. "What use could you and your cousins have for a weapon? Especially now that you have such a successful delivery business?" He nodded over to the *Master Viktor Is A Genius Self-Propelled Rocket Wagon XXI.* "Any old scoundrel can draw a weapon, goblins. But only you can pilot that miraculous wagon."

He had a point, Oli had to admit. Except…

"Weapon no for goblins, weapon for Big Boss," Oli explained. "We use special wagon to take weapon to Big Boss. Goblins stay in delivery business, Big Boss stay in weapon business."

His cousins nodded at that as, after all, it had made perfect sense. Oli patted himself on the back for being so smart. Maybe smart as Gob, even.

"You don't have to serve the Big Boss," Sherrock said, his words tentative.

"Goblins serve Big Boss," Hob said, speaking slowly like he was explaining it to a toddler.

"Yeah!" Lin Two added with a raised fist and a cheer. "Goblins always serve biggest boss around!"

"Who says you can't be the biggest boss around?" Sherrock shot back and the thought hit Lin Two with almost a physical force.

Gob choked back a sudden laugh.

"Need it really be said? My cousins struggle to pick their own noses without guidance.

Sherrock ignored him.

"The only Big Boss you need is that voice inside your hearts, goblins. That voice that tells you what *you* want to do."

Oli frowned at that, but the big stompy rock man had never been mean to them, so maybe it was worth a try? He did his best to turn his ears inward and see what the voice inside him had to say.

"…voice say Oli hungry. And maybe should do arson later."

"Are you sure that's what it's saying?" Sherrock prodded. "I chose to believe there's more to you than that, my wriggly little friend."

"Well then you've chosen quite wrong," Gob said with a mean laugh. Oli's stomach churned at the sound and he found himself with an overwhelming urge to give Gob a good and nasty poke right in the ribs.

A slight smile pulled at Sherrock's lips then, or maybe it was just the most recent puff of pipe smoke obscuring his face as it passed.

"Anyway, I think you should pay attention to Man and those wondrous little water stones of his. They—"

Nestlecles stepped back out of the pocket dimension in a puff of dust. He coughed as he waved it away.

"Sorry about that, I really need to do some tidying. Anyhow, I know you were sent for the Key, but while you're here…"

"Oh no," Oli said and pressed his face into his hands. "No again."

"No, no, I don't want to impose, it's just the mail's just been so unreliable since the war really heated up and I just have, like, three little things. And you're already going that way," Nestlecles said, then held up three packages. "This one's just a letter to my friend, Mishalob. And this is…" He read the label. "Some sort of sourdough starter the Dark Lord ordered forever ago? I don't know why it ended up here." He looked at the last item. "And I don't even know what the deal is with this one. It came via priority fortnight delivery." He held it high, then squinted as he read the cover. "*His Imperious Majesty The Dark Lord Sarusomal and the Humble Barkeep Rodrigrar Drown the World in Shadow and Sorrow: An Aspirational Fiction, Part II*. Does that make any sense to you all?"

"Just throw in wagon please," Oli said, massaging his brow as he felt a headache starting to come on.

"Really, I don't even know how this Rodrigrar fellow got the address here." Nestlecles tossed the items into the wagon, then grew serious. "Anyway. You were sent for the Key?" He asked it with a little smile. "Allow me to... give you a hand with that." He whipped his arm from inside his robes to reveal, well, something held tight in his grasp.

"That no Key!" Lin One said, scratching his head. "That... a hand?"

"Think fast!" Nestlecles said and tossed it to Oli, but he was still trying to figure out what Sherrock wanted with Man and the Weeping Stones, so he fumbled the catch. The hand's dusty old index finger snapped off as it hit the ground. "Oh, uh, oof." Nestlecles winced as he scooped up the finger and tucked it in a pocket. "Don't tell the Dark Lord about that, huh?" He gave a nervous laugh. "Our little secret?"

Oli picked up the brittle thing to find it was exactly like Lin One had said. Not a key at all but an old, bony hand. There was still some skin on it but it was shriveled and wrinkled.

"It like wet beef jerky man," Oli said. "But no wet."

"Good for back itches maybe," Hob said, leaning in to examine the thing's yellow and too-long fingernails.

"Ooh, ooh! It like book!" Robert chimed in suddenly. He pulled away from the genie—whose back was turned while he wrote strange and undecipherable symbols on a floating chalkboard—and hurried over. "Robert read!" He pointed to where rough letters had been cut into the back of the hand. "Ka-la... kl-ah-ah... klaa-ta-uu!" He shouted and pumped a fist in the air. The genie spun around, eyes wide with excitement.

"Come on, Robert! Please, please. Lords of the Lamp,

guide him!" He cheered the biggest of the goblins on as he sounded his way through the word. But he'd only gotten one. There were two others.

"Uh…" His confidence wavered. "Ba-ra-aa-da?" He sighed. "Robert no read good yet."

"But he read a word! You all heard it!" the genie shouted, gesturing around with an accusatory piece of chalk. "I did it! The little cretin can read now!" He spread both arms wide and tilted his head back. "Free me from this wish!"

Nothing happened.

More nothing, until a stream of curses Oli didn't recognize spewed from the genie. He didn't understand what they meant, but from the sound of them, it wasn't anything good.

"Right, well." Nestlecles looked thoroughly lost. "Clearly you all have a thing going here and I don't want to butt in, but if you're going to take the Key to the Dark Lord, it's best I give you the instructions."

"It okay. Goblins no need know," Oli said and the others nodded along.

"*I* might like to know," Gob interjected.

"Goblins do deliver for Big Boss," Oli reminded him. "Because… well, because it what goblins do." And for the first time, saying it didn't feel true. Somewhere, deep in his subconscious, a new thought was forming. But goblin brains weren't really equipped to handle complex thoughts, so Oli brushed it aside.

"Whoever holds the Key must know the instructions," Nestlecles said and crossed his arms. "It's the rules."

Oli rolled his eyes.

"Then goblins can to leave?" He found he didn't want to be around the mean sorcerer any longer than necessary.

"I will hurry you on your way," Nestlecles said with a

nod, then produced a scrap of parchment. "Okay, the instructions." He coughed to clear his throat. "When once more Lock and Key are near, speak thee such that all may hear, the words upon thy cursed hand, and doom abyss upon the land," he began, taking on a singsong rhythm. "Lock and Key once more will meet, the seven seals will be complete, set free will be the hungering heat, and all your foes will know despair."

In the wake of his reading, silence fell about the space. Until Sherrock gave a polite, quiet cough.

"Um... despair?"

"Huh?" Nestlecles turned to face him.

"You said despair?"

"I did."

"Not... defeat?"

"What?" The sorcerer's brow scrunched in confusion.

"I just thought..." Sherrock mumbled the rest.

"What? What did you say?"

"No, no, it's fine, it's just you had like a rhyme scheme going." Sherrock nodded along to the syllables as he recounted the instructions. "Lock and Key once more will *meet*, the seven seals will be *complete*, set free will be the hungering *heat*, and all your foes will know... " he waved his hand, encouraging Nestlecles to finish.

"Despair."

"*Defeat,*" Sherrock insisted.

"Alright Master Poet," Nestlecles said with a mocking tone. "When you invent your ultimate weapon you can write your own instructions, how's that?"

Sherrock fired back some retort, but Oli wasn't listening. He couldn't shake that thing about Man and the Weeping Stones? And despite his best efforts, that pesky thought he'd pushed down kept floating to the surface.

Man.

Weeping Stones.

Wet.

Other goblins. Dry?

Weeping Stones make water. Water... make sand wet? Make mud? No, that wasn't quite it. There was something more.

The curse!

The realization hit Oli with the force like the time a great gargle oak had come crashing through the roof of his hovel.

"Weeping Stone water is break curse!" Oli shouted, unable to hold back his discovery.

"It doesn't matter if it doesn't rhyme, that's not the point," Nestlecles was shouting at Sherrock. But Sherrock wasn't listening anymore, he was smiling at Oli. Nodding, even. Encouraging him to go even further.

"The power doesn't come from the rhyme, it comes from understanding the instructions. The rhyme's just there for..." Nestlecles paused. "Wait, what did you say?"

"Weeping Stone water is break curse!" Oli shouted again, then rushed over to Man who stood in the middle of a growing puddle. Everywhere the water touched, Nestlecles' cursed sand was receding. Almost as if running from the wet, leaving only a slosh of mud behind.

"What is that?" the sorcerer asked, frowning. "What's happening?"

"Stones still talk to Man?" Oli asked and his cousin nodded. "Man can ask stones make more water?"

He was silent a moment, ears turned inward.

"Stones ask salty or fresh?

Oli shrugged.

"Fresh?"

"Stones ask how much?"

Oli smiled wide.

"Lot. Lot water." And before he could get any more words out, the trickle of water running from the Weeping Stones exploded into a roaring torrent.

"Whoaaaaaahhwooo!" Man shouted as he was lifted off his feet, then propelled around the room by the deluge. Everywhere the water hit, Nestlecles' cursed sand sloughed away. A group of a dozen sandfolk took blasts full in the chest and instead of falling into grains, this time the sand was washed from them—revealing living flesh beneath.

The people yawned, then pried their eyes open, faces drowsy as if they'd just had a centuries-long nap which, as a matter of fact, they had.

"No, no, no! Stop that!" Nestlecles shouted—until a hand came down on his shoulder. He was spun around to find himself face to face with Delphine, her body fully freed from its sandy prison.

"I've waited a couple hundred years to do this," she said, then socked him across the jaw. At least one tooth flew free as he spun, then collapsed to the sand. Or, what had been sand and was now rapidly being replaced by mud.

The sandfolk that hadn't been touched by the water rushed forward to protect the sorcerer.

"Waaahhaaahooo!"

They made it about five steps before Man rocketed by and soaked them. He continued about the place, bouncing off the walls, the ground, and even the ceiling at one point when the force of the water blasted him straight up. Inevitably, though, gravity won out and Man's echoing cheer followed him back to the ground. The impact was enough to knock Man free of the stones.

"Thank for give Key!" Oli shouted to Nestlecles. "Goblins take to Big Boss, but stomach no like you."

If Nestlecles heard, he gave no indication beneath the

dog pile of formerly sand people—who were now just regular people—building on top of him.

"I knew you could do it!" a gravelly voice called and Oli turned to see Sherrock holding the stones and drenched in water, but smirking nonetheless. "Nestlecles' curse worked by denying water to the people, so the best thing to undo it was water freely given," he said. "I knew you'd figure it out, kid."

"Uh…" For lack of anything else to do, Oli nodded. "That it. Oli… Oli know that."

Sherrock dug a little patch of ground out and planted the stones in it. When he stepped back, they stayed in place, still issuing forth a torrent of rushing water.

"Stones say they happy," Man said, pouring water from his ears. "Stones like make fresh water here."

"Well, it's not the wellspring," a voice said and Oli turned to see Delphine knee deep in the quickly forming river. "But it just might work."

As she spoke, the little depression they'd all been standing in began to fill. And to flow toward the cliff. Except, they weren't in a depression, Oli realized, but an old dried-up canal. And the cliff had once been a waterfall. As he watched, it became one again as the rising water fell off its edge.

There was a dry pool there—but it wasn't dry for long as the falling water splashed into it, frothed and foamed, then spread through a network of canals leading across the rest of the city. Everywhere the water went, sandfolk were washed away and people were reawakened. And more, the buildings—once old and decrepit, began to change. The water swept by and took with it the years of neglect that'd reduced them to ruins. Proud, strong homes and businesses and temples were left behind, looking for all the world as if all they needed now was a fresh coat of paint. Plants sprouted, as well, as the water passed and the city of Sandlantis awoke from its slumber.

"Whoa…" Oli said, mouth agape as he took in the sight. Somewhere deep inside, he started to feel all warm and fuzzy, which was new and weird.

The water hit the far wall of the underground canyon and then a great tremor ran through the earth. Oli was near bucked from his feet as the great sandstone column beside him cracked, then teetered, then collapsed to one side. It ripped a great chunk of the ceiling away and for the first time in centuries, true sunlight poured into the city.

"Arrest that goblin!" A shout from behind and Oli turned to see Sergeant Lastrof running toward him. "Don't let him get away! Don't let—"

A roar drowned her out as Lin Two revved the throttle on the wagon.

"Maybe Oli hop in now?" she asked. "Goblins go?" She pointed at the fallen sandstone column which happened to have made what was probably a mostly serviceable ramp up and out of the city. "Goblins go?" Lin Two asked again and Oli beamed.

"Goblins go."

THIRTY-FIVE

At The Risk Of Being Overly Modest

After so long in the stuffy corridors and endless sand of Fortress Isolgar, the fresh air of the desert surface was a refreshing change of pace. Or, at least, Oli imagined it would be once they got there. Lin Two had the wagon at full throttle but it wasn't moving as fast as it used to. Maybe that was because of the steep ramp they were climbing, or maybe it was because of how bumpy said ramp was, or maybe still it was simply because the toppled over pillar had never meant to be used as a ramp in the first place. It was definitely one of those.

Nonetheless, the *Master Viktor Is A Genius Self-Propelled Rocket Wagon XXI* managed to launch itself up the ramp, to the surface, then right off the end of said ramp in a flaming arc. There was one brief, beautiful moment of flight—the wind in Oli's ears, the blue sky above, the desert below—then the wagon slammed down to the ground. Its airspeed fought against the speed the ground wanted it to go and the result was a screeching spin—the screeching mostly coming from the goblins holding on for dear life. The momentum finally subsided when the wheels on one side stuck fast in deeper sand and the whole wagon rolled over. Wood crunched, metal groaned, and the goblins were thrown clear off.

Oli pulled his face from the ground and spat a mouthful of sand as his vision steadied.

"Cousins okay?" he called, stumbling to his feet. "No get squished?"

The first response was a whinny from Horse who, it appeared, had somehow landed on his feet. Probably it was easier when you had four of them, Oli thought.

"Lin Two good," the sand beside Oli said as his cousin emerged from it. She fished around behind her a moment, then pulled Lin One up as well. The rest of the cousins were scattered about, but in a hurry, Oli gathered them all up.

"Come cousins, need dig!" he shouted, pointing to the wagon. "Must to make stand up."

Getting the sand away from the half-buried rocket wagon turned out to be the easier task, seeing as next they needed to flip it upright. Hob stared at the impossible feat before them and blew air through his cheeks.

"Genie man help flip wagon?" he asked with an expectant look.

"Does it look like your idiot cousin knows how to read yet?" the genie snapped back.

"Hob no know," he said with a shrug. "Hob no can read either."

The genie gave an exasperated sigh, but didn't stop Robert from trying to flip the wagon over.

"Big Boss flip wagon?" Lin One asked, then peeked up toward the sky.

"Big Boss help goblins!" Man said, arms spread wide as if the Dark Lord himself were reaching down to pick them up.

"Big Boss no help goblins," Oli said as another thought bobbed to the surface of his mind. Seemed they were doing that more often now. He wasn't sure he liked the sensation. But he was sure of what he said, despite the aghast looks of his cousins.

"Big Boss no help goblins," he said again. "Goblins help goblins. Come, we lift!"

It took some arguing still, but thankfully Gob agreed and managed to shout everyone into place on the same side of the wagon and heaving at the same time.

"And... lift! Lift!" Gob shouted, giving a cadence to their struggle. "And lift!"

"Arrest... arrest those... goblins!" a weak shout came from behind. Oli looked over his shoulder to see a thoroughly winded Sergeant Lastrof stumbling up the ramp. "With all... due... haste," she managed between wheezing breaths.

"*Lift!*" Gob called one last time and the wagon gave

way a little, groaned, then momentum took over and it rolled the rest of the way up.

His cousins started to cheer, but Oli cut them short with his panic.

"In, in! Get in! We go! Goblins go! Goblins go now!" He swatted at his cousins, chasing them into the wagon, then scooped their new packages from the ground—and most importantly, the Key—then climbed aboard.

Seeing them so close, Sergeant Lastrof found her second wind and managed to up her speed to a determined trot. Two of her most dedicated officers emerged behind her—or maybe they were her most in-shape.

Not too far off to the side, Oli could just make out the leaning stone heads where they'd begun this whole misadventure. Beside them milled a flock of saddled terror birds, their reins staked into the ground.

Neither Lastrof nor her officers made for them, though. Instead, they did a stumbly, trotting run right at the goblins and their stationary wagon.

"Lin Two!" Oli shouted. "Go please! Go now!"

"Trying!" she shouted back, but the throttle lever was snapped clean off. Finally, she jammed a finger into the mechanism then pushed forward. The engine roared to life and they exploded forward with a surge of flame—is what would have happened had the wagon been in something approaching working condition. Unfortunately, it'd been mistreated by goblins for days on end so instead of a rocketing blast of flame, what they got was something closer to a puff of smoke, a low grumble, and just enough momentum to get the wheels turning.

"Oh no you… don't," Lastrof puffed as she was forced to increase the pace of her trot to something approaching a canter. "Stop… stop what… " She gave up trying to issue commands in favor of just tucking her head and focusing on running. Her officers weren't able to keep up and both collapsed. Lastrof wasn't so easily beaten, though. She stretched one long arm out, fingers splayed as she reached for the back of the wagon.

Closer…

She could almost reach.

Just a bit… closer…

"Excuse you! I'm trying to teach here," the genie snapped, then smacked her between the eyes with a hard-back edition of *I Can Read My ABC'S*. Lastrof went down with a surprised grunt and would have rolled dramatically a few times if she'd been running at all fast. Instead, she just kind of plopped.

Hob blew a raspberry at the fallen sergeant and Lin One scooped a handful of sand from the bottom of the wagon and chucked it at her.

Grunting through the distinctly book spine-shaped welt rising across her face, Lastrof clenched her fist and staggered to her feet. She would have dwindled from view, then, as the goblins roared toward the horizon, if they had in fact been roaring toward the horizon. Instead, they were still within earshot when one of her officers shouted about getting the terror birds.

Lastrof's eyes lit up at that and a wicked smile pulled across her sand-stuck face. She turned to the stone heads, ready to retrieve her mount. But there was a figure there. A stone man next to the stone heads.

Detective Sherrock Stones.

He had all the terror birds' reins in one fist.

"What are you doing?" Lastrof snarled.

"Something I may very well come to regret." He took a long pull of his pipe. "Though, at the risk of being overly modest, I must say, I'm rarely wrong." And with that he released the reins, then clapped his stony hands together.

The resulting crack sent the birds jumping and squawking as they scattered about the area.

Sergeant Lastrof howled and chased the nearest one. Meanwhile, Sherrock met Oli's eyes. The golem wrapped his knuckles over his heart then tilted an ear down as if listening for something inside. When he was sure Oli had seen that, he smiled, then raised his pipe in a small salute.

THIRTY-SIX

Chaos Wagon

"But how are we 'sposed to walk on goop?" the guard sergeant asked, and it took every ounce of resolve in Germund Stonemixer to stop from face palming.

"Ooh, maybe stepping stones?" one of the cadets answered, waving a hand in the air. "Me sister-in-law's got this little pond whatsit and she plopped stones down so you's can walk across w'out getting your fancy slippers wet." He paused, frowned. "Not that I make a habit o' wearin' slippers, mind you, fancy or otherwise."

"No, no. Nothing like that," Germund said and the guard cadet looked relieved that no one was accusing him of an overfondness for slippers. "The putty rock looks like 'goop' now, but it won't *stay* that way," he explained for what had to be the twentieth time that morning. It was bad enough he kept getting sidelined to answer questions from every curious passerby, but now every new shift of the guards was curious too.

It's okay, he told himself, trying to stop from fuming. Questions are good. Questions are the precursor to under-standing. He took a long breath and steeled his resolve once more.

"Putty rock will change the world," he said, launching into his trusty spiel. "You see, it's—hey! Keep out of that!" A gaggle of children were huddled over the far edge of the 'goop' and drawing anatomically implau-sible images in it. "Get them away from there!" Germund shouted at his assistants who ambled over to chase the kids away. "And someone please smooth those... drawings," he said, gesturing at them. "I won't have my crowning achievement despoiled with—what was that?"

"What was what?" the guard sergeant asked, brow furrowed. The cadet next to him frowned suspiciously at the putty rock.

"*That,*" Germund said as he heard the sound again. Or, more specifically, the voice. Stiff, measured, and—he shuddered at the thought—giving driving directions. He spun, peered out the gate, and...

"Bright Queen's mercy. Close the gate! Hurry! Close it!"

"What are you shouting about?" the sergeant asked, but there wasn't time to explain. Already they were too close. Germund threw himself against the door, heaving with all his might as, just down the road, a smoking, shak-ing, rattling mess of a rocket-powered wagon approached.

"Not… again," Germund growled as he shoved with his full might against the gate. "Assistants, help me!"

They loitered about, seeming just as confused as the guards.

"Boss, is that…?" Another voice from behind and through his straining exertion, Germund could make out two bakers who'd frozen midstep.

"Bright Queen's mercy, not again!" they cried, then rushed to set down the massive cake they carried and throw themselves against the gate as well. The additional weight was enough to get the thing moving, but not fast enough to close before the goblins and their chaos wagon arrived.

"What's that look like to you?" the guard sergeant asked his cadet as they both peered through the slowly closing gate. "Some sort of wagon? On fire?"

"Oh no. Oh no, no, no!" A piping, panicked voice and a mouse of a man threw down the boxes he was carrying in order to help close the gate. "Stay away from my manuscript you monsters!" he shouted and pushed with all of his might. Between the four of them the gate creaked, groaned, then swung shut with a resounding thud.

The city's defenses had stood against more than their fair share of sieges and natural disasters. There was no reason to doubt them and yet, as the roaring outside grew louder, Germund found himself backing away from the gate and chewing on his lip.

The gate would hold, surely?

The roaring grew to a fever pitch and he threw himself to the side. Instead of a resounding crash, there came that odd, stiff voice again, just audible on their side of the walls.

"Alternate route found! Turn right onto unnamed road. Turn right!" it screamed and then there was a squealing of wheels, a groaning of wood, and a great whooshing of air just out of sight.

* * *

"Come now, push! Get it on there," Xander called as his laborers fought and strained to get the modified blast forge mounted on the rear of the carriage. Lord Maricelli had graciously allowed his stables to be converted into a work-shop so Xander could focus on his task.

"I don't think it's going to fit, sir," the head laborer said as his crew cursed and sweated.

"It'll fit," Xander said, his tone stuffed to the brim with confidence. "I designed it to fit," he said, quieter this time. Though, truth be told, the equations weren't really working out. Even with all the modifications he'd made, the blast forge still weighed a quarter ton and that was without accounting for fuel to feed it. It really didn't provide much thrust—certainly not enough to offset its weight—but, well, Lord Maricelli wanted his carriage exactly like... like that monstrosity they'd seen. That beautiful, terrible monstrosity.

But it was okay, everything was fine. Xander was the foremost inventor this side of the Everblight and he'd prove it. So what if his forge didn't explode with eardrum rupturing force? It still shot out some... burps of flame. And besides, who needed all that spectacle and foul smoke? His design was better because even if it was a bit lacking on thrust, well, that's what all the sails were for. And also the air paddles. Then, when the wind was blowing right, and a full complement of servants were rowing, and maybe a few horses were pulling up front, well then, those goblins and their ridiculous wagon had better watch out!

Ha! The thought was enough that Xander almost let

out a little cheer. Except, someone was already cheering. No, screaming.

Xander scanned his laborers, worried what he'd find, but the sound was coming from further away. Looking out across the perfectly manicured lawn, he could just spy the Kings Way Bypass, and on it, a hurtling plume of smoke.

The wagon! Gods above, it was back!

"Spyglass!" Xander snapped, hand splayed behind him. "Spyglass!" he shouted again before it was plopped into his palm. Raising it to his eye, he turned the dial and brought the distant creation into focus.

It was in terrible shape. A smile spread across Xander's face.

"Oh, would you look at that?" The engine casing was all beaten and cracked such that fire spewed from all the wrong places. And the smoke coming out was entirely the wrong hue. Looked like the machine was burning itself up. The wheels, too, were bent out of shape and missing spokes. Even the chassis of the thing was battered so much as to be unrecognizable. Still, it was moving faster than a thoroughbred at full gallop.

"Look at it! It's shedding pieces by the moment!" And then Xander let out a cheer. "Where's Lord Maricelli?" he called, lowering the spyglass. "Quick, someone send for him! He must see th—"

There was a crash from all too close and Xander turned in time to see his blast forge come tumbling free of the rear of the carriage. The sudden change in weight caused the front end to tip forward and slam into the ground. The impact spooked the horses and they took off at a wild gallop, eyes crazed. The wind was blowing against them, however, so just as the carriage crept free of the stables the sails snapped taut and yanked it in the opposite direction. The resulting groaning snap was decidedly not fine as the carriage was ripped in two.

"Xander?" A chilling voice from behind. A lord's voice. "You sent for me?"

* * *

"We ha-ave bo-ooks," Henchperson Seventy-Six said, smiling wide at the stack cradled in the cold, gray flesh of his arms.

"No '*ha-ave bo-ooks*'," Henchperson Fourteen corrected, focusing on remembering to speak clearly and smoothly, like Left was teaching them. "We have... books." He nodded as he sounded the sentence out bit by bit. Yes, that was correct. "Henchpeople speak... better now."

"Henchpeople no long-ger... *longer* speak like Master Percival make," Henchperson Fourteen said, frowning as he focused, then smiling when he got it right.

"Left will be proud of us when we get home," Henchperson Seventy-Six said, eyes turned toward the horizon where Castle Melkior was just drawing into view. "The library excursion has been a success."

Their plodding steps continued down the road and their plodding conversation along with it, neither perturbed by the confused stares of the mammoth riders and wagons passing by. Surely, though, they were an odd sight. There were plenty of strange things one saw along the road, but two massive humanoids made of re-animated flesh, seemingly stitched together at every joint, were among the strangest. Right up there, in fact, with a shuddering wagon full of goblins hurtling down the middle of the bypass with no apparent understanding of the incredibly important term "lane."

At the approaching sound, Henchperson Seventy-Six's ears perked up, straining the stitches that kept them on.

"I know tha-at… that sound," he said. "It is the *Master Viktor Is A Genius Self-Propelled Rocket Wagon XXI.*"

"I do not like that name anymore," Henchperson Fourteen said. "And it is no longer Master Viktor's wag-gon. Sorry. *Wagon.*" He turned around as he spoke, careful not to drop the stack of books.

"Goblin friends!" the Henchpeople said in unison. They moved to wave, but seeing as they were overburdened with books, it was the best they could do to give a little wiggle.

"Henchpeople!" a cry came back, but the wagon didn't slow.

"Pull back throttle lever to slow fuel to the engine and enter neutral, please," Henchperson Fourteen said.

"No can, sorry!" the goblin they recognized as Oli shouted as the wagon heaved and shuddered.

Henchperson Seventy-Six frowned as he kicked up into a stiff jog, the books bouncing along with him.

"Why can you not slow?" he called.

"Goblins go home! Back to Kingdom of Darkness. But must go quick!" Oli shouted from the back of the wagon, leaning out to be heard.

"Why must you go quick?"

"Goblins in trouble!" Oli shouted, then pointed. As he did, a screech came from behind and both henchpeople turned to see three police officers astride some sort of large, seemingly flightless birds. The creatures should not have been able to keep up with the *Master Viktor Is A Genius Self-Propelled Rocket Wagon XXI,* but it was clear to both henchpeople the wagon had seen far better days.

"Out of the way, freaks!" a policewoman shouted as

she rode past, nearly knocking over Henchperson Fourteen and his books.

As quickly as they'd appeared, the goblins, their wagon, and the police officers were gone, rushing down the road and out of sight, a panicked mammoth trumpeting as they passed.

Henchperson Seventy-Six felt a frown pull at his stiff face as he processed all of that.

"Goblin friends are in trouble? We-e must he-elp!" he said, losing grip of his pronunciation as concern stirred in his stomach. "Bu-ut ho-ow?"

* * *

"Commander Argont, sir? It's urgent!" a soldier burst into the tent, throwing the flaps wide and flooding the space with daylight.

"Bright Queen's mercy!" the commander swore as pain stabbed into his eyes. Used to be he considered that phrase closer to a blessing than a swear, but lately, well, a lot had changed, hadn't it? "What do you want, son?" he growled while, internally, *the voice* had it's own thoughts on the matter.

Do not suffer this insolence! You are an officer! A nobleman! Seemed it'd been doing that more and more these days. The commander found his hand was on the hilt of the dagger. When had it gotten there?

"Come on, soldier. Out with it!" he snapped to distract himself from the thought.

You cannot distract yourself from me, Argont. We are one. Our destinies are intertwined.

"There's been a message sir, through the Web. Top priority. It's from a… Sergeant Lastrof?"

"Lastrof? What does she want?" Argont made the

gesture to summon the Web. With a few flicks of his finger he found the correct strand, then on it, the message. "What is this nonsense? 'Rocket-powered goblins?' She lost her mind?"

Everyone has except you, Argont. And me. Us.

The commander strode from the tent, ignoring the dagger.

"Armolas!"

"Sir!" the elf snapped to attention.

"Look down there, son. Tell me, what do your elf eye —" He stopped, took in a breath. "Sorry. What do your non-racially specific eyes which happen to be better than ours see?"

The elf sighed, then turned and stared across the rolling hills and farmland.

"I… well, sir."

"Out with it."

"Well it's kind of like if you strapped a bunch of fire-works to a wagon?"

THIRTY-SEVEN

The Manufacturer Is Not Liable For Any Damage Sustained From Use Of Vehicle Outside Of Its Intended Purpose

The good news was the wagon had stopped trying to take flight every hundred feet. The bad news was that was on account of the side falling off. It'd happened all at once with only hours of creaking and groaning by way of warning. The silver lining was the wagon weighed less overall so now it moved faster, right? Still not fast enough to outrun Lastrof, though.

Lin Two had run the engine day and night and yet Lastrof and her two officers were always visible in the distance, leaned over their terror birds and riding hard. Every so often they'd fallen out of sight—and the goblins would rejoice—until they reappeared on fresh mounts. But soon, it wouldn't matter. Soon, Oli and his cousins would be back within the Kingdom of Darkness and the agents of the Bright Queen would be powerless.

"There is a slowdown on your route," Iris said suddenly. Oli looked up from where he'd been bundling loose bits of wood and metal to throw at Lastrof if she got close enough.

"Slow down? No slow down."

"Go faster!" Lin Two agreed, but kicking the throttle lever forward had long stopped working. The original lever had snapped off in the escape from Sandlantis, so for a time she'd used her finger to replace it, but then Horse had generously donated one of his ribs. It did the job well enough. The engine, however, was on its last leg. It spluttered and bucked for all it was worth, which at this point, wasn't much.

"There is a slowdown on your route," Iris said again, this time as the road turned through a copse of trees, then emerged to show there was something in the way ahead.

Soldiers in shining armor had flipped two wagons across the road and were standing around them and waving torches. One of the men had a whistle and was blowing hard on it, the shrill cry echoing in Oli's ears.

"What they want?" Lin One asked.

"They want us to stop," Gob said with mounting dread. "It's a roadblock! Lastrof must have called in support."

"No can stop now," Oli cried. "Almost home!"

"Make wagon jump again!" Hob suggested from the back. "Jump over mean soldiers."

"Wagon no jump anymore," Lin Two said, shaking her head. "We go around."

"Where around?" Oli asked, a panic building in him

now as Lastrof and her officers emerged from the trees behind. "No road to use!" And there wasn't. The soldiers blocking the route ahead were positioned right between two deep ditches.

"Can you find an alternate route, Iris?" Gob called as he scampered up to the floating head. "A back road or something?"

"Alternate route found!" she replied with a hint of pride and the goblins cheered. "In fifty feet, turn left onto unnamed road." The cheers died out as she continued. "Warning! The *Master Viktor Is A Genius Self-Propelled Rocket Wagon XXI* is not rated for backcountry travel. The manufacturer is not liable for any damage sustained from use of vehicle outside of its intended purpose."

Oli spotted the unnamed road ahead and suddenly everything made sense. Even for a goblin, calling the 'alternate route' a road was generous. It was closer to a rockslide waiting to happen.

"Need make decision," Lin Two called nervously as her eyes flitted from the roadblock to the dangerous path and back. "Need make decision now!"

The soldiers were sprinting toward them now, swords in hand. And behind, Lastrof and her officers were picking up speed.

"Left!" Oli shouted, then helped Lin Two pull hard on the wheel.

"Hold on to something!" Gob shouted then grabbed the back of the running board for support. The whole thing splintered in his hand and fell away. He grabbed Oli next, who grabbed Lin Two, who was glued to the wheel, fighting to keep it straight as the road beneath them turned to gravel, then rocks, then the worst kind of mix of loose dirt, downhill slope, and tree roots. The wagon bounced and shook, vibrations shooting through it like a barrage of earthquakes.

On the upside, they had found a way to go faster: gravity.

"You are now on the fastest route," Iris said, though even her floating head was having significant trouble staying in place as they rocketed downward.

"Maa-aaayy-beee wwwee-ee slow doow-wn!" Oli called, his voice bouncing with every furious shake and tremor as the wagon transitioned from driving to outright sliding.

For once, Lin Two agreed. She pulled back on the rib bone throttle lever and the whole thing snapped off in her hand.

"No again!" she cried.

"Brakes!" Gob shouted. "Use the brakes!" He pulled the cord to activate them and all at once the wheels went from bouncing to screaming. Then smashing into splinters and shooting off to either side.

"In two hundred and fifty feet, take the second creek bed on the right," Iris said, but Oli couldn't hear her as the wagon belly flopped onto the slope with a crash and his ears filled with a shrill, grinding sound. Oli was by no means a wagon expert, but he was reasonably sure that wasn't an indication of everything going exactly as it was supposed to.

The wagon skidded sideways, engine spluttering, and the whole thing threatened to tip over into what was sure to be a catastrophic roll.

"Look!" Hob cried suddenly, pointing from where he'd stumbled into Oli. "Home!"

The slope was still whipping by below them, but Oli did his best to focus his eyes and look where his cousin was pointing.

"Home!" Robert cried as well, the unplanned detour down the side of a mountain freeing him—if only temporarily—from the genie's relentless tutelage.

"Home!" Lin Two cheered and then, finally, Oli spotted it. The Swamp of Sadness and Sweaty Under-things! It lay just beyond the bottom of the mountain, off to the southeast. The sight of its impenetrable canopy and gas spewing waters brought an ache to his heart, made the little goblin realize just how homesick he'd been this past week. But the swamp was not their destination. Even the wagon seemed to know that and steered itself away, toward the opposite side of the slope where a great plain spread before them.

The Plains of Abandoned Hope and Paralyzing Fear. Normally they were a desolate place, but now, it looked like a party was underway. Or, two parties, really, though from the look of things, both sides looked eager to rush forward and join together into one big party.

Even as his vision jumped and bumped, skidded and shook, Oli could make out both sides. Nearest their path was a massive host, adorned in white and beige with banners flowing in the wind. Their tents were organized in neat, orderly rows, and war mammoths and siege engines dotted their ranks as a great many soldiers—at least twenty more than Oli could count—organized themselves into battle formations.

The Bright Queen and her Army of the Just.

And across from them was the other party. This one a heaving mass of darkness that buzzed and howled. The soldiers there seemed to jitter and shake, like shadows from a campfire cast on a dark wood. If they were individual soldiers, it was hard to tell as their forms shifted and merged, then split apart again only to merge again some-where else. When Oli squinted, at the center of the force he could just make out a singular point of swirling dark. The rest of the horde gathered around it, like water about a drain, if said water was made of oozing oil and half-coagulated blood. It was the center of all that was evil and foul.

"Big Boss!" Oli cried and now it was his turn to point. "Big Boss, goblins coming! Have Key! Goblins do it!"

But of course, the Dark Lord was too distant to hear. Nonetheless, looking down the slope, Oli could just make out a path around the edge of the plain that would lead them right to the Big Boss.

"Goblins do it," Oli said under his breath. "Goblins have Key and bring."

"In fifty feet, use the second creek bed on the right to—oh no." Iris' stiff voice conveyed little panic, either because it wasn't capable of such emotion or there simply wasn't time. Either way, her floating head blinked, grew fuzzy around the edges, then disappeared entirely as the wagon broke apart and her gem popped free of its socket beside the steering wheel.

The boards beneath Oli's feet gave way next, then the last nails and bolts holding the wagon together broke apart in what almost seemed a coordinated affair. Then the world was a spinning, bouncing, crashing cacophony of sounds and images and a couple rather nasty bumps.

When Oli finally rolled to a stop he was at the bottom of the mountain. Planks of wood, his cousins, and one rather large section of engine came rolling down after him. He dodged the debris and managed to slow a couple of his cousins, lest they go bouncing off somewhere else.

Horse somehow made it down in a stumbling sort of run, his undead hooves kicking at the shale-covered mountainside to slow his descent. Lin Two came next, squealing as she chased Iris' gemstone, reaching to save it from its frantic bouncing trajectory. It pinged off the side of Gob's head and Lin Two flung herself into the air to catch it on the ricochet, then crashed down into a pile of debris.

Robert was the last of the group to arrive, along with the genie, though largely because the genie was levitating them both while beginning a reading lesson on something called "bowels and condiments."

The last pieces of the *Master Viktor Is A Genius Self-Propelled Rocket Wagon XXI* slid down the slope and Oli's stomach felt all wrong at the sight. Felt like he'd eaten an underripe newt. All churny and bubbly and… sad. The word hit him all at once. He was sad. And he didn't like it. A nasty feeling. It was almost like how he'd felt when deciding to betray Nestlecles, but not exactly. That had been something else. Something brighter and active. This was dark and slow. Creeping, almost. Oli decided immediately he didn't like feeling this way. But it was appropriate. The wagon had been a good one and done everything it could to help them. Oli didn't want to see it gone.

The corner of one of his eyes was wet, then. What was that about?

"We miss you, wagon," a voice said and Oli turned to see Lin Two beside Horse. She held Iris' gemstone in one hand and had the other slapped to her brow in a sharp salute. "Rest in pieces," she said, voice shaking.

"We're going to be the ones in pieces if we don't get moving!" Gob shouted as he climbed to his feet. But too late.

A screeching squawk tore through the debris field and Oli turned to find Lastrof and her two officers looming over him from the backs of their terror birds.

All of them were sweating and panting but had wands in hand. At least, those that had hands. The birds couldn't very well wield a wand and honestly, avian intelligence wasn't particularly suited for spell casting.

"Don't move another step!" Lastrof growled as she blinked through the stinging sweat dripping into her eyes. "I've had five hundred miles of your nonsense and if I have to tolerate a single stride more of it…" She swallowed hard. "Well, the Bright Queen won't much mind if I only deliver six goblins. Or five." She jabbed her wand in Hob's face and the sadness in Oli turned hot again. Like it had with Nestlecles. Turned into something that needed a fiercer name. Like… hot sad. No, meaner. Mean sad! No, how about…

Mad.

Oli was mad.

"No to threaten cousins," he said and his little voice did its best impression of a growl. He reached for his curse-mark and as he did, a voice whispered inside his head.

Yessss. Call forth your magic, puny one. Call it for real this time. Call it with anger. With righteous fury. Enact your justice on those who have wronged you.

The voice was sharp as nails across his ribcage and as it spoke, Oli could see a vision of his shadow cousins hacking and slashing, ripping and tearing into Lastrof and her officers. Could see blood splattering across the ground and hear cries of pain echoing down the mountainside. Could see Lastrof ripped to bits and—

No.

What are you doing? the hissing voice inside cried.

Oli shook the sights and sounds from his head. He didn't want that. And while he'd summoned his shadow cousins a half dozen times prior, something inside him now knew that if he summoned them while mad, it would not be like the other times.

Do not turn your back on your potential! You are a servant of smoldering shadow! A courier of cataclysm! You are—

"Oli no mean," he said and his little goblin hand fell away from the cursemark. "Oli no do hurt."

Lastrof smiled at that, knowing she'd won. After all, goblins were just goblins. What could they do besides start a few fires, cause a bit of trouble, then get caught? There was a reason no one paid attention to them, even if this little family had tried to prove otherwise. Goblins were pathetic, and weak, and really, she should have had this triumph long ago. But it didn't matter, the Bright Queen would reward her all the same. She would be—

The tree behind her exploded and the ground shook as a massive creature charged. Something wrapped around her waist, then the world spun as a crushing force squeezed tight and hefted her into the air.

"Bright Queen's Mercy!" she tried to shout, but already her ears were ringing with a deafening sound. A trumpeting blast.

Her officers just had time to cry out before their birds panicked, bucked them off, then sprinted away.

"Ah, ah! Drop those wands," a cheery voice said as the gargantuan foot of a decidedly blonde mammoth pinned one officer down.

"Mam?" Oli asked. "And Flan!" he cheered as he spotted the smiling rider. His cousins joined in, jumping up and down and hollering.

"Well howdy there, little fellas!" Flan called back in his usual singsong voice. "And don't you move an inch, pigs!" he snapped as he faced the officers. One was pinned beneath Mam, and Lastrof was all wrapped up by Mam's trunk, but the last was still free. Wand in hand, he'd scrambled to cover behind a downed tree.

"Don't make no trouble and there won't be no trouble," Flan warned him with a stern gaze.

"How you here?" Oli asked. "Why you here?"

"Well I came for y'all, of course!" Flan said with a laugh. A spell whizzed up at him and he ducked under it. "Someone put out word on Crag's List. Said you guys were in trouble. Something about the police?" He produced a sort of little shield and deflected the next spell, sending it hissing off into the woods. "Never much cared for the feds." He frowned at the firing officer. "Them and their weigh stations. And their overzealous fruit import laws!" He shouted that last bit as he deflected a spell right back at the officer. "And I was headed this way with a delivery anyway," he finished with a shrug.

"You is serve Big Boss?" Oli asked, eyes wide.

"Who?"

"He means the Dark Lord," Gob explained.

"Oh, no."

"You is serve Bright Queen, then?" Oli asked next, suddenly worried.

"Nope." Flan laughed. "I'm an independent businessman," he said, hiking a thumb to his chest. "I serve myself. And besides," he leaned down for this part. "The world's bigger than them two, you know? Work in the hauling business long enough you meet all sorts. You learn life ain't all that black and white so much as it's a spectrum."

Oli wasn't sure what colors had to do with anything, but apparently Flan didn't work for the Big Boss, and he was helping them anyway so that was good, wasn't it?

A frenzy of spells interrupted Oli's deliberations and Flan was near knocked off Mam under the assault.

"I guess I better see to this," he said through gritted teeth. "You kids get on your way now, yeah?"

Oli's cousins didn't need to be asked twice. They burst

into motion, hurriedly forming a ladder to climb onto Horse. But Oli couldn't leave just yet, even if the Dark Lord was in sight.

"Flan and Mam be okay?" Oli asked, another new feeling pulling at his stomach.

"This won't be the first time I've had a run in with the suits," Flan laughed. "Go on, now, get!" He turned back to the last officer and rolled up his sleeves. "You ever been given a wedgie in armor, son?" he cackled manically, then leapt clear of Mam's back.

THIRTY-EIGHT

Good Spooky

Goblins are excellent navigators. When it comes to going, there are few finer. Arriving, though, is a whole other matter. And arriving where they actually intended to? Well, that's right out.

Had Iris not been stuck in jewel form—and jammed deeply in Lin Two's pocket—she would have proposed an alternate route. Any other route, really, than the one the goblins had chosen. Though, perhaps *chosen* was too strong a word for what had really happened. It'd been something closer to several minutes of incoherent screaming, pointing, and then when Horse had had enough, galloping in the direction that'd felt most correct.

Luckily there were helpful drums beating and hell horns wailing down on the plain, signaling where the Dark Lord's army was assembled. Lin Two pulled on Horse's reins and did her best to get them going mostly in that direction. Not directly, though, seeing as the Bright Queen and her Army of the Just were still in the way. No, they'd have to go around that army then come into the side of the Dark Lord's. Simple enough, though both armies looked to be readying to charge at one another. If that happened, well, they'd figure it out. Probably.

"Faster!" Oli called, jumping up and down on Horse's back, but their ignoble steed was already at full gallop. So much time aboard the *Master Viktor Is A Genius Self-Propelled Rocket Wagon XXI* had somewhat redefined Oli's conception of fast. "And no get too close to bad people," he added.

Lin Two's face scrunched up like a shrivelstoad releasing its pollen.

"Me thought we going to bad people?"

Oli pointed to the Dark Lord's army.

"We go to bad people, not *bad* people," he said as he pointed to the Bright Queen's army.

That didn't seem to clear the confusion up.

"No go to *scary* people," Oli said and nodded at the forces of Good.

"We go to scary people instead," Hob said.

Oli sighed.

"Mean people there!" He pointed sharply at the Bright Queen's army so Hob and Lin Two and also himself would understand.

"But mean people there too," Hob insisted, pointing to the Dark Lord's ranks.

"You confused, Hob," Oli began, then realized he was

just as confused. Or, maybe his cousin had a point? He'd never thought about it, really. They all served the Big Boss but the other servants of smoldering shadow had never been particularly nice to Oli and his cousins. Certainly not like Flan had been. Or the Henchpeople. Or even Sherrock Stones, for that matter. But there'd be time to think on that later. They'd come this far, now all they had to do was get the Key to the Big Boss.

"Okay, Horse. You can do!" Lin Two said, slapping his bony, animal skin covered neck in support. "We almost there. You do good! You—"

Oli was flying. And not in the good way.

Faster than his goblin brain had been able to process, a ballista-launched javelin had come whipping in and scored a direct hit on Horse. The result was a rattling explosion of hay and bones as the undead horse shot apart in all directions—and his passengers went flying.

The ground smacked Oli in a decidedly unfriendly manner, then hit him a few more times until he finally stopped rolling. Even then, his eyes swirled a few moments longer, spinning in their sockets.

"Horse!" he cried when he was able to process what had happened. "Horse okay? Horse be okay!" Hay floated to the ground as he scrambled through torn animal skins and loose bones until he found Horse's skeletal head. By some miracle of the Dark Lord, the steed's eye sockets were still glowing.

"Horse okay!" Oli shouted, hugging the skull tight. "Horse be okay!"

And then Lin Two was beside him, reins still in hand but no longer connected to anything.

"Horse…" she began.

Oli held up the skull with a weepy cheer.

"Horse okay!"

Lin Two threw the reins aside and hugged the skull. Its eyes flared a bit at that but due to a distinct lack of a body, that was all.

"Yes, well, I'm glad Horse is okay," Gob said, backing up toward them. "But you won't be able to say the same for us in a few moments." He pointed.

"Uh oh," Hob said. "Bad people here."

"Bad people?" Oli asked hopefully, but as he looked up, he realized it was the other bad people—the good ones.

They'd strayed too close to the Army of the Just and now a detachment had broken off from them and was in the process of surrounding the goblins. Soldiers in gleaming armor and carrying heavy weapons. And not the nice kind of weapon, these looked to be the extra mean kind.

Oli swallowed as the soldiers surrounded them completely.

"Hands in the air!" one of them shouted. "And drop your weapons!"

A spearhead poked Oli in the shoulder but he held tight to Horse's head, defiant.

"No be frighten, cousins," he said, poking his little chest out. "Big Boss help goblins! Big Boss just over there!" But even as he said it, he realized how much distance there was still to go. And the Big Boss hadn't helped them any time they'd needed it so far.

Oli peeked over to Robert and the genie. Despite everything, they were still in a reading lesson. The soldiers were attempting to separate the two, but every time someone got close, their face went slack and they fell to the ground, snoozing.

"Genie man help goblins?" Oli squeaked.

"One wish at a time, kid," he snapped back.

"Wish take too long!" Oli snapped back. "Maybe Genie man no good at teach!"

"Why don't you do it, then?" the genie shouted back. "You come try to teach this rock to read!"

"Robert no is rock!" Oli growled. "Robert can to be smart! Robert can to read!"

"I don't know what you're talking about, but stop it!" The closest soldier raised his spear in Oli's face. Oli slapped it away, then reached for his cursemark.

Yesss. That's right. The voice was back. *Use your anger. Wield it. What other option do you have?* And as it asked the question, visions of violence filled Oli's mind. Visions of his shadow cousins hacking into the soldiers and of the plain running red with blood.

There is no option left to you, goblin. Become a true servant of the Dark Lord. What else is there for you in this world? No one wants you. No one loves you. The voice paused to laugh, long and low. It was a cruel sound, and a growl tinged its edges. *No one even appreciates you.*

As if he could hear the voice, the soldier in front of Oli stepped forward.

"It's time you…" He paused. "Is something… whistling?"

There was a shadow on his head and growing by the moment. The whistling rose to a fever pitch then *wham!* Something about the size of a spooky ghost urn and moving at roughly the terminal velocity of a spooky ghost urn smashed apart against the soldier's helmet.

He went down in a heap, but before his body even hit the dirt, icy fog was spreading across the ground, rolling outward in slow moving waves. And from it rose a familiar looking family of ghosts.

THIRTY-NINE

An Injury To One Is The Concern Of All

"Scary ghost family?" Oli asked, his face numb from shock. Or maybe it was the chilling fog that coated the ground and rose to his waist. "Why you here?"

"They... they came to help us?" Gob asked, disbelief in his voice. "Well that doesn't make any sense." He frowned. "They don't serve the Dark Lord."

The fog parted to reveal finger-width letters scraped into the soil.

"Friends help friends?" Gob read, then shook his head. "They're not our friends. Are they?"

"Goblins help ghosts, now ghosts help goblins!" Lin Two cheered. The ghosts rose up from the mist, taking the closest thing to physical forms Oli had seen as they placed themselves in a defensive circle.

Terrified cries went up from the Bright Queen's forces at the sight.

"Foul creatures from the beyond!"

"Damned souls conscripted into the Dark Lord's service!"

"Is that Uncle Rick?"

Angry, frantic cries.

"We'll send them back where they came from, eh, lads?"

"Evil sorcery is no match for pure hearts!"

"I hated Uncle Rick!"

Someone chucked a javelin. It passed right through the foremost ghost and came out the other side as a translucent, vague impression of a javelin which hit Gob in the chest—and dissipated like candle smoke in a stiff breeze.

The foremost ghost waved a finger at the soldiers and as she did, an invisible hand drew more letters in the dirt. They were too far away for Oli to read—not that he could anyway—but the soldiers' faces went pale as they read the message.

"That's how it's gonna be, huh?" one shouted back. "Let's have at it, then!"

But something was whistling again. Oli looked up to see a massive figure plummeting toward them. It was shiny —made of some sort of metal?—and shaped like, well, like a big person.

Soldiers scrambled out of the way as the figure came crashing down, a fist and one knee making contact first such that it landed in a really cool looking crouch.

"Whoa," Oli said with a little gasp as the impact caused a shockwave that bowled several soldiers over.

Debris and dirt rained down for a moment, but as the dust settled, Oli got a better look at the thing.

It was a metal giant, two or three times taller than a person and held together by all manner of welded joints and driven rivets. A hatch on the back popped open and Oli was treated to a view of complex inner workings far beyond his understanding. Until a head leaned out.

Gray, slack features, with stitches all over the skin, and little jolts of electricity running below the surface.

"Wo-ork together?" it asked as the slack features pulled into a smile.

"Henchpeople?" Oli asked, but his brain was well behind his mouth.

"Henchpeople!" Man shouted, jumping up and down. It took a moment for Oli to realize he was pointing up. Up to where the sky was filled with little white dots, growing bigger by the moment. They were some sort of sheets? Filled with air and slowing the descent of—

"Henchpeople!" Oli cheered. Dozens of them, each dangling beneath a sheet. They began to touch down all around the goblins and Oli had never been so happy to see so many cobbled-together reanimated corpse people. And even better, they had weapons! Probably? They carried neither swords nor spears, but strange cylinders strapped to their backs with wires and cables running from them to weird, metal stick things that looked kind of like the spouts of watering cans. One henchperson swung the device overhead and instead of water, the spout spewed a swirl of howling flame.

"An inj-jury to one is the con-cern of all!" he shouted.

The soldiers of the Bright Queen gasped and stumbled back as the other henchpeople echoed the cry and released similar bouts of flame.

"No gods, no masters!" another cried, then turned to Oli and nodded. "Just cousins."

There was a warmth in the little goblin's chest, then, unlike any he'd felt before. Even more than the first time he'd met Horse. He tried to say something back, but his heart felt too full, and his mouth was doing this weird shaking thing, and he just couldn't get the words out right. Oli settled on a nod and slapped his hand against his forehead in the sharpest salute he could manage.

If the Bright Queen's forces had faltered before the ghosts, now they looked to be actively worrying if they'd renewed their life insurance policies. Especially when the henchperson-piloted metal giant rose up to tower over everyone. Doubt ran through the forces of good in a visible ripple. Soldiers shifted from foot to foot, spears lowered, and even the banners were abandoned by the wind, left to droop limply.

"Wait..." Oli said suddenly as a thought hit him. "Have question." He frowned at the ghosts then the hench-people, then furrowed his brow. "How all come so fast?"

"When Seventy-Six and Fourteen saw you on the road, we knew we had to act," the nearest henchperson answered. "So Left and Right used the Web to mes-sage everyone who left you good reviews."

"That smart!" Oli chirped. "But no answer question?"

"Well, that nice ghost family and us weren't the only ones who decided to come. Someone else wanted to help, and offered us a lif-ft, too."

One single, low note echoed from the skies. It was a reedy, bird-like sound. And then the henchperson was smirking. There was a massive crash next, the ground bucked, and the soldiers of the Bright Queen screamed in panic as the biggest newt in the world landed with a roar and a plume of fire.

"Hail and well met, dragon-friends!" she growled and the air shook with her words. Even the genie was momentarily distracted from teaching.

"Whoa, a dragon," he said, eyebrows high. They furrowed next, though. "Why do I feel like I know you?"

The dragon smiled at the goblins—her gaping maw curling open to reveal a forest of teeth—then turned to face the soldiers of the Bright Queen, or, those she hadn't already crushed in her calamitous arrival.

"Thou reek of righteous honor and performative good deeds," she said and the resulting wash of flame rolled across their ranks and sent them fleeing.

"Goblins is saved!" Lin One cheered and bounced up and down. Her cousins joined her, even Gob, who had a permanent look of shock plastered across his face.

"Goblins is saved!" Oli cheered, arms in the air. "Thank friends, thank!" He'd never felt so happy, so loved. It was enough to bring a tear to his little oily eyes. Enough to make him squint. Or maybe the squinting was on account of that strange point of impossibly bright light that was getting closer? Why was it human-shaped?

FORTY

The Might To Be Found In The Meek

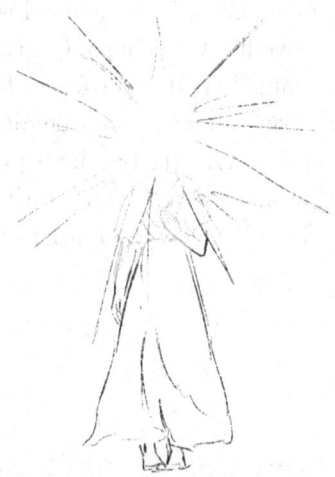

It's said the hottest thing in existence is dragon fire (despite the protestations of a couple chili pepper farmers and the winner of last year's Miss Kingdom of Darkness pageant). Staring at the thing approaching them now, however, Oli was pretty sure *she* was the hottest thing in existence. And not in the good way. More in the 'slough your flesh from your bones, reduce what's left to ash, then burn that as well' kind of way.

It was as if the sun had been condensed down to human size, then taken the form of a woman. As if Oli had never known true light until this very moment. As if the very moisture of his eyeballs was boiling off. No, wait. That last bit was actually happening.

"This bad. This very bad," he said as he rubbed his sizzling eyes with his knuckles.

"Bright Lady..." Lin Two said, staring despite the pain.

"That's not just any bright lady," Gob said, dread in his voice. "That's the Bright Queen."

Oli was no wordsmith, but in the moment, 'bright' a rather underwhelming description. He'd have worked on a better one if his tiny brain wasn't presently being cooked in its own juices.

She strode across the plain and the world was brighter for it—literally. She glowed with such intensity that even the sun's light looked shady in comparison and was burned away.

She might've been tall, she might've been fair, she might've had imperious features, but Oli really couldn't say. In the wake of her arrival, about all he could say was "this bad," "this very bad," and also "ow, ow, ow why head feel like boil from inside?"

The sight of her was so overwhelming it was suffocating—for Oli and his cousins. For her own forces, the Bright Queen's presence on the field of battle was inspiring. Seeing her stride toward their enemies, they found hope in their hearts again—and a deep desire not to let their beautiful queen down.

Oli wanted to run but his feet felt like they were melted to the ground, and he couldn't stop staring.

"So you're the ones Lastrof warned me about?" the voice sounded in Oli's ears and rebounded around inside his head. The queen was too far for him to physically hear and yet her words were impossible to ignore. "Funny little creatures, aren't you? Some might even say insignificant. But that's where your power lies, doesn't it? So often we overlook the might to be found in the meek."

"Oli have no might," he said but even in his own mind the words were burned away, so forceful was the Bright Queen's presence.

"You have impressed me, little goblins. You eluded the best of my servants, even the detective."

That wasn't entirely how Oli remembered things happening, but the Bright Queen seemed interested only in what she had to say.

"Oli!"

"It's a shame you serve my nemesis, we could have used your talents. Yet another tragedy of the Dark Lord." She sighed then—an impressive thing seeing as she was a hundred paces away still, but Oli heard it clear as could be.

"Oli!"

"There will be many tragedies here today, I fear. But that is the cost of banishing evil once and for all."

"Oli!" Someone was shouting his name. Lin Two, he realized, as she slapped him. "What you do?" she cried, staring into his eyes with concern.

Oli shook himself awake and it was only then he realized he could control his body once again. And the Bright Queen wasn't calmly striding toward him but locked in combat with his allies. His friends.

The ghosts swirled around her on one side, tendrils of ice and walls of fog washing against her radiant brilliance only to be burned away. She cast out a hand and the ghosts were scattered before a shimmering light and forced to regroup several paces back.

The henchpeople picked up the slack, however, drowning the queen in an ocean of snarling flame. It got within a pace of her before a golden orb flashed into existence. It shielded her, boiling, popping, and shining as brightly as the queen herself. In the face of such radiance, it was the fire that was burned away.

The henchpeople weren't yet done, though. Their metal giant plunged into the fray, punching at the queen with mechanical, steam-powered might. She caught the blows in her open palms and redirected them to the side, each of her movements as graceful as if waving to adoring crowds while on parade. And all the while, her advance on the goblins continued.

"Thou stink of righteous self-belief and unhealthy beauty standards!" the dragon roared and soared toward her. "Mine nostrils can hardly bear the stench!"

"Perhaps you should go somewhere else, then?" the queen suggested and, with a wave of her hand, the air in front of her split apart. For a brief moment, Oli found himself staring at somewhere completely different. A tropical coast with drooping palm trees and gentle crashing waves. The dragon's momentum carried her right into the picturesque scene then, with a snap, the portal closed and the dragon was gone.

"That should handle her for an hour or so," the Bright Queen said, a self-satisfied smile creeping into her face. Or maybe Oli imagined that last bit seeing as looking at her directly was likely to burn his eyes from his head.

"Oli! What wait for?" Lin Two shouted, shaking him now. "Goblins go!"

"Goblins go?" Oli's thoughts came slower than usual.

Things picked up a bit though when one of the hench-people stepped in front of him, blocking his view of the Bright Queen. Only then could Oli think freely.

"Goblins go-o," the henchperson said. "We will handle this."

"It no safe!" Oli protested.

The henchperson pulled a lever on his weapon and it clicked in a way that somehow sounded both cool and dangerous.

"Nothing worth doing is." And with that the hench-person spun and unleashed a burst of flame into the approaching forces of Good.

"Goblins go!" Oli shouted as he ran the other way.

Probably it was a good idea seeing as everyone else was going too. Just, in the wrong direction. Seeing the Bright Queen's army charge, the Dark Lord's forces had done the same. Now, they rushed past the goblins, weapons held high as they plunged in to battle their sworn enemies.

It was all Oli could do to lead his cousins in a weaving, frantic sprint through the stampede of orc feet, and troll feet, and even some creatures so foul as to not need feet.

Ahead, through the chaos, Oli could just make out a looming shadow. A darkness foul and ancient. The Big Boss. And they had a delivery for him.

* * *

No, no, *no*! Those pesky goblins had shown up at exactly the wrong time!

It was the last thing the Lieutenant of Lament needed seeing as already the day had veered off plan. First of all, Dr. Viscous had deployed his troops in entirely the wrong place, but somehow, that was still better than Warlock Dan who'd failed to show at all. All those resources they'd sunk into his geistsword experiment and for what? A no-show on the day of days? And then what of Nestlecles and his sand-folk army? The lieutenant hadn't been foolish enough to rely on them, but Nestlecles always had a way of coming through when it counted. Not today, though. No, today was a disaster. A disaster the goblins were making worse by the moment.

The Lieutenant of Lament cursed under her breath as her long-prepared battle plan fell to pieces.

All that work to get the Legions of Smoldering Shadow arrayed just right, to bait the Bright Queen's forces into an open battle, and not to mention, dam up the volcano so at just the right moment it could be unleashed to sweep through the forces of Good.

All of it ruined.

The Army of the Just had followed their queen in charging the goblins. Then the Legions of Smoldering Shadow, already jumpy enough as it was, had followed suit. Now the whole battle was wrong, being fought off to one side and out of range of the volcano trap.

But... the goblins were back. Could they possibly have...?

The Lieutenant of Lament nearly perished as the thought crossed her infernal mind. A moment of focus, though, and she realized the implications.

If the goblins had somehow succeeded and returned with the Key, then it wouldn't matter. The Dark Lord could join it with the Lock and unleash his ultimate weapon! The Army of the Just would become the Army of Dust. Or, something like that. It wasn't her job to know the specifics of how the ultimate weapon worked. It was her job to serve the Dark Lord. A job that, admittedly, hadn't been going all that well of late. But by whatever infernal gods there were, the goblins were back and if they had the Key, well, the Dark Lord didn't *need* to know it was them who'd returned it, did he?

A little lie never hurt anyone.

FORTY-ONE

Wriggly Little Lies

"Stay where you are!" a voice boomed.

Oli was in the middle of darting between another orc's legs when something reached out and tried to grab him. His naturally slimy coating did its thing, though, and he slid free. But the attempt was enough to get him to look back and see a familiar suit of infernally cursed armor.

"Ms. Lieutenant of Lament!" he said. The instinctive smile that jumped to his lips made it look he was happy to see her, but his stomach seemed to have a different opinion as it gurgled uncomfortably.

"I said stop running!" she shouted and spread her arms wide. As she did, each piece of armor broke free and spread out to form a wall in front of the goblins. The disparate pieces were linked together by some sort of shadowy, oil-slick substance. The sight was enough to stop the rest of the goblins.

"That's... better," the amorphous shape said, then cleared its throat as the pieces of armor all clicked back into place and the lieutenant reassembled herself.

"Good news, Scary Lieutenant of Lament lady!" Oli chirped, ignoring the feeling in his stomach in favor of focusing on said good news. "Goblins be couriers of cataclysm and bring Key! Goblins do good for Big Boss!" He paused, frowned. "Or do bad for Big Boss, maybe?"

Questions of semantics didn't seem to bother the lieutenant, nor the dozen troll guards waiting behind her. She snapped her fingers and the guards stomped forward, hands out to capture the goblins.

"What game this?" Lin One asked as he darted between a set of massive hands.

"No time for games!" Man added. "Bright Queen lady too close!" And he was right. Even facing away from her, the edges of Oli's vision were burning with radiant light.

"If can please excuse," Oli said as he shot from a troll's grasp like a wet bar of soap. "Goblins take Key to Big Boss, thank!"

"No, I think not," the lieutenant growled as she stepped forward, then clocked Oli on the cheekbone with a backhanded blow. The force of it knocked him onto his back and before he could get up, a troll foot came down heavy, pinning him to the ground.

"There we go," the lieutenant growled. "Finally."

"Please to let go, thank," Oli said, vision still a bit blurry.

"Goblin want be let go," the troll said, looking at the lieutenant. "That okay?"

"No, of course not!"

The troll nodded, then frowned at Oli.

"Sorry, slippy one."

Oli grunted and reached for his cursemark, but he was planted flat on his back and couldn't reach it with the troll's tree trunk-thick leg on his chest.

"Why do this?" Oli cried as the rest of his cousins were cornered and pinned. And now his stomach was properly churning. "Why do this?" he snapped again.

"Nothing personal, kid," the lieutenant said, then paused. "Actually, no. This is personal." She crossed her arms. "Now where's the Key?"

"No have Key!" Oli said and blew a raspberry at her.

"You already said you did."

"Was lying!"

"No, you're lying now. Search them." She gave the order and the trolls set about patting and prodding. One poked Robert particularly hard in the stomach and he burped up the book Nestlecles had asked them to deliver on behalf of Rodrigrar.

"If you don't mind, I'm trying to teach here!" the genie shouted. "Actually, wait. No, it's easier this way," he added, then bent down in front of Robert and continued quizzing him on vocabulary words. Pinned down as he was, there was no escape from the test.

"What's this now?" the lieutenant asked, but not about the genie. Somehow, that didn't seem to interest her half so much as the book. "*His Imperious Majesty The Dark Lord Sarusomal and the Humble Barkeep Rodrigrar Drown the World in Shadow and Sorrow: An Aspirational Fiction, Part II.* 'A gift for the Dark Lord from his humble servant.' This isn't the Key, I don't think…" she began, then paused. "Wait, is there more inside his stomach? Are you… don't tell me you had the big one swallow the Key?"

"Slimy ones be clever," one of the trolls mused.

"No, they're idiots." The lieutenant snapped her fingers. "Go on, poke him some more. Get the Key out of there."

"*Oof oomph urgh!*" Robert protested but there was no stopping the packages he'd swallowed from coming up. The letter addressed to Mishalob first, then the Dark Lord's jar of sourdough starter next. The troll paused and side eyed his boss.

"Is that all of it?" the lieutenant asked scooping them up.

Robert coughed, then gagged and Oli could see there was one more thing inside him, stuck in his throat. Acting without thinking, Oli bit the leg of the troll holding him.

"Yow! Slimy ones be bitey!" the monstrous creature said, his tone wounded.

Oli scrambled over to Robert and pushed away the hand that'd been poking him.

"You have Key! No hurt Robert more!" He covered Robert's mouth, then whispered. "No more vomit, cousin."

"This… is the Key?" the lieutenant asked, holding up the letter with a confused frown.

"No, that letter for Mishalob," Oli said. "*That* Key."

"That?" The lieutenant raised a questioning eyebrow.

"Uh huh."

She picked up the sourdough starter. It was a mess of sticky, beige goop jammed into a glass jar.

"Well, it *is* addressed to the Dark Lord," she said, turning it over.

"Key inside. Nestlecles say only Dark Lord can to open," Oli lied. "Scary goop protect it."

"That no what Nestle—" Robert began but Oli clapped a hand over his mouth again.

"Something tells me you're lying," the lieutenant said, looking Oli straight in his eyes. "So I'm taking these. This one's definitely just a letter, though." She let it fall to the ground as she turned to stride away, then after a few strides, stopped to speak over her shoulder. "And if you're still lying, well, we can always cut you all open. In fact, maybe we will even if you are telling the truth." She laughed at that.

"Big Boss no let happen!" Oli shouted back.

The lieutenant laughed even harder then as she turned back to face them.

"Do you think the Dark Lord actually cares about you? Cares what happens to you?" The laughing was hard enough to shake her armor now, its heavy metal clinking and clacking. "You're not special, you slimy little freak. You're a *goblin*, and goblins are like... I don't know, mosquitos. You serve no purpose, not even as food for more impressive creatures. You just..." She waved her hand idly. "Annoy. Squirm and squeak until someone finally swats you." She stopped laughing then. "And when I get back, I'll personally do the swatting."

"Big Boss no let!" Lin Two yelled back and everyone else joined her.

"Big Boss like goblins!"

"Goblins make Big Boss proud!"

Oli sucked down a breath to join in, but it caught in his throat. Stuck fast because, suddenly, he wasn't so sure it was true. His cousins sure did, yelling and shaking their little fists at the lieutenant's back. All except Gob. Their eyes met a moment and Gob simply gave a sad little shake of his head.

"It's great to be a goblin if you want to be forgotten," he said, and there was a sadness in it Oli hadn't noticed before. "Not so much if you want, well, anything else."

"Goblins no deserve be forgotten," Oli said and there was a rush of adrenaline in his veins then. And a bad idea forming in his head.

FORTY-TWO

One Last Lamentation

All around there was chaos and fighting. The Lieutenant of Lament strode toward the Dark Lord as the Legions of Smoldering Shadow surged past in the other direction, hurrying to join the rapidly intensifying melee at the front line. They didn't have to run far, though, seeing as said front line was moving closer by the moment, driven by the Bright Queen and her ridiculous Bright Knights. Even the cloudy sky above had parted to cast down perfectly brilliant sun beams on them. Whoopity doo. So special. So full of themselves. And soon to be, so dead.

The Lieutenant of Lament dropped to her knees as she arrived in front of the Dark Lord. In his presence, the sounds of the battle fell away. The burning heat of the Bright Queen numbed. For a perfect few moments, all grew still and quiet.

"My Dark Lord Sarusomal, Master of Deceit, Corrupter of the Just, He Who Even the Shadows Fear(™)," the lieutenant said, head bowed and arms out. "It is my sincerest pleasure to deliver unto you, the Key!"

Of course, she wasn't entirely sure which of the items it was, so she presented them both. After all, the Dark Lord was craftier than a gnome in a hobby shop and it would come as no surprise to learn he'd disguised his ultimate weapon as an ordinary object. Wasn't that what all Dark Lords did anyway? Turned the most evil of things into golden rings or hide them in talking journals, or pet snakes or whatever? With the power of the Dark Lord's deception, the Key could have just as easily been the book with the overly descriptive title as the jar with the weirdly beige goop inside. Or… maybe even the letter she'd discarded? The lieutenant suddenly wondered how good an idea that'd been. Perhaps she should go back and get it, just to be sure?

The thought floated around in her mind, stewing a long while. Too long, as it happened. Why wasn't the Dark Lord saying anything? He should have definitely said something by now, right? Perhaps he was just in that much awe? Yes, certainly that was it. He hadn't expected such good news as his ultimate weapon delivered directly into his hands. Even he, in all his dark wisdom, hadn't dared to hope such a victory could be possible. But it was! And it was all because of her, the lieutenant knew.

She allowed the Master of Deceit another moment to gather himself. Probably he was preparing something dramatic to say. Some important words with which to forever cement this historic moment.

Any second now...

* * *

Somewhere off in the battle, there was an agonized scream. Though, funny enough, it didn't come from the direction of the fighting, but back toward the Dark Lord. Strange, but Oli didn't have time to worry about that. He was too focused on saving his cousins and himself.

"Okay, slimy one. You get back down now," the troll Oli had escaped from said and raised one massive foot. "Lieutenant said so."

"Oh, right." Oli did his best to look innocent. "Sorry. Will to get back down, but first have itch."

The troll frowned.

"Huh?"

But Oli had already pressed a thumb to his cursemark. Not out of anger this time. No, as he called forth the shadow servants, he focused on only one thought: saving his cousins. And maybe himself.

The nasty, angry voice did not return. Oli's mind was blissfully silent, just the way he liked it, as the ground cracked and split around them. From the sudden crevices, six familiar damned souls crawled free.

"What you done now?" the troll above Oli asked. "Bad goblin! Tricky goblin!"

"Hello shadow cousins! Good to see!" Oli chirped. "Please to make trolls go away."

"With pleasure, liege," came the hissing reply. The trolls bristled at it and released the goblins in favor of taking fighting stances. They were massive creatures and more than formidable opponents. None of that helped them overly much, however, as the crevices opened wider and more shadow hands reached out to drag them in.

"Is there anything else, liege?"

"No, thank," Oli said and the souls nodded, then with a sinister sort of glee, dived into the crevices after the screaming trolls. The ground sealed back up behind them with a grinding finality.

The genie was still shouting vocabulary words and Robert still looked sick from being forced to barf up the packages. But there was one more inside him.

"Robert no hungry anymore," he mumbled, expression nauseous.

"Sorry, cousin," Oli said, empathizing with him a moment before slapping him on the back until the last package came up.

The cursed hand hit the ground like some kind of shriveled and waterlogged spider. One of its fingers was still missing from where Nestlecles had dropped it and Oli picked it up gently to avoid breaking any more.

"We deliver to Big Boss!" Oli said, holding the Key high. "We deliver to Big Boss and get credit!"

"Deliver to Big Boss then put Horse back together," Lin Two said but there was no excitement in her tone. Something else instead. Hurt, maybe? She missed Horse. And Oli found he did too.

"We deliver then to remake Horse," he said.

"Deliver to Big Boss then friends no more get hurt," Man said, looking to where the Bright Queen had swept the henchpeople and ghosts into one squirming, half-conscious pile.

"We deliver then friends no need fight more," Oli agreed and suddenly these reasons felt more important than getting credit. Felt more important than appeasing the Dark Lord. "Goblins live to serve biggest boss around," he said, reminding himself.

"But goblins no have friends before," Hob added, sad eyes turned to the allies who'd come to save them.

"Goblins no been give gift before henchpeople give wagon," Lin One said.

"Maybe..." Oli paused, unable to give voice to the thought.

"Maybe goblins don't need to only serve the Big Boss," Gob said, finishing what Oli had been on the brink of conceptualizing. "Maybe goblins can serve themselves, too?"

Oli physically recoiled at the thought. That was a dangerous thing to think and even more dangerous to say. But even as he was cowering from the thought, Robert pushed past the genie to shout his approval.

"Goblins can do what goblins want sometimes!"

Oli took in the faces of his cousins as they all nodded. He looked down at the Key next, then up to where they were supposed to be going. To the Dark Lord. Previously he'd been a swirling cloud of shadow at the head of the army, but now he was moving. Toward them!

The Dark Lord! The Big Boss! He was still a good fifty paces away but striding closer, his magmatic eyes wide at the sight of his ultimate weapon in Oli's hands.

Oli's heart leapt at seeing his lord again. Or, well, he'd expected it to. Instead, it sort of did the opposite? What was that about? He was pretty sure his insides couldn't move that much but it really had felt like his heart had dropped. Or... recoiled? And his stomach, too. It was churning and gurgling, and growing worse with each step closer the Dark Lord came.

Oli's mind twisted itself into new shapes to process

what was happening. That was the Big Boss! So why wasn't he excited? Why did he feel... well, bad? There was no other word for it.

He'd traveled all this way and waited all this time to make the Big Boss proud; to be a good courier of cataclysm! He'd been useful, and so had his cousins. So then why did the sight of the Dark Lord leave him feeling bad? Just like—he realized with almost visceral force—just like he had when near Nestlecles.

The feeling seemed reflected in his cousins' faces as well. They all sort of looked around at one another. Oli wasn't gifted when it came to intuition, but in the moment, he had the distinct impression they were feeling the same as him.

"*Klaatu!*" Robert shouted suddenly.

"Huh?" The words broke Oli from his thoughts with the force of a slap. It took him a minute to regain his senses. "What mean?" he asked Robert, who was hanging over his shoulder now. But the mountain goblin wasn't looking out at the Dark Lord, but down at the Key in Oli's hands.

"*Klaatu!*" Robert said again, then pointed at the words carved into the desiccated flesh of the hand. "It make sense. Robert can read it!" He ran a finger along the letters, sounding them out. "This one go '*ka*' and this one '*la*.' Then '*a*' and '*tu*'. *Klaatu!*" he chirped, a wide smile across his face.

"Robert... read?" Oli asked, excitement building in him. "Robert can to read?"

"Robert can to read!"

"Wait, wait, wait!" the genie rushed over. "Explain that again. And speak loud and clear so everyone can hear," he added, eyes turned toward the sky. Oli didn't see anything up there but some clouds and sunbeams, but whatever.

What he did see, however, was the Dark Lord only twenty paces away now and closing the gap quick. He held the Lock in hand, the golden ring reflecting the fires of the battlefield. The sight drained away the happiness Oli felt at Robert's accomplishment. His stomach gurgled again.

Oli looked to the Bright Queen next and his stomach churned even more strongly. Last, he looked at the hench-people, the ghost family, and the dragon. His stomach settled and something like warmth rose up inside. Oli felt... good. Happy.

He looked to his cousins last and found all except Robert were looking back at him. As if waiting for something. For him to decide something.

Gob was the only one to move. He simply gave a long, slow nod.

"Goblins serve biggest boss around," Oli said, explaining what everyone knew. Except, this time when he said it, it didn't feel true. He tried again. "Goblins... serve goblins? Goblins do what goblins... want."

As he said it, words rang in his head. A memory that brought back Nestlecles' instructions. *When once more Lock and Key are near, speak thee such that all may hear, the words upon thy cursed hand, and doom abyss upon the land. Lock and Key once more will meet, the seven seals will be complete, set free will be the hungering heat, and all your foes will know despair.*

Oli lingered on that a moment, then set his brow and fixed Robert with a hard stare.

"Please to read words on Key."

Robert nodded excitedly, then looked down at the shriveled hand Oli held.

"*Klaatu!*" he began, obviously remembering that one. "*Ba-ra-da!*" he sounded that one out confidently. "*Nuh—*" He paused, frowned. "N...ewtcake? Niktoad?" He hissed, then worked through the last word letter by letter. "Ah!"

His eyes lit up. "*Klaatu barada nikto!*" He shouted it and pumped both arms in the air. "Robert read! Robert can to read! Robert—"

The sound was drowned out. Or, swept away? It was hard to say exactly what happened. All Oli knew was suddenly the world had been reduced to a single point. He could see nothing beyond the shriveled, cursed hand. Then it moved, the fingers cracking and snapping like tree branches coming to life. The hand spasmed violently, then turned and latched onto Oli's wrist.

"Ah! Bad hand bad!" he cried. It didn't listen. Perhaps unsurprisingly, seeing as it had no ears.

The hand squeezed tight and Oli's naturally slimy coating oozed up between the fingers. Something in his wrist popped next and then the hand let go. All of its fingers pointed up at once. Well, all except the index finger, as that'd broken off back in Sandlantis. The *remaining* fingers pointed up as one, then the middle finger gave a long, loud crack and snapped clean off.

Oli yelped as it fell to the ground, but the finger wasn't broken, it was moving under its own power. As if it were tied to a fishing line the finger shot across the ground, pulled by an irresistible force toward the Dark Lord—and the Lock held in his hand. The little golden ring.

Like an arrow striking the bull's eye, the finger launched into the air and—before the Dark Lord's magmatic eyes could finish going wide—slid right into the ring.

A perfect fit.

The ring exploded outward, circles of flame shooting away in rippling, roiling waves that bowled everyone over. Everyone except Oli and his cousins. The waves parted before reaching them. All around the earth was blasted and torn, soil ripped up and tossed into the air. Beneath

Oli's feet, however, the grass was still green. Or, at least, that particularly dismal shade of yellow-brown only found in the Kingdom of Darkness.

"What have you done?" the Dark Lord cried, his voice distant and echoing through the roar of the fiery waves. He kept shouting until the waves of fire stopped, then reversed course. Everyone who'd been bowled over was suddenly sucked in toward the ring. As he was closest to it, the Dark Lord was first. He'd been holding the ring but in the blink of an eye—and with a sickening crunch—the ring was holding him. Or, something like that as the inside of the little golden trinket had become a swirling void. The Dark Lord was a good eleven feet tall but that didn't stop the ring as it crunched him smaller and smaller, then sucked him into the abyss.

His most trustworthy officers came flying in next, then various orcs and trolls, and then Oli spotted the first glints of bright armor. Soldiers of the forces of Good. All of them hit the ring and as their mass joined it, the trinket grew. The abyss contained within its band howled and consumed soul after soul. And then the Bright Queen herself whipped by, her light burning, brilliant, painfully bright—until she too was crumbled up and sucked in with a sound Oli found uncomfortably close to a slurp.

Above it all, someone was cheering.

The genie. Oli turned to find him dancing in place.

"I did it!" he howled. "I *did it!* The idiot can read!" For whatever reason, the magic man seemed entirely unaffected by the ring and its all-consuming abyss. His eyes were, instead, toward the sky as he shook a fist. "There's no denying it now! I did it!" he cheered.

Another shout, next, and Oli saw the henchpeople's giant machination being dragged toward the ring.

"Oli use second wish! Oli want second wish!" he

shouted all at once as he grabbed at the genie. "Magic man save dragon and henchpeople and also ghost family!" he shouted hurriedly. "Send back home, make safe!"

"That's a lot for one wish, kid. But I don't even care right now," the genie said with a smile. "How I've waited for this day. Wish..." he raised his fingers and snapped, "granted." The henchpeople and ghosts vanished at the sound. Presumably the dragon too was saved, wherever she'd been sent.

The genie smiled at him. It wasn't a happy smile so much as one of relief. And there was definitely a bit of insanity pulling at the edges of it after so long an ordeal.

"May we never meet again, kid," he said, then dissipated in a poof of golden light. His hands were the last to disappear, both middle fingers raised at Oli until those too vanished.

"That strange way say goodbye," Oli mumbled, but returned the gesture for fear of being rude. But by then huge swathes of earth were being ripped free and sucked into the ring. Even the clouds above were caught in the vortex, swirling around and around until they too were dragged down and into the abyssal nothingness.

FORTY-THREE

And Then There Were Goblins

Just about everything in sight had been destroyed. The goblins were still standing in the middle of their little patch of yellow-brown grass, though. And the sun hadn't been sucked out of the sky—but, was it a bit dimmer now? Oli couldn't be sure.

What he could be sure of was that the Plains of Abandoned Hope and Paralyzing Fear needed a new name. First of all, they weren't really plains anymore, were they? Looked more like some sort of strip mine if no one could agree on exactly where to begin digging. Huge swaths of land had been ripped up and, seemingly, consumed by the ring.

Speaking of which, the little trinket still hung in the air. It'd returned to its normal size now and was spinning slowly in place. The abyss inside was still visible, but even as Oli watched, it faded, then winked out of existence entirely. The ring gave a little flash of gold—a bit too much like flashing a smile—then fell to the ground, entirely normal once more. Oli was left standing with the desiccated hand, now less two fingers, but otherwise, still intact.

And the Dark Lord was gone. The Big Boss. Squished up and sucked into his own ultimate weapon. Oli expected to feel bad about that, expected his stomach to gurgle and churn.

It didn't, and that was weird. Weird, but somehow, meaningful? As if agreeing with that thought, in the distance there was a great groan and then the Citadel of Shadow and Sin collapsed in on itself.

The Dark Lord and his Legions of Smoldering Shadow were gone. So to the Bright Queen and her Army of the Just. Did that mean the Eternal War between good and evil was over? Oli's goblin brain wasn't equipped to handle such complex thoughts. All he knew was the scary people were gone and he and his cousins were left.

"What, uh, what do now?" Lin Two asked, Horse's head and Iris' gem held in her hands.

"Uh… Oli no know." He frowned at that. Once, their lives had been purposeless, but not like this. They'd served the Big Boss, even if that had taken the form of waiting for orders that never came. Then, in a whirlwind they'd been given a purpose and a destination and a time limit. There'd been so much to do. Too much to even keep up with. Oli had just gotten used to being… what was the word? Ah, busy. Right. Oli had just gotten used to being busy and now, as quickly as it'd all started, it'd ended. Now there was nothing once more. Just waiting, but there wasn't even a Big Boss to wait for this time.

There was a cough from behind and Oli turned to find Gob standing with something in his hands. The letter the Lieutenant of Lament had tossed to the ground. The letter Nestlecles had wanted them to take to Mishalob.

Gob looked at it for a long moment, then up at Oli.

"One last delivery?"

FORTY-FOUR

A Wriggly Little Ending

The Swamp of Sadness and Sweaty Underthings had never felt quite so swampy, nor sweaty, as when the goblins had finally returned home to it. It was good to be home. But just like it felt extra swampy and extra sweaty, Oli had to admit, it also felt extra sad.

Being home was good—the best part of any journey, Gob had told them. And he was right. It was nice to be home. But at the same time, home felt a little less like home after having seen so much of the wide world. It was hard to love home as much now that they knew exactly how much

346

was out there beyond the borders of the swamp. And also, that the Dark Lord they served had been chewed up and swallowed by his own ultimate weapon.

"Me wonder how Henchpeople is?" Lin Two asked, her feet kicking idly in the murky water. Everyone had been a bit mopey of late, so Oli had insisted they all head down to their favorite mud pool to splash around then maybe catch some newts. And when they went back to their hovels, he'd cook up his nan's infamous newtcake. "Maybe we go visit?" Lin Two added hopefully.

"It long walk," Oli said, pausing from where he'd been doing his best to convince his cousins to jump in by rolling around and loudly espousing how good it felt today. "And goblins no know the way."

"Iris know way!" Lin Two held up the gem, then gave it a little shake. But, as had happened every time they'd tried, the little floating woman didn't appear. Either she was broken or just didn't want to come out.

"Cousins, look!" Gob shouted as he bounded over. "My masterpiece… is complete!" He gestured dramatically to a collection of sticks loosely held together by vines.

"What is?" Lin One asked, twisting his head to see it from a different angle.

"A new body for Horse, of course!" Gob grabbed the skeletal steed's head from the shore and ran back to his creation. And now that he'd mentioned, Oli could kind of see how Gob's work was vaguely horse shaped. Just took a bit of squinting.

"Prepare yourselves for wonder!" Gob said then raised Horse's head high. He held it up a moment as Hob blew raspberries in something close to an approximation of a trumpet. "And… there!" Gob placed the head atop the stick-body.

"Horse?" Lin Two asked, eyes hopeful.

The ignoble steed's eyes still glowed in their sockets, but he was just a head and on their own, those didn't move much—unless toppling to the ground counted as Gob's stick structure collapsed in on itself. Gob winced and Hob's trumpeting spluttered out.

"Horse!" Lin Two scrambled over and scooped up the head. "Stick body no work!" she hissed at Gob.

"Sorry…" he said, voice low. "I was just trying to help."

"Remember when do deliveries, cousins?" Robert called from where he was sitting waist deep in the mud. "We do best deliveries! Go many places!" He smiled at the memory, and it was then Oli noticed the mountain goblin had their old Crag's List strand open. He'd been reading the reviews again. A favorite pastime seeing as he could read now but there were no books in the swamp.

"Ooh, ooh! This good review! Remember this?" Robert asked, then cleared his throat. "'Expeditious and elevated. Courier delivered package ahead of schedule and with a gilded refinement most befitting our stature.'" Robert stumbled over some of the words as he read, but if nothing else, the genie's lessons had been thorough. Probably Robert could read even better than Gob now. "'All noble families should seek to employ a company of such class in future, though exemplary dedication so fine as this may come at a cost beyond the means of *some* so-called nobles. Five out of five stars.'" Robert beamed as he finished. "Five out of five stars, cousins! We did good! Ooh, and look this one! This favorite review!" He cleared his throat again. "'Delivery arrived ahead of schedule, but courier's reckless driving caused significant damage to our facility. Three out of five stars. We will be filing a claim with courier's insurance.' That one good time," Robert finished, smiling. But as always happened when he stopped reading, the colorful memories in his head faded and were replaced with the muted blacks and weeping grays of their considerably charred swamp. "We should go on more adventure." He looked to Oli. "Goblins need one more adventure."

"Delivery job was fun," Oli said and even he reminisced on it happily for a moment. "But no have wagon. Is break." And then even he gave into the somber mood.

No! He didn't want to think that way. Sure, all of their neighbors might have been obliterated by unknowable dark magic, and sure, they might have been separated from their new friends by boundless miles, but they were goblins and they were home. This was where they belonged. Best they make the best of it. "Goblins have good adventure!" Oli said, smiling at the memories. "But goblins belong in swamp."

"But what do without Big Boss?" Man asked, looking up from where he'd been making a mud castle. It looked a lot like the Citadel of Shadow and Sin—and in a few moments, collapsed much in the way the real one had.

"Well…" Oli pondered the question. "Maybe goblins be own Big Boss?"

"If we're going to be our own Big Bosses, then I say we get on the road!" Gob insisted. "Who needs a wagon or an ignoble steed? We have feet, right? And we have each other." He gestured around, trying to get everyone excited. Oli appreciated the effort but it was wasted. "We'll just pick a direction and start going, yeah? Find some trouble along the way!"

"Ooh, and maybe do some deliveries?" Robert asked. "Or find library?"

"I'm sure we can—"

A trumpeting call blasted through the swamp so

sudden and so loud Oli near jumped out of his skin, then landed face down in the mud with a splash.

"What that?" he shouted, spitting mud. "Goblins in danger!" He reached for the cursemark instinctively, before remembering it'd disappeared along with the Dark Lord. "Run cousins!" Oli shouted as he prepared to cause a distraction and buy them time.

"What's the hurry, y'all?" a voice called out with a laugh. A voice that stopped Oli in his tracks. He paused, frowned, then turned to find a smiling human atop a massive blonde mammoth.

"Flan! Mam!" he called, then sprinted at them, arms open wide.

"Friends come to visit!" Hob shouted, also running, and then all of the goblins were in motion. In moments, Mam's furry sides were covered in a sticky barrage of small goblins.

"Whoa there, whoa!" Flan laughed. "It's good to see y'all too."

"Why come?" Oli asked, pulling his face from Mam's thick fur. "It good see you, but why come?"

Flan smirked.

"Well, I wanted to check in on my favorite upstart haulers, of course," he said, then smiled wider and leaned in close. "But I'm here on business, too."

"Bisusness?" Lin Two asked.

"Bisusness," Flan nodded. "I have a delivery."

"Who for?" Oli asked and Flan chuckled.

"You know anyone else that lives in this swamp?"

Oli thought hard a long moment.

"Delivery is for Thing That Waits Beneath The Mud?"

"No, man." Flan rolled his eyes. "I have a delivery for y'all!"

"No see it on Mam," Robert said.

"Well, strictly speaking, Mam couldn't deliver this one. But we wanted to be here when y'all got it anyway." As he said it, Flan clapped his hands.

From far away, a sound echoed through the swamp. It bounced off the trees, skipped across the water, and finally, arrived in Oli's ears with tickling vibrations. It was a deep roaring. A humming thrum. A gurgling bellow.

And it was getting closer.

"No..." Lin Two said, eyes going wide. "Wa... wagon?" she said, voice quiet as if she barely dared to speak the question.

"Oh, no. Y'all broke that one real good."

"Oh." She sagged inward.

"This is a new wagon." And as Flan said it, the thing roared into view. There were no roads in the Swamp of Sadness and Sweaty Underthings but this vehicle didn't seem to mind that one bit. Huge wheels with tightly coiled springs behind them kept it mostly level as it roared over marsh and mud, rocks and brambles. The back end had an engine like the old wagon, but this one looked a bit slimmer. It roared just as loudly, though, and spat an even more impressive plume of flame out behind it.

"It... it beautiful!" Lin Two said, wiping tears from her eyes as the wagon pulled a hard turn then skidded to a stop that sprayed mud over everyone.

"Hello, goblins," a stiff voice spoke. A henchperson, driving the wagon! He waved stiffly. "We heard what happened to the last wagon."

"We sorry for break," Oli said, ears down.

The henchperson waved away the apology.

"That was merely the prototype. We've improved on the design now," he said, his gray features pulling into a smile. "And thanks to all the marketing you did for us driving the wagon all across the land, we've had *considerable* interest from buyers." He hopped down then slapped the side of the wagon where a name was written in swirling, gold text. "Allow me to introduce the pride of the Hench-people United in Labor and Purpose Local Chapter Zero Zero One. This, goblins, is the *Master Viktor Was A Tyrant (and Dr. Viscous too) Labor Is Entitled To All It Creates Self-Propelled Rocket Wagon XXII!*" He paused to catch his breath, then nodded. "And we'd love for you to have it."

Lin Two's scream of delight was beyond incomprehensible as she sprinted madly forward. She leapt clean up to the henchperson's face and smothered him with a slimy hug, then before he could even gag, scrambled over his head and leapt into the driver seat.

"It beautiful! It best thing me ever seen!" she screeched.

"No," Oli said walking over with a smile. He placed Horse's skeletal head on a little nub sticking off the front, then adjusted it slightly so it hung evenly. "*Now* it perfect."

As he was slotted in place, Horse's eyes flared brightly.

Lin Two gasped, then dug around in her pockets to produce Iris' gem. And, sure enough, there was a slot in the wood for her just beside the steering wheel. Lin Two slotted the gem and with a snap and crackle, the translucent, blue floating head reappeared.

"Hello, I'm Iris, your personal navigator and interactive guide to—" she paused, taking in the goblins. "Oh, hello again."

"Now it perfec*ter*!" Lin Two cheered and then all the goblins rushed the wagon in a gleeful, mad scramble.

Robert hadn't moved, though. He was standing alone, the corners of his eyes wet.

Oli climbed into his old place beside the driver's bench, then nodded at his biggest cousin.

"Maybe you right, Robert. Maybe goblins need one more adventure."

Afterword

Knightman Alex want Oli to thank you for read book. Also say please to leave review. No need many words, but nice words please. More good reviews mean more clients for goblins. What else suppose do with shiny new wagon? Thank!

Please to leave review here:

Oli also suppose say if want news from Knightman Alex, mailing list is to be here:

https://authoralexknight.com/news

Oli give big thank to you. Oli love you.

Also by Knightman Alex

—Fantasy—

Wriggly Little Hands

You just read this one!

The Far Wild

Skyships, big egos, and an expedition gone awry in the most dangerous wilderness known to humankind. *The Far Wild*'s a fantasy thriller where even the plants are trying to eat you.

Servant of Rage

Kill an heir, claim their magic. But at what cost? *Servant of Rage* is an epic fantasy about honor, brotherhood, and the sinister magic that'll push them to the breaking point.

* * *

—LitRPG—

Rise to Glory

Pro eSports, fantasy quests, and the world's most popular VR gaming tournament. *Rise to Glory* is an underdog story of found family and maybe getting that iced coffee sponsorship.

The Nova Online Trilogy

Spaceships, alien planets, and a pinch of dystopian conspiracy. The *Nova Online* trilogy's a twisting adventure where the world's hottest VR game might just bring down the government.

Also available in an ebook and audiobook boxset.

Acknowledgments

From day one, *Wriggly Little Hands* has been a joy to create. I've tried to approach every step with the reckless optimism of Oli and his cousins. And just as Oli wouldn't have gotten very far without his cousins, I wouldn't have gotten anywhere without mine. My *publishing cousins*, that is, who joined me in the runaway rocket wagon that was the creation of this book.

In no particular order, I want give big thank to:

Erin Anthony, for her endless patience every time I ran into her office with some dumb joke to tell

Eric Schnier, for being infinitely funnier than me, jerk

Bethan Hindmarch (@BethanMay on social), for her extraordinary editing, for finding every typo I hid in here, and for being this book's cheerleader from day one

Ivan Shavrin (https://www.instagram.com/ivan_shavrin_art), for his artistic genius in creating this book's cover and map

Andrei Bat (https://99designs.com/profiles/bandrei), for making my wriggly little title look just perfect with his typographical wisdom

Kellan Moss (kellanmoss.com), for her—honestly—too adorable work creating the chapter header art

Dorrie Sacks (https://soundbooththeater.com/team/dorrie-sacks/), for helping Oli find his voice, and for bringing to life so much of this book, including Lin Two and various female cast

Justin James (https://soundbooththeater.com/team/justin-james/), for just outright rocking his roles as Robert, Lin One, and various male cast—and for fielding my unending questions with endless patience through the audiobook creation process

Gary Furlong (https://soundbooththeater.com/team/gary-francis-furlong/), for his excellent work as Man (the goblin), Flan (the man), and various male cast

Ryan H. Reid (https://soundbooththeater.com/team/ryan-h-reid/), for playing both parts of the loveable duo of Hob and Gob (it's pronounced *Johb*!), and various male cast

Jeff Hays (https://soundbooththeater.com/team/jeff-hays/), for bringing the heat as the Dark Lord Sarusomal, the friendly darkness as the shadow cousins, and for working so many unknowable magics at the helm of Soundbooth Theater

Christopher Ragland (https://christopherragland.com/), for once again lending his approachable yet enrapturing narrational talents to one of my insane books, this time as Detective Sherrock Stones and the Genie

Tiana Camacho (https://soundbooththeater.com/team/tiana-camacho/), for keeping us on route as Iris, the Bright Queen, and various female cast

Andrea Parsneau (https://soundbooththeater.com/team/andrea-parsneau/), for her unrivaled work as the biggest newt in the world as Ankcaulagraung, Fire Wyrm of the Blazing Eternities, and also the Lieutenant of Lament and various female cast

Everyone at Soundbooth Theater (https://soundbooththeater.com/) who worked their wriggly little butts off to turn this goofy story of mine into something truly special!

Brook Aspden-Li (author of *Gamified*), for his cherished friendship and mutual geeking out over Sir Terry Pratchett's works

G.D. Penman (author of… just so much, but we'll go with *Hat Trick* because it'd be Oli's favorite), for their eternal wisdom, innuendo, and general mentor character energy (which *will* see them killed off in act two of my life)

Ryn Striker (author of again, so many books, but let's go with *Dungeon Core Online*), for the constant writing chats and meme exchange

And finally… **you, dear reader.** Without you, I couldn't make a living writing silly books full of dumb jokes. It's my favorite thing in the world. Thank you.

About the Author

Alex Knight is filling good books with bad jokes one sentence at a time. As an author, his work includes *Wriggly Little Hands, The Far Wild, Servant of Rage*, and more.

As an aspiring twin, he's not making much progress (but remains determined).

Alex grew up a sunbaked, outdoorsy Floridian and has lived in several places around the world including many of the on's—London, Boston, and currently, Houston.

When he isn't writing, he's likely lost in a wetland, falling down in his novice hockey league, or playing pinball. Oh, and gaming. Lots of gaming.

Catch him online at: www.authoralexknight.com

www.ingramcontent.com/pod-product-compliance
Lightning Source LLC
Chambersburg PA
CBHW010513100726
47903CB00009B/2724